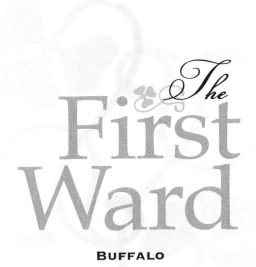

The First Ward

BUFFALO

FINGY CONNERS & THE NEW CENTURY

RICHARD SULLIVAN

Visit www.mutualrowingclub.com

Books
by Richard Sullivan:

The First Ward II:
Fingy Conners & The New Century

by
Richard Sullivan
Copyright © 2012-2018 by Richard Sullivan and
Montgomery Ewing Publishers

Montgomery
Ewing

This book is dedicated to my sister,

Barbara Sullivan

ACKNOWLEDGEMENTS

The Sullivan Family Historical Archive
Fultonhistory.com
Ancestry.com

Margaret M. Sullivan
Dennis C. Sullivan
Mary Lou Woelfel
Craig Cooper-Wyble
Thomas J. Higgins
Anette Weitzel
Steven Whelan
Lenny Kamp
Sonja Stieglitz, nee Grażyna Dyląg,
Michelle Bennett Stieglitz

Advocates of Murder: Death Before Divorce
by Charles Boswell and Lewis Thompson
Pediatrics 12:414-419, 1901
Snap Shots On The Midway by Richard H. Barry
The Railway Age, Volume 32.
Marine Review
Review Of Reviews vol. xii
The Chief, by David Nasaw

The National Archives
The Library of Congress
The staff of the Buffalo and Erie County Public Library
The staff of the Buffalo and Erie County Historical Society
The Buffalo Express
The Buffalo Courier
The Buffalo Commercial
The Buffalo Times
The Buffalo Courier and Republic
The Buffalo News
The Buffalo Star
The Buffalo Evening News
The Buffalo Advertiser
The Buffalo Catholic Union and Times
The New York Times Online
The Detroit Free Press
The Amsterdam Democrat
The Amsterdam Sentinel
The Fulton County Republican
The Chicago Tribune
www.buffalohistoryworks.com

Mark Twain's Buffalo residence, 472 Delaware Ave.

MRS. ANTHONY G. WORCKENER of Frie, Pa. better known as
CHIQUITA, The Doll Queen
C. B. Ridenour Studio, 914 Arch St. Phila

Chiquita, The Doll Lady on the Exposition Midway with her 17-year-old new husband.
Opposite page. top: The Electric Tower dominates the Grand Court Esplanade at the 1901 Pan American Exposition;
Opposite page. bottom, President McKinley's assassin.

Put Me Off At Buffalo

"Put me on at Buffalo,"
Said "Fingy" Conners, soft and slow
And so they did, for "Fingy's" way
Is what the bosses need today.

What! You don't know who this party is?
Well, listen to a story
That circulates in Buffalo
To add to "Fingy's" glory.
He isn't to the manner born,
But has the planks aplenty
And when a ten is all they ask
He hands them out a twenty.
He has a mighty yearn to be
A social luminary,
But up to date the swagger set
Is just a wee bit wary.
To catch the fashionable eye
And please the social powers,
He set across his spacious lawn
His name in gorgeous flowers.
Such art and beauty, "Fingy" thought,
would sock 'em in the plexus
And make him solid socially
From Buffalo to Texas.
A swagger lady, driving by.
Observed the combination:
"Poor man," she sighed "poor man
he thinks
He is a railway station."

L'Envol

In politics they put him on
At Buffalo, and star him;
But socially they put him off
At Buffalo and bar him.

—From the *New York World*

Fingy Conners circa mid-1890s

THE FIRST WARD

Synopsis: The Story Thus Far

Brothers James and John ("JP") Sullivan were placed in the Buffalo Orphanage in 1863 by their destitute mother after their father died in the Civil War. The Union Army had no record indicating Pvt. John Sullivan was ever married or had children, and because of this oversight the family was denied a pension. Out of desperation, Mary McGrady Sullivan took a new husband, an ex-and future convict named Halloran just in order to survive and reclaim her sons. Living in Halloran's saloon at the edge of the Buffalo River, life for the Sullivan brothers was almost as violent outside the home as in.

Their "friend" and neighbor, an arsonist and bully named Jimmy Conners, left school at age 13 to escape the clutches of the police and sail on the Great Lakes aboard passenger steamers as a cabin boy. In the ship's galley one day on a dare his friend Kennedy chopped off Jimmy's left thumb with a meat cleaver. Jimmy Conners raced all over the ship screaming, "Me fingy! He chopped me fingy!" providing him the nickname that would follow him throughout the rest of his life.

Fingy Conners returned to his Buffalo home as a young adult and due to the convenient sequence of deaths of four family members, who all died within less than two year's time, he inherited all of their estates, which included a saloon.

Dock-walloper Fingy had witnessed the desperation and disorganization among his fellow longshoremen and conceived the idea of contracting with a shipper to exclusively handle their freight, promising lower costs and an end to labor unrest. He accomplished this by hiring and paying his workers from his saloon, arranging for those who spent the most of their meager pay in his tavern on drinks to be the first hired on again to work the following week. The desperate competition fostered by this ploy plunged First Ward families further into poverty and desolation, not to mention alcoholism. Soon other shippers took notice of the cessation of labor unrest on the docks, lower costs, and higher profits. Ultimately Fingy Conners cornered the market on contracting workers, expanding his saloon-boss schemes to the point of becoming a millionaire. Thousands of First Ward families soon found themselves trapped under Conners' heel in indentured servitude.

In addition to owning half the ward's residents, Fingy also came to control its politicians, as well as the Buffalo Police Dept., who guarded the polling places on election day while hired thugs assaulted anyone trying to vote for any candidate other than Conners' choice.

Laborers James and JP Sullivan were determined to escape the First Ward's downward spiral. James founded the Mutual Rowing Club in 1881, which became the social hub of the ward, and joined the Buffalo police department in 1883. His younger brother JP unscrupulously won the office of Alderman of the First Ward in 1890, acting recklessly for his first few years, beholden as he was to his sponsor Fingy Conners and various other political demons. In 1899 there a great labor strike was called against Fingy Conners in which the Alderman finally turned his back on Fingy, standing instead with the strikers and thus forever altering his historically-precarious alliance with Conners.

The humiliating loss of the Great Scoopers Strike, as it was called, polarized Fingy Conners, who swore revenge on all his enemies. Now a multi-millionaire and the single largest employer of labor in the United States, he drafted a scheme to rain economic devastation down upon the entire city and bring to ruin the upcoming mammoth Pan American Exposition of 1901.

Alderman John P. Sullivan mid 1890s

JANUARY 1, 1900
00:04

"My God, man!" Annie Sullivan screamed. "Watch out!"

She held tight to her agonized husband.

As rockets raced skyward on their futile conspiracy to become one with the stars, and firecrackers ignited and exploded and bounced wildly about on the frozen pavement in celebration of the brand-new century, the speeding Fitch ambulance carrying the stricken Alderman and his wife began to slide sideways on the icy cobbles.

The horses, spooked by the aerial explosions and pulled off balance by the momentum of the careening wagon, its wheels failing to adequately grip the street, stumbled. One fell. The other, dragged down by the weight and momentum of his partner could not help but follow, screaming. The ambulance turned over ejecting the driver who landed sickeningly on his head with a resounding crack as loud as any accompanying pyrotechnic, killing him instantly.

John P. Sullivan and his wife Annie collided painfully with each other inside the wagon as the ambulance tobogganed, but they remained contained within it.

The dead man's partner, ambulance attendant Malcom Weber, found himself badly bruised, but no bones had been broken in the crash.

The Alderman's brother, following the ambulance at a three-minute distance in his sleigh, soon came upon the horrific scene. The Detective had some twenty years' police experience dealing with the unexpected and the gruesome, but when catastrophe involves one's own family, emotions have a tendency to override a man's professional detachment, his practiced calm and cool flying out into the ether. Jim Sullivan was gobsmacked by the scene.

The ambulance had crashed just a few yards from a firebox. Responding automatically to the emergency, Jim ran to it and pulled the alarm. The driver's head was cracked apart, he observed as he stepped over the man's splayed lifeless form on the street, his brains eerily exposed in the ugly yellow arc light. Soon a steamer and a ladder wagon came shrieking from the hose company on Chicago Street, tearing toward the Elk Street site of the accident.

The Alderman was in severe pain. Annie was bruised but uninjured she assured Jim through tears, though doubtless she was quite shaken.

The Fitch Hospital was alerted and a second ambulance was quickly dispatched.

Jim helped the firemen carefully remove the Alderman from the overturned conveyance. He did his best to comfort his brother. The vehicle's windows, reinforced with chicken wire, were fractured in a spider webbed pattern, but resisted shattering as designed.

Both horses were bruised but not gravely so. The entangled team was unattached from the overturned vehicle so that the firemen could right the ambulance. The equines were becalmed, then treated, then reengaged. The smarting attendant examined the Alderman but could not determine if he'd suffered any serious injuries as he had already been riddled with pain when they first arrived to fetch him. Annie was now wailing and crying, discombobulated, as fully worried for her husband as she was for her secret passenger.

The couple were transferred into the second ambulance and continued on their ill-fated race for the hospital. Jim followed. The dead conductor was loaded onto his original ambulance, this time riding in the back, his gaping head tightly wrapped to contain his brain matter within. He had lived but four short minutes into the new century.

The telephone sounded at the Mutual Rowing Club boathouse a little past one o'clock. Because of the noise of the continuing New Year celebrations, it went unheeded for ten rings until Junior perceived its jangle over the music, horns and revelry and finally unhooked the earpiece.

His sister Nellie happened to be watching him from across the way as his face transformed, stricken with the news.

He bolted across the room and hooked Nellie's arm, steering her through the crowd, past the Christmas tree, beneath the mistletoe, down the stairs and out the door.

"That was Ma! Uncle's ambulance crashed," he gasped. "You go stay with Ma, Nellie. I'm going to the Fitch to be with Pa."

Nellie felt as though she'd been shot. She lingered as Junior ran to fetch the Alderman's sleigh, minding each step carefully as she rounded the corner of South and

Hamburg Streets so as not to slip on the icy walk. She waited in front of the house until her brother had hitched up the horse and disappeared down the street before she opened the door to step inside. Zeke, the black Labrador retriever invisible in the dimness, was only evident by his excitedly wagging tail colliding with her knees. She let him out and waited until he finished peeing on the front gate, too distracted to scold him. As the dog ran back inside past her she firmly shut the door. There she would await further news while comforting her mother.

Annie sat on a gurney at the hospital having her bruises attended to. Suddenly she began to cramp badly, almost doubling over from the pain. She looked down, then felt with her hand, quickly withdrawing it in horror. Blood seeped from her vagina. She jumped up and screamed.

"Tell me, are you pregnant, ma'am?" asked the alarmed doctor.

Where am I?" abruptly shouted Alderman Sullivan awaking from a terrible nightmare. He tried to sit up, but weakness prevented the effort.

His head pounded with migraine.

In his disturbing phantasm he had found himself in the company of his father, a man he had no actual recollection of. Pvt. John Sullivan of the 49th NY Vols. had died in the Civil War when the Alderman was just a baby cradled in his forsaken mother's arms.

In his dream he and his father were conversing together atop Louis Sullivan's masterwork, the terracotta-faced Guaranty Building, fourteen stories up on the roof. He had been frozen with a fear that his father might fall from there, and tried to dissuade him from getting too close to the edge. He even felt a vague suspicion that his father might purposely try and jump. He was anxious and apprehensive, clinging to the surface, terrified of the height, dizzy at being so high up, the adventure being such an unnatural one. He had no idea how they had arrived there, but felt that as long as he kept his father talking that nothing bad would happen. As they spoke about nothing much of consequence, his father walked over to the steel skeleton of the two-story weather tower bolted to the corner of the roof. There, clinging to its brace work, he leaned out and over to have himself a long look down at the smoky city below.

The war veteran marveled aloud that from that vantage point he could actually look down squarely upon the highest pinnacle of the spire of St. Paul's.

"I can still recall when St. Paul's was the tallest structure in the entire Niagara region. Now we're high above it. Can ye believe it, son...I..." As his father spoke, mid-sentence the Union soldier nonchalantly stepped off into empty space and disappeared.

JP was horrified. He wanted to flee, to find the stairs and get himself down from there as fast as he could, but was more urgently compelled to investigate in order to verify his worst fear. He crawled haltingly toward the edge on his hands and knees, too vertiginous to stand upright. Loose scree painfully embedded in his palms and knees. He peered uneasily over the edge into the abyss to witness a crumpled human figure in orange lying far, far below on Church Street. A street-cleaner's cart lay shattered into pieces all around him, brooms broken, a blizzard of paper litter fluttering slowly down like giant snowflakes to cover the lifeless musketeer. The Alderman wondered why his father was dressed so oddly, in a Union Army uniform of bright orange wool.

"There, there. You're still at the hospital, Alderman. Just lie back and relax. You are in good hands. Dr. Park will be in to see you shortly."

"But...what's happening to me?" he asked.

Nurse Margaret Mary O'Neill just smiled.

"Dr. Park will be in to see you shortly."

"Where's Annie? Where's my wife?"

"Remain calm, sir. Dr. Park will be in to see you shortly."

She pulled the drape around his bed not quite fully closed, then exited the room.

A minute later there came a sudden commotion.

"Papa!" the voice loudly whispered as the Alderman saw a young girl's figure run past though the gap in the drape.

"My little Margaret!" barked a gruff voice from a few feet away.

The Alderman was not in a private room.

He worried suddenly that he might be in a public ward, recalling the noisy, confusing stressful experience of being hospitalized after his leg had been crushed on the docks when he was a young man. He didn't sleep for weeks back then, what with all the noise, the midnight interruptions by staff, and the occasional screams of someone or other in terrible distress.

"Hurry!" whispered the girl, as the Alderman saw three more children quietly rush past the narrow gap in the curtain.

"Be quiet, you kids, or they'll know we're here and kick us all out!" young Margaret scolded.

It was the first time they had seen their father since the accident.

Ed Moylan was a yard detective for the Lehigh Valley Railroad. He'd encountered more than his share of roughs in the course of his job, that of policing the Tifft Farm railyard. His task was to remain alert for those who might be emboldened to break into cars to loot the contents or for vagrants secreted away in the darkest corners attempting to evade detection. He'd had guns, knives, swords, bayonets, clubs, daggers, and even an old musket aimed straight at him, mere seconds away from reuniting him with his maker, but had blessedly remained unscathed except for a few knocks and bruises here and there.

But on December 26th, right at the tail end of the century, something occurred while moonlighting across the border over in Ridgeway, at the Crystal Beach amusement park. There he supervised construction of the much-ballyhooed Scenic Railway attraction at the famous Canadian resort. With its promise of wicked turns and thrilling sheer drops, the Scenic Railway was the number one topic of talk in any conversation addressing the upcoming summer season of 1900. Workmen were rushing to complete it.

As Ed Moylan stood atop the steepest drop's apex during his inspection, a gale-force gust of arctic wind blasted off Lake Erie and invaded the volume of his heavy woolen overcoat transforming it into a sail of sorts and toppling him from the towering height. He instinctively reached out to grab a handhold as he fell, but his wrist became lodged tightly in a crook where a number of support beams all joined together. Gravity, velocity, and the weight of the man's stout frame, along with the unfortunate torque of his arm at that exact moment all conspired to tear the limb right off his body.

He fell into a deep frozen pillow of fresh snowdrift with a muffled thud, bleeding profusely from the void and suffering great pain and shock. Fellow workers dug him out before he could suffocate. They abandoned the severed arm where it fell, the skin so pale as to almost camouflage it against the snow, errant blood globs the only clue as to its whereabouts. Ed's back was severely sprained and three ribs had cracked. He was lucky to have survived.

Margaret, his eldest, tried not to take notice of the empty gap her father's arm once occupied as per her mother's explicit instructions as she stood by his bedside.

"Can I see it, Pop?" cheerfully asked Eddie. The boy was just turning twelve and not at all afraid to investigate the missing limb.

"Edward!" snapped his older sister.

Eddie continued to stare in fascination.

More figures, those of a pregnant woman carrying a little girl and a young boy clinging to her coat, passed the cleft in the drape quickly as she softly cried out, "Ed! Oh! How's my lovely Ed?"

Norah McCarthy Moylan sat her five year old Frances on the bed so as to lean up against her father on his good side, and then bent over to hug her husband. As the sound of kisses filled the air, Frances hopped off the bed and looked about the room in curious assessment.

"I'm alright, Norah. I'm just itchin' to get back to work, that's all. The doctor said I should be able to leave here in a day or two."

"Already? Are you sure, Ed? Where is he? Can I speak to him?" Norah asked.

"Dr. Park will be in to see you shortly," slurred the male voice from behind the closed curtain in mocking imitation of the nurse.

Little Frances grabbed the valance and flung it open.

"Hello there gittle wirl," garbled the woozy Alderman.

"Hello," said Frances, brightly.

"Frances! Come over here. Oh, I'm sorry sir. We didn't mean to disturb you. Frances, come here. Now."

"That's all right, Missus. I have a quite a br...brood of little ones of me own," JP smiled hazily.

Ed Moylan struggled to upright himself, lopsided and grimacing with pain. He might no longer possess a left arm but he could still feel it there nevertheless, still move it, still attempt to use it. This was the first good look that JP had taken of his roommate.

Dr. Roswell Park walked into the room at that moment, surprised to see all the children as youngsters under the age of 16 were barred from visiting patients. He said hello to the roomful in general, and then focused his attention on JP.

"Alderman Sullivan, how are you feeling today?" asked the doctor.

"Not especially very well at all," replied JP quietly. "My head is splitting."

Nurse O'Neill entered the room right then and was surprised and perturbed by the crowd. She announced to all present, "Hospital rules are clear. No children are allowed to visit patients. You will all have to leave. Now."

Dr. Park did not interfere for he had an important discussion to conduct with the Alderman and privacy was preferred.

"All right," said Norah. "Ed, I'll take the children outside and Margaret can keep watch over them there for a few minutes so you and I can visit for a little bit. I'll be right back."

"Quickly!" announced the nurse, clapping her hands together as the children all rushed to kiss their father and were herded out by their mother.

"I'll be right back, Ed," she assured once more as the family exited.

Dr. Park drew the curtain closed around the Alderman's bed.

Nurse O'Neill attended to the armless Ed Moylan.

"Could you help me sit myself up, ma'am?" Moylan asked her.

Nurse O'Neill arranged pillows behind him and helped brace his remaining arm as he struggled to attain a more vertical position.

"Alderman," said Dr. Park in a lowered voice, "I've spoken to my colleague Dr. Buchanan at the St. James Hospital at Hornellsville. Dr. Buchanan is a specialist and he recommends we take you there. He has had more experience with your malady than anyone else in the state."

The Alderman was not happy to hear this.

"*Hornellsville?* Where the hell...where the hell is *that?* Isn't that way out...in the Finger Lakes Region somewheres?"

JP had been jolted out of his stupor by the disturbing proposition.

"Well, south of the Finger Lakes, yes. But not all that far. A couple hours."

"Why there? That's out in the middle of nowhere. We have many a fine hospital right here in this city, Doctor. Why would any specialist of worth be working way out in the hills in some clinic in the sticks? I'd think any man worthy of his salt would be practicing in an institution where he might make best use of his talents! Hornellsville? Really! Come now!"

"His family lives there, Alderman," said Dr. Park. "He is one of the hospital's founders, along with Father James Early. It's a new Catholic hospital, small, yes, but that is no adverse reflection on the quality of care. Dr. Buchanan's son is a cripple, you see, and Hornellsville is his family's home. He chooses to work there. It casts no dispersions upon his abilities. He's a genius, actually. You need to have this surgery, and he's the best there is."

"But Dr. Park!" wailed the upset Alderman. "The prospect of surgery is frightening enough in a big city where we have all the latest equipment! What kind of modern facility could they possibly have in Hornellsville?"

"Trust me, Alderman Sullivan. If I thought for a moment there was anyone in Buffalo who could resolve the problems you are experiencing, I would not hesitate. But if you are to fully recover, you need the best available surgeon, and that would be Dr. Buchanan. I promise you, Alderman, you will receive exceptional care."

Dr. Park paused a few moments to gauge the confusion on JP's face.

"I'll be back in an hour or two, after I find out more. Until then, just consider the idea. Mull it over a bit. We'll discuss it in more detail later, and then you can let me know your decision after you've had the opportunity to talk it over with your family."

"All right. Thank you, doctor," weakly sighed the exceedingly infirmed Alderman.

Dr. Park then moved on to Ed Moylan.

He drew the curtain around Moylan's bed. There was a small Lehigh Valley flag attached to his bedstead, a black diamond shape on a red field with "LH" in white, the black diamond a symbol for coal, the line's chief haul.

"Mr. Moylan, I'm going to have a look at your shoulder now to see how it's healing."

The doctor peeled back the dressing to gauge how readily his handiwork verified his skill.

"How soon can I get outa here, Doc?" barked Moylan.

While Dr. Park gently reapplied the dressing he said, "It's only been a week since your accident, Detective Moylan. I'll have another look at it tomorrow. If there is still no sign of infection I will discharge you. But you will have to remain very, very quiet at home in bed for at least another week. This is a very serious injury, and complications might well arise. It is of the utmost importance that the area be kept scrupulously clean and that it suffer no further trauma. You must be very careful to keep the region covered and protected from any sort of jolt, or impact, or jostling as it tries to heal. No rough stuff. No holding the children, much less carousing with them."

"I gotta get back to work, Dr. Park. I got a lot o' mouths to feed."

"What did the railroad tell you about that?" inquired the physician cautiously, doubtful that a man who had lost an arm could any longer police over a tough environment like that of the infamous rail yards.

"It'll be a fight all right, I'll admit," barked Moylan. I'm plannin' on marchin' into that yard office with my head held high. They're not goin' to get rid o' Ed Moylan so easily, I'll tell yous that much."

"That's the spirit!" Dr. Park enthused, gladdened that Moylan was taking his tragic circumstance so well. Lesser men had sunk toward depression and drink over such an injury, and few could ever hope to return to their previous work after suffering such a debilitating loss.

"I'll still be tougher with just one arm that most of them other hot house petunias over in the yard who got the use o' both, I promise yous that much."

Dr. Park laughed out loud.

"I don't doubt that for a moment, Detective. Give 'em hell."

Ed Moylan tried to sleep, but in truth he was worried sick about his future and that of his family. He wondered when the tragedies in his life might end, or at least ease up a bit. The long-awaited rewards he'd worked so hard and waited so long for had yet to show themselves, in his job, in his 11th ward politicking.

He'd tried unsuccessfully for over year to get answers from the government concerning the death of his brother Michael Moylan Jr., and now with nothing else to occupy or distract him, all the painful questions reemerged.

Ed was notified by the Navy almost a year previous that Michael had gone missing. He had mysteriously disappeared from the USS DuPont where it lay at anchor at Bristol near Newport, Rhode Island on the previous January 18th. It was thought at first he had deserted. But Ed knew of no reason why Michael would walk away from the military as he loved the Navy. Furthermore, certainly if he had deserted he surely would have allowed his wife and family know where he was. The family feared he was injured or dead and quickly petitioned the government to launch an investigation before too much time had lapsed. But based on the government's suspicious statements that men aboard his ship had claimed they had overheard Michael talking about deserting, they stuck fiercely to that assumption despite having no evidence.

Then on April 6, winter ice having cleared, his badly decomposed body was spotted in the water just off where the ship lay. The Navy quickly buried him at Newport, reporting no findings as to the cause of death nor any evidence of foul play. Ed suspected his brother was done in by those who claimed he had spoken of deserting, and demanded the Navy question those men who had made these claims.

The Navy was maddeningly unresponsive. They dug Michael's body up at Newport and shipped his remains back to his wife and parents in Silver Springs N.Y. Ed knew in his heart that his brother, who had served in the War with Spain honorably, had been murdered. But the American government ignored the Moylan family's pleas. Michael and Sarah Moylan were asked to give their son in battle for their country, but their country refused to give the Moylan family the basic respect of investigating their son's suspicious death.

HORNELLSVILLE

The Alderman had been administered laudanum to ease both the anxiety and the physical discomfiture of the rail journey to Hornellsville. Yet he winced and cried in pain when carried onto the train securely strapped to a cot. The click-click of the wheels as they passed over the joins in the rails recalled the rhythm of a metronome, lulling him to a fitful sleep. He didn't remember anything at all about the rest of the journey, of who he was with, nor of his admission to the hospital.

The hospital structure was of wooden fabrication looking rather more like a pleasant country resort inn than a medical clinic. It featured a large shaded veranda spanning the front and a stately three story tower structure ten feet wide by twelve deep crowning the entrance.

JP awoke in a large pleasant room appearing very little like a hospital ward. There were two other beds, both iron, both empty, and both neatly made up with chenille bedspreads. It took him a while to make sense of it, where he was and why he was there.

"So. You're awake, finally," said his brother, lowering his newspaper into his lap.

"Oh!" The startled Alderman hadn't noticed him sitting there.

"The doc says you came through the operation like a racehorse, whatever that suggests. I assume he meant it in a positive way, judging by his tone. How're ye feelin', JP?"

"Oh. A little like...Rip Van...Winkle. Only not quite as, uh, alert," he slurred, haltingly.

"They gave you laudanum to keep the pain from the surgery at bay," Jim explained.

It took a few seconds for JP to absorb it all.

"Is Annie here?" he asked.

"She was here, but after you came out of surgery the doc told her you'd be delirious for a few days and said she might as well go home to be with the kids. Hannah's been watchin' over the troops in the meanwhile, so don't worry. Your girl Sophie's there too, doing what she does, and the two together have everything in proper order."

"Is Annie here?" JP repeated.

Jim paused before answering the same question again, realizing the laudanum was affecting JP's mind.

"No, JP. She had to stay home with the kids."

"I was hoping to see...to see my Annie's face when I woke up. Instead, here's your...big ugly mug," JP smiled groggily.

Jim ignored the dig. He wouldn't worry his brother with reminders about Annie's injuries. She may have suffered no broken bones in the crash, but the trauma was great nonetheless. She was beaten and bruised and had lost a baby neither of them knew for certain she was pregnant with. At any rate, Annie had no business traveling the great distance to come all the way out here to visit him.

"The doc told me to leave and go home too, but I wanted to stick around a while. He said you wouldn't even stir until tomorrow, yet here you are, awake. So this is a good sign, that you're conversant already."

"Is Annie here?" inquired JP.

"No, she's home taking care of the kids."

"Oh. When can I go home, do you think?" asked JP hazily, his voice barely above a whisper.

"JP, you just got sliced open for Christ's sake. You'll have to ask Doc Buchanan about that. He's gone home for the day. He'll be back in the morning. But my guess is you'll be here for at least ten days or so."

Jim looked at him expecting a response, but JP had fallen fast asleep again. He was snoring.

The detective sat stiffly in his side chair, watching his younger brother breathe steadily. He looked so old now. This latest illness had removed whatever semblance of youth that lingered on the nearly forty-year-old alderman's face, making the eight-years-older Jim feel all the more ancient himself.

A nun of the Mercy order of Sisters rustled in, dressed in a nursing nun's habit of pure white, with a large stiffly starched semi-circular white bib, crowned veil, and a huge black rosary affixed to her waist cinch. In contrast, the teaching nuns of the same order dressed in a black habit.

"Detective Sullivan, you should go back to Buffalo now to your lovely family. It will be two days or more before your brother is even coherent," the kindly nun soothed.

"No sister," Jim countered, "I believe you're mistaken. He was just speaking to me a minute ago."

"Yes, but he will have no memory of that, Detective, nor of your even being here at all. He will be kept sedated for several days. So whether you are here or not, it won't matter to him the least bit because he will have no memory of such things until we cease the opiates. I will make it my personal mission to carefully watch over the Alderman for you. I promise. I'm sure your own family must miss you very much."

Jim smiled at her kindness. "My family is lying right here, Sister."

Upon this correction the nun returned his smile, faintly. She surveyed the scene for some moments, then said, "All right. I will bring you some soup then, Detective. You must eat something."

"Thank you, Sister. That would be welcome. Is there a telephone I can use, here at the hospital? I'd like to call my wife."

"Certainly. It's downstairs in the office. The cost of the call will be added to the Alderman's bill. There are long distance toll charges to call Buffalo, you're aware of that?"

❧❧❧

"Operator, can you ring Frontier 0043 in Buffalo?"

"One moment sir, while I connect you."

After a few clicks, three minutes and two rings, the telephone at No. 16 Hamburg Street was picked up.

"I have your party on the line. Go ahead, sir," counseled the operator.

"Hannah? Hello? Can you hear me?"

"Yes, dear. The line is very clear. Where are you? Are you still at the hospital?"

"Yes. Still here."

"Annie's been home for an hour already. We just put her down to bed, poor thing."

"Well, I'm still with JP," he replied. "But please try and talk Annie out of coming all the way down here to visit, all right? With the laudanum JP has no memory of her even being here—none at all. She needs to stay home instead, and get all the rest she can."

"I agree, Jim. I'll have a talk with her about it. Are you coming back home? I'll send Junior down to pick you up at the terminal in the sleigh. Just tell me what time he needs to be there."

"Honey, I don't feel right about leaving him here all alone tonight, even if he doesn't remember from one moment to the next. I'm sorry. I'm going to spend the night here, just to reassure myself. Then if he seems all right I'll leave for Buffalo first thing on the morning train. How are the kids doin'? The baby?"

"The baby still has that cough," she fretted. "The wind's been blowin' all the smoke in our direction, and even with the storm windows installed that poison still manages to work its way in."

Hannah had become quite rabid about germs, cleanliness and pollution upon losing three toddlers. She had been reading in the Buffalo Sanitary Bulletin that the illnesses that killed her babies might have been worsened or even caused in the first place by unsanitary conditions and habits. Her hands were raw from washing them continually with Fels Naptha soap, and Junior and Nellie were irritated by her insistence they wash theirs "every five minutes!" as Nellie complained. Nellie had bought her mother a box of Cuticura Soap, a much gentler alternative, but Hannah was convinced that only Fels Naptha, which she also used to scrub the floors, possessed special germ-killing properties that the gentle Cuticura did not.

Hannah was acquainted with other families who'd produced many children yet had not lost a single one, Tom Nunan and his Jennie for example. She thought about it constantly. Hannah concluded that she herself must somehow be to blame and pledged to never again lose another child.

Hannah had taken to tying fresh cheesecloth weekly around all the faucet spouts to catch any errant dirt or rust that might come in through the pipes. Within the first week she was horrified to see the white cloth become almost blackened, berating herself for not taking up the precaution much earlier. She boiled water for drinking when they ran out of bottled Crystal Water. She bought a charcoal filter to improve the taste of water she used for cooking.

The Alderman had mocked her for the extravagance of purchasing bottled water, despite her informed choice, which was supported by much recent published evidence. Annie soon insisted that they too have bottled water delivered as well. The infamous tightwad was forced to relent.

Hannah compelled everyone in the house, even visitors, to wash their hands upon entering, and she used rubbing alcohol to daily wipe down all the doorknobs in the house, the ice box handle, the entire telephone box, the toilet seat and chain pull and all the cupboard pulls, in order to sanitize them. Within months of initiating this regimen she was rewarded by the family's suffering from fewer colds and general ailments as a result of these novel practices. She insisted the rear windows be closed even in stifling heat to keep out the coal smoke of passing trains as they chugged by right behind the house. Lake Erie winds applied this locomotive soot directly to the exterior batten and in summer clogged the window screens so heavily as to block even the most insistent cooling lake breezes. Additionally, almost six years after Johnny's drowning, the children were still strictly forbidden from walking anywhere close to the banks of the river or of any canal or slip or ditch, a difficult feat in a city cut with nearly as many waterways as Venice.

"Is David okay then, Hannah? Is he sick?"

"No, Jim, the baby's fine. He's playing with Junior and Nellie in the parlor as we speak, and he's laughing. I'll keep a close watch over him. Don't worry. You take care of your brother. I know how to get ahold of you, so don't fret. I promise to place a call if I need you."

"Okay. I'll be home as early as I can tomorrow."

"Goodnight, husband," said Hannah softly.

"Goodnight, dear wife."

❧❧❧

"Detective?" the nun's voice softly woke him.

"Why are you sleeping in a wooden chair? The beds are empty. Here, you can undress and sleep in a bed."

"Are you certain it's all right, Sister?"

"Of course it is."

The following morning Jim awoke to the rough noises of a different, older nun attending to JP, this one lacking every particle of the saintliness of the previous. She cradled a pile of clean folded sheets tightly in her arms against her breast as if expecting to ward off some imminent attack.

"Who told you that you could sleep in a hospital bed?" Sister Mary Seraphim snapped accusingly in a nasty shout, her bitter personality undisguised.

Jim sized her up instantly, having encountered her type all too often in the past. Jim may have been a product of the city's public school system, but had been well versed in the reputation of some of these more monstrous nuns during the many times he had returned truants to their classes.

"You do not speak to me in that tone, woman. Understand?" barked the policeman. "Take a civil tongue."

"There are rules in this hospital, sir," she sneered, fuming officiously, "and these beds are for our patients, not for overnight guests! There is a hotel located right down the street! I've got better things to do than clean up after the likes of you!"

Detective Sullivan gave her a damning look.

"Sounds to me like you could use a good dose of what you so-called 'Brides of Christ' have been forbidden from ever gettin'," sniggered the Detective, sizing her up and down for effect. "Deprivation has made you into quite a sour old crab apple, that's evident enough. But you chose the life you did, so direct your frustrations elsewhere, lady."

"How dare you! I will have the director remove you from this hospital instantly!" the offended witch hollered.

"Yes, I do well know your embittered sort. Just because you've attempted to disguise your true nature underneath that costume doesn't mean the world doesn't plainly recognize the evil beast that dwells within. You seem hardly less foul than Satan himself."

The nun, livid and unaccustomed to any challenge, much less open vilification, angrily shot out of the room in search of the hospital's overseer.

JP giggled. He may still have been in a stupor, but not so addled that he failed to recognize his brother's ventilating the family's shared repugnance regarding a peculiar type of nun.

"That one's hardly no Sister Patricia, now is she?" JP chuckled, citing a sainted nun universally revered in the First Ward.

"Hardly. How are you doin' there, JP? Feelin' any better?"

"I don't know. Where am I, anyway?"

"You're still in the hospital in Hornellsville, remember? They got you on laudanum to keep the pain down, that's why you're so groggy."

"Take me home, will ya, Jimmy? I don't like it here."

"We'll just wait for the doctor, and see what he says. Okay?"

JP didn't respond. He'd drifted off to sleep again.

Jim Sullivan rose and gathered his things for the long train journey back to Buffalo. He paused at the threshold to take in a departing look at his brother, making sure he was still breathing. Then he left for the depot.

On and off thereafter JP half awoke numerous times, not at all sure of exactly where he was or why. He wasn't positive, but he could have sworn he saw Sister Seraphim leaning over the bed that Jim had slept in, thoroughly sniffing the sheets.

BELFAST, NEW YORK

The substances administered to deaden his pain and calm his fears had the disquieting effect upon the Alderman of producing imaginings so luminous that they seemed more authentic than real life itself. His vivid hallucinations were accompanied by a luxuriance of scents and sensations, exquisite in their nature, as well as a most welcome and miraculous disturbance—that of collecting together the beloved dead in reconciliation with the living.

His mother Mary McGrady-Sullivan-Halloran lived and breathed once more, as if she had never departed her loving sons. She hummed her favorite ditties, tunes which by that time had almost all but faded from the Alderman's memory while she fiddled about baking her ginger cakes and stirring her Irish stew, attending to baby Dennis. Half-brother Daniel Halloran once more smiled his famous grin, a mischievous smirk expressed as much in the asymmetric curl of his lips as in the sparkle of his crinkling eyes, a mannerism that had once lit up the First Ward like a pharos. JP witnessed Daniel rowing the perfect race in his scull, being awarded the winning trophy, then marching inland a few blocks to recite his wedding vows in a grand ceremony conducted at the foot of the altar at St. Brigid's. There, Mary and John Sullivan looked on, beaming. The Union soldier nursed his musketball-wounded arm in a sling but otherwise appeared quite fit. The evil stepfather Peter Halloran, the dreaded *ollphéist* who had tortured the family for twenty years, was excised from the Alderman's dream altogether as if he had never at all existed. Peter's son Daniel had been reincarnated instead as a full-blooded Sullivan, the authentic progeny of the two who truly loved each other. The Alderman smiled, recalling the time when, so ashamed was Daniel, so degraded had he been by his father Peter Halloran, that for a time he listed himself in the Buffalo Directory, while still living at his father's address, as Daniel Sullivan. Peter had become outraged over this slight, taking no responsibility for his son's estrangement.

❧❧❧

Detective Jim Sullivan braced himself against the familiar jolt of suddenly walking outdoors into the cruel blast of sub-zero arctic winds and horizontally blowing snow. He quickly bounded away from the little hospital toward the train depot. He was worried about his brother being so far removed from the visits of family and from their encouragement, so vital for one's speedy recovery. He looked up at the blackboard as he entered the small pot-belly stove-warmed waiting room. The train was on schedule. He checked to make sure he had his rail pass in his breast pocket. At the distant sound of the locomotive he exited, pacing anxiously to keep warm on the frigid platform as his convoy made its approach, eager now to get home and see Hannah and the kids. The temperature hovered at twenty degrees below zero. The hairs in Jim's nose instantaneously froze solid and crackled with each draw of dry arctic air through his warm moist nostrils as he waited for the iron beast to halt.

He climbed aboard his car and expelled a relieved sigh as the wheels began to grind laboriously forward, slipping at first on the icy rails as the engine struggled to gain traction. The ride back home was relaxing, the countryside lovely. The fierce wind had stopped and a light snow now drifted lazily toward earth. He napped on and off as the car gently rocked back and forth.

The clouds parted. The morning sun shone brightly on the newly fallen bone-dry snow covering the landscape. Trains passing each other in opposite directions kicked up a wild sparkling blizzard of powder as they shot past each other, propelling millions of tiny glittering flakes gloriously up into the brilliant sunlight. Young boys lingered by the tracks here and there along the route among the pretty little towns as the train raced by so that they might exchange a mittened wave with a heroic engineer or some friendly traveler they might compel to engage in a greeting.

❧❧❧

Alderman Sullivan's opium-infused delusion drifted in the direction of cousin John L.

The Champ was entertaining his captivated admirers at the Mutual Rowing Club boathouse on South Street, smoking expensive cigars end to end, and downing whiskey in quantities that directly contradicted his professed training credo. It had been John L. Sullivan who, soon after the Mutuals' first boathouse had been completed, suggested to the brothers that they broaden the scope of the rowing club to include boxing in order to fill the void of physical inactivity created by the long dark freezing winter months. It was a logical suggestion in a ward where pugilistic skills were a basic means of survival. It was John L. himself who had plotted the club's ring with a stick of chalk, deciding its location and pacing it out by carefully placing one famous foot in front of the other.

Whenever he came to visit, John L. coached the ward's lads in the Mutuals' boxing ring, then afterward boasted of his innumerable exploits both recent and ancient to an awed audience of star-struck boys and men who'd collected there like swarms of summer canal flies.

Lately upon each occasion of an impending John L. arrival, JP and Jim didn't even inform the family until the date was almost upon them. Previously, such news would spread like wildfire and bring forth a gaggle of hangers-on near the corner of Hamburg and South Streets in anticipation, the turnout interfering with the normal flow of riverside traffic for days.

In his delirium the Alderman recalled that Michael Regan was at that time an upwardly ascending sergeant due to make captain at any time due to his alliance with Fingy Conners. The Mutual Rowing Club was in its early eighth year of incorporation. Growing up with the Sullivan brothers on Louisiana Street, Regan had forged with them a friendship so tight that even daylight couldn't come between.

Back when the name John L. Sullivan first began to appear reverentially in the newspapers and in the utterances of an admiring populace, Regan was dazzled to discover that the Sullivan brothers were family to the great bare-knuckle boxer. And so it was, before the wives were told of any of John L.'s visits, before the kids had any idea that John L. was on his way, Mike Regan was informed on the sly that John L. was on approach. He found himself as excited as he had been as a boy by the imminent promise of Christmas.

By 1887 periodic indulgences in whiskey, tobacco and all too many willing women had worked lethal damage on John L. Sullivan's marriage to Annie Bates. Too, these things had eaten away at the canon of strict discipline that had represented the foundation of the Champ's tenet. His visits to family in Buffalo by this time were both shorter and fewer in number and smacked more of nostalgia and of a longing for the good old days than anything other.

John L. had historically exhibited a poorly-disguised admiration for Hannah, something that did not go unnoticed by Jim Sullivan, a frustrated and disillusioned Buffalo Police Department patrolman at that particular stage. John L.'s flirtatious manner with Jim's bride was neither subtle nor respectful. The men came to exchange brutal words one night after one too many drinks.

Jim called the great John L. Sullivan a has-been.

The Champ, infuriated by the deadly accurate insult, went packing that very evening. Jim was left deeply troubled, regretting the familial rift, but not the reason for it. Hannah was relieved of the discomfiture wrought by the Champ's too-obvious attentions, despite her secretly being flattered by them. The week following their falling-out, Jim Sullivan received a most soul-searching letter in which the boxer poured out his heart and apologized profusely for his covetous manner. He promised nothing of the sort would ever happen again, and once again pledged to stop drinking.

This family upset proved a watershed event, compelling John L. to reevaluate his ponderous overindulgences in drink, his adulterous relationship with longtime mistress Ann Livingston, and his partaking in far too much rich food and too many fine Cuban cigars. The Champ was obliged to take a long hard look at his now off-kilter life.

He concluded that if he wanted to recapture the heady feeling of being John L. Sullivan and all that the name had once stood for, that he would have to get himself back in the ring and fight once again.

❧❧❧❧

JP's dreams continued to waft and drift among and through mostly pleasant illusions, undiminished even by a crying patient in the next room. He relived the wonderful day when the brothers and Mike Regan journeyed together in the early summer of 1889 to cheer on John L. in Bill Muldoon's barn out in Belfast N.Y.

The Western New York hamlet was so tiny that the trio were the only ones who got off, or on, the train when it lingered its few minutes at the Belfast platform. They'd arrived late in the day when the sun was just dipping behind the hills. With cicadas loudly buzzing and irritating dragonflies flying much too close to sweaty faces for comfort, there was nary a breeze to cool the summer's humid heat. They checked into the town's little hotel, respecting John L.'s trainer Bill Muldoon's strict early-to-bed, early-to-rise regimen. Muldoon was preparing the champ for the battle of his life against Jake Kilrain. It was to be the fight of the century, the very last world title contest fought under the London Prize Ring rules. The final bare-knuckle heavyweight title bout. John L.'s last hurrah.

The innkeeper apologized to the three men in advance for the Muldoons' parrot.

"Why? Does it live here at the hotel?" asked JP.

"No, thank God. It lives at Muldoon Farm. But you'll be hearin' that bastard bird just the same."

Just the previous year John L. had taken seriously ill. On his thirtieth birthday, October 15th, he arose from his certain death bed after nine weeks of terrible sickness and summoned a cab to take him to his father Michael's house at 8 Parnell Street in Boston, where he intended to die.

The Champ's physician warned him he would never survive the ten mile carriage journey, but from the moment he arrived in the embrace of his father's home, he began to recover. John L. had suffered from typhoid fever, gastric fever, inflammation of the bowels, heart trouble and liver complaints. A few weeks after arriving at 8 Parnell Street, feeling much improved but still on crutches, he felt well enough to again begin contemplating a future for himself.

The woefully weak and physically disabled John L. was inconveniently called upon at this ill-timed juncture to answer the challenge of Jake Kilrain that Sullivan either defend his world championship title or forfeit all claims to it.

Though by the end of the year the most egregious signs of his illnesses had dissipated to a promising extent, the still-languishing John L. Sullivan nevertheless traveled to Toronto on January 7, 1889 to sign articles to meet Kilrain in or near New Orleans the following July 8th.

This meant he had exactly six months to accomplish the impossible—to somehow restore his sick, tortured and defiled body to world-champion fighting condition.

John L. was still weak enough that he had asked cousin Jim Sullivan to meet him in Toronto to lend support both physical and emotional. Jim took the train from Buffalo across the International Bridge.

After an absence of several years, former manager Jimmy Wakely had again taken the helm as John L.'s steersman. Wakely engaged Charlie Johnston, an infamous Brooklyn gambler, to back the champ for expenses, for John L. in early 1889 was totally broke once again.

Once the Toronto business was wrapped up and the papers signed, and despite his frightening appearance and obvious poor health, John L. insisted the two cousins ditch the other men and go out on the town by themselves to celebrate the signing.

John L. commenced drinking more heavily than Jim had ever seen him, surpassing all previous benders. Many hours later they ended their marathon in the bar at the Queens Hotel on Front Street where John L. was staying. When John L. began vomiting blood there, Jim Sullivan engaged the assistance of two hotel employees to help carry the Champ up to his suite. Jim put his cousin to bed, then fell asleep on the divan, exhausted by drink and his day's trials. The following morning Jim hoisted the barely-hung over John L. onto a train back to Boston, and then immediately afterward boarded the train home to Buffalo. Head pounding, he fitfully slept the entire two hours.

A few days later back in Boston, the champion's concerned manager Jimmy Wakely visited the Michael Sullivan home on Parnell Street. John L. was there in disastrous physical shape, shaky on his pins from "incipient paralysis." He was sluggish, dyspeptic, short-winded and grotesquely fat. Furthermore he was in a desperate state of depression that bordered on neurosis. He was unable to keep food down and he continued his heavy drinking. All involved were compelled to agree that John L. was a complete wreck.

Wakely had engaged the services offered by renowned wrestler and spartan tyrant Bill Muldoon as a physical coach. Wakely persuaded John L. to leave Boston and join Muldoon on his farm in Belfast N.Y. to begin training for the momentous fight ahead. When John L. staggered off the train in Belfast accompanied by Wakely and Johnston, trainer Muldoon was on the platform to meet them.

Muldoon couldn't believe his eyes.

Appalled at John L.'s having ballooned up to 240 lbs., Muldoon experienced second thoughts. He was doubtful he could accomplish the miracle expected of him by his employers and he told them this right then and there on the platform. The men looked panic-stricken for a few moments. Muldoon suddenly conceived a challenge and proposed a wager.

"I will accept no fee if Sullivan should lose to Kilrain, but if he should win, my fee will be $10,000," he announced.

Wakely and Johnston agreed to Muldoon's proposition on the spot without any hesitation, and as the departing locomotive's coal smoke enveloped the group, they shook on it.

With grim resolution Bill Muldoon, who believed with a religious conviction that the human body was a sacred temple, imposed one final demand. He pivoted to stand face to face and nose to nose with the defending champion, so close in fact that he could feel his own hot breath ricochet off Sullivan's face as he spoke.

"John L. Sullivan, you must obey me without question or argument or you can just turn around right now and get back on the next train," he demanded.

John L. accurately read the dead seriousness in Muldoon's forbidding grimace.

"By the way, when's the last time you saw your own dick?" Muldoon asked him in a shaming tone.

John L. looked down at his enormous belly which hung prodigiously over his belt. "All right, Mr. Muldoon. I am all yours. No arguments," promised the Champ.

At first John L. was so weak upon his arrival in Belfast that he took to his bed. He was unable to keep any solid food down at all, save for a few spoonfuls of oatmeal. Muldoon was sympathetic and solicitous, never leaving the champ's side. He knew that before he could begin repairing John L.'s thrashed body he would first have to rebuild his self-confidence and spirit.

The pugilist was placed under virtual quarantine. No visitors were allowed for the first few weeks who had not been pre-approved by Muldoon. John L. drank nothing stronger than milk and ate gruel and the most basic of foods in small portions. Coffee and tea were forbidden, as well as cigars and all alcohol, save for an occasional ale.

Muldoon slept in the same room as Sullivan because he didn't trust him. As soon as he felt better, John L.'s promises predictably began to fall by the wayside. There were but two saloons in the small town. Muldoon had approached the proprietor of each tavern and warned that they would have him to personally deal with if they should ever serve John L. Sullivan a single drink.

One evening, Muldoon, distracted by his wife's having suddenly taken ill, was given the slip, and John L. sauntered into one of the town saloons. The barkeep thought twice, then figured that between the two, he'd rather incur the wrath of Muldoon later on than that of Sullivan at that particular instant, and poured him a whiskey. John L. had finished his second drink and was just starting on his third when Muldoon stalked in. Without uttering a single word and entirely devoid of facial expression the trainer pointed to the door. Sullivan thought for a moment, then put the drink down and walked out the door into the black night. The two walked back down the road to the farm in complete silence.

John L. started up the porch steps, but Muldoon gently took hold of his elbow

Bill Muldoon, John L. Sullivan's trainer.

THE FIRST WARD II

and guided him instead around to the barn, still wordless. Muldoon stripped himself to the waist, then stood there waiting until Sullivan got the message and did the same. Then he laid into the Champ, twisting his arm behind him, back-heeling him and slamming his great heft to the earth. Muldoon's victim strained his neck to look around and assess his livid face, contorted with anger and contempt.

"All right, Bill," he gasped. "I won't never do it again!"

The rebellious incident was Muldoon's signal to commence fulfilling his agreement in earnest: the real work of rehabilitating John L. Sullivan had begun.

❧❦❧

John L. had warned his cousins when they'd asked to visit him that if they expected to spend any time with him in Belfast they would have to keep up with and train alongside him: Muldoon's orders.

JP was apprehensive, what with his foreshortened leg making running any more than a few yards unmanageable. Michael Regan was an enthusiastic member of the Mutuals but hadn't ever actually been an active participant in any of the clubs' athletic contests, and himself was overweight by thirty-five pounds or more to boot. Only Jim Sullivan was up to the task fully, his being compelled to run daily in order to corral law-breakers, but he did wonder just how serious his cousin was about his claim of "getting into the best shape of my life," for John L. had left in his wake a sorry history of fully celebrating his every victory by partaking of all life's most damaging pleasures as reward.

Bill Muldoon's farm lay nestled postcard-pretty just a few short minutes' walk from the Belfast Hotel. It quartered horses and contented cattle along with two barns and a spacious cottage painted snow white, surrounded by lilacs and red-edged white peonies in bloom, with thick lawns as green as Ireland itself. Skirting three sides of the house a wide shady veranda furnished with easy chairs, a porch swing, hammocks and potted geraniums imparted the welcoming appearance of comfort and ease. A line of young maple trees shaded the house from the hot sun of late spring.

Bill Muldoon was himself a champion wrestler and athlete, handsome and fit, his mature rosy cheeks indented with boyish dimples, eyes brilliant blue. He was an enthusiastic fan of John L., and when he'd first heard that the Champ was intending a comeback, he formed the idea of responding to an overpowering calling. Muldoon would offer his farm and his expertise as a trainer in a quest to restore the Champ to fitness and his rightful station in the athletic world.

John L. liked to complain that Bill Muldoon was a harsh taskmaster who he nonetheless obeyed unquestioningly in his pursuit to preserve his title. But truth be told, concerned townsmen at all odd hours had more than once come knocking to fetch Muldoon to drag Sullivan out of one of the saloons where he'd escaped while Muldoon was distracted by other business, or soundly slept.

At a bit past eight o'clock on the morning following their arrival, the Sullivan brothers and Mike Regan mounted the two stairs to the Muldoon porch and knocked on the screen door. Bill Muldoon came to the door and greeted them like the intrusion he believed them to be, informing the men they were late.

"Yous shoulda been here by six."

He invited them into the cool interior nonetheless. The sun was already hot.

"We already finished our two-mile run and had our breakfast. Your cousin is gettin' his rubdown now. It will still be a few minutes yet. Have yourselfs a seat and I'll go tell him you're here."

Muldoon disappeared into the back of the house as the men turned to the sound of a knock at the screen door. Not knowing what else to do, JP hopped over and asked the young lady standing there if he could be of service. He opened the screen door a foot and accepted a letter of introduction that she handed to him.

"I am Nellie Bly, from the New York World newspaper. I've come to interview Mr. Sullivan."

"Well, I'm Mr. Sullivan, Miss Bly. How lovely of you to have traveled all this way just to see me," effused the First Ward's candidate for Alderman with face straight. Jim and Regan joined in the farce, nodding affirmatively in an official manner, expressionless.

Bly was taken aback for a moment, confused by the sight before her of a slight man of average height, thinning reddish hair and unusual taste in footwear. She looked down at the enormous orthopedic shoe. The men all laughed.

"Didja see the look on that young gal's face?" the Alderman would later joke whenever retelling the story.

Five uncomfortable minutes later, Muldoon appeared with John L. He enthusiastically shook hands first with his cousins and then with Mike Regan, the men all smiles and shoulder punches. Nellie Bly remained seated. She was then introduced to cousin John L. by the Alderman.

"Mr. Sullivan, I would like to shake hands with you, also," Bly said to the Champ, standing at her chair. John L. stepped forward and took her hand in his, the unmistakable look in her eyes not at all unnoticed by the other men present. Nellie ogled the imposing presence of the Champ, for some reason having anticipated seeing him outfitted in training togs rather than his cheviot coat and vest and slippers. As she accepted his grip, she took a good look at his hands. She wrote later they were smaller than she'd expected for such a large man. Although quite thick, the fingers were straight and shapely, the closely trimmed nails oval and pink. She later confided in the visitors from Buffalo that she had been as impressed by John L.'s height and his broad shoulders as she was his gentle manner.

"I came here to learn all about you, Mr. Sullivan, so will you please begin by telling me at what time did you get up this morning?" asked Nellie Bly.

The three visitors shouldn't have been at all surprised by the reporter's presence, considering the great international interest attending the upcoming bout. But they had arrived naïvely expecting to have John L. all to themselves, or at least, not to have to share him with some upstart female and be compelled to curtail their language and manners because of it. They had envisioned a manly weekend free from the social constraints demanded by the presence of more delicate company.

Nellie Bly unleashed an avalanche of questions on the Champ, questions both insightful and inane, but mostly the latter. The Buffalo group excused themselves to "go have a look around the farm." John L. gazed longingly after his cousins, betraying in his eye who he'd prefer to be spending his time with at that moment. Bly was the third newspaper person to visit that week, and her questions were identical to all those of the previous male reporters.

"Be ready at half past ten, lads," John L. called after them. "We've got our 12 mile run-and-walk to tackle then. Care to join us, Miss Bly?"

John L. well knew what her answer might be even before she demurred.

❧❧❧

JP roused a bit now and then in his hospital bed as he relived the explorations of that lovely day in his delirious miasma; the Muldoons' big dogs rolling over lazily onto their backs in the open barn doorway in expectation of belly-rubs as the men stooped to oblige them while discussing the future bout; a shrieking fight between two roosters breaking out; huge horseflies buzzing menacingly around the neighing steeds, their tails wildly swatting against the winged villains' landing and biting. Everything was permeated by the pungent essences of the Upstate hinterland.

"Interesting how much better shit smells out here in the country," JP recalled saying to his concurring companions.

"That's because it ain't human," replied Mike Regan, citing personal experience.

Nellie Bly wanted to know how much the Champ had earned so far in boxing. He replied that it was close to $600,000, give or take. What did he wear in the ring? "Knee pants, stocking and shoes, and no shirt." What did he eat? "Oatmeal for breakfast, hot meat and bread for dinner, cold meat and stale bread for supper."

He added "I used to smoke the livelong day, but since I came here to Bill Muldoon's, I haven't seen a cigar. Occasionally Mr. Muldoon gives me a glass of ale, but it doesn't average one a day," or so the Champ claimed.

When the time came for their run, Mrs. Muldoon took over the entertaining of the famous Nellie Bly on the veranda as John L. changed into training clothes. JP and Mike Regan followed lazily in their distant footsteps as John L., his cousin Jim, and Bill Muldoon went galloping off into the pasture followed by the dogs.

"I weighed 240 when I arrived here, Jim," wheezed his cousin, "and now I weigh 215. By the day of the fight I will weigh in at 195," said the champ, already out of breath. "Muldoon keeps an eagle eye on me, him and his missus."

Ninety minutes later, the champ's route almost completed, JP and Mike Regan short-cutted across the pasture to the end of their circuit to meet up with the joggers a quarter mile from the house, where by that time the three had had their fill with running and slowed to a lazy amble. The larger dog, a huge handsome mastiff mix, had backtracked to rejoin the two laggards, JP and Regan, early on, he deciding not to follow his master the entire 12 miles. The bulldog on the other hand completed the entire circuit and looked desperate for water.

The group walked casually along the dirt path, crossing from side to side to take advantage of whatever shade was available. Fallen leaves crackled beneath their feet, dust was swirled up by their shoes, and a crushed squirrel, pregnant, the victim of a heavy dray's wheel, lay disemboweled among her unborn in the dusty track, flies laying their eggs inside her and her little ones. The dogs sniffed and tasted the mess thoroughly, then moved on.

"Just how many of these reporters have come out here to see you so far, Johnny?" asked cousin Jim as he and Muldoon avoided stepping on the squirrels.

"Too many, that's for damn sure," coughed John L. "But this bout has piqued interest like never before, and I can't fight forever, Jim. I'm gettin' old, cousin! I got to look to the future and try my hand at other things. The more famous these reporters can make me now, the more opportunities I'll have once I retire from the ring. So, I'm willin' to talk to 'em all, time permittin'."

JP and Regan caught up to, but lagged behind, Jim and John L., talking training with Bill Muldoon. Neither shy nor retiring, Regan asked how much Muldoon was charging the champ for his services.

"I don't make any money by doing this, Mike. I was anxious to see John L. do justice to himself in this coming fight. It was a case of a fallen giant, so I thought to get him away from all the bad influences and to get him in good trim. I do admit I've had to fetch him a time or twice from the saloons after he sneaked away. He'll gladly tell anyone willing to listen that the training is ten times worse than the fight itself. And he might be right. This is the healthiest place in the country for him right now, and Belfast is one difficult town to reach. Just ask the reporters! Both of these things are desirable for training. On his journey down here he had secured a private railcar, yet there were more people entering his car than any other. Next time, when we all go to New Orleans for the bout, we'll keep our car's doors locked and none but John L.'s backers and representatives of the press will be admitted."

Nellie Bly met them on their return at the top step and started in with a hundred questions for both John L. and Bill Muldoon. Having already exhausted poor Mrs. Muldoon, the lady of the house was relieved to have the indefatigable journalist out of her hair. The World's famous reporter had to get back to New York City soon.

"Mr. Sullivan is the most obedient man I ever saw," Muldoon boasted to her as if reciting from a memorized script. "He hasn't asked for so much as a whiskey or a single smoke since he came here and he takes what I allow him without so much as a murmur. It is a pleasure to train him."

Muldoon had learned a thing or two about public relations during his own years on the mats.

❦❦❦

As the Alderman's lovely dream coincided with the hospital's lunch hour, his stomach began to growl. The sisters were late with his soup and bread. With the scent of the coming meal filling the air, the Alderman's mind wandered through the white cottage inventorying the Muldoons' simple treasures. The bucolic surroundings were in brilliant contrast to those of Hamburg Street in the filthy First Ward with its perpetual industrial stench and round-the-clock haze of soupy gray air.

In the Muldoons' unembellished den was a welcoming rattan lounge for afternoon naps and rocking chairs for pleasant company. The walls were lined with photographs in frames, more than a few of Modjeska, with whom Muldoon had traveled. There was what appeared to be a bar, with a bare rack behind it on the wall, emptied of what may have been bottled spirits so as not to tempt John L.

Apparently free of modesty, there were quite a number of photographs of a younger Bill Muldoon himself in the nude, posed in the manner of classic Greek statutes of antiquity, as befitted his then-enviable physique. There were scrapbooks and albums scattered about, filled with photographs of famous athletes, including a number of the great naturalist strongmen Hakenschmidt and Sandow, the men intimidating due to their unusual beauty, if such a word be used to describe a man.

The two famed naturalists were exceptional in this regard, not resembling any human male form that anyone had ever actually encountered in real life outside of an art museum. In their photographs they truly exceeded the classic standard that had been preserved in the ancient sculptures of Greece and Rome, sculptures that had lately been disparaged by scoffing modern critics as representing nothing more than idealized fantasy versions of the actual humans who had posed for them.

Hackenschmidt's photographs especially countered this assumption, giving credence to the possibility that the men and women represented in ancient sculptures, rather than representing some idealized imaginings of the artist, were perhaps in truth depicted accurately as they truly existed at the time after all.

Scrapbooks brimmed with Muldoon's professional history to the point of spilling over, containing news clippings of the wrestler's athletic conquests. Additional books on the Muldoons' shelves, leather bound, bore authors' names such as Yeats, Bryant, Longfellow, Whitman and Shakespeare.

Lunch was called.

The Alderman re-imagined drifting toward the Muldoons' bright pretty dining room, the large table set in white linen and beautiful white bone china devoid of any embellishment, the colored waiter standing quietly at attention. On both sides of the room the windows were wide open to the gentle breeze of that summery day, providing beautiful views out toward the flower-filled garden. A tamed forest of maples and elms thickly repelled the sun's stifling rays. In birdcages along the room's perimeter sang yellow canaries, and in a large brass cage placed in the open window a green parrot clung to the vertical bars and shrieked "God damn you bastards!" joyfully out over the countryside.

A pork roast fragrant with rosemary and mustard seed was brought out, with braised potatoes and asparagus for the guests, the spuds forbidden to John L. They laughed and talked, interrupted by Nellie Bly's tiresome questions. Luckily she would have to be leaving soon after lunch.

❧❧❧❧

JP's dreamy reliving of that day was almost entirely accurate rather than the result of pharmaceutical amplification. He had found it remarkable that the Muldoons' barns were kept cleaner than many people's own homes. One barn was fitted out after the latest improved athletic training methods. Two horses were stabled at one end in immaculate stalls while training equipment occupied the rest of the space. A rugby ball hung suspended from the ceiling waiting for John L. to beat the tar out of it daily, pretending it to be Jake Kilrain's head. A Herculean medicine ball of ponderous weight tempted, promising to tax the abilities of the men who hefted it back and forth to each other. A white wrestling pad covered the floor in the loft where John L. and trainer Muldoon clambered up and grappled every afternoon. In the corner stood a rack with dumbbells and several sizes of Indian clubs. Fastened to the wall was a chest expander.

"There you go Alderman, said the nun as she set the tray on the table. "Can you sit upright to eat? Would you rather sit in the chair?"

JP was not so loopy as to be unaware of how loopy he was.

"Uh, uh, umm... Oh, hello. Was I asleep?"

"Yes, Alderman. Can you sit up now?"

"I don't know. Leave it there, will you, Sister? Let me think about it for a while. Is there any cake?"

❧❧❧❧

As the morning special from Hornellsville raced into Buffalo and the snow turned from country white to city gray, Jim began preparing himself to disembark. A few hundred yards ahead a one-armed railyard detective dragged a struggling young man across the tracks quickly in order to get out of the way of the fast-approaching behemoth. Ed Moylan, on his way to the Tifft Farm rail yard office to reclaim his job, had collared the youth loading up a haul of fifty journal brasses from a compromised freight car.

"Let me go, you circus freak!" shouted the man-boy a half second before the single-armed man brought the butt of his pistol down hard on his skull. The youngster collapsed, dazed, but the iron grip of the railway detective elevated him to a more or less upright position again and half-dragged his sorry carcass a full quarter mile through the snow toward the Tifft Farm office. Moylan's ribs were shot through with pain, as they were yet unhealed entirely.

"I'm back, Boss!" Ed Moylan lustily shouted to his wiry superior as he entered the warm room attempting to disguise his tormented and winded condition. He threw his capture to the floor. "Here's a present for ya, Jess. Happy New Year. Caught this here thief makin' off with a load of journal brasses from an Erie car."

Jess Maloney just stood there, speechless.

He was having his first look at Ed Moylan since his employee had lost his arm. In truth he never expected to see him again, especially not here of all places. He assumed Moylan would be spending his final days at home, a cripple and a recluse, attached to a gin bottle.

The man-boy lay moaning on the floor.

"Shut up, ye little shit!" Moylan threatened. "I ain't near done wit' yous yet."

"Uhh...yeah. Okay. Good work there, Moylan. Yous all right?"

"Course I'm all right. Why wouldn't I be? I ain't gonna let a little inconvenience like this stop me from doin' my job," he said, nodding downward to indicate the void. "That ain't what you was thinkin' was it Boss?"

Maloney scratched his temple. In fact he had thought exactly that, but was now forced to reconsider as he faced the undefeated Ed Moylan.

"Want me to drag his ass down to the precinct or what?"

"No, I'll telegraph the cops," replied Maloney. "This might be the same lad who's been hittin' the yards pretty hard lately. The coppers'll be only too happy to drop by and escort him to his new lodgings, I'm sure."

"What's on the ledger for today?" Moylan asked.

Still wondering how to handle the newly reconfigured Ed Moylan, yard manager Maloney's normally smooth syllables tripped a bit on their way out.

"Uh, um...Johnson's out with consumption, so between you being out, and him, we've been really short-handed lately," Maloney said, pausing to reconsider his choice of words.

"You just take up Johnson's schedule, Moylan. But stick close to the office and come back on in when you see the coppers show up. They'll need to take your statement on this little asshole. You warm enough? Come, sit by the stove a few minutes. There's coffee."

"No. Yeah, sure I'm warm enough. In fact I'm sweatin' thanks to our boy here."

Ed pulled out his handcuffs and dropped his knee securely on the man-boy's back.

"Oof!" expelled the criminal in response to the shock and the pain.

"Hands behind your back!" Ed Moylan demanded.

The culprit obeyed and skillfully, Moylan, to the astonishment of his boss, deftly clicked the cuffs around the prisoner's wrists in a fluid one-handed motion. Maloney's lingering doubts concerning Ed Moylan's ability to resume his job were quickly melting away.

In anticipation Ed had practiced for two days on his sons at home, and when they had tired of the game, he practiced on eager little Frances, handcuffing the children over and over again, until he was able to perform the maneuver one-handed and swiftly.

Maloney was quite impressed.

"With only one arm, Moylan, nobody woulda blamed ya if you'd a just shot 'im," laughed the yard manager.

"Nah. He might have a family at home waitin' for him," explained the one-armed man, freshly awakened to his own mortality.

❧❧❧

Jim waited patiently for the train to come to a complete stop at the Terrace Station. On his last trip he had jumped off as the train still moved and slipped on the icy platform, almost going under the deadly car. Such accidents happened all the time, but Detective Sullivan never thought it could happen to him personally. But it just about did.

Before heading home he stopped in first at Police Headquarters, it being located just a few steps from the Terrace Station.

"How's the Alderman doin', Sully?" asked Superintendent Bull as Detective

Sullivan walked in.

"Yeah, how's JP doin'?" echoed Chief of Detectives Patrick Cusak in his Irish lilt. Cusak had been noticing Jim Sullivan's work favorably more and more lately, impressed by his resolve and his photographic memory for faces. The match had been clinched when Cusak learned of Jim's boyhood friendship with the great Mark Twain and found himself seduced by Jim's stories about the man.

"I ain't real sure. He's doped up real good still. Can't even finish a sentence before fallin' back t' sleep. But his doc says he's doin' great and expects a complete success."

"The Democrats are waitin' so tell him to hurry the hell up," said Supt. Bull. "Says so right here in the newspaper."

The boss showed Jim the *Buffalo Express* news article stating exactly that. JP was the chairman of the Democratic Executive Committee, and they were waiting on his recovery and return to set a meeting to prepare amendments to the party rules. His unfortunate illness was also bad timing due to the fact that JP needed to be present at the new year's organization of the city government's new Common Council.

"Well, you're just in time," said Bull. "There's been another shooting on Mansion Row, and we need to keep it quiet, considering the names involved. So I'm sendin' yous down there with Cusak to investigate."

"Okay, but give me a minute to call my Hannah first," Jim said, heading for the telephone box. "I just got off the train and came directly here. She's worried sick," he lied.

Cusak whispered, "Psst! We'll be stoppin' at yer house on a detour, Sully, if ye don't mind. Bull's coffee is pure shite, ye know. Ask yer Hannah if she wouldn't be mindin' puttin' on a nice pot fer us."

THE FIRST WARD II

WHAT IF?

"The folly of *what if*," stated Annie," is that people are always convinced that if they had only done things differently that the outcome would have been better, when in truth it's just as likely the outcome might have been worse, or at least, just as unsatisfactory in a different way."

"Worse? How could it possibly have been worse, Annie?" shouted Hannah angrily. "I lost three babies. I managed to keep them alive for two years or more, and then they just up and died! Each one. My first three did just fine, but the next three died, all at the same age. Why? What did I do so wrong? What changed in me?"

Hannah was suffering another dark episode. It was happening more and more these days, Annie noticed, always when Jim had to go out of town.

"That's not what I meant, Hannah. You are deliberately searching for ways to blame yourself. You can't go on doing that!"

Between keeping vigil over his brother in the hospital and scurrying about retrieving and delivering suspects and prisoners all across New York State and beyond, Jim had been absent quite a bit during the preceding eighteen months.

Hannah was alone in that big house with only little David for company much of the time. Junior and Nellie were in their teen years now, out and about in the world, busy with school activities, creating a life independent from the family. Hannah was feeling isolated and abandoned. With little David thankfully having survived—and having passed the heretofore dreaded age of two years still thriving—Hannah's worried mind had wandered more and more away from concern for him and toward other things. Unfortunately those other things were her four dead children. She renewed her self-flagellation for the drowning of seven year old John. She thought of two dozen things she wished she had done differently that very day, as futile as such an exercise in hindsight was. And who knows why or how the babies got sick? Only God could say, all had agreed. None of it made any sense.

In her mind Hannah meticulously went over the weeks preceding when each toddler became ill, reexamining her every move, her every decision. Did she not boil their drinking water or Hygenia bottles long enough? Did she not wash her hands often or thoroughly enough? Did she not fetch the doctor soon enough?

Annie had lost just one baby to Hannah's four, and Hannah was convinced that there must be some logical reason for that. Tom Nunan's wife had five babies and all were healthy and happy still. Was it the smoky air right here across the street from the ironworks? The filthy water in the river just yards away? Are germs floating on the air, infecting her family living so close to the polluted air and water?

"Hannah, JP and I live one house closer to both the river and the smokestacks than you do. You *must* stop torturing yourself!" Then, in an attempt to steer Hannah's mind away from the morbid thoughts, Annie got an idea.

"Why don't we take the children out to the Exposition property to see how they are progressing with the Pan? We can do that this coming Sunday," she proposed brightly.

"The Pan" was popular shorthand for the 1901 Pan American Exposition. The ambitious work of clearing and leveling the site adjacent to Delaware Park and the digging of lakes and canals had begun during the winter. Temporary rail tracks were laid down to bring in the mountains of building materials that would be required to construct the colossal undertaking. The urban railways had added extra streetcars to accommodate the additional thousands of workers commuting to the site. Men from all over the East and Midwest had emigrated to Buffalo in hope of finding work. The city was booming, changing and growing on a daily basis.

Annie had succeeded in calming her.

Hannah herself was aware that she was adrift. She felt it in her gut. She realized she was spending too much time by herself. She was disheartened that the older kids didn't need her the same as they used to. She was sick of keeping her mind occupied with thankless repetitive housework. The Church had offered some comfort for a while, but again she was turning away from it, angered by the things she witnessed firsthand, angered by Jim's stories of that hypocrite of the pulpit Father Brian O'Brien, repeatedly arrested on Canal Street for laying with prostitutes. He also told her that the new priest from St. Stan's was lurking down there as well in the Chinamen's opium dens. She was sickened by these stories. She felt personally betrayed by the hypocrisy.

Additionally she was remembering how intruded upon and resentful she felt when Jim would stop by the house unexpectedly with Mike Regan or Pat Cusak or John Geary. Then she'd holler at him for dragging some of the Mutuals home for a beer or two after she'd just finished mopping the floor.

"You've got that expensive boathouse right there back of our house! Why aren't you dirtyin' that place up instead of tracking up my nice clean floors?"

And so Jim stopped bringing the boys over, and now she missed the clamor and the laughter and the banter, their gentle kidding and scintillating gossip. These days she'd welcome all of it. Or any part of it.

"Be careful what you wish for, Hannah," Annie always liked to say.

Annie was right again.

When Jim came home from work that day she stood straight and tall as he collapsed at the kitchen table with a cold bottle of Beck's.

"I need to apologize," she said.

"What for?" he asked.

For...for bein' an idiot! For tellin' you that your friends weren't welcome here. For me sayin' my clean floors were more important than any of it. I miss them and I miss you. You can invite them back anytime you want. I don't know what's gotten into me lately, Jim. Honestly!" she said, disgusted with herself.

"I think I know," Jim countered. "The older kids aren't home near as much as they used to and you got more time on your hands now to think about unpleasant things. Don't get mad at me now Hannah, but I think you need a hobby, and I don't mean bringin' home more stuff needin' cleanin' and polishin'."

"Maybe you're right."

"Yeah, I am right. The house used to be full of people and noise. Nowadays we hear an echo when we talk to each other. Nowadays I think you might not even mind it so much if my brother came over to visit once in a while."

She fell silent at that.

"Of course *he won't*," Jim continued, "not since you pulled that knife on him here in the kitchen."

"I didn't pull a knife on him! I just...I...I just..."

"...pulled a knife on him," Jim reiterated.

"Well, he knows I never woulda shanked him, I mean...you know, for *real*."

"Well, I'll say this much for ye, Hannah. You sure know how to clear a room."

THE HAMBURG-MAIN CANAL

The agitated conversations among politicians and clerics concerning finally doing away with the fetid Hamburg-Main Canal and the human vermin attracted to its environs had reached such a crescendo that a plan of action was agreeably formulated and a general consensus reached.

Invigorated citizens congratulated themselves on their good work and shook hands. The worried-sick mothers of mischievous unruly fence-scaling boys sighed in relieved gratification. The Railroad Men salivated at the prospect of the coming bonanza, a central corridor of reclaimed land on which to run new rails, the promised bounty of which was the one and only sustenance capable of truly nourishing their empty souls: greenbacks.

Brothel managers panicked. The Far Eastern proprietors of the city's most notorious opium dens took to the streets fitfully discomfited. The sanitation department scrambled madly for a plan to reroute the flow of human waste heretofore allowed to mindlessly gush down the sewers toward an ignominious and disease-breeding culmination into the Hamburg-Main.

The venerable old canal was the furthest reach of the world-famous Erie Canal that had been almost single-handedly responsible for the early settling of the nation. Rather than being cleaned up and restored, as had been the plan of conservationists, it was contrarily to be stricken forever from the maps. Rather than realizing the dream of many a Buffalonian, that of enhancing the historic maze of waterways, slips and canals that spider-webbed the municipality so that the Queen City might rightfully claim her station as the Venice of America, the canals and slips instead were being systematically filled in one by one.

Only those aeronauts who had sailed the cloud-free rising currents high above the city in their lighter-than-air craft were acquainted with the true breadth and beauty that was the result of the Herculean efforts of the three previous generations of citizen planners, diggers, and haulers who engineered the awe-inspiring system of watery arteries. Only their eyes from a certain altitude could gather in and ascertain the sheer scope of the endless interconnections of ditches, estuaries, bottlenecks, slips, conduits, firths and trenches that lay out far below in such profusion as to fill their field of vision with awe and reverence for the men and women who excavated, navigated, labored and lived upon them.

On any given sunny late spring day with the blazing orb bouncing its reflections like a billion sparkling diamonds off the breeze-ruffled surfaces of these man-dug arteries hundreds of feet below them, there was no more beautiful sight in America or Europe to these airmen. The sky sailors could practically feel the cool kiss of the billowing clouds of mists rising from the plunge of the grand falls of Niagara. They could see the vast schools of silvery pike and salmon undulating below them just beneath the surface of the mighty Niagara River, the fish valiantly fighting the current of the great flow in its determination to pull them back downstream toward a deadly end over the raging precipice. In one grand sweep of their gaze the airship pilots could gather in a complete census of the population renowned locally as Canal Rats, those who made their homes on the thousands of barges, arks, ketches and tugs, sloops, packet boats, scows and steamboats that jammed the watery surfaces of the vast liquid arterial reticulation of the great megalopolis that was Buffalo, New York.

Good riddance, sneered Jim, as he stood on the rickety Louisiana Street bridge traversing the disgusting Hamburg-Main. He'd had his fill of dead bodies, sexually violated children, hopeless criminals and vast black clouds of biting summer insects in his almost-daily travail of policing the tenements that lined the stagnant deadly aqueduct. All of these horrors, he determined, were somehow directly related to the poisonous fumes exhaled by the thick black liquid that had been at some point in seemingly ancient times navigable fresh water.

The Hamburg-Main's undulating vapors were visible to the naked eye rising up in the summer's heat from the nasty one and a half mile-long gash that had long ceased to be viable as a route of navigation by craft of any sort. The trench had accumulated inestimable tons of garbage, scuttled canalboats and deceased dogs, dead horses that had cruelly expired on the streets in the very throes of their thankless labors, and the putrid human effluence of the city's toilets. These very same vapors were now claimed to be responsible for the recent wave of smothering deaths among local babies whilst they slept.

Like a swarm of giant iron arachnids, the earth movers, bulldozers and steam shovels would soon descend on the First Ward from all points south and east in an invasion of military amplitude and fervor in order to do away once and for all with the choleric scourge.

Jim lingered, lost in recollection on the very spot where his newlywed immigrant parents had first disembarked from their Erie Canal packetboat on their arrival in the city fifty years previous. The darkness had snuck up on him so stealthily that the detective was startled to find himself enveloped in its shroud. He descended the wooden planks of the bridge hastily and headed back down Louisiana Street toward the police station. The night was inky in the absence of any municipal lighting in the area, with only a faint moon filtered by clouds and the intermittent luminous glow of a window lamp lighting his path until he delivered himself to the gloomy arc-lighted yellow illumination of Seneca Street.

HANNAH IN THE COURTROOM

Late that afternoon when Jim arrived home from work for the day, his niece Molly Nugent was quietly playing Parcheesi with his daughter Nellie in the downstairs parlor as Zeke happily guarded over them. Jim kissed his bride for meeting him at the door with a welcome bottle of beer, cuffed the kids and bent down to greet the excited dog who swiped him a few strong licks on the lips. Then he and Hannah discussed the situation upstairs in the kitchen.

Even though the girls remained one floor below, Hannah rose from the kitchen table a number of times during their conversation to double-check the closed swinging door that separated the kitchen from the dining room to make sure that neither Molly nor Nellie had sneaked up behind it to eavesdrop.

Hannah's brother David Nugent, Molly's father, was scheduled to be sentenced to prison the following morning. Molly had been practically living with her cousins during the trial, and was so frightened about what might become of her father that she had erupted in hives, which she had been itching in the night to the point of bloodying herself.

Hannah refused to attend any of the court proceedings. She was filled with shame for what her brother had wrought and prayed night and day for his suffering victims.

The previous October, pistols at the ready, David Nugent had led his gang of 16 thugs on a raid, boarding an unloading ship at anchor down at the Minnesota Docks, the whaleback *Mather*. Silently stealing aboard late in the afternoon, they went from open hold to open hold raining down an estimated two hundred rounds of gunfire upon the concentration of unsuspecting vulnerable men hard at work below. When the captain readied to pull the ship's whistle to summon help, Nugent leveled his pistol at his head and dared to orphan his children.

It was an onslaught so outrageous and cruel that even in the city where Canal District atrocities often didn't make the front page anymore the population was incensed. Even worse that it was all the work of Fingy Conners, who continued to exercise free rein in his terrorizing of the First Ward despite all the transgressions he had regularly committed in the two decades leading up to the Grain Scoopers Strike the previous Spring.

Hannah's relationship with her younger brother had always been discomposed. Their mother had died. Their father then remarried their mother's sister. Then he died. Then their aunt-stepmother died. All three died within the space of four years when the children had barely started school. They were then farmed out to relatives in the ward, separately. Though they lived just one block apart, they seldom saw one other. The Sheas, with whom Hannah lived, knew only too well how troubled David Nugent was, and did all they could to keep the siblings from spending too much time together, lest Hannah become tainted. They feared David's explosive temper, but were troubled even more so by the proposition of what the young wilding's cunning influence might do to jeopardize his sister's promising future.

When David was in his teens and at his most impressionable, he'd attached himself to Fingy Conners, attracted by the wild folk tales told all around the ward about the pugilist saloonkeeper—tales that turned out to be true and more so.

He began hanging around outside Fingy's saloon after throwing a rock through his expensive plate glass window, Fingy threatening to rip his arm off but secretly admiring the boy's moxie. Soon Fingy had David running errands for him. David proved himself reliable and loyal. The willing lackey worked his way under Fingy's skin and the two came to establish a relationship that was far more like father and son than anything less. Fingy acted as demanding matchmaker between his timid niece Minnie Hayes and the reluctant David Nugent when David was of age. They married, cementing permanently with a family bond the profound loyalty that existed between Fingy Conners and David Nugent. Hannah did not want to attend her brother's wedding to Fingy's niece, so troubled was she by David's relationship with Conners, but such an affront would have electrified the ward and been interpreted as nothing less than a direct insult against both Fingy and her brother. So she went.

In a sensational trial where spectators had to fight it out among themselves daily to gain a ticket for a prized seat in the courtroom, David Nugent had been found guilty the previous December of the vicious crimes he was charged with. Not even Fingy Conners, with all the police captains, politicians, high-powered attorneys and judges he had tucked in his vest pocket could sway the jury chosen from among the laboring men of the First Ward from its findings.

❧❧❧

"May I go with you to the court tomorrow, Jim?" Hannah asked her husband. Jim was very surprised.

"Why sure, honey, of course," he said. "What made you change your mind? I haven't even heard you so much as speak your brother's name in a while."

Hannah was feeling differently, now that things had come down to a hair's breadth.

"It's possible I may never see David again. I can't let him go to prison with me not acknowledging him. I feel compelled to be there. Not just for Molly's sake, but..."

She stopped mid-sentence.

"But because he's your brother, regardless of his deeds," finished her husband.

The look on her face said it all.

"Yes, dear. I'm really frightened for him."

The weeks-long trial had provided opportunities for the curious to come have a look for themselves, but the sentencing was different in that it was a one-time event. There was a near-riot among the populace to gain access to the criminal act's penultimate culmination.

As family, Hannah was accommodated respectfully. Jim wore his uniform, and the couple entered through the side entrance, which was guarded against the throngs by Headquarters men. Michael Regan was there in the doorway conversing when the couple arrived. They all smiled nervous smiles, the men tipped their hats, and Hannah held her eyes downcast as she entered the courtroom and maneuvered toward the defendant's table. Hannah sat directly behind her brother where David's wife Minnie awaited them nervously with a reserved smile. She was glad to see them. The women exchanged a quick hug. Minnie sat on Detective Sullivan's left, Hannah on his right.

"How are the boys?" asked Hannah. "Will they be here?"

David and Minnie had three sons older than little Molly.

"No," Minnie said. I didn't want them to see their father like this."

Minnie Nugent harbored mixed feelings about her husband's only living sister never having come to the trial, even though it was Hannah who had taken charge of little Molly so that the Nugents might be together in the courtroom. Minnie knew that the Alderman's servant girl could have watched over Molly a time or two, freeing Hannah to at least make a representative show of support. David Nugent spoke little to his wife about his troubled past, or about his relationship with his sister for that matter. Minnie's knowledge of such things were derived almost entirely from the questionable versions offered by her Uncle Fingy rather than from her own spouse.

As Hannah and Jim seated themselves, David slouched forward head-down in deep conversation with attorney Hoyt. Fingy Conners flitted from Judge to court officers to friends and allies like a busy bee as Hannah and Jim got situated. David was alerted to the commotion of the arrivals in his periphery and turned around to see his sister sitting behind him. A look of extraordinary tenderness and relief came over his face. His eyes watered.

"Thank you for comin', both of yous, and fer takin' care of our Molly," he said. Minnie nodded and smiled in accordance.

David Nugent's once unshakable display of solid bravado and confidence had on this day disintegrated into a façade thinly masking misgivings and genuine doubts about his ultimate fate.

In all the years of their acquaintance Fingy had controlled every situation. No man working under Fingy Conners had ever been jailed longer than a day or two for any crime, no matter how egregious, before being sprung. David Nugent was the first ever to actually go to trial, but then again, the sheer ambition, audacity and hubris of his vicious attack could not be expected to result in anything less. Additionally, Fingy Conners' loss to the scoopers and the union's allies in the Catholic Church and city government the previous May had cracked the very foundation of Fingy's power base. No longer did the invincible armor of infallible certitude or *fait accompli* surround the amply-nourished ego of Fingy Conners.

David had of late begun experiencing dreadful nightmares about prison; forced labor, poor food, freezing cold prison cells. Worst of all, he began to have night terrors concerning falling victim to thugs who might rape him and indenture him into a living hell of imprisoned subservience over which Fingy held no power nor could provide any protection.

David had become fearfully aware just how vulnerable he would be without Fingy Conners, for Fingy was newly setting into motion an audacious plan that would wholly transform his family's life, shock the entire state of New York, and wreak economic devastation upon the city of Buffalo. With David shackled in Auburn Prison, and Fingy and his family beginning a new life as far removed geographically as sentimentally from the old, David feared he would be abandoned and forgotten, left to rot, forever.

Minnie excused herself to visit the ladies' facility. Her uncle remained at the front of the courtroom conferring animatedly with the Judge. David first turned and checked to make sure Fingy was out of earshot, then spoke to Hannah and Jim.

"I don't know what I'd a-ever done wit' out the two o' yous. I know you'll watch over my Molly if I go to prison, you've more than proven that."

"David..." Hannah began.

David continued. "Wait, Hannah. I'm afeared Molly and her mother'll fall under the wrong influences if I get sent away. Fingy...Fingy ain't exactly the best idea of what's a good parent, if you know what I'm gettin' at. I'm afeared fer Molly. I got my regrets. I don't want nothin' to happen to 'em. Will yous take Molly, if ye can? Please?"

Jim was surprised at the request, but before he could even think, Hannah replied, "Of course we'll raise her, Dave, just like our own...because she *is*. We're a family, all of us. But what...what about Minnie?"

Dave looked around again. "You might already realize that Minnie's a-scared o' Fingy, Hannah. And I think you know that Molly likes spendin' as much time with yous as she can, while Minnie busies herself wit' other things."

They waited for Dave to finish his thought.

What "other things" Hannah wondered silently.

He didn't elaborate any further.

"I wish I hadn't a-done it Hannah, ya gotta believe me. We was all drinkin' all the livelong day from one saloon t' the next. Drinkin'. Carousin'. Talkin' tough. One-uppin' each other. Gettin' pissed mad. And then the devil got in me, and I thought the oremen were doin' us wrong, disrespectin' me and Fingy, an'..."

His agitation was increasing.

"They was callin' us a bunch o' dirty scabs and..."

"Hey Dave," interrupted Jim. "Remember me? I was *there*. I saw what you did. All the people in the yard told me what you and your gang done from the beginning. So stop bullshittin'. Take responsibility."

Dave turned once again to gauge Conners' whereabouts. Seeing that Fingy was still busily engaged, Dave licked his lips nervously, then burst out with an astonishing revelation.

"Fingy's plannin' on movin' everything and everybody to Montréal, Jim! You gotta tell the Alderman! He's takin' my Minnie and my Molly and the boys, too! Everybody! He wants his revenge on Buffalo and everybody in it and for a thousand miles around. He's talkin' right now with some big businessmen, investors and bankers in New York and Pittsburgh and Chicago t'all put up half a million dollars to build a whole lot of grain elevators up there in Montréal, and move the whole business kit and caboodle—t' fuckin' Canada! I don't wanna live in no Canada, Jim! Or lose my girls to that godforsaken place, especially not them French frogs! They ain't gonna be speakin' no French, my wife 'n' kids, I kin tell yous that much!"

Jim was stunned.

The night the strike ended JP had theorized that Fingy was planning as much, but nothing since was heard about it. Now David's bombshell was heart-stopping.

"Fingy's come to figure that the power that the scoopers was able to gather together and bring against him during the strike last May was because how close this city is, everybody tied up the way they are, related to each other, goin' to church on Sunday, helpin' each other. Fingy thinks any two or more people who aren't with him is plottin' against him. Fingy wants to punish everybody he thinks is after him, which as far as I can figger, is everybody. He don't trust this place no more. What would somethin' like that do to this city, Jim?" he asked, his face twisted in fear and uncertainty.

Even Dave Nugent, most of whose neighbors and relatives made a living from the grain business or on the docks in some form or other, had scant idea of the extent of the damage that would surely result from such a scheme if successfully carried out. William J. Conners was creating a plan to try to steal the entire grain business away from the city—the grain-milling capitol of the world—outright, leaving everyone, especially those in the ward, stranded, without jobs or any hope of getting a job, out of nothing more than sheer greed and revenge.

"I don't want Molly growin' up no Canuck! Or worse, a Frenchie! I want her here wit' her family. Wit' you, Hannah, and Jim an' the kids, you're her family! Please, take her."

Hannah was confused.

"What would Minnie have to say, Dave?" asked his shocked sister. "She's Molly's mother! She's not going to give her little girl up."

"Minnie don't wanna go noplace neither! She's never been anywheres away from Buffalo in her whole life. All her friends is here. Yous are here. The girls she went to school with. Everybody. We talked about it. She's afraid Fingy'll make her pack up and go wit' him if I get locked up in a prison. So, I been tryin' to figure some way to make it so's Molly has to stay here for some necessary reason, and then Minnie will have to stay here with her too, to take care of her, o' course. I got money put away but not enough to support them more 'n two years or so. Then what? I just haven't figgered that part out fully yet. I was thinkin' of payin' a doctor to say Molly has some medical condition that can only be treated in Buffalo. I don't know. But if I just know that Molly will be safe with yous, it'll provide me with some peace of mind."

❦❦❦

The judge's gavel banged. The court was called to order and the stiff sentence read: two years in Auburn Prison. Dave shot to his feet in a panic, attorney Hoyt trying to restrain him. Hannah and Minnie grabbed each other and cried. Fingy leaned over and bellowed loudly to Dave, so all could hear, "Dis ain't over by no long shot! Hear me, Dave? We's gonna fight dis. Yous ain't goin' t' no prison, I will promise yous that much, little Davey!"

Attorney Hoyt had anticipated well and was exquisitely prepared with an interminable list of legal complaints, grievances, protests and a grand show of indignant bellowing outrage, all of which succeeded in getting the sentence reviewed.

David braved a smile. Minnie hesitated not fully understanding what had transpired. They embraced. Fingy took possession of Minnie's husband, putting his arm around his shoulder and walking him out to the encouraging instigations of a number of well-wishers on the street. Minnie followed behind like some afterthought.

She turned to look at Hannah.

"Come with us," mouthed Hannah silently, beckoning with her arms.

A sad smile came over Minnie's face and she shrugged and mouthed back, "I can't." And the little group disappeared out the door.

"We'll have a talk with her later Jim, when she comes by to collect Molly."

But Jim's mind wasn't on Molly, but rather on the thousands of men and their families who would be thrown into financial ruin if Fingy followed through with his scheme. The cataclysm resulting from such a move would prove an unprecedented debacle for the city.

"Let's go home to Molly and the kids, Hannah. I got to make plans to go back out to the hospital and have a talk with JP and see if he knows anything about this."

FINGY IN MONTRÉAL

The following morning found Fingy Conners pondering the great Canadian river's mighty waters, stilled now by a roof of ice. It was one of the colder winters within anyone's memory in Québec.

Sleighs glided effortlessly across its surface, ice bridging the Saint Lawrence from bank to bank, but standing there on rue Mill, fresh off the overnight train and surveying the imminent site of his newest obsession, Fingy Conners could vividly reimagine that which he'd initially set his eyes upon the previous summer in Old Montréal. The site was perfect for the location of the first in what was envisioned as a virtual city of towering Conners grain elevators, a project that would visit upon his enemies in Buffalo his ultimate reprisal.

"Dem scoopers t'ought dey had it bad workin' under me, did they now? Wait til dere ain't nobody left in Buffalo fer 'em t' work fer at all. Dat'll teach 'em. Dey tink deir kids is hungry *now?* Jus' yous wait!"

Buffalo's grain scoopers made up only a small measure of the intended receivers of his vicious retribution. Fingy Conners was planning on delivering a bombardment of malevolence; Alderman John P. Sullivan, Mayor Conrad Diehl, Father Patrick Cronin and Bishop James Quigley were all singled out to reap his ruthless animus.

At the time of his first visit to Montréal the previous June, the awesome breadth of the mighty St. Lawrence had dwarfed whatever idea the maps had given Conners as to the suitability of the superb route, expansively wide and very deep at most points from the Great Lakes all the way to the Atlantic Ocean. The amply expanded possibilities offered by such a natural passage over that of the Erie Canal made Conners' giddy.

"Dese fuckin' Canucks dey don't know what dey got here, which is all the better fer me, eh, Kennedy?"

John Kennedy just nodded, awestruck. Fingy's carefully practiced refined diction always evaporated completely whenever he was secure in the company of his longtime First Ward intimates.

The Québecois driver of their sleigh did not speak much English, let alone the First Ward dialect—not that Fingy had any compunctions about hurting anybody's feelings. After all, he himself possessed Canadian citizenship, his father Peter having been born in Canada, then returning his boy there to reassert his birthright at first opportunity. Peter Conners wisely foresaw advantages of dual nationality for his son.

The site at Montréal's Ville-Marie offered everything Fingy Conners would need: a dominating presence on the river, undeveloped except for the shacks and shanties of Montréal's newest immigrants from Europe littering the spot now, and offering an ideal situation for an ambitious developer such as he.

The neighboring tenements dotting the area surrounding Ville-Marie were crowded with unemployed Irish, French and Scots, offering an unlimited and malleable potential labor force.

The city's environs surprised him as to their age. Montréal was two hundred years older than Buffalo, and its history was displayed especially in the merchants' quarter with its fine customs houses, meticulously cobbled streets, and lovely European churches.

Canada was the future. He'd come to realize this while sailing down the St. Lawrence the previous summer. The United States had been compelled by geographical circumstance to dig a sad little ditch between Albany and Buffalo at enormous expense both to construct and to operate, and requiring an army of men to upkeep and maintain. Canada on the other hand cradled the magnificent Saint Lawrence, a natural highway, God-given, awe-inspiring, ennobling, needing neither maintenance nor management, and literally flowing with possibilities. On its banks Conners would construct a metropolis of grain elevators reaching for the heavens, the first of many such complexes to come in his newest international empire.

Within just a few days now, once the scheme was fully digested in Albany, the project to divert the lion's share of America's lake grain trade over to the St. Lawrence route would be certain to panic New York State officials as had no other scheme in the transportation field, ever. Some were sure to even become downright suicidal over it. Fingy relished the thought.

Unquestionably, Conners' revolutionary Montréal development would not be without profound influence on the canal commission appointed by New York Governor Teddy Roosevelt. This board would in response prepare a hurried report, that in accordance with the recommendation of Governor Roosevelt, would be quickly submitted to the state legislature. The State's counter-plan would be to transform the shallow aqueduct that was the current Erie Canal into a "great inland waterway,"one that would accommodate ships, rather than just barges; an artery that would rival the St. Lawrence.

The sheer absurdity of the State's idea would make Fingy guffaw in derision.

New York State's delusional plan would call for an initial outlay of at least $50 million, which included a large sum for the damming and regulating of the Mohawk River so as to supply a much increased volume of water to the improved waterway.

Such an ambitious renovation might accomplish all that the friends of the canals would expect or hope for, opening the Erie Canal to much larger craft, facilitating navigation and enabling boats to make the trip from Buffalo to New York City very much more quickly, and at the same time carry increased cargo tonnage. This would expand the capacity and traffic of the Erie Canal and thereby cheapen transportation by water, with which transportation by rail had already caught up, but now threatened to surpass in economy.

The problem was, although equal in some respects, there were distinct inarguable advantages to shipping by rail: the shallow Erie Canal froze over quickly in winter, completely halting traffic for as long as six months—half the entire year—whereas the rails operated year 'round.

Within a week, once Fingy's plans were widely known, the New York State Canal Commission would consider the continued viability of the Erie Canal to be as equally threatened by Fingy Conners as by the railroads. Something drastic would need to be done about both if the seventy-five-year-old Canal and the vast industry it spawned were to survive.

The Canadians themselves had as well recently been energized by Conners' threat. Conners' papers of incorporation had been filed, compelling the hurried organizing of a new Toronto transportation company to develop a plan to compete with Conners' so as to keep the Americans out. Principals in this new Canadian company included Toronto M.P. George H. Bertram, Ottawa M.P. Alex Lumsden, and Montréal Senator Pierre Forget. They had first descended on Montréal the previous summer after initially getting a whiff of the Conners' plan. Mistakenly, they were not overly concerned at first. But upon visiting Buffalo they came to realize that they had woefully underestimated the threat. Once their information-gathering efforts began revealing troubling understandings, the Canadian group scrambled to gather sponsorship.

The Canadians' impression, and it was a widespread one, was that the American syndicate might demonstrate too tender a regard for the commercial interests of Buffalo and the U.S.A. over those of Canada in Conners' Montréal endeavor.

In addition to the emerging competing Canadian syndicate, Fingy also had to reckon with the powerful hostility of the Canadian Pacific Railway, hell-bent on retaining in its own hands as much of the expanding grain business of that country as possible.

Even if Fingy succeeded in his scheme to include some Canadian capitalists in his syndicate, the Canadians were going to do all in their power to prevent the infamous American's securing of any concessions.

Sir William Van Horne, president of the Canadian Pacific, had come out in an interview declaring that "Canadians themselves can attend to the transportation matter without American interference." That utterance, being interpreted, revealed to Conners that the Canadian Pacific was trying to block his bid and gobble up the elevator business in Montréal for itself. There was also talk in Canada of the government stepping in and building elevators.

Fingy as usual had everyone running around every which way in utter discombobulation like rats in a dark cellar after the lights were suddenly switched on.

By this time the Barnett & Record Co. of Chicago, engaged by Conners, had practically completed all arrangements for beginning work on Conners' first elevator at Montréal. In the January 25, 1900 edition of the *Marine Review*, it was stated that "work will begin within the next few days." The article elaborated further, saying that the structures were to be constructed of steel, concrete and wood, having a capacity of 3,000,000 bushels, and the bins were to be of concrete of the Pierre Monier type, as near-fireproof as possible. The entire Conners plant, the article claimed, would be completed by November that year.

It was generally understood, both in Canada and the United States, that if full advantage was to be taken of the newly enlarged St. Lawrence canals, and if Canada was to get her share of the export trade in grain and flour over this route, that the facilities for transfer of these commodities to ocean vessels at Montréal must be greatly improved.

Despite the grand dreams of the Canadians, no north-of-the-border powerhouse version of Fingy Conners existed there; no Canadian possessing his single-handed determination and influence, his money, his extreme self-confidence, his dominance, his violent threatenings, or his extraordinary conviction.

Conners' scheme was one of considerable magnitude.

It contemplated the through-shipment of grain from the northwest to European points by way of the great river and its lately improved St. Lawrence canal route. His plan was to give to Montréal the advantage of such elevator and dock facilities as presently prevailed in Buffalo, to be accomplished by the organization of a company in Canada and by the cooperation of Canadian interests with the gentleman of Buffalo who proposed to furnish capital for the enterprise.

Conners had already put $200,000 into the scheme to immediately construct the first elevator and steel freight houses in order to stake his claim and prove his seriousness in making Montréal the new Buffalo. This would return Buffalo to its deserved fate, to the throes of the Great Depression of 1893 or worse. He didn't want to delay, to await the approval of the mercurial Canadians. His plan was to begin building on the site immediately to make it more awkward for the Canadians to consider disapproving his plan.

Hungry and cold, the two former First Ward visitors elected to depart from the site of the newest Conners enterprise and have the hired sleighman drive them through the snowy cobbled streets of old Ville-Marie to find a cozy spot to enjoy a meal. As they proceeded they surveyed the existing saloons closest to the new elevator site for possible venues from which to continue Fingy's wildly successful saloon-boss system, recently forbidden to him in the U.S. The very underpinning of his past and continued financial successes, the saloon-boss system had been newly outlawed in Buffalo, a personally devastating outcome of the scoopers strike.

Québec, however, was virgin territory, ripe for Conners' exploitation. Desperate, easily-intimidated, competitive, alcohol-loving immigrant laborers were the key to his fortune, and Montréal was overflowing with them.

On the Rue de Marguerite d'Youville a certain saloon caught Fingy's eye. The duo stopped and entered. It was of solid fabrication, soundly constructed of heavy timber and stone block, not dissimilar in floor plan to the wood frame Conners Hotel on Buffalo's Ohio Street, it too having an equally adequate bureau attached. They handed the proprietor Conners' Buffalo Courier business card adorned with his photo, the image picturing him much more refined and becalmed than his appearance at present, bundled, crimson-faced and angry as he was due to the biting cold.

After grunting goodbye to the indifferent saloonkeep they drove on without any particular itinerary in mind other than finding a suitable restaurant. They passed the Bouthellier warehouses which were employed for storing potash, a bleaching agent for export to England. The warehouses were a far cry from the depressing haphazard thoughtless counterparts that existed in Buffalo, these of Montréal having façades of cut stone, pediments, and *œil-de-bœuf* windows. Not far away a wildly extravagant elegant and colorful building was being erected in the Flemish style, and upon asking, Conners was told that it was to be a fire station.

"A fire station! Yous mean a hose company, fer firemen? Why, in Buffalo, we'd never throw away money on something so fancy! It's a waste of capital dat could be put to better use!"

Kennedy, the childhood detacher of Fingy's digit and source of his nickname replied, "I think it's fantastic, Fingy. Golly. Look at this place. I love this town!"

As they proceeded they halted once more for a few minutes to observe final touches being applied to the headquarters of the Grand Trunk Railway Company on McGill Street, a masterpiece of architecture boasting majolica bas-relief glazed earthenware tiles being installed that day in the vestibule.

"I'm freezin'. Let's cut the sight-seein' crap and get us some grub," ordered the Boss.

The driver recommended L'Auberge du Pierre Calvet, on the rue de Bonsecours, which had been established in 1725. Fingy had been in the best private clubs in Chicago and New York, but nothing compared to the solid dignity and atmosphere of the Auberge, with its massive stone walls, fine oil paintings, huge roaring fireplace, exquisite French wines and the intoxicating aroma of roasting suckling piglet and *pommes de terre au gratin*. The two old friends spent four hours there, seduced as much by the brandy as the cuisine and atmosphere, and talked over plans of domination and relocation.

"I t'ink I might could convince Mary to move her big fancy ass up here t' Montréal," Fingy winked.

Mary A. Jordan Conners was a West Seneca girl, having revealed herself after her marriage to Fingy to be the quintessential social climber, the epitome of America's *nouveaux riche*, a woman enthusiastically seduced by everything French. She was also quite aggressive and demanding in her husband's achieving even more than he already had, "for the sake of the children," she transparently claimed, rearranging one of her silk Parisian gowns, which were worn by her as daily fashion rather than reserved for special occasions.

"Every day must be lived and enjoyed to its fullest as if it were a special occasion. What good is life if we cannot always partake of the very best?" justified the native of the little two-room frame cottage on West Seneca's muddy Main Street.

The two childhood First Ward allies, who had sailed aboard the Great Lakes freighters and shared dreams together as boy-stewards, gently clinked their brandy snifters together as they gazed out the window at the horse drawn sleighs gliding noiselessly up and down busy snow-covered rue de Bonsecours.

"To Québec," toasted Kennedy, "and to an even grander future fer us to come."

As Kennedy continued his enthusiastic spiel, Fingy's mind disengaged from his friend for a moment to set to figuring out how to best gather his publicity resources so as to present his plan in its most favorable light, despite its certain terrible consequences. At every stage of his life Conners always managed to have a willing contingent of apologists and clarifiers sitting at the ready who would take whatever his latest assault on humanity was and spin it into something more or less positive.

Fingy Conners had recently set up a charity meant to aid the poorest agonized souls of the First Ward, who of course were imprisoned in their misery to begin with precisely due to his cruel business practices. He was richly praised far and wide for this new philanthropic turn by those who chose to suddenly forget exactly why such an emergency fund was needed in the first place.

His own newspapers—the *Enquirer* and the *Courier*—of course trumpeted the news of his generosity and compassion throughout the region while his telegraphic services delivered his praises to a hundred other newspapers across North America eagerly looking for any tidbits of interest they could parrot in order to fill their pages.

Besides his own news organs, what was perhaps more troubling was that so many others were additionally willing to take up his banner with praise, even members of the local Catholic clergy who had demonized him heatedly from the pulpits just a few months previous. They now conveniently sidestepped the evils he'd initiated, evils that they were only too well acquainted with, in order to newly paint Fingy Conners as a caring philanthropist in spite of the naked facts, as if a leopard could suddenly change his spots.

Fingy learned that the most effective way to quell the angry voices within the Catholic Church was to become a generous contributor of cash. Cleverly, knowing that his charity was now in place and operating caused those who might benefit from it to suddenly become uneasy about riling the man. In reciprocity, despite all he had done and still planned to do, Conners would be honored in 1904 with a two-page biographical spread in Thomas Donahue's deluxe encyclopedic *History of the Catholic Church in Western New York*, a copy of which almost every Catholic family in the area was urged from the pulpit to purchase.

"William James Conners...is a remarkable example of a well-earned and well-deserved success..." begins the torrent of praise within its Catholic pages.

Fingy Conners was a brilliant observer and manipulator of the human condition, a world-class chess player as adept at moving kings and queens as he was pawns and Catholic bishops in whatever direction most favorable to his interests.

GET WELL WISHES

Alderman Sullivan was feeling much improved, fidgeting with his get-well cards, moaning on and on about how his life was in limbo due to his illness. Annie, still feeling weak and unsettled from the loss of her baby, sat in a straight-backed chair across the empty room distracted, bored by his prattle and transfixed by the beautiful view of the snow-covered hills outside the window. She was wondering why she'd bothered to take the train all the way out to Hornellsville only to see her husband more interested in the well wishes sent by strangers' secretaries than with news of his own family.

"You do look so much better now, dear. I'm so relieved," she whispered gently.

"Dodged a bullet yet again, me love. Death seems to follow me wherever I go Annie, droolin' down the back of my neck like some crazed bull mastiff raging with hydrophobia. But it can never quite sink its rotten teeth into me, can it? I should've died fifty times over by this stage in my life, but I haven't yet, have I? See? I am getting better. I told you. Didn't I tell you?"

"Yes, dear, you surely did."

The room was studded with flowers in vases from the Mayor, the Governor, fellow aldermen, the Pan-American Exposition Directors, members of the Common Council, and the Mutual Rowing Club.

"See, Annie? It's not just the Democrats who are lost without me. Even Roosevelt feels the void created by my absence!"

He held up the tiny card that was attached to the greenhouse roses sent from Albany by the governor, or more accurately, the governor's secretary in charge of such niceties.

"They need me for the Pan-American!" he bragged.

"Dr. Buchanan said you might be discharged day after tomorrow if you keep improving at the rate you have been, so be cautious, JP. Try and stay in bed. These floors are icy. I brought your hairy slippers for a reason. You don't need another relapse."

The slippers were ridiculous, the insides brimming with curly auburn bison fur spilling out in such abundance as to almost trip the wearer. They were handmade in a little teepee or some frontiersman's cabin out on the plains in Nebraska someplace, JP explained, his fascination with the personalities of the West expressed this time in his choice of footwear. Perhaps because he couldn't wear normal shoes, or wear shoes in a normal way, he was fascinated by their outlandishness.

JP was frustrated by all his illnesses and confinements to bed over the years. So much precious time lost, he worried. He had nearly died even as his first successful campaign for city alderman was coming to its logical conclusion. That was a close call. To have worked all those years toward that single goal, only to be close to death as election day approached, and he, silenced, unable to strike back at his opponents and political enemies. He never forgot those who'd kicked him when he was down and helpless. He made sure they paid.

"The children are doing well," Annie said, having waited in vain a half hour for him to bother to inquire. "They miss you."

"Oh, that's nice."

He was fixated on other things. More important things. The Common Council. The Democratic Executive Committee. The Pan American Exposition. The Sullivan Ice Company. The Mutual Rowing Club. Annie should have taken it as a compliment of sorts, his being so secure in the knowledge that the family ran like a well-oiled machine with her at the helm. She had shielded him from far too much family responsibility, she realized too late. His children needed their father more than they ever got him. But she knew all too well that as long as she continued to have everything efficiently under control, he'd feel free to focus his energies elsewhere.

Maybe she could change that.

"That's good, Annie. Good to hear. I can't wait to be back home to coach my little team."

He was determined to have nine children, so they could form a family baseball team. As captain of the Buffalo Aldermens, the informal team made up of the city fathers that played at the Island Beach grounds, he took the pastime much too seriously, considering all the other responsibilities that he had assumed already.

"I hate to leave you, JP, but Hannah has been run ragged taking care of both of our families, as well as David Nugent's, and I'm anxious to get back before that blizzard hits. I'm so happy you're nearly well again."

Chicago was already buried under two feet of snow and the telegraphed warnings from the west were ominous. Trainloads of individuals were being left stranded on the tracks from Wisconsin to Ohio right in the middle of nowhere.

"Of course, my love. I'll be fine. I have a pile of papers to look over. You just hurry home so you can outrun the storm."

"The whole idea of bed rest, JP," she reminded him, "is *rest*. *In bed*. You do understand that, don't you?"

He just smiled. She bent over and kissed him. He was sitting in a chair next to his bed.

"Now climb back in and I'll cover you up. Stay warm. Do what the Sisters tell you to. We all need you at home."

She glanced back as she stepped out the doorway to smile a last goodbye, but his head was already buried in his papers.

A cold blast hit her in the face as she walked out onto the veranda. A carriage was waiting to take her to the nearby station.

"Don't you have any enclosed carriages?" Annie asked the driver, annoyed and shivering. "This weather is dreadful!"

"We do have one ma'am, but it's already been hired. Sorry. The drive to the station will only take just three minutes."

❧❧❧

JP held his precious cards in his hands, the celebrity signatures reinforcing his lofty stature as conceived in his own mind.

"Best Wishes For Your Recovery. Best, Conrad," came from the Mayor.

It was just over a year previous that the Mayor had sent a letter to the Board of Aldermen containing recommendations which called into life the Pan American Exposition Company. As Council president, Alderman Sullivan offered the resolution at the meeting of the lower house, directing the Corporation Counsel to draft a special act giving the Mayor power to appoint a committee to attend at the birth of the new enterprise. This was adopted and the Board of Councilmen at its meeting the following afternoon endorsed the action of its colleagues.

The Mayor then appointed the members of the Provisional Committee, which included three other alderman besides JP, as well as the city's top business leaders, and as well too, the man who had his finger in just about every pot these days, Fingy Conners.

JP shuffled through the cards again. There was nothing to be found from Conners. No get well wishes. No flowers. They were having their predictable periodic differences of opinion these days. Conners was supposedly spending time in Québec on business, it was said. The idea registered quizzically in the alderman's still-drugged mind. *What kind of business would Fingy have up in Canada?* he wondered. He'd forgotten all about his realization of such the night of the Scoopers Strike ending.

JP resumed filing through the deck of well wishes: "T.R.", read the signature on the governor's card. JP didn't dare call him "T.R." to his face, and Roosevelt never made himself so familiar to JP as to encourage him to call him anything other than "Governor Roosevelt."

Almost exactly one year before to the day, JP had boarded the Empire State Express for Albany with Mayor Diehl, Fingy's attorney Bill Hoyt, Judge J. Henry Metcalf, Alderman Kennedy, and the various major boosters among the city's businessmen, led by George Urban and J.N. Scatcherd.

They were headed to the capitol to present the Pan American Exposition bill for approval. Chairman Brackett of the State Judiciary committee asked Judge Metcalf to explain just what the bill which the committee had under consideration was intended to accomplish.

Judge Metcalf cleared his throat as he stood and faced his audience in the Assembly Chamber and began to explain the bill in detail. He had not proceeded very far when Mr. Brackett interrupted that he did not believe that there was any opposition to it and suggested that a vote be taken. The vote resulted in a unanimous agreement to report the bill favorably without amendment. This decision was greeted with enthusiastic applause by the Buffalo boomers.

The committee next marched across the Grand Staircase and down the barrel-ceilinged hallway to meet with Teddy Roosevelt in the Executive Chamber. Various members took turns explaining the object of their visit. Alderman Sullivan, well aware that he was a Democrat standing before the Republican Governor, humbly asked for the Governor's pledge of approval of the bill. Roosevelt replied that he would take a look at the bill and if he had any questions, he would get back to them on it.

Mr. Urban interrupted tactfully, explaining that the need for haste on the Governor's part was caused by the efforts of the city of Detroit to secure the exposition for the state of Michigan. Alderman Sullivan explained to Roosevelt that it was necessary they raise half a million dollars by the following Saturday night, and they needed the Governor's approval in order to get moving on that.

"Then I will rush it right through," Teddy boomed, looking JP straight in the eye. "Buffalo is obviously the rightful place for such an important exposition."

❧❧❧❧

JP glanced out the window of his hospital room and noticed that it still had not begun snowing. He was sure that Annie would make it home all right, without the train experiencing any delay from the approaching blizzard. He opened once again the card from little James, their youngest, barely six months old. It was covered with embossed violets and smelled of that flower's scent. Annie had imitated a child's scrawl in signing it: "Get well soon Pa, we miss you. Love, James."

JP placed all the cards in a neat stack on the bedside table, then pulled the covers up around himself.

"I've got to get out of here," he mumbled to the empty room.

Just as he began to doze off, the nasty Sister Seraphim came in with that day's issue of the *Buffalo Express*.

"Here's your newspaper, Alderman Sullivan."

"Thank you, Sister," JP said with a wink, never considering for an instant whether winking at a nun was appropriate for he had never attended parochial school. He fully meant to place the newspaper aside until later and settle in for a nap, but the headline caught his eye: NUGENT SENTENCED.

The sub-headlines set his mind to stirring: TWO YEARS IN AUBURN THE PENALTY IMPOSED, and below that, HOYT IS STILL FIGHTING.

Fingy's top attorney and JP's fellow Pan-American Exposition committee colleague Bill Hoyt was intent on exhausting every legal source to save his client. He planned to make an appeal.

County Judge Emery imposed the sentence, and JP mused about Nugent's destination, Auburn State Prison, practically a second home to the Sullivan brothers' abominable stepfather, the late Peter Halloran. For various despicable offenses committed before and throughout his marriage to his mother Mary, including plunging a kitchen butcher knife into her neck right in front of the children, Peter Halloran had come to know that particular prison as he did others very well through the decades.

Ashamed of his sordid history Halloran was not. Peter Halloran delighted in relating disturbing recollections of his adventures behind bars at the place he called "the castle" for its architectural resemblance to such an edifice. The young JP had figured this made perfect sense since every castle had a dungeon in which to toss its worst scoundrels.

JP continued reading.

The *Express'* story told of the fight that attorney Hoyt and second attorney Shire had waged in defending his sister-in-law's brother on the charge of assault, first degree. They objected to the indictments. They objected to the jurisdiction of the court. They held that the grand jury that found the indictments was irregular and unauthorized. They fought against David Nugent's arraignment to plead. They had the trial put off many times. They exhausted their challenges of jurymen. They quibbled and objected and took exceptions throughout the trial. They opposed District Attorney Penney at every point. They produced a wonderful number of witnesses who swore on Nugent's behalf. They took exceptions to the court's charge, and when the jury reported the verdict, they moved for a new trial. They delayed the arguments on the motion for over a month. Judge Emery denied the motion and appointed the day of sentencing.

When Nugent was arraigned for sentence, Attorney Hoyt demonstrated that his resources were still not exhausted. He objected to sentence on all his old grounds as to alleged irregularity of the court, the grand jury and the indictments, and additionally on one new ground, the novel argument that the case should have been tried by a United States Court. He argued that the scene of the alleged crime, which was the armed assault upon Polish ore handlers in the hold of the steamer *Mather* lying at the Minnesota ore dock, was under Federal jurisdiction. The court overruled his objections. Then Hoyt moved for an arrest of judgment. Judge Emery denied the motion.

Hoyt then made a plea for leniency. As a testimony to Fingy Conners' extraordinary talent for manipulation, Hoyt presented a statement signed by ten of the twelve men on the jury asking that Nugent be set free with a $250 fine as his only penalty. Hoyt called the court's attention to the evidence as to Nugent's previous good character and asked the court to be merciful.

The *Buffalo Express* story reported that Judge Emery imposed sentence in these words:

LO EVENING

BUFFALO, N. Y., WEDNESDAY, JANUARY 17,

NUGENT'S SENTENCE IS FOR TWO YEARS.

Sent to Auburn Prison by Judge Emery This Afternoon--Appeal May Be Taken on Certificate of Reasonable Doubt.

David J. Nugent was arraigned for sentence before Judge Emery at 2 o'clock this afternoon. He was convicted in County Court in November last of assault, second degree, after a long and stubbornly fought trial, on an indictment charging him with assault, first degree, in shooting John Möth, an ore handler, in the hold of the whaleback Mather, in the riot on the docks in June last.

Judge Emery was on the bench at 2 o'clock, ready to take up the case, but Nugent and his counsel, William B. Hoyt, were late in arriving. District Attorney Penney appeared for the people. The court room was crowded with scorners and curious spectators. None of Nugent's political friends were present when court opened.

Nugent was dressed in a neat suit of gray worsted, with a dressy brown overcoat and appeared perfectly cool.

Before the District Attorney could take his record, Attorney Hoyt raised his usual technical objections to the indictment of Nugent, the jurisdiction of the court etc. He made a new point by claiming that the case was more properly under the jurisdiction of the United States Court. He made a motion that the taking of the record be arrested.

"I'll deny that motion," said the Judge.

The record was then taken. Nugent said he was 32 years old, married, a hotelkeeper by occupation, and lived at 490 South Park avenue. He said, in answer to question, he had never before been convicted of any crime.

"Have you any legal cause to show why the sentence of the Court shall not be pronounced on you," asked the court clerk.

"I have none," replied Nugent. "Mr. Hoyt will take care of that part of it."

PLEA FOR CLEMENCY.

Mr. Hoyt then arose and made a strong plea for leniency. He referred to the

guilty of a serious crime. Now some of the jurors have asked that you be fined only. I could sentence you to serve five years in prison, and to pay a fine of $500 as well.

"It is unpleasant to sentence a man in any case. But the law directs what must be done in such a case. The verdict means that you went into this host with a drawn revolver and shot into the hold upon a mass of poor, inoffensive and unarmed men. It is your good fortune that nobody was killed."

"Such crimes cannot be punished lightly or our laws and the authority of our courts would be defied at will, and render no protection to the community. It is most fortunate for every person that night on that boat that no one was actually killed when the charge would be mere serious.

"Nevertheless, there is a possibility which the jury seem to have considered in recommending you to mercy, that you may have acted under great excitement, without understanding fully the effect or consequence of your acts.

"The court after much consideration has come to the conclusion to give you the benefit of the doubt in that respect, and also the doubt raised by previous good character and not impose the extreme penalty of the law. In imposing the penalty which the court will pronounce, it is deemed by the court that due weight has been given to the recommendation of the jury at the time of the rendering of the verdict.

"It is proper for the jury to make that recommendation whenever deemed proper, and it is the duty of the court to heed the same, and the court believes that due consideration and due weight have been given to the recommendation of the jury for leniency.

NUGENT'S SENTENCE.

"The sentence of the Court in your case is that you be confined in the State's prison at Auburn at hard labor

"Nugent, the jury by its verdict has found you guilty of assault on the lesser charge of assault in the second degree. Your boarding of the Mather with a gang with loaded pistols drawn is a clear indication of planning and forethought, which fits the criteria for the original charge of assault in the first degree.

"The jury has now seen fit to show its mercy, however misplaced that might be, by finding you guilty of this lesser charge, that you were concerned in the commission of the crime which resulted in the shooting and grave injury of Mr. Molik on the boat Mather.

"While acting as jurymen the members of the jury decided that it was their duty, from the evidence presented, to render their verdict, and performed that duty. Certain members of the jury, now, as individuals, have signed a paper asking that you be let off with a fine.

"Under this verdict you could be sentenced to imprisonment for five years and in addition be fined $1000, but the fact that jury has recommended you to the mercy of the court is to be taken into consideration in fixing the penalty for your crime.

"It is a very unpleasant duty to sentence a man, and especially a man who has a family and who has heretofore borne a good reputation, but the court must do what the law requires, and the court believes it to be a plain duty. In view of the enormity of the offense of which the jury has found you guilty, to impose a more severe punishment than a mere fine.

"According to the evidence in this case which the jury must have believed in order to have reached this verdict, you, being armed with a loaded pistol and having gathered a number of men who were likewise armed, took forcible possession of a vessel lying at anchor in the harbor of this city which was wholly entitled to the protection of our laws, and fired or caused to be fired, shots at innocent unsuspecting men densely confined within the hold of this vessel with nowhere to run and no way to protect or defend themselves.

"Such crimes cannot be punished lightly or our laws and the authority of our courts would be defiled at will by lawless men and afford no protection to the community. It is most fortunate for every person present on the boat that night that no one was killed, as if anybody had been killed the charges would have been more serious.

"Nevertheless there is a possibility which the jury seems to have considered in recommending you to mercy, that you may have acted under great excitement without understanding fully the consequences of your acts. The court has concluded, after much deliberation, to give you the benefit of the doubt in that respect and also the doubt always raised by previous good character, and not impose the extreme penalty of the law.

"In imposing the penalty which the court will pronounce, it is deemed by the court that due weight has been given to the recommendation of the jury at the time of rendering the verdict. It is proper for the jury to make that recommendation whenever deemed proper, and it is the duty of the court to heed the same, and the court believes that due consideration and due weight have been given to the recommendation of the jury for leniency.

"The sentence of the court in your case is that you be confined in the State Prison at Auburn at hard labor for the term of two years."

Nugent jumped to his feet in shock as his wife and sister cried out. Fingy in contrast looked confident and stoic. Quickly Attorney Hoyt took a few moments to calm his client and his client's relatives, then proceeded.

Hoyt immediately asked for a certificate of reasonable doubt upon which to make an appeal, which was granted. Hoyt then asked for a stay of execution of the sentence for 60 days, which was also granted.

This allowance and the posted bond of $5000 would allow David Nugent to remain a free man until a decision could be reached on his appeal. If the appeal were granted, Bill Hoyt could easily get an order allowing Nugent to remain free until the appeal is determined.

"The attorney seems to be confident," the *Express* editorialized, "that he can secure a new trial for his client."

JP put the newspaper down just as his brother walked into his room. Sister Mary Seraphim contorted her face in an expression of undisguised contempt at first sight of the policeman, then imperiously stormed out.

"Hello brother!" cheerily called JP. "It's awful late in the day for you to be in this neck of the woods."

"I had to return a boy to his mother in Hornell before the storm hit. Well, I didn't *have to*. A patrolman could've done it. But it gave me the opportunity to come see you, being right in the next town over. Any news about your release from the clutches of these Angels of Misery and Death?"

JP laughed. "That ugly one certainly knows you've got her number. She treads very lightly around me."

"She looks to be a character straight out of Ma's horror stories about poor Aunt Bridget!"

"That she does, Jim. She looks like she'd be right at home slave drivin' at the Magdalene Laundry."

"I wouldn't be a bit surprised if that's exactly where they scraped 'er up from," snarled Jim.

The Detective paused to appraise his brother. "I gotta say, JP, you do look a little less like death-warmed-over today. I mean, compared to last week. I almost stopped by Holy Cross cemetery to pick out a fancy little headstone for you last Tuesday."

"Oh, what a sweet gesture, Jimmy. I thank the dear Lord for ye every night before I go to sleep. Keep in mind I'm partial to rose granite."

JP picked up a little hand mirror from the table, a sample submitted by a company wanting a concession for souvenirs for the Pan Am Exposition. He studied his gaunt face briefly.

"As distinguished as ever," he concluded, as they both laughed.

"Doc Buchanan says I can go home day after tomorrow perhaps. He will let me know for certain late today, so I'll call to let you know."

"I have to go to New York tomorrow, JP, so I can't be here. I'll send Junior down here so you'll have company on your way back."

The detective knew JP would need someone to literally lean on, and to help carry his bag, but his proud brother would never admit to that.

"I'm perfectly capable of going home on the train by myself," defensively stated JP.

"Oh no you're not, Alderman," said Dr. Buchanan as he walked in on the conversation. "Someone must accompany you on board the train, and then guide you home, right up to and *inside* your front door. And then stand there to make sure you climb into your own bed. That's an order. Or else we can just keep you here."

"All right, then! This matter seems to have been settled," chuckled the detective. "So, your favorite nephew it will be, JP."

"I'll see you in the morning alderman," the doctor announced. "I'll be leaving for the day, now, gentlemen. Good afternoon, Detective. A pleasure to see you, as always," smiled the doctor.

"Likewise Dr. Buchanan. Thank you for everything," Jim responded sincerely.

The doctor's footsteps could be heard descending the staircase.

"Will Junior be able to come here? Did you talk to him already?" asked JP.

"Of course he will, JP. Junior will do anything for the family. You know that."

"What's he been doing lately?"

"He's obsessed with photography these days. He wants to build a little developing closet in the cellar to process his plates. He's all excited about a photo exhibit opening tonight at The *Express'* news office. I might go downtown with him if I get back in time, storm permitting, if my train's not held up."

JP displayed the newspaper containing the story he'd just read, and mocked, "Say there, Detective, have you read the very latest about your famous brother-in-law?"

Jim nodded his head. "I was there. In court. With Hannah."

"Hannah went to court?"

"Yep. It finally hit her that if he were sent to prison she might never see him again. That idiot deserves prison, JP. A long, long sentence."

The unfairness of the world never ceased to dishearten the detective.

"There is only so much bad meat a man can digest," he lamented. "At least Hoyt didn't try and present some cowardly defense, like insanity, or claiming to be defending the nation against hordes of Polish invaders, or some such malarkey. Too many malcontents try to justify the worst characteristics of their nature by cloaking their acts in the guise of religion, patriotism or some outlandish definition of morality to try and deflect from the true nature of their deeds...even to try and get away with murder. At least I have to hand that much to Hoyt."

"But on the other hand, Jim, what were those jurors thinking? They want to let that lump of horse shit walk free among their own families? Don't those people fear for any of their own when they're sitting there recommending that someone like him be allowed back on the streets?"

"People have to get it through their fool heads, JP, that prisons aren't meant to punish—they're meant to *separate*. Prisons are cages that we've constructed for the purpose of segregating and confining those animals who have forfeited their right to live among the rest us due to their violent behavior. And Nugent has more than proven that such a separation applies to him. Prisons exist for the purpose of keeping the rest of us, our defenseless children, our old people, safe from harm."

JP nodded in agreement.

"Well, you're preaching to the choir, Jim," he said, and then recalled a saying his mother had oft recited time and again throughout her life. "Remember what Ma used to say: 'What determines the true character of any man is the character of the men he chooses to defend,'" he quoted.

They both fell into silence for a few moments, thinking about their late mother.

Jim continued. "Amongst that fool jury were laborers, or the sons or fathers of laborers, who themselves could just have easily been the victim of Dave's insanity. What could explain their sudden sympathy? I am always perplexed by seemingly good people believing they are less likely to someday be victims of criminals than be criminals themselves. It's as if they're saying, 'If I stand up for the man who committed this act, and I find myself in a similar predicament one day, I will already be on record for declaring that transgressions such as this should be forgiven. Then it is more likely that I might be forgiven as well.'"

"Hedging their bets?" JP guessed.

"Yep."

"Fingy bribed them," JP summed up.

"Undoubtedly."

"But if Nugent does go to prison, will you and Hannah keep Molly?"

"JP..." Jim began, haltingly. "Dave told me and Hannah something disturbing in court yesterday. That's really the reason I came today."

"Okay. Well, what did Nugent say?" JP wondered.

Jim expected JP to have some idea about what he planned to say, so he paused to allow his brother a comment.

"What? What is it?" asked the alderman, claiming having heard nothing of any particular concerning nature.

"Have you heard anything new to bolster that hunch you told me about the night the Scoopers Strike ended? Remember? About Fingy moving to Montréal? Seems like he's been hatchin' a scheme with millionaires in Chicago and New York to move the entirety of Buffalo's grain business to Canada."

The alderman was as yet a bit discombobulated and didn't quite understand.

"What? ...what do you mean, Jim? I..."

"When Hannah and I went to Dave's sentencing yesterday and Fingy was preoccupied Dave told us that Fingy had gathered together investors from all over the East and they were planning on building what Dave called "a metropolis of grain elevators" on the river in Montréal. This would mean the grain trade could completely bypass Buffalo by way of the Welland Canal, stealing Buffalo's entire grain business away to Canada. David said Fingy is in Montréal right now surveying the sites on which he plans to erect all these new elevators, and that he might have already begun building there."

"What? Oh my God! So that's the business in Montréal I've heard about? I thought it was something more trivial. Are you kidding? Why, that fucker!" snarled JP.

"Fucker is just a particle of what that murderin' bastard is, JP. So you haven't heard nothin' about this at all? Don't you recall your tellin' me this very thing the night of the scoopers strike ending? You said you thought Fingy was plannin' on movin' his business to Montréal."

"Me? No! I...oh, wait a minute. Okay, now I remember. I was just throwing out ideas back then, don't you know? You and me, we'd been drinking and we were celebrating and happy, and I was just considering some theories..."

"Well, it seems your drunken 'theory' was correct." Jim said.

"I haven't heard a single detail about Montréal until now. Just some general gossip about him conductin' some sort of new business up there. Oh my God. We could all be ruined. This city could be ruined. Oh! And the Exposition! News like this could knock the wind right out of that entire thing—end it right here and now!"

"That's exactly what you said to me that night last summer. I can't believe you forgot. Remind me never to take laudanum."

JP continued his rant.

"And after all the work and money we've put into it so far. All those subscriptions that all those people, hardworking people, the little students in the schools, have paid for!"

"Well, JP, I think you need to call some of your friends and talk about what this means. Can he actually do this? I mean, does he have the power to actually divert Buffalo's business away from the city?"

"My God, how typical! Really! How am I surprised by this? The man is a prominent member of the Pan American Exposition Company at the same time that he's plotting a scheme that will sabotage that very thing! He would have to move his ass out from this city entirely in any case, lest a bullet surely find him, if not a bomb."

"Well, since you can walk downstairs by yourself now, why don't you telephone a few people to see if others know what Fingy's up to. I gotta get home before the storm hits."

Jim stood and put his coat on, then wrapped his wool plaid muffler around his neck twice.

"Already? I'm bored to tears and jumpy as a racehorse. Can't you just sneak me out under your coat?"

"I'll see you at home day after tomorrow, JP. Make a few calls, rattle some cages, and then get some sleep."

"I won't sleep until I'm in my own bed with my arms around my Annie."

"Bye. You heard me. Try and sleep."

"All right. Bye."

Jim disappeared out the door while JP began calculating who he needed to call.

As he descended the oak staircase the Detective passed Sister Mary Seraphim on her way up. She completely disregarded him despite the narrowness of the stairway. In his mind he pictured her bouncing back down the stairs head over heels. How good it would feel to set that apparition in motion.

He continued to delight in the fantasy of the nun's mortal tumble as he trudged toward the station.

THE MAGDELENE LAUNDRY

The train was not crowded. Jim had already read all the newspapers. Feeling unsettled, he noticed an irritation at his back. He turned to look. The leather seat wore a clean slash in it, most likely from a bored young vandal's pocket knife, he surmised. Stuffing had been removed, leaving an uncomfortable void. He got up to find another seat more accommodating. The car was warm, the windows frosted over with a pattern faithfully imitating a forest of beautiful ferns etched in ice. This miracle of nature always enchanted him, but others seemed not to take much notice.

People on board were quiet. He closed his eyes.

His conversation with JP had reminded him of the terrible fate of Aunt Bridget. He hadn't thought about the story for years. He thought also of the pernicious Sister Seraphim back at the hospital, wondering what turned her into that damaged thing she'd become. Then he began to recollect his mother's emotional telling of the story of his late father's younger sister, the aunt he never knew. She always wept whenever she told Bridget's tale, even though the two had never met.

❧❦❦❧

In Limerick, there exists a house of horrors still in full operation, even now into this new century, infamous throughout the South of Ireland. It is the Good Shepherd Convent and Magdalene Laundry, a place of enforced servitude of young women, unspeakable cruelty and unfathomable sadness.

It stands in Clare Street on the very site of Farrancroghy, the place of public executions in the 16th and 17th centuries. "You best be good or we'll else send you off to the Good Shepherd!" parents at their wits' end would threaten their misbehaving children, and the children would immediately fall silent.

The Sullivan brothers' father's sister, Bridget Sullivan, had been seduced by their parish priest in Ennis when she was just fifteen. That pious agent of Christ left her with child. While performing the insidious act he whispered that he loved her, and promised he would take care of her. Instead, the shame of her pregnancy and the ruin that such a revelation would surely bring the priest as well as to the parish he would lose dominion over summoned into being an evil collusion between Ireland's Catholic Church and Bridget's father to pack the little girl up like so much garbage and deliver her to the nuns at Good Shepherd.

The shame of such an immoral failing in that society at that time was intolerable, and girls of her type, for she was indeed seen as being to blame, were sent to the nuns at Good Shepherd Asylum where they would give birth in secret and live out an anonymous, shamed, and pointlessly cruel life behind high gray walls topped with shards of broken glass meant to keep them from escaping. No one need ever know.

Many such girls, made pregnant by their priests, their doctors, their own drunken fathers or brothers, were discarded there. Other unfortunates banished to Good Shepherd had not become pregnant at all, but were placed by families who perceived that their raped daughters had been made unmarriageable by the act, as they were now forever tainted. One such star-crossed unfortunate who Bridget labored alongside in the convent laundry had been sodomized repeatedly at only age eleven and afterward dragged here by her rapist brothers.

Such a blighted victim was deemed from the day of her assault forward to be an actual moral danger to Irish society, and so she was removed from it, permanently.

No policeman had arrested these girls. No lawyer had represented them. No court tried or sentenced them. No Judge reviewed the case. No challenge was permitted. No release or parole date was ever set. Imposed complicitly by the Holy Catholic Church of Ireland and the families of the unfortunates, it was a life sentence for most, particularly for those who could not survive the desolation and deprivation of their unjustified imprisonment. The barbaric Medieval Ages that were ancient history elsewhere in Europe had yet to see their end in St. Patrick's land.

John Sullivan was horrified for his younger sister. He had plotted scenarios within which to garotte the guilty priest and sink his sacrilegious bulk, rocks filling his pockets—and a few more shoved up his arse for good and proper measure—beneath the river Shannon. He shadowed the priest for some time and learned his routine. On a visit to his Kerry cousin Michael Sullivan across the estuary in Abbeydorney, the two discussed the particulars. John had hoped to find a way to pull it off immediately before his departure for Queenstown, to be safely aboard a ship on the high seas before they found the decomposing vow breaker, if indeed they ever did.

He was infuriated with his father and ashamed of his mother for agreeing to the diabolical solution. He promised himself he would find some way to make things right for Bridget and her baby. It was a calamity, he railed, "...we Irish having to fight off both the Church and the British!" The social mores of that time and place, and the might of the Catholic Church allowed that this cruel course of action be followed. Any girl who'd been ruined in this way whether by romantic seduction or violent rape had to be expunged.

Months before he left Ireland to emigrate to America, John made application for permission to visit with his sister and her baby. It was a daunting and complicated process, requiring meeting a long list of preconditions, making written permission of the nuns a dozen weeks in advance, and then finally obtaining the approval for the visit from the Bishop himself.

The very Sunday before John was to embark for Queenstown, he was finally notified that he could come to the Good Shepherd Asylum to say his good-byes to Bridget and his nephew.

The famine that had devastated Ireland was still raging. John Sullivan's involvement in the failed Young Ireland Insurrection, exacerbated by the famine, drove him to seek a new life in the New World.

"People in Ireland aren't even acting in their right minds anymore. They're barely human," he told his friends, "with merely surviving another day their sole and overriding preoccupation."

As draconian as the nun's Good Shepherd Asylum was, most people accepted that a girl who was defiled was doomed anyway, and unless placed in such an institution would otherwise never survive. She had stigmatized herself and besmirched her family by becoming someone's unwitting victim. Getting one's self pregnant in a country where living breathing children were already dying from starvation by the tens of thousands was considered a terrible enough sin for moral reasons, but substantially worse now because it meant literally taking food out of some other starving child's mouth, a child legitimately born of parents properly sanctified by the Holy Church.

"At least these girls and their babies had food and shelter," cowardly people could tell themselves, in an attempt to assuage any feelings of angst and misgivings they may have felt as the stories of what went on behind those walls circulated. Some brazen townsfolk even acted as apologists for the conditions by praising the nuns for providing some semblance of a life and an education to girls who otherwise, they claimed, would have remained homeless and illiterate. They failed to recognize, or perhaps never knew, that the girls were slave labor, never paid a cent for their exhausting servitude.

"Certain professions, such as politicians, policemen, priests and nuns attract more than their share of a particular kind of damaged person to their ranks," Mary McGrady would later tell her eldest son and future police officer Jim as he grew up. "And all kinds of formerly abused and discarded little girls were to be found inhabiting the costumes worn by nuns in convents, those rotten apples disguised inconspicuously among the good," she warned. "And you will see, Jim, if you go through with your plan of becoming a policeman, that you'll find yourself working side by side with some very damaged boys as well, boys who were cursed with the most cruel and abusive kinds of parents, and suffering the most frightening living conditions. And these boys will take their anger, that which they should rightly be venting on the very people who damaged them, and instead land it squarely on the backs of those perceived as weaker than they, over whom, as policemen, they have been awarded free rein to victimize without penalty."

It was obvious that the more cruel and bestial of the Irish nuns of the Good Shepherd Asylum of Limerick had themselves been similarly damaged, and thus acted much the same toward the inmates as they themselves had been treated, the result of the distress they experienced upon seeing their own torture reflected in these young girls' faces. Some of these nuns had themselves been raped. Others were made to feel worthless and unwanted as children,. The nunnery provided one of the few avenues available to cast-off girls of that period to be respected and be cared for without stigma or shame.

Those who found refuge cloaked in a nun's habit would however find no true refuge from the sufferings of her own past other than burying it deep within her betrayed heart. And like most other human beings lacking the courage to confront those who hurt them, they instead lashed out at weaker targets, those they felt safely superior to, those they believed had no avenue of recourse against their assaulters.

Bridget Sullivan was not allowed a visit with her brother unsupervised, but the nun who was her chaperone, Sister Bernard, was a kindly lady, and made a great fuss of having to unexpectedly step out of the visitors' cell twice during the thirty minute visit, providing the siblings the privacy to say what they needed to say.

"But can't I hold little Michael, Sister?" John Sullivan asked the nun.

"Oh, no, that is not allowed," she admonished. "But as you leave today, my son, your sister will be waitin' on the balcony with that tainted little fellow and you'll catch a glimpse of him then."

"But I would like to hold him in me arms, Sister. He's me nephew!"

"No, I'm sorry, young man. You cannot. Those are the rules here, and they must be strictly obeyed."

The nun at that point, appearing to be overcome with emotion, rose again and left the cell.

John watched as the door closed so he might speak in private. He was trembling with fright at the prospect of having to tell his sister that he would soon be leaving for America, possibly never to see her again.

"Sister Bernard, she's one of the nice ones," said Bridget, after the nun walked out. "But she's insulted now because ye didn't genuflect to her."

"Genuflect? Are ye coddin' me now, Bridget?"

"No, Johnnie, I'm not. We must genuflect each time we encounter a nun or priest here, and sometimes that's more than a hundred times a day."

John was appalled. The very same Irish priests and nuns irate about the requirement to bow or curtsy to British royalists expect their fellow Irish to bow to them?

"Johnny," Bridget sobbed, "they won't allow us see our babies ever again once we've weaned them! At holy Mass on Sunday is the only time the others can even catch a glimpse of their older children, when the little ones go up to the altar rail to receive their communion. How will I ever recognize him at that age? How will I know him? Soon I will not be allowed to see or hold my little Michael, and I am so disconsolate over that prospect, that I think I might hang myself!"

John was horrified.

"No, Bridget. Ye mustn't! I will find a way! Trust in me! I promise ye, I will find us a way!"

His mind raced. He would be leaving two days hence, but now that Bridget's predicament was made so painfully real, and extreme, Bridget so upset and John Sullivan so helpless in the short term to do anything about it, he completely lost his nerve to tell his sister of his plans.

He looked down at the tortured hand he was comforting. Bridget's fingers were red and cracked from scalding water and bleeding from scrubbing laundry all day. They stung and burned from the lye soap. Bridget had hoped to master the preliminaries of making lace, another source of income for the institution, so she might leave the Magdalene Laundry and its back-breaking labor behind.

"We all work just like slaves in the laundry, John. The sisters take in tonnes of laundry, terrible laundry, from the hospitals, prisons, and butchers. We have to sort and mark the whole infectious filthy mess when it comes in, and we're not allowed to wash our hands. I'm afraid to even itch meself, for fear of disease. It's a horror just to touch it. We have to handle other people's soiled knickers and underthings, baby clothes thick with shite and sick. 'Tis an afflicted business, John. We aren't allowed to speak at all, we must only pray and scrub, they remind us, scrub and pray our dirty sins away."

Bridget's eyesight was not clear, and she told how the nuns were cruel in their assessments and demands. Her hesitation in reciting in catechism class was not due to stupidity, as the nuns had berated, but rather the result of her seeing a blurry form where others saw a crisply defined written word. Her lace-making attempts could never come anywhere near to meeting the nuns' standards because she could not see well enough to achieve such fine work. She concluded she might find herself doomed to working in the nightmarish laundry for the remainder of her days.

"One poor little girl who I made friends with here returned only just last week from an eleven month hire up in Tyrone. The nuns sold her to a farmer and his family. She had to sleep on a pile of straw in the hallway, and every morning she had to be awake before everyone else, to light the fire and clean up every bit of straw before the others came downstairs. She had to go out in the freezin' cold without warm clothes to bring in the cows and milk and tend to them. And the farmer violated her over and over, and now she's back here, again with child, and the nuns treat her as if she were a prostitute! They placed that poor little girl into his evil clutches, and they took his filthy money for it, while she herself received not a penny for her labors. She's not to blame for any of it! This is a prison, John, and we are no better than slaves. We are white slaves! I have been incarcerated, and my baby will soon be taken from me and incarcerated here too, or sold away from me. I am not a criminal, John. My baby is not a criminal, he's my son! I hate our father! I hate our mother! How could they discard their own daughter rather than kill the priest who did this to her?"

John's head was spinning. He wished he could say that his father's betrayal of his own child and his conspiring with the Church surprised him, but he could not. The emotional distance their father maintained from his own children had left all his offspring chronically insecure and fearful. Their father had himself been orphaned at an early age. He was never loved. He was not capable of giving what he himself had never been given.

"I realize things are terrible now, Bridget," said her increasingly panicked brother, not quite knowing how to process these alarming new revelations. "But where could ye possibly go? What would ye do? Father will not allow ye back home. I have no resources of me own as of yet, but I will. I promise I will. People are fightin' tooth and nail for rotten scraps and dyin' by the thousands from hunger in this famine. How would ye and the baby survive? There is no food in this bleedin' country! As bad as it is in here, ye can't be livin' with yer baby somewhere out in a peat bog, eatin' dirt!"

Silently to himself John chastised Bridget for a moment. He wondered how his sister could ever allow that priest to do this to her. *Why didn't ye fight and scream!?* he wanted to yell at her. But he was all too familiar with the overpowering dominance of the Church and how its leaders squashed the common people in both body and spirit as if they were of no more value than insects.

When they were children everyone for miles around knew that the neighbor down the lane, a man of certain influence, was raping his own daughters, yet the Sullivan children were required to tip their caps and greet him respectfully as they passed him. But the neighbors whose son had resigned from the priesthood, they were told they must cross to the other side of the street and cast down their eyes when it was that family whom they passed.

The hypocrisy was suffocating the country.

Sister Bernard returned. It was time to end the visit. John held Bridget tightly.

"I promise, Bridget. Remember that."

Bridget was escorted out first, and up the stairs. Then a few minutes later, John was shown out the door into the courtyard. Once outside, the nun pointed upward. There on the second floor balcony stood John Sullivan's sister Bridget, dangling baby Michael in her outstretched arms as if in offering, alongside three other girls doing exactly the same thing with their babies. A stern nun stood behind them, prompting them, ordering them, admonishing them. The group was cruelly on display.

"This is their shame," loudly announced the nun from the balcony, her ridiculing voice echoing off the incarcerating walls glistening with shards atop. "They are showing ye their sin. See, now? Mind ye the sight of these girls! It is here with us they've been left, holdin' the baby."

"That's where it comes from, Jim, that saying, that expression," his mother had told him after finishing her story. "The warning was, 'don't be left holdin' the baby.' The nuns meant it, literally."

Once he and his new bride Mary McGrady had become settled in Buffalo, John Sullivan from County Clare posted letters to his sister Bridget back in Ireland, and to his parents. He pledged to work hard so he could get Bridget and her son on a ship headed for America. He thought this would satisfy his parents, having Bridget and Michael clear across the Atlantic rather than just over the Sarsfield Bridge. But his pledge did not elicit the expected result.

John wrote more letters to Bridget, promising her that by early 1854 at the very latest, and perhaps even sooner, he and Mary would have enough saved to give her and Michael a new start, a new life. "Just hold on, Bridget," he implored.

But Bridget did not reply.

Perhaps she had no money for posting a letter. Or perhaps more likely, after opening and reading them first, the nuns kept John's letters a secret from her, preventing Bridget from ever seeing them for fear of losing an industrious and profitable worker. John's message may have been anathema to the sisters, for Bridget's hands were needed more than ever in the laundry, times being as hard as they were; people's filthy knickers were the convent's main source of revenue.

In 1852, a letter had arrived from Ireland from John's parents that for quite some time extinguished any joy that John and Mary Sullivan were feeling over their first baby's approaching birth.

Bridget Sullivan had hung herself from a coat hook one rainy midday in the Magdalene Laundry as the others ate their porridge lunch.

The nuns buried her anonymously, away from prying eyes in an unmarked mass grave, mixed in with all those other young sinners who had preceded her. The only record left of Bridget Sullivan was a notation of her name on a list of the deceased in a ledger tucked away in the back on a musty shelf in the Good Shepherd Asylum in Limerick, Ireland, where it would lay unread and forgotten for the next century and a half.

FINGY

Fingy Conners liked to boast that he had emerged from his mother's womb already a brawler, delivering precisely targeted haymakers with both fists clenched and punching. As a baby it was said he flailed and kicked and hit at his parents so forcefully and unerringly that at the age of just a few months his mother found herself avoiding picking him up or holding him. Little Jimmy Conners was a baby who seemed to have little need or tolerance for tender touches, coddling, or a mother's comfort. Mary Scanlan Conners even postponed changing her baby's diapers for as long as possible, for the undertaking always proved a scatological battle.

Just as did the Rockefellers and Vanderbilts, Andrew Carnegie and JP Morgan, Fingy Conners held with a religious fervor the unwavering conviction that he was created superior to all those around him. That it was God's will and His choosing that Fingy Conners should succeed wildly and be a leader of men. That anyone who might oppose him was in effect contradicting God's plan and therefore deserved to be crushed.

Many of the nation's very rich were unabashedly partial to Charles Darwin's axiom of natural selection as it pertained to the ascendant stature of a certain caliber of human. One's applying this logic established the converse as well. The corollary, mostly whispered, being that the poor were such due to their genetic inferiority. This concept, that they themselves were solely responsible for being poor, initiated rage among the lower classes, motivating them to stage work stoppages and strikes and fueling their crusade to form powerful labor unions.

To Conners and those whom he considered his peers—even as those "peers" scoffed at the absurdity of the street thug's claim of being equal to their stature—labor unions were evil. Unions stood in the way of the natural order of things, in the way of progress and innovation. And profit. The laborer's true and only place in life, these superior men claimed, was to be a barely-surviving cog in the great wheel of industry and to be grateful for being allowed even that much. Men working 84-hour weeks amid deadly conditions in Andrew Carnegie's steel mills were paid but $10. That seemed just about right to Fingy Conners, for if they were worth more, they would have certainly risen above the rest just as he had.

Conners turned his back on institutional education at age 13 in order to ply the cobalt-blue Great Lakes as a steward and cabin boy less out of boredom with school than in response to a calling to satisfy his profound restlessness and get on with the seeking of his destiny as he perceived it. And to get away from pursuant police.

Struggling to read by lamp light in his tiny bunk at night deep in the ship's hold, he became convinced of the ideology of Manifest Destiny, the belief whereby the lands and resources of the North American West were created solely to be at the disposal of superior men, the assets existent for the sole accruing of superior individuals' wealth and power. Conners extended this philosophy to every area of his life, whereby everything was there simply for the taking, as was only apropos for one as exceptional as he by way of his grabbing it from whomever happened to be holding it at the moment.

During his travels on the inland seas he observed how crucial those waterways were proving to the growth of the two nations that shared them. Other men were mining, harvesting, grazing and exploiting the resources of the North American West, but Fingy Conners saw clearly the link that was the transporting of all these resources to the consumer. At every port in which the boy's ship stopped to off-load or take on freight, desperate laborers duked it out with each other on the docks for the privilege of earning a few pennies an hour breaking their backs. He was fascinated and disgusted by the competition among the masses for the most menial of jobs. He knew in his soul he was never meant to end up one of these.

As he grew into adulthood, it became apparent that Fingy's own special brand of brilliance was in his corralling, bullying and controlling of men and the exploitation of the unfortunate circumstances in which they found themselves. His first taste of power came at the age of twenty three when on the wave of one of the numerous labor upheavals that plagued Buffalo's docks he rose overnight from lowly longshoreman to assume leadership of his own gang. To establish his authority among older and larger men, he addressed the detachment of freight handlers waiting for the turn-to from their freshman boss to start them off on their initial toil.

"If dere's a mudder's son in dis here gang dat t'inks he kin lick me, let 'im come up and do it right now," he challenged. It was a commonplace enough provocation, for men on the docks rose to become foremen and retained that position largely through their readiness to use their fists on all comers.

A muscular man over six feet tall stepped up to respond to the ultimatum.

"So, you t'ink yous is good a man as me, Pat?" asked the neophyte boss.

"Tis within an inch of yer life I'll surely be after baitin' yous, Fingy Conners, just as soon as ye take yer coat off," boomed the grinning Irish longshoreman to the prompting cheers of his fellow workers.

"Well den, Pat, yous is fired. I won't be havin' me no man in dis gang wot t'inks he kin lick me."

Among the roustabouts of the First Ward it was a given that a boss longshoreman must be a boss walloper first and foremost; that a foreman must prove his mettle by licking every member of his gang and retire from that position the moment he proved no longer up to the task. And so with a mixture of brute force and cunning that would become his formula for success, Fingy Conners began his steady and unstoppable rise from relative illiteracy to the apex of power and wealth to become one of the largest individual employers of labor in the United States.

He accomplished this by instituting a system perfected from his string of saloons from which men were hired, paid and fired. A portion of their weekly wage was paid not in cash, but in the form of brass slugs which could be redeemed for one thing only, alcohol at a Fingy Conners saloon.

The laborers who spent the most money over and above their brass slugs each week in his saloons were the first to be hired again the following week.

His boss longshoremen and boss grain scoopers, most of whom ran saloons of their own, were installed by Conners to manage the many gangs of common dock laborers. These bosses earned their lucrative and profitable positions in part by buying all their beer for their saloons from Fingy's Magnus Beck Brewery, and in another part by functioning as Fingy's goon squad.

On the docks a scam was initiated early on whereby each boss longshoreman would create a number of nonexistent employee positions on his work gang. A fixed rate would be bid to unload a ship. Come payday, that money would be divided equally among all the men, including the phantom workers. The boss pocketed the wages of these phantom workers for himself. Because few men worked more than a week or two for the same boss, they would be unfamiliar with the other men on the gang, and never suspect the scheme.

The boss longshoremen additionally were an instrumental cog in Fingy's self-perpetuating machine by their freely distributing brass checks among their penniless gang for use as advance credit to purchase drinks at Fingy's saloons to ensure their future hiring. Hot and thirsty, needing to unwind, hesitant of going home to face their spouse's certain wrath with pockets empty, fearful of being without work the following week, the tokens' temptation was oftentimes too great to resist.

A vicious form of competition was inaugurated in Conners' saloons as much for sport as for profit whereby Fingy would pit two or more customers against each other for what he claimed was the one remaining work position available, telling each that the other man was ahead in his tally of drinks. Broke, their families starving, Fingy would extend credit to these men in the form of his famous brass checks, effectively guaranteeing their running up a sizable tab to be deducted from their upcoming pay. This system guaranteed that only a minimum of the pay his laborers received would ever find its way past the tills of Fingy's saloons to the wives and children of the toilers.

Beginning in the 1880s, striking dock workers and the saloons in which they held their clandestine meetings were terrorized by imported thugs that Fingy scraped up from the gutters of New York, Chicago and Cleveland. These hoodlums would take up clubs, bats and bricks and apply them forcefully to the heads of striking or unionizing laborers, systematically cleaning out the resorts where the union men gathered and destroying the premises to teach the saloonkeeps a lesson about what happens when someone crosses Fingy Conners.

The Buffalo Police Department did not intervene.

In 1899 the Grain Scoopers Strike resulted in the first ever defeat for Fingy Conners, dealing a death blow to his extremely profitable saloon-boss system. From the inception of the Scoopers Strike onward, with the event's inspiring the firing of missiles and bullets, it had become dangerous for Conners to show his face in his First Ward contractor's office. His army of lieutenants, led by Hannah Sullivan's brother David Nugent, carried out his commands.

Conners, having become a millionaire, purchased a stately mansion on Buffalo's millionaires' row, Delaware Ave. At this particular time, Buffalo had more millionaires per capita than any city in the world.

One Saturday late, a street railroad company which had a line crossing Delaware Avenue near Conners' new mansion was about to make repairs. The company delivered a wagonload of rails to the site, dumping them with a terrific racket in the dead of night to the alarm of the local sleeping residents. Conners' new neighbor Harry Hamlin, a millionaire more famous for being a Buffalo police officer than for the source of his wealth, remarked to his startled wife, "That must be Fingy Conners moving in."

Shortly after Conners had taken possession of his new home, Mrs. Metcalf, one of the social elite of Delaware Avenue, passed Fingy's house in her carriage. Conners had ordered his gardener to plant his name in letters a couple of feet high in flowering foliage on the lawn in front of his mansion for all to admire.

"Goodness!" exclaimed Mrs. Metcalf, appalled at the gaudy display. Examining the floral legend through her lorgnettes she called aloud, "The poor man must think he's a railway station!"

When enemies smirked over his obvious lack of formal education and mistook his dockworker diction for stupidity, he would challenge their assumption with the retort, "Brains? I can hire all the brains I need for $20 a week. Brains is as cheap as tenpenny nails."

At his first public banquet fresh from his dock days, Fingy had quickly gulped a spoonful of scalding hot tomato soup, whereupon he immediately expelled it in a heavy spray all over the white linen tablecloth. The table fell silent, and he knew his act had been a gross breach of table manners. Suppressed laughter rang from both sides, to which Fingy blurted, "I suppose yous fellows woulda swallowt it and burned yer insides out, and said nothing, would yous?"

By the turn of the century, Fingy Conners' business interests had expanded to include urban railways, the paving of streets, dominion over three newspapers as well as a state-of-the-art printing plant, ownership of the Magnus Beck Brewery, the directorship of two banks, a 350-acre poultry farm in Angola NY, extensive real estate holdings and various industrial concerns. He sailed a fabulous yacht, which rivaled in luxury that of J. Pierpont Morgan's, taking it around the Great Lakes to attend to his various enterprises in Detroit, Chicago and beyond. It also served as an instrumental tool in isolating those men with whom he had urgent business dealings, attracting them initially with the *Enquirer's* luxurious offerings and a leisurely cruise, but then not allowing the ship anywhere near shore until they had agreed to terms benefiting his own interests. With his move to Delaware Avenue, he abandoned his former customary haunts of comfort and began to frequent the city's first class cafés and resorts where he established a reputation as a spender and the wearer of large diamonds and loud raiment. He disowned his "Fingy" moniker and demanded that he be addressed as the "Honorable William J. Conners."

A new friend from the loftiest of his high-end hangouts, The Buffalo Club, whose members included President Grover Cleveland, took him aside and said, "Jim, you are making a fool of yourself wearing so many diamonds. It's positively vulgar."

"I heard that before," Conners said testily. "But, b'gosh, I notice that thim wot has thim wears thim, and thim wot hasn't, doesn't."

But quick to see the wisdom behind the criticism, the gaudy display soon disappeared from his shirts, ties, and most of his remaining fingers.

Conners had dabbled in politics in the 1880s, seeking the Republican nomination for alderman of the city's 1st ward in 1881, but was defeated. His Mariners Home saloon on Louisiana Street, inherited from his late father Peter Conners, became the haunt of the small time politicians and ward heelers of the neighborhood, and he used their influence to propel his way upward. Known as a Black Republican, party lines meant nothing to him, and sometime after his defeat for alderman, he turned Democratic. His own explanation for this turn of loyalties was explained in his newspaper the *Buffalo Enquirer* the day after he bought it:

> He left the Republican party not from personal motives of jealousy
> or disappointment, but because he believed that the progressive forces
> of the country were at that time arraying themselves on the side of the
> Democratic Party, and those are the forces in which he has faith. But Mr.
> Conners is thoroughly independent and liberal in his political views.

With his wealth attained and his political ambitions expanded, Conners developed a hankering for power and for the prestige that power bestowed.

He even began to substitute, when necessary, the pugilist's use of brute force as his preferred modus operandi with more genteel methods effected through bluffing, shouting and intimidation, for as much as he might be tempted, he knew he wouldn't get very far by beating the pulp out of the cultured elite. Upon them he would instead be employing less violent but no less fearful methods. The common man was a different story; on them, the older methods continued to work best.

As a young boy, Jimmy Conners had made no friends except for one: John P.

Sullivan.

Younger, smaller, slighter, lacking in aggression, Conners nonetheless was impressed by JP's tenacity and his willingness to put up with his moods and patiently suffer his domination and violent outbursts. JP Sullivan had been blessed with the instinctive gift of personality. He was a peacemaker and diplomat by nature, in contrast to Jimmy Conners' warmonger. JP delighted in making people laugh, whereas Jimmy Conners delighted in making them cry. Some men are born without the ability to hear or see, others with cleft pallets or a club foot. Fingy Conners was born without any need or desire to be liked.

JP understood Jimmy Conners as did none other. Instead of running away from him like most kids, he quietly backed off just out of arm's reach until the outbursts and flailing subsided and the bounteous nature that was the texture of many a youth who had known abuse at the hands of adults, a trait which only JP Sullivan was able to discern beneath Conners angry exterior, surfaced. Peerless bully that Conners was, only JP Sullivan was capable of unearthing in the complicated and enigmatic hoodlum the humbling emotions of remorse and regret.

For the first twenty-four years of his life, up until he married Catherine Mahany in 1881, the one and only person to whom William J. Conners had ever uttered the words "I'm sorry," was JP Sullivan.

THE RUMOR

"Do you think you can use your influence to get me a position at the Pan-American, Uncle?" asked Junior.

They sat side by side on the speeding train, having departed the hospital at Hornellsville for Buffalo. JP cast off his blanket when Junior tried covering him with it.

"I'm not an invalid, boy!" he blustered.

"I know you're not, Uncle, but my mother made me promise I'd cover you so's to keep you warm, and now I can truthfully say that I tried and failed," Junior clarified with a conspiring smile.

"Oh. Hannah said that? Oh well, all right then." JP then pulled his blanket back up to his chin as there was an unwelcome draft in the car after all.

"Well, what kind of position are we thinking about here, Junior? Perhaps you might be an assistant to the manager at the New York State building? Or the Art Museum. Yes, that's it, the Albright! You're interested in photography now, your father tells me. You could make some good contacts at the Art Museum."

The New York State building and the Albright Art Museum were the only two Pan-American Exposition buildings that were being constructed to remain on site permanently after the close of the fair.

"I was thinking more of a situation in one of the beer gardens," replied Junior.

"The beer gardens? What ever on earth for, lad?"

"For the money. The gratuities. I read a story in Collier's a while back where at the Chicago Columbian Exposition the waiters at the beer gardens made forty dollars a day in tips. And that was during bad economic times."

He had also read in this Chicago veteran's published account that there was much to be found in the way of frivolity and good times in a position at such a venue as well, but he didn't want to reveal that to his uncle so as not to give the impression of his being unserious.

"But son, think of your future. A waiter? Where could that ever lead? No place! The friends you would make at the State building or art museum could well initiate a life-long career!"

"What kind of career, Uncle John?"

"I don't know—a politician, or some other position in government, or a respected artist. I was door-keeper in the State Assembly when I wasn't much older than you are right now. You might well have the opportunity to meet Roosevelt and all kinds of other influential men. I'm sure President McKinley will be attending the exposition. You could meet him as well."

"But what kind of skills do I possess that would garner me such a prestigious position, uncle?"

JP laughed and nudged his nephew. "Nepotism is the only real skill a man needs at the outset, Junior. You let me worry about the rest once we get your foot in the door."

❧❧❧

Hannah Sullivan, in order to ease the discomfort that came from feeling unneeded now that the Alderman was home and Molly Nugent was back with her parents, left the house on Hamburg Street to pay an afternoon visit to Our Lady of Perpetual Help Church.

She left little David next door with Annie's servant girl Sophie. The elder children were at school. Her housework was done, or at least that portion which would be most noticeable. When it came to housework Hannah believed there were two levels of accomplishment: good, and good enough. As of late, good enough was good enough.

There in the echoing dimness of God's house, where the faint zephyr of holy incense from morning Mass still lingered in the air, she found comfort despite her inability to believe. In the afternoons the church was empty save but for a scattered half dozen women, each sitting solitary in an empty oak pew, isolated, desolate, and ensnared by her own singular agony.

Religion is a testament to the stupidity of humans, she reminded herself as she looked around. She thought she truly believed that, and yet here she was.

Hannah dropped a nickel into the coin box for the poor and lit a candle in front of the statue of St. Jude, the patron saint of desperate cases and lost causes. In recent years when she prayed at all it was exclusively to St. Jude, for God Himself had long since abandoned her.

She sat in her pew, watching as the flickering of the rows of votive candles at the foot of the various saints projected eerie illuminations upward, manifesting upon their plaster faces animated expressions akin to those of living beings. She detected the mournful sniffling of a woman she had only known previously in passing. She tried to ignore it, but observed that the woman's burden was so ponderous that her head was weighted down and bowed so low as to almost be cradled in her own lap.

Other solitary churchgoers cast an errant glance or two her way, but embroiled as they were in their own personal torment, they ignored her. Soon enough two of the afflicted exited the church, and suddenly, being closest in distance to the weeping soul, Hannah found herself drawn to the woman's suffering. She decided to be charitable and go to her.

"Are you all right, missus?" Hannah whispered softly.

The woman, Mary Lambert, looked up in wonder to see that it was the very spirit she considered most kindred who had come to comfort her. God was indeed listening.

"Oh, Mrs. Sullivan!" Lambert revealed, "My husband is spending his nights away from me with a woman out in Orchard Park. I am all alone now. He has lost all interest in me and in our marriage. Tell me what to do!"

Hannah was taken aback to be included in Mary Lambert's humiliating secret, but more so to be asked to provide her a solution.

"Mrs. Lambert," she softly murmured, "I am so very sorry. I truly am. But I hardly know you or your husband. I have no right to tell you what to do."

Mary Lambert's eyes flashed at the perceived hypocrisy for one little moment, but then softened, for Hannah seemed at this instant to be her only hope for consolation.

"But Mrs. Sullivan, what did you do when this happened to you? How could you stand it?"

Hannah jolted as though knocked hard sideways.

"Mrs. Lambert, I beg your pardon, but I have had no such experience. You must have me confused with some other."

"Why, you're Detective Sullivan's wife from Hamburg Street, are you not? Everyone already knows hereabouts, Mrs. Sullivan. It's common knowledge. No need to be evasive. I sincerely want your advice and encouragement. Please!"

Hannah's blood was set to boil.

"Mrs. Lambert, wherever did you hear such a lie! My Jim has never been unfaithful to me!"

"Oh, my dear, sweet darling! How could you not know? He sees that young Scots woman from the florist shop on Elmwood Avenue!"

"Mrs. Lambert! I never! How dare you involve me in your terrible misery! I am sad for what you must be feeling, but do not make the mistake of thinking that my Jim would ever do what you husband has done. I demand that you tell me right now where you heard of this!"

Hannah was standing upright now, leering contemptuously down upon the crumpled woman. Her impassioned whispering was now audible to the other visitors.

"Perhaps we should go outside, Mrs. Sullivan."

The two left, Hannah so upset that she nearly left her bag behind.

Mary Lambert revealed that she had heard the story from Evelyn Rundle from Katherine Street. Hannah immediately turned on her heel and headed three blocks over to pay Mrs. Rundle a surprise visit. Rundle was a timid woman who did not suspect why Hannah Sullivan might be knocking on her door, so she opened it with a smile.

"Why are you spreading vicious lies around the ward about my husband, Mrs. Rundle?"

Evelyn stood there dumbly, trying to comprehend the situation, stammering for an answer, praying that Hannah would retain her dignity.

"Why, Mrs. Sullivan. The wanderings of your husband are common knowledge. We all thought you knew!"

"I know of no such thing! My husband is at home every night, Mrs. Rundle, and he is a good man. How dare you!" Hannah looked good and ready to punch Evelyn Rundle in the eye.

"But Mrs. Sullivan, I was told this by Jennie McCree, the downstairs maid at Fingy Conners' mansion on Delaware Avenue! She told me it was common conversation around the Conners' dining table, spoken by Mrs. Conners herself at a dinner party recently where Alderman Kennedy and your very own brother David Nugent and his wife were guests!"

Hannah fumed. *That filthy bitch!* she thought silently, picturing in her red-hot imagination the hardened prim face of Fingy Conners' second wife.

Hannah stormed off Evelyn Rundle's porch and hurried her way toward home, wondering what to do. How could Jim be spending time with another woman without her knowing anything of it? He was home every night, and often stopped in at the house many times throughout the day—even during working hours as he passed that way on his police duties. Then she thought about all the out-of-town errands he had been running in recent months, delivering or taking possession of prisoners on the train to towns and cities across the state, or to Chicago, sometimes being away overnight. Her heart sank a bit. She had never even thought to question Jim's word.

She pictured herself immediately storming over to Delaware Avenue to confront the source, but thought better of it for the time being. Before she risked humiliating herself, she needed to confront Jim with the gossip.

Knowing she had to rid herself of the fearsome burden she now carried, Hannah went next door to see Annie even before stopping at her own house. With a squirming infant refusing the breast writhing in her exhausted arms, Annie looked to be at the end of her rope. Hannah knew the feeling well. Annie asked Sophie the servant girl to leave the room with the older children, including Hannah's little David.

"Mama!"

"We'll be going home soon, Davey, in just a few minutes. Go with Sophie," Hannah assured her son.

Hannah related the story to Annie, then found herself crying hard for the first time in quite a while.

"That just doesn't sound like Jim to me, Hannah."

"No?"

"No, Hannah. Do you remember," soothed Annie despite her ongoing battle with the infant, "when little David was born? And as he got older, you were terrified he would die when he reached age two, like little Hannah Jr. and Daniel and Catherine? You put David in ruffled dresses and finger curls. Your Jim was so anxious to show off his youngest boy, his little man, but you fought him tooth and nail to keep little David in dresses and long curls for God knows how long. For two years or more anyway, as I recall. And Jim allowed you to have your way."

"All right. I remember," she said stiffly.

"And do you recall why you dressed David in girl's clothing and had his hair in ribbons, even though people haven't done that with boys since, well...since the war between the states?"

"Yes."

There was a period of silence in which Annie waited for her to continue her thought, but she did not.

"Well, say it, Hannah. Say the words."

Hannah wiped her tears and cleared her throat.

"Ahem. All right. Many Irish once believed that the devil was out to steal their boy babies, and so they dressed baby boys in girly frills and ribboned curls to fool the boy-seeking devil into not taking their child, because Satan didn't take girls."

"And do you really believe in that malarkey, Hannah? Or did you ever?"

"Well," she explained, "I never really believed in that particular superstition, no. But I had lost three babies and I was terrified it would happen again, and I couldn't bear that. So...I didn't think it would hurt anything."

Annie paused a second to look her friend kindly in the eye.

"I think it might have hurt Jim, Hannah," said Annie seriously. "He wanted to show off a new son, but you had him dressed like a daughter and wouldn't even let David out of your sight, so fearful were you that something or someone would take him. You wouldn't even allow Jim to take him over to the boathouse to meet the fellas—fifty feet away!"

"I was desperate, Annie," she whined. "And perhaps a bit...barmy... in the head."

"Well, no, you weren't barmy, Hannah. You were terrified, and no mother on earth who had herself lost children would ever fault you for that. But Jim patiently stood by and allowed you to have your way, as much as he'd rather his baby son look like a little boy. He let you have him in the way you needed to have him without any fight or recrimination. Do you recall that? Because he knew what was going through your mind at the time. He put your welfare ahead of his own desires. Jim is not the kind of man who would take a risk of losing his family, Hannah. *Not ever.*"

"But what if I drove him to it, Annie, with all my feeling blue and my bedlam and my crazy distressing about everything? What if I drove him away, like my mother drove away my father?"

"Well...all right. What if we consider that—about what you would do if you found that this rumor was true? If he admitted he had seen another woman, and said he was sorry. Would you allow him forgiveness, admitting as you do now that you may have driven him to it?"

Hannah's face grew red as she ruminated for a few long moments.

"Forgiveness. I don't know. What is that, exactly Annie? Is forgiveness the dictionary definition of the word, or something else altogether? Forgiveness from my experience is re-trusting those having proven themselves previously untrustworthy. Allowing those who have already proven to us that they can hurt us to have the opportunity to take another shot at us. It is the delusion one is under that the person who has demonstrated they're capable of wounding us terribly will never do it again, if we will only just 'forgive' them.

"Forgiveness in such a case would seem have to be defined as taking Jim back and just giving him another chance...one more chance to hurt me, betray me. Only when the damage of hurtful people is absolute, complete, do they finally let you be, leaving you collapsed in a crumpled pile while they go off and find themselves a new victim as willing to overlook and reduce themselves, their own wants, needs and desires, as you!"

Annie was rendered speechless for a moment. "Oh, my, God."

Annie recoiled, and more than just a little bit. "What in heaven's sake is going on with you, Hannah? Inside that head of yours?"

Hannah's agitation had flown up suddenly and in great volume, like a splash of muddy water from a puddle some speeding automobile just raced through. Hannah had obviously given this particular subject far more thought than Annie ever suspected.

"Hannah, compose yourself! This might only be gossip. In fact I would bet money on it. If that Rundle woman is correct and this slander did come from Fingy Conners' horrible wife, then for God's sake consider the source! She is an awful woman! She's from *West Seneca*, for cryin' out loud! *West Seneca!* She grew up barely surviving on onions! You know what them people are like out down there. They're dirt farmers at best. Your Jim is a good man! A good family man."

Hannah began to apologize for bothering Annie with her problems.

"Hannah! You stop that right now. We may not be blood, but we are sisters all the same. Don't ever apologize for coming to me. We two need each other."

Hannah stood and summoned a weak smile, then patted Annie on the shoulder that didn't have baby spit-up all over it.

The women kissed. Hannah called for little David and made her way out with him to their house next door, glancing over across the river toward The Island where a giant ship was spewing grain into the massive new concrete elevator just constructed, guaranteed fireproof, it was claimed. *We'll see about that*, thought Hannah, recalling some of the spectacular window-shattering explosions of the past. Its cloud of rising grain dust was dramatically back lit golden by the lowering sun. The river stank something awful of iron and oil and dead things. Hannah was doubtful if the age of disastrous elevator fires caused by the spontaneous ignition of grain dust would ever really become a thing of the past.

Having two hours to torment herself with Evelyn Rundle's claim and to compound it with recollections of other terrible upsets of her past, by the time Jim made it home she was seated collapsed into her own folded arms on the kitchen table, sobbing.

She told him of the rumor. He listened patiently, calmly.

"Hannah," Jim said firmly. "I love you. I realize I have in recent times not been paying you proper attentions."

He lowered himself and put his arm around her shoulder.

"I am...well, embarrassed...as a man...to admit that my powers and appetites may not be what they once were. But I have no interest in other women, Hannah, honestly. My fidelity and loyalty is yours and only yours. No one else's."

She could see a fury begin to rise behind his eyes, it bubbling and boiling, he formulating in his mind his own suspicions and ideas about the origins of such a nasty story even as he was calmly comforting her.

"You and I have been through too much together for me to be anything other than what I promised you I'd be, Hannah. You have been tolerant and kind and considerate to me during those long intervals when I was tormented and drawn into myself and feeling as though I had all but lost my way.

"I am a police detective, sweetheart. It's in my blood. And I need to know from you where you heard this rumor. I will track down the origin of this lie and I will put a stop to it."

Jim's eyes were watering now from equal parts emotion and vengeance. This reaction, unanticipated, put a sudden fright into her. So she lied.

"I don't know just yet Jim. I heard it from a woman on Katherine Street who told me she heard it from someone who heard it from someone else, and so on and so forth," she rambled. "I will ask more questions tomorrow, and when I discover the source of these stories I promise I will tell you."

It occurred to Hannah that if Jim ever suspected that the source might possibly be Fingy Conners himself, there might be hell to pay.

The following morning Hannah read the social notices in the *Express* to see if she might discover some opportunity for a convenient encounter with the second bride of Fingy. There was no mention therein of any doings connected with her name. Hannah sent the children off to school, then went next door to talk with Annie before leaving little David with her and Sophie. Hannah could not speak freely about her intentions in front of the servant girl. Annie was preoccupied and overwhelmed with the children. Hannah longed to have Annie's opinion of her plan before she set out on her provocative errand. In many ways she and Annie were opposites, but this contradiction often revealed its fullest value when complicated matters needed opposing points of view in order to be best understood. But today, Annie's wisdom would not be available.

"I have some errands to run downtown Annie, so I will speak with you later. I'll be back by the babies' nap time to fetch David, to be sure."

"You aren't by any chance going into the Wm. Hengerer Company, are you?" asked Annie. "I have a jumper I'd like returned but I haven't had any time."

The last thing Hannah needed was to be sidetracked from her essential purpose, and at first she took charge of the package, not having an excuse not to. But then she abruptly changed her mind.

"Annie, no, here. I can't. I'm sorry. I can't take this for you right now." She handed the package back. "I'll explain why later on when I get back home," she said, silently casting sidelong noddings in the direction of the servant girl.

Annie understood the code. Hannah left. Annie walked to the window, baby bent over her shoulder, patting his back to encourage a burp. She stood there, between the curtains, and watched as Hannah boarded the Hamburg streetcar in front of the house.

She was concerned.

❧❀❧

Hannah was required to transfer twice in order to reach the Conners mansion. The West Ferry Street car stopped just yards from the Conners' entry gate.

She approached the solid front door, its great volume resembling a castle's drawbridge, and pulled at the ponderous brass knocker, sniggering as she employed it due to its being cast appropriately in the form of a huge clenched fist. It must have weighed a good two pounds. The door opened. The Irish servant girl Jennie McCree recognized Hannah immediately but pretended that she did not.

"Yes, may I help you?" she lilted.

"Is Mrs. Conners to home?" asked Hannah, a difficult-to-maintain pleasant smile on her face. Her keen peripheral vision at that very instant perceived the flash of the sunlight's reflection off the sheen of an expensive yellow silk gown as Mary Jordan Conners, formerly of West Seneca, spied her from the inner reaches of the grand home and took refuge in the shadows.

"Mary Jordan! I see you in there!" shouted Hannah.

The servant insisted, "Ma'am, she's not at home."

Jennie tried to block her way. "You'll have to leave now," the house servant dictated, attempting to close the door on the guest. Hannah pushed back with a strength anchored in her unrelenting intention as the servant called out, "Mrs. Sullivan! Stop. You have no right!"

Scorning the servant's shanty Irish origins, the maid being a product of a shack at The Beaches constructed largely of driftwood, flotsam and jetsam, Hannah would not lower herself to respond to her. Instead Hannah steamrolled toward the inner sanctum. As she turned the corner there stiffly stood Mary Conners, terrified and indignant.

The former Mary Jordan had set her determined sights on Fingy Conners from the moment she first heard of his first wife Katy's illness. After Katy's death Mary doggedly pursued him. She did not relent until Fingy had given in to her fierce pursuits and the whisperings of her storied talents and agreed to a union. The rumor had been that during her earliest days in West Seneca, Mary Jordan had cultivated a reputation for a certain ability most sought after by men, a technique that made her renowned in the gossip circulating at certain south-of-the-city saloons.

"Who in God's name do you think you are, Mary Conners, spreading vicious gossip about my husband to your guests sittin' around your own dining table in this very house—including my very own brother!"

Mary was stunned to have been found out. She cursed that damned David Nugent under her breath. Hannah, not suspecting her brother in the least, turned right then and cast her accusing steely gaze upon the hovering servant, assigning the guilt to her. Mary Conners immediately realized how the story might have spread so widely. Perhaps it wasn't David Nugent—or Jennie McCree either—but it was clear that the dissemination was the work of either a guest or a member of the staff.

"How dare you burst into my home, Hannah Sullivan! Everything your brother has said about you has now come to be proven as I speak in the here and now!"

"How dare I! You are joking to be sure, Mary Conners! You will pay dearly for your disgraceful lies!"

"They are not lies, Hannah Sullivan. Perhaps you should grow up! Perhaps you should be cognizant of your proper station!" she sniffed haughtily.

"*My* station!" How about your own station formerly, one of which being the rear of the West Seneca rail station to be exact, from what I hear to be true! And the entire police force knows the tale as well, Mary Conners! Do you think that your marriage to Fingy Conners erases the disgraces of your past? Do think that men do not talk loud and long about women such as yourself?"

The servant had taken flight, making a show of her hasty exit, but stopped and hid just around the corner, listening and smiling, hanging on every word.

"I have it on good counsel that the Pan is combing the hinterlands for unique attractions for the Midway. Perhaps you could resurrect your talents of renown and exhibit yourself there! With your husband himself sitting on the Exposition board of directors I'm certain he could intervene on your behalf."

Hannah was surprised at herself, that she was capable of being so vulgar and crude, but did not regret it.

"You, Hannah Sullivan are the most horrible woman in Western New York, if not the entire state. No wonder your husband's famous cousin talks about you behind your back!"

"You mean, no wonder he talks about me while he has you flat on *your* back! John L. told us all the details of your shamefully pursuing him!" she fabricated off the cuff. "That man can have any woman he wants, so why in heaven's name would he settle for the likes of you?" Both women were being driven at the moment into a frenzy of concocting wild accusations.

"Listen to me well, you Canal Street strumpet!" yelled Hannah. "You will take back your stories about my Jim and tell your friends that you were mistaken, or as our own John L. would say, the gloves will come off! You think you have some protection in your husband's not caring what others think about him? Well I can guarantee you, since I myself have known him from the time he was a small boy, that he will not stand for the kind of shaming that you have brought upon yourself if made public! Perhaps he can overlook your past in the privacy of your bedroom, but he will not stand for being regarded the fool, seduced by a cunning harlot with intentions even less honorable than her reputation!"

With that, Hannah turned to leave. She spotted a Chinese vase from the Ming period on a Chesterfield table surrounded by other *chinoiserie*. She picked up the vase and flung it hard against the wall, shattering it and ripping the imported French hand-painted wall paper that depicted a bucolic Bois de Boulogne scene with its lovely waterfalls in the early spring.

"My God, you are an evil woman! Where do you think you are? This isn't one of your customary resorts on Ganson Street, Hannah Sullivan! This isn't the Swannie House, where you might be allowed to get away with such drunken shenanigans the likes of these! I am going to call the police right now!"

"Fine, Mary Jordan from West Seneca! Just make sure you ask for Detective James E. Sullivan by name when you do call, or better yet, Michael Regan," Hannah retorted, laughing. She strode out feeling a good foot taller than when she'd walked in, and as she passed, the look of awe and admiration on the servant's face sealed her victory.

Hurrying from the Conners home, head held high, Hannah was nearly knocked over by a crazed-looking character at the corner of West Ferry Street as she rushed to board the waiting streetcar home. He didn't bother to apologize. The primal expression on his face troubled her, so she didn't ask for amends.

Stash Molik had taken a streetcar from Kaisertown, down Broadway, up Main Street, then walked some distance in a zigzag pattern to reach Fingy Conners' mansion on Delaware Ave. He did not want to be seen disembarking from a trolley anywhere near his final destination.

He scoffed again when laying his eyes on the magnificent house built of the miseries of laborers like himself and his recently disabled brother. He was unarmed—this time. Men of his lowly caste lurking around on Delaware Ave. brought unwelcome attention from the police. He needed to be clever about this. Careful. Meticulous.

His eye was drawn to the semi-circular portico flanking one side of the Conners mansion as an opportune point of entry. *That freakish Irish animal needs to be put down once and for all*, he fumed silently.

Molik had visited this same spot three days previous, trying to look inconspicuous, waiting for Fingy's auto to come out of the carriage house to carry him off on his daily business. He studied the features of the chauffeur. The driver wasn't a common house servant. He recognized him as one of Conners' lieutenants, almost certainly carrying a pistol. Molik's intention was to get to know Fingy Conners' movements so he could obtain a precise and deadly vantage point from which to blow his brains out.

Stash Molik's brother was only recently out of the hospital, but he would never function properly again. The wounded man had a wife and five children to feed, and rent to pay.

Stash was a laborer too, and like his brother, barely able to feed his own. And now the Moliks were reduced to begging for money from their Bielicka cousin Bronisława who had gone and married that damn German, Schutkeker, the butcher operating the shop at the Broadway Market. Wilhelm Schutkeker was in better financial stead than most, even with his own four brats to raise. Bronisława gave her wounded cousin what she could, or so she claimed, which to Stash's eye wasn't nearly what she was able. Herr Schutkeker was determined that his children not end up laborers or anything close to it, and was resolutely tight-fisted.

The Moliks were not happy in the least that their cousin had married outside her nationality, especially uniting with a man who acted as if he believed that all Poles, other than his own wife, were inferior.

Buffalo's struggling Polish population had immediately stepped forward upon first report of David Nugent's heinous crime to offer aid to victim Molik and his family and support their countryman in his quest for justice. For the time being, people were willing to help as best they could. The terrible deed was yet vivid in their minds, and the recent headlines announcing the Court's conviction of Fingy's lieutenant for the act had brought some satisfaction, if not compensation. But what will happen when people begin to forget? What new atrocities wrought by Fingy Conners and lesser hoodlums might obscure this crime, replacing it in people's hearts with some newer, fresher outrage? What then will become of the Moliks and their children?

Stash would have preferred a less public arena within which to kill Conners, one affording a more certain escape.

Conners rarely ventured into the First Ward anymore save for an occasional dash into his Nugent's Hotel and its adjacent contractor's office in disguise. He had been pelted with dog shit and a variety of sharp-edged missiles whenever recognized down there. He was certainly too good for the Mutual Rowing Club these days. The First Ward's crowded and densely built environs offered plenty of places ideal for an assassin to lurk, as well as plenty of men who looked enough like Molik among whose scurrying about Stash might evade detection. But Delaware Avenue—now *that* was a challenge. Molik stood out like a sore thumb on the wealthy boulevard that saw little in the way of pedestrian traffic.

As an alternative, hunting Conners downtown might well provide the cover of dense crowds that Molik desired, but Conners was customarily tightly surrounded by his lieutenants as he went about his business there, and those men all carried pistols. The only predictable activity that Stash Molik could familiarize himself with was Conners' leaving his home in the morning and returning in the evening. But that venue left him vulnerable.

"Just what the hell do you think you're doin' here, Molik?" asked Detective Sergeant Jim Sullivan.

"Uh, nuttin'," responded the startled Pole.

Sullivan seemed to appear out of nowhere. The detective's stealth shocked Molik, who had convinced himself that his own careful movements had gone undetected thus far. Sullivan possessed a flawless memory for faces as was often noted in the newspaper stories detailing his sleuthing prowess. Molik's confidence in his anonymity had now been compromised. He would need a disguise of some sort. Or a different plan altogether.

"Jus' lookin' for work, dat's all, officer. Dere's so many big houses here side by each. I'm knockin' on doors to see if anybody got a job for a good worker like me."

"Get yer ass outa here, Molik. Nobody around here hires workers off the street, much less dirty polacks. You know that as well as I do! Get back to Kaisertown, and don't let me see your stupid bug-eyed polack face over this way ever again."

Molik resentfully grunted and walked off in the direction of Main Street.

The Detective had quickly spotted Molik's laborer's garb as he emerged from across the street where he had just called at the Milburn Mansion. There he delivered a red envelope containing an urgent letter from his brother the Alderman to John G. Milburn, the president of the Pan American Exposition Company, relating to a serious matter of crisis involving Fingy Conners.

Milburn's stately home occupied the opposite, northwest corner of Delaware Avenue and West Ferry St., while Fingy's was just a stone's throw away, directly across the street on the southwest corner. Jim studied Fingy's mansion before walking up the walkway, trying to imagine what Molik had been looking at, or more relevantly, what he might be planning.

He had an inkling.

As he approached Conners' door, he cleared his throat and steeled himself for what he had to do next.

Mary Jordan Conners glanced out the window in time to see him and nearly tripped on the oriental carpet at the sight of the Detective approaching her door.

Oh my God!, she thought to herself. *First Hannah appears at my house to threaten me, and now just five minutes later, she sends her husband!*

Jim was wearing his uniform. She saw he was carrying his pistol on his person. A cold chill flashed through her, as she feared the encounter.

"Jennie!" she called in a loud whisper.

The maid appeared instantly.

"Tell that policeman that I'm not home. Go! Go to the door!"

The knocker banged and after a few beats, the maid opened the door.

"Is Mr. Conners at home?" asked the Detective.

Mary was in a wild panic now, realizing Hannah's husband wasn't here to confront *her* about her accusations, but rather was going to appeal directly to her husband instead. Mary hid around the corner, where she could have herself a good peek and hear all that was being said. She felt as if she might faint.

"No, sir. Mr. Conners is not home as yet. Can I tell him who called?" she inquired, despite knowing exactly who the officer was.

"Um. No, I'll come back, or perhaps I'll catch him at his office in the morning. Will he be in town tomorrow?"

"I believe so," the maid replied as she began to close the door.

Just at that moment, David Nugent screeched up to the entrance. Fingy and Kennedy, just back from Montréal, emerged from the automobile. Fingy eyed his old nemesis warily, and Jim exchanged nods with his brother-in-law. Indoors, Fingy's wife Mary was dissolving into a puddle of apprehension.

If only that man had delayed coming home from his trip for just another two minutes! Mary fretted, cursing Fingy.

She wondered for a moment if it would be best if she just ran and hid herself somewhere, but instead concluded it might be wiser for her to take the situation in hand so she might better control the direction of the conversation. She quickly came to the door.

"Oh, hello Detective Sullivan," she said sweetly. "And you too darling. You're home early," she effervesced to Fingy. "Welcome." She completely ignored Kennedy and Dave Nugent.

Conners instantly knew something was up as Mary never came to the door to greet anyone. She believed it beneath her dignity. "People come to me," she loved to boast. "I don't go to them."

"Whaddya want Sully?" asked Fingy, offering him a piece of Juicy Fruit gum.

"Well, Jim," he said, unwrapping it, "It's not at all good," the detective said, throwing a dirty look in the direction of Mrs. Conners. "I'm afraid I have been sent here on a very uncomfortable mission, one that you're not gonna like. Nor me neither, for that matter," he warned as he popped the gum into his mouth and shot Mary Conners another disdainful look.

"I'm really sorry that I have to be the one to bring this unpleasantness to your door."

Mary's eyes were nearly popping out of her head. She couldn't believe Jim Sullivan was going to confront her husband right there in her presence, with the maid and Kennedy and Hannah's own brother standing right there, as if she were invisible.

"This is all a misunderstanding, Detective!" Mary Conners blurted, interrupting. "I never said any such thing, and I have no idea why Hannah doesn't believe me. Why, she forced her way into my house like some intruder and broke my antique vase! And damaged my French wall covering! Didn't she, Jennie?"

Jennie nodded weakly.

"I have no idea how such a terrible story started or why she thinks I had anything to do with it. But I did not! In fact, I am insulted that she or you would even believe such a terrible thing!"

She was trembling, wringing a linen handkerchief between nervous fingers.

Jim looked at Fingy and Dave Nugent, pretending to be searching for some clue as to what Mary was talking about, while Fingy was assessing Jim's expression for the same reason.

"What in hell are yous talkin' about Mary?" growled Fingy, recognizing rotting garbage when he smelled it.

Fingy's bride looked at Jim Sullivan to try and read his face, but the wily detective remained pokerish.

Suddenly the befuddled Mary realized she'd been had. She tried to cover. "Well, uh, darling, Hannah Sullivan had heard a terrible rumor and, uh, got it into her head somehow that it originated from me and...and she came here a little while ago and screamed at me like I was an absolute nobody, and she threw a horrible tantrum and the girl and I had to ask her to leave the house at once!" she babbled, looking to Jennie McCree for support. The maid nodded obediently in forced agreement.

And just what was that rumor, Mary?" grunted Fingy.

"Oh, dear. I couldn't repeat it. It was very unlady-like, and..."

"Mary Jordan! Yous tell me right now what the rumor is so's I don't gotta hear it fer myself out there on the goddamned street!"

"Well, uh. It was something to the effect that, um, Detective Sullivan here was, uh, had been seeing, a...a younger woman over on Elmwood Avenue..."

"Jesus Christ Almighty, Mary!" he shouted. "How is it that you seem to always get involved in this kind of malarkey?"

"Darling, I had nothing to do with it, and had not heard any such rumor of the kind myself until Hannah showed up at my door just a short while ago!" she lied.

Fingy looked to the maid whose face was beet red, her eyes cast down to the floor. That told him all he needed to know.

"Mary, I will deal with you inside! And yous too, McCree!" The maid was thrown into a panic suddenly, now drawn into the drama and fearing her position was in certain peril.

The women slinked into the house and shut the entry.

With the heavy thud of the door Detective Sullivan began giggling uncontrollably, and Fingy joined in.

"Women!" derided Fingy, shaking his head.

"You don't gotta convince me," laughed Jim.

"Wish I coulda bin here to witness it when things started flyin' about, Sully!" said Nugent. "You know how my sister goes once she gets goin'!"

"Don't I though, Dave," said Jim, still in stitches.

"Well, then what's it yous came to see me fer, Sully?" said Fingy.

"Oh, I gotta deliver you this," the Detective said, handing Fingy a subpoena.

"Shit," swore Fingy. "What the hell?"

"It's from Judge Murphy, for you to appear. In person. Skinny Pat McMahon from the scoopers union's suin' you for criminal libel."

The President of the Union was utilizing one of Fingy's own classic methods to get him.

Fingy grew hot under the collar. "That one-eyed fucker!"

"Now, Fingy, we both know any patrolman on his beat could have presented this to you. But they sent me down here special to personally deliver it. Now what does that tell you?"

Fingy looked at the subpoena, then looked back at Jim blankly.

"How's I'm supposed t' know wot that means?" he spewed angrily, nearly losing his cigar stub, then threw open the door. The group disappeared inside, slamming it behind them.

Jim turned and walked back down the granite block pathway and onto the Delaware Ave. sidewalk. He was eager to head directly home to hear Hannah's version of the day's events. He could hardly wait.

When Fingy, Kennedy and Dave Nugent entered the house and the door was snugly shut, Mary became apoplectic, pouncing on her husband's weary bones, demanding in exasperated gasps that Fingy do something about that horrible Hannah Sullivan and her "entire low-brow family!" in retaliation for her unforgivable invasion of the Conners Sanctum.

There was an uncomfortable silence for a moment.

"I happen to be her low-brow family, *Mary*," scornfully reminded Dave Nugent. "And my little Molly is her family too."

Mary shrunk back momentarily from her gaffe.

"Oh. I never meant..."

Mary's gossip, uttered tipsily to dinner guests at the dining table during an interval when Fingy had excused himself to visit the bathroom, had recirculated to at long last reach his ear weeks later. Even the old dock walloper himself did not relish the specter of the sort of beehive tempest that this feud between the two women could well ignite.

Mary Conners was one of the few people, if not the only one, who Fingy ever gave in to, and she had become overconfident in her ability to harangue him into getting her way. But at this particular juncture, Fingy drew the line.

"Mary Jordan Conners!" Fingy shouted, his face contorted in florid rage. "You fix dis, damn yous t' hell! Wot is wrong wit' yous anyway? You go and apologize to Hannah Sullivan! You hear me? You do it!"

Hannah's brother drove home the point with a steely stare, then walked toward the kitchen with the maid for something to eat. The two slyly touched hands as they went.

❧❧❧

At that very same moment, Mayor Conrad Diehl and John P. Sullivan, the Alderman still weak from his illness, were arriving at their clandestine destination in Ontario to meet with Willie Van Horne of the Canadian Pacific Railway.

Van Horne was visiting the Niagara Frontier to confer with Pan American Exposition President Milburn and officials charged with overseeing transportation planning, as well as to deal with a lingering problem affecting his company's Niagara Falls, Ontario office.

The Railway was keen on the business prospects of accommodating hordes of Canadians, their numbers stretching from the Prairies to the Maritimes, about to stampede their way to Buffalo to attend the Pan.

Willie had the previous year considered a proposal received from the Alderman that the Canadian Pacific Railway build an exhibit at the Exposition. But Van Horne had the greater picture in mind. He thought his energies would be better spent trying to convince the government of the largest of all the Pan American nations to construct an imposing national building at the Pan to promote the expansive country and its industries as a whole. Something spectacular that would grandstand Canadian pride and the nation's tremendous accomplishments, a structure as large as the planned US Government Building, or perhaps even bigger.

The most land-rich of all the Pan American nations was the only one that had yet not contracted to participate in the Exposition. Even Japan had signed up to erect a beautiful pavilion in spite of the fact of that country being located well outside the hemisphere. The Philippines and Hawaii would have buildings as well, and there would be an African Village filled with black natives and another peopled by the Esqimaux of the Arctic. Inscrutably there seemed to be no enthusiasm from Canada to represent herself despite the zeal demonstrated by every other nation in the Western Hemisphere. Willie believed there was still time to sway the powers-that-be in Ottawa, but confided that as a native-born American himself he was still puzzled at times by Canadians' reticence when it came to its dealings with the United States.

Willie's visit could not have been better-timed, proving both serendipitous and providential. He had retained a suite at the Iroquois Hotel, and had come over to the Alderman's house for dinner the night before, reuniting with Annie, who was his second or third cousin, depending on who was doing the calculating.

The dinner had been strictly arranged by her to be a purely social family evening. Annie demanded there be no shop talk whatsoever. Since Willie had scheduled business in Niagara Falls the following day, the Alderman thought he and the Mayor should take advantage of that opportunity to meet Willie across the border and discuss the gravity of "the situation" far enough away from Buffalo on the Canadian side where no one was likely to scrutinize their presence. For their meeting they settled on the distracting holiday atmosphere provided by the massive Clifton Hotel where droves of happy tourists would be bustling about helping to divert attention away from the seriousness of the plotters' intent.

Fingy Conners' secret plan to exact his revenge on the city that had tried to rein him in him was a secret no longer. During the previous twenty-four hours, businessmen and politicians all up and down the eastern seaboard had been brought to a panicked state by the emerging news of Fingy's intended scheme.

Until his unprecedented loss to the scoopers union the previous May, Conners had amassed an impressive record for the triumphant accomplishment of evil. Now however, his ego freshly wounded and his voracious accumulation of wealth slowed just a tad by the scoopers fiasco, he was determined to reestablish his dominance over, and ruin upon, all those who were involved in opposing him, especially Mayor Diehl and Alderman John P. Sullivan.

This latest explosion of Conners' fury exceeded every previous blast to now include the City of Buffalo in particular and the United States of America in general.

The spreading news was galvanizing the East. The loss of Buffalo's Great Lakes shipping industry and the grain processing and transfer business would be devastating. Coincidentally too, if Conners was successful, it would also usurp the Canadian Pacific Railway's lucrative grain and freight business within Canada itself, as the waterways would be favored over the rails in Conners' project as the chief mode of transport.

Willie Van Horne took a few deep gulps of his Molson. "So, how much do you both already know about what Conners is up to, exactly?"

The Mayor replied, "He's out to ruin the economic foundation of our fine city. And believe you me, the ripples from such a brick tossed into the pond will spread fast, far and wide. After his defeat in the scoopers strike last May he traveled immediately to Montréal, I'm now told, to propose a deal with Canadian interests to build half a dozen mammoth grain elevators there."

"I am aware of that meeting," offered Willie, calmly.

"You are? Wait. Last May you were aware of it?" asked the Mayor.

"Yes."

Mayor Diehl then rustled around in his pile of papers and pulled out the latest issue of the *New York Commercial.*

"This article in the New York paper is interesting," understated the Mayor. "It quotes your friend James Hill of the Great Northern Railroad regarding 'The Montréal Conners Contract, Recently Signed.' Allow me read an excerpt to you:

"President Hill says 'That agreement will kill Buffalo as a commercial centre and prove disastrous to the same interests at New York, Boston, Newport News, Baltimore, Galveston and Portland. The diversion has begun and cannot be checked. There is no remedy that I can discover at this time because a point has been reached when the men who carry the scheme through have stolen a march on the interests that have been concentrated so long at the lakes and seaboard, and have felt too secure in their longtime prestige.'"

Conners planned to divert all the lake ships into the Welland Canal before ever reaching Buffalo and ship instead through Lake Ontario to the St. Lawrence, completely bypassing the United States and all the interests that thrive there on the grain and freight trade.

"His plan apparently was to corner the market, as they say," explained Willie, "to try and control the very bread of life, literally. The grain that Conners' had his eyes on isn't just that from America's heartland, remember. A good portion comes from the Canadian prairie provinces, and Canadians—especially we of the Canadian Pacific Railroad in particular—never had any intention of allowing this usurper to steal our harvest or the shipping business that goes along with it. Conners believed that in Canada he would be safely out of the reach and the eyes and the examinations of the likes of Teddy Roosevelt and his enemies in Congress."

Van Horne, the American Hero of the Canadian Pacific Railroad, went on to recite the astonishing statistics.

"The contract as I learned about it some time ago called for the expenditure on Conners' part of close to 4 million dollars at Montréal for grain elevators and warehouses, with a capacity of 9 million bushels. The operations of his company will involve the employment of a large fleet of vessels of the special canal type, for which construction has already begun.

"There are already contracts to construct two steamers of canal size at the plant of the Bertram Engine Works in Toronto, and the construction in England of four steamers and four tow barges.

"The contract with the Montréal Harbor Commission grants him three pieces of property which are, needless to say, among the choicest in the harbor at Montréal, affording ample space for the transfer of millions of tons of freight. The contract also calls for new elevators at Port Colburn on Lake Erie, which as you know is the western terminus of the Welland Canal, as well as the deepening of the harbor at that point so that large lake vessels unsuited to canal trade can transfer grain and other freight there to be carried down to Montréal by the smaller craft. These latter would engage in either through-traffic from Chicago and Duluth to Montréal, or simply in Port Colburn to Montréal trade as conditions may warrant.

"In return for these grants, Conners agreed that after the harbor at Port Colburn has been deepened, at least 25 million bushels of wheat the first season, and in every season thereafter 35 million bushels or the equivalent in freight will be transported to Montréal and handled through his facilities there, employing over a thousand men initially, and many more once all the facilities are up and running."

"Jesus Christ!" whistled the Mayor. "Lord knows, this could entirely sink the Pan-American Exposition."

The Alderman said, "I sent my brother this morning to deliver a report to John Milburn at his home, Conrad, addressing how all this might affect the Exposition. I'll hear from Milburn by morning tomorrow at the latest I'm sure, if not this very evening. I did not mince words. I told him that this was a catastrophe in progress. He may have some insight on how to stop Conners."

"Well, Gentlemen, it sounds like you two are ready to call out the troops...but you don't have to. I assure you—it's not going to happen. We've been following Conners' plotting for months. He thinks because he enjoys Canadian citizenship that he's a real Canadian. We don't quite agree. His contracts aren't legal."

The Alderman had initially called this meeting with Willie and the Mayor to propose some ways to stop Fingy, not realizing that Willie was quite a few steps ahead of him already. JP had had no intention of allowing Fingy's venture to move forward without a battle and he believed his ace in the hole was Willie Van Horne. And he knew that Willie Van Horne's ace in the hole was Canadian Prime Minister Sir Wilfred Laurier, a close friend, confidant, wily former attorney, and an unwavering champion of the expanding Canadian Pacific Railway.

Laurier may have had his hands full supporting the war in South Africa and gathering his political forces to bring the Yukon, Alberta and Saskatchewan into the Confederation, but the threat of Conners was so audacious and presumptive that Laurier relished participating in the opportunity to dispose of the little wharf turd once Willie had informed him about what was transpiring.

"This Conners person has no friends here," Prime Minister Laurier told Willie, "No one he can buy, no one he can threaten. He's out."

Willie Van Horne had been looking forward to meeting with the Mayor and the Alderman in order to calm them and to fill them in on what he had accomplished thus far...and perhaps to help them draft their own plan for revenge, turning the tables on Fingy Conners for once. After years of hearing tales about the ogre, Willie wanted to participate in helping topple him from his pedestal.

"Megalomaniac." Willie laughed. "Yes. That's the precise word I was searching for. Megalomaniac!" snorted the international rail tycoon, describing Conners with amused disgust. "That man's sick."

"Yep," conceded the Alderman. "In light of his most recent erraticisms, the title is more than fitting. I've known Fingy Conners since I took my very first steps as a small child holding my mother's hand, whereupon he immediately pushed me down to the ground and made me cry. Me dear departed mother nearly tossed the little fucker into the Ohio Basin at that point, she liked to recall."

"Oh, if she only had," countered the Mayor, wistfully.

"Gentlemen, what your little friend Conners now has on his hands, and doesn't know it yet, is what our British friends would call a sticky wicket."

Willie took another gulp of his Molson ale and savored the cold golden brew's welcome tickling effect as it foamed down his warm throat. "This should be fun to watch," Willie cackled.

The men laughed right along, relishing what was inevitably to come.

"I got meself a good taste of finally entering into some real combat with Conners during the scoopers strike," said the Alderman, nodding his head in recollection, "after a lifetime of sidestepping and dancing around to avoid him. And now he's boasting that I'm as good as ruined. Not to my face, of course," chuckled JP. "but certainly in his newspapers. We've been at each other's throats on and off before, but this time he's hell bent on total annihilation, and we just have to put a stop to this lunatic. And you're the man I realized could make it happen, dear Willie."

"That I am, cousin," Willie Van Horne grinned widely with no lack of confidence. "Happy to help."

The conspiring men all clinked glasses and laughed.

Perhaps Fingy forgot, or maybe wasn't even aware, that Willie Van Horne was family to the Alderman's wife. Or more likely, he knew but simply didn't care, so cocksure was he of himself.

"The Prime Minister would never consider such a deal as Conners', gentlemen, not for a second," stated Willie, "nor will the Canadian Pacific Railway. I've a good mind to just sit back and allow Conners to go ahead and spend a few million or so building us a lovely elevator facility before we kick his ass out of the country for good."

JP and the mayor were visibly relieved.

"Are you saying, Mr. Van Horne," asked the Mayor in disbelief," that all the gloom and doom we've recently heard and all we've read in the newspapers is wrong?"

"Yes, Mayor. Conners will never operate in Canada. I suspect all these positive reports you've quoted to me here and all the gloom and doom are all the products of Conners' own publicity machines. He seems to be dedicated to planting fear in people, you know, as his standard modus operandi. And owning two large newspapers he certainly has the wherewithal to accomplish that."

"Whew!" the men expelled in unison.

"I came here with all my fears and concerns and my head filled with ideas on how we might stop this man, and all along you'd had him already stopped?" asked JP.

"Well, he is stopped, I assure you. He just doesn't have any inkling yet. But until the work is done nullifying the contracts and educating his naïve Canadian backers, it can't yet be stated officially, and that could take a few months still. Meanwhile, Conners will continue to throw his money into a doomed project without realizing it's all for naught. Surely we can all gain some satisfaction from that. But just between the three of us, right here and now, it's exactly that—finished.

"Conners spent a lot of money contracting the building of those ships, drawing up plans, clearing land and improving facilities, laying foundations, and it brings me great joy that he has done so and will continue to, because he will lose his shirt on this deal. And those business partners of his in Chicago and elsewhere? No telling how much money they will lose between now and the official announcement. Those saps will think twice before they ever become bedfellows with Conners again."

"I'd give anything to be the one to break the news to him," mused JP. "What a real knife to the gut that would be! How good that would feel after all these years of all of us just standing there forced to take his shit!"

The Mayor reminded, "There's that Exposition Directors' banquet coming up in May at the Iroquois. How thrilling it would be, as you stood to make your toast in front of all two hundred of the city's most important men, JP, to raise your glass with all eyes upon you, including Fingy's, and you saying, "And, oh, by the way Fingy, me wife's had a little chat with her cousin...you remember, the President of the Canadian Pacific Railway? And he in turn had a little talk with his good friend Laurier, you recall? The Prime Minister of Canada? And together they decided that Canada won't be makin' yer acquaintance any time soon. Sorry you went ahead and spent all yer fuckin' money for nothin'.""

The men roared.

"Keep something crucial in mind gentlemen," summed up the railway man. "This news is completely secret, and if maintained as such, will present us all with investment opportunities based on information that no one else has. As people go forward thinking that Conners will succeed, as some men panic and others' plans are laid, you could well become rich betting against him. This could be a rare opportunity for you both to secure your families' financial future. That might be the greatest revenge of all."

❧❧❧

As a young boy growing up right around the corner from his future wife, the Alderman had been fascinated by Annie Saulter's army of cousins and friends-of-the-family spread across the nation as they were far and wide. When they came to visit in the summers to stay with the Saulter clan to see Niagara Falls, the neighborhood was newly enlivened with fresh perspectives and odd colloquialisms and funny accents from California, Tennessee and Illinois, to name but a few.

Willie Van Horne was older than Jim Sullivan by ten years, older than JP by eighteen, but over the decades they had all become close during his visits, with Willie proving himself a trusted ally. Willie was not quite as fond of the Alderman however as the Alderman was of him, truth be told. Confiding in Jim one year at an early Fourth of July Mutuals Regatta, he said that he believed that somewhere along his chosen path, John P. Sullivan had bargained away a substantial portion of his soul.

"Annie could have done better," he declared of his cousin with some regret in his voice.

Jim did not defend his brother.

❦❦❦

William Cornelius Van Horne had been an Illinois farm boy until he was eight years old, acclimated to rising with the roosters and tending the livestock in sub-zero winters. Having developed a greater sense of responsibility than most boys his age, the steadfast worker took on additional encumbrances voluntarily, much to his father's pride. When the family moved to the big city of Joliet in 1852, Willie's father was relieved to be able to retire his son from the never-ending toil of a family farm. He wanted his boy to get an education and to be exposed to opportunity. Not entirely unselfishly, Willie's father knew he himself would be getting old one day, and a parent's best insurance policy for old age might well prove to be a successful child, ably secured with property and money in the bank and occupying a stable place near the upper reaches of the social pyramid.

And succeed Willie Van Horne did, beginning with employment as a clerk with the Michigan Central Railway when he was just 13 years old. From there he rose to the position of superintendent for the Chicago and Alton Railway, and in 1882 was appointed general manager of the Canadian Pacific Railway. He won the vice presidency of that Canadian enterprise in 1884, then became its president four years later.

The American, Willie Van Horne, was now a Canadian hero and a legend in his own time for his envisioning and overseeing the construction of Canada's transcontinental railway—the entire four thousand mile length of it. Willie himself ceremoniously piloted the locomotive engine that inaugurated the first trans-Canadian Atlantic-to-Pacific journey. He was the first to consider the country's railway as an integrated communications and transportation system. He lobbied the railway's shareholders and directors to create a telegraph service, stringing lines that paralleled the railroad's right-of-way from coast to coast, and to establish a lucrative freight delivery business as well.

Like Alderman John P. Sullivan, Willie Van Horne felt quite comfortable straddling the international border with one foot on either side, working on behalf of both American and Canadian interests, and it was this international vision that finally warmed Willie to the Alderman as the politician rose to claim ever increasing power. From the time Willie first received the effusive letter from the Alderman trumpeting Buffalo's ambitious Pan American Exposition plans, he set out to make sure his firm would benefit most fully from the international fair. Fortuitously, this very endeavor coincided with another issue of far greater and more immediate concern to the Canadian Pacific Railway: Fingy Conners' planned infection of that country with his unique recipe of poison.

"That man knows no boundaries!" boomed Willie. "He professes no loyalties to anyone but himself; not any political party, neither to any national flag! I daresay he's determined to gobble up the entire planet if we allowed him."

Fingy Conners cared not one iota what anyone else on this earth thought of him, and that was his greatest strength. Even the worst of men seem to harbor in some lonely corner of their hearts or minds some speck of fear of rejection; a fragment of themselves desirous of others' acceptance. Everyone wants to be liked. Everyone except Fingy Conners.

"HOP" SULLIVAN

Fingy Conners was already hard at work on a plan to purge Mayor Conrad Diehl. That would be easy enough given the power and breadth of the voice of his newspapers. But getting rid of Alderman John P. Sullivan might prove somewhat trickier, although not impossible. "Hop" Sullivan had endeared himself to his First Ward constituents for all time by at long last publicly ramming heads with Fingy during the scoopers strike and mustering troops both political and religious to try and bring an era of unstoppable Conners tyranny on the docks to an end. The gauntlet had been thrown down.

The Alderman was by his very nature an affable sort, skilled at telling jokes and making disarmingly clever comments at the most unexpected times. He would drop a *bon mot*, and it would be followed by a full second or more of silence as listeners considered the odd remark, until suddenly the group would erupt in great, prolonged gales of laughter, delayed as they always were by the unusual delivery and cleverness of his utterance.

He had become increasingly popular with the passing years and excelled as a tireless self-promoter. He colluded with the press, especially the *Buffalo Express*, to create charming or humorous stories about his exploits, principally those involving his large family.

JP was enthusiastically social and humanely inclusive, having accumulated hundreds of friends among all classes and cultures while skillfully managing many an iron in the fire simultaneously, as his Annie was always quick to guilt him over. He patiently fulfilled promises of employment for his constituents, who would intrusively knock on his door day and night at No. 12 Hamburg Street, much to his family's irritation. He developed the successful strategy of inviting the job-seeker inside and employing a speedy routine borne out of necessity and practice, one that would allow him to stand tall in their eyes, yet dispatch of them quickly. He would pick up his Frontier telephone in his little home office that had been set aside for this very purpose, which was not hooked up to any line, and pretend to speak with whomever might be the opportune provider of a solution for his seeker. He would feign a positive response, then in short order dispatch the visitor with a handshake and a smile. Then later at a more convenient time, he followed up with the actual provider to see what he could do about getting the man work or the problem solved.

He himself employed a good many First Ward men during winter in his own business of harvesting Lake Erie ice—a small army actually. Always in his mind were the stories of the kindnesses of his predecessor David Clark of the Buffalo Ice Co. and the generosity the man had bestowed on his parents, and later also on himself and his brother. David Clark's originality was the compass that guided John P. Sullivan in the conducting of his own ice business, now the largest such private enterprise in Western New York.

The Sullivan Ice Company's paychecks were accepted the same as cash throughout the ward and beyond, their backs often covered with a dozen endorsements or more before finally reaching the bank. The check that initially went to the ice company employee was then signed over to the relative he owed money to, who signed it over to the grocer, who signed it over to the plumber, who signed it over to the carpenter, who signed it over to the dry goods store downtown until ultimately finding a nest at the bank. If the check had circulated too long into the autumn season, when the Sullivan Ice Co. bank balance was precariously low, especially if the previous winter had been too warm for a good ice harvest, sometimes a man would find the check he had accepted as being as good as cash would not be immediately honored by the bank.

One day the Alderman was enjoying a brew at Jimmy Murphy's crowded Blazing Rag saloon on South Street, just around the corner and down a jog from his home, when an irate man dressed in a very neat checked suit entered looking especially agitated. He went from man to man showing each his piece of paper and inquiring if any of them knew who "John P. Sullivan of the Sullivan Ice Co." was. They all did, of course, since the Alderman was standing right there, but none betrayed him. The irate man held a check that the bank had turned down. It was November and cold weather was only just arriving. The ice company's funds were depleted.

"Sullivan always makes good on his checks, sir, eventually," the man was told at the bank. "But you might have to wait until the ice crop comes to harvest before we can cash that for you."

The man had inquired around the neighborhood and was told that the Blazing

126

Rag was one of Sullivan's customary watering holes. He bounced from one Blazing Rag customer to another, asking the same question, until he reached the little red-haired man in the derby hat and cane, wearing the giant orthopedic shoe.

"Say, fella, do you know anything about this man Sullivan? I accepted this here check as payment because I was told it was as good as gold, but the bank refuses to cash it. I need to find this scoundrel! Do you know anything about him? What he looks like?"

"Well," said the Alderman, stroking his chin as he displayed a far-off thoughtful look, "He's a damned good looking man, I'll promise you that much! Quite charming they say, and just about my height. And he walks something like this."

And with that, Hop Sullivan turned and made his way out the door with the characteristic gait that provided his nickname, his limp an accompaniment since his younger days. The entire Blazing Rag erupted in laughter.

The irate man looked puzzled for a moment, and then his eyes widened to saucers. "Was that *him?*" he asked of no one in particular to even greater laughter, and quickly pursued the Alderman out the door.

"Sullivan! Hey! Is this you? Is this your check?"

The Alderman stopped and turned on his cane, and when the man caught up with him the jokester accepted and examined the note, holding it up to the light, squinting his eyes, inspecting both sides repeatedly. Then he said, "Well, by gosh, I do believe that is my signature! I'll be damned!"

"So, what are you gonna do about it? I accepted this check because I was told it was as good as gold! But the bank won't even cash it!" shouted the frustrated creditor.

"Well, not gold perhaps, my friend," said the Alderman, "but silver, certainly."

And with that the Alderman took out his change purse and counted out three and a half silver dollars, despite the personal agony that such an act visited upon the infamous tightwad.

The man accepted his silver and grumbled, "Now, there's a fine how'd you do!" and stormed off toward Elk Street in a huff.

MAY 16. 1900

Fingy Conners' luxury yacht *Enquirer* steamed westward through Lake Erie's calm waters. Upon his most recent return from Montréal by rail, he immediately set sail for Chicago to confer with his partners in his ambitious Montréal project.

The Commodore, as he insisted he be addressed, was served a whiskey in his stateroom by his chief steward, along with toasted crumpets slightly burned—as was his preference—and spread thickly with creamery butter and loganberry preserves. His ever-present cigar stump never left his mouth. He was able to sip his whiskey and even to some extent munch his crumpets with the soggy butt still somehow firmly embedded in his lips.

He held the glass to his eye and looked through the ruby red glass rim, with its beautifully scrolled "Yacht Enquirer of Buffalo" proudly emblazoned on it. He looked around the elegant suite, just to see how it would appear if he should decide someday on a whim to have it all redone in red. The bottom half of the tumbler was of the finest deep-cut crystal, providing a firm grip on rocky seas for tipsy drinkers.

His intention this particular trip was to use the opening of his newest offices in Chicago on River Street as a pulpit to preach his latest plan to the newspapers, and thereby scare the shit out of everybody in Buffalo, and those well beyond.

The *Enquirer* was a fabulous vessel by anyone's standards, but Fingy was especially proud of the validation provided by the framed clipping hung in the salon for all to see, cut from the *Mariners' Report* magazine.

The article pictured gathered together the top ten luxury yachts in the United States, and there among the giant private craft owned by the Astors, the Vanderbilts, J.P. Morgan and the like, was William J. Conners' spectacular *Enquirer*, the noble photo having been snapped by Mr. George Hare.

Conners had first met Hare at the launching of his ship on June 14, 1896. Hare was present to photograph the festivities for the *Buffalo Express* for its Illustrated Sunday edition. As the ship careened down the launch and slid into the water at the Union

Dry Dock Company's slip, Hare's two cameras recorded the spectacular sight. Once it had hit the water with a tremendous slap, propelling an explosion of spray going as high as her smokestack, the gorgeous ship righted herself and sat the water like a duck.

Fingy had used a rare bottle of Veuve Clicquot Champagne to christen the $75,000 ship, as sad thirsty eyes watched the exotic bubbly drain wasted into the filthy harbor waters. The *Enquirer's* hull was of steel construct, the decks of white pine with deck trimmings of brass. The hull was painted white from head to stern, giving the ship its nickname, The White Flyer. Her length measured 144 ft.; the water line measurement 123 feet; 17 1/2 ft. beam and 10 ft. hold. She was fitted with a triple expansion Hodge engine with cylinders 10 1/2, 17, and 23 by 16. The electrical apparatus was of the very latest pattern. The dynamos were automatic, and anywhere from a single light up to four hundred could be lighted or extinguished at will. The search light was of 7,500 candlepower, and the rigging gaily dressed with 200 colored globes of electric luminescence. The yacht was of 140 tons burden. She boasted a Taylor water tube boiler and the contract with the builders called for a speed of 18 miles an hour, but the *Enquirer* would prove to significantly exceed that rate.

The exposed woodwork of the boat was of solid mahogany and the interior of curly birch with the exception of Fingy's private stateroom which was paneled in bird's eye maple.

Conners had recently purchased a spectacular Captain's bed from one of the early luxury steamers being dismantled in New York that had plied the lakes, a ship he himself had once served aboard as a boy. He remembered being jaw-dropped upon first seeing the bed as a thirteen-year-old. He had carried a tray up from the galley to the ship's Captain, a man who especially disliked Fingy, attesting to the keenly intuitive sort he was, much experienced in encounters with scoundrels of all sizes and ages.

The Captain's bed was a spectacular creation, a four-poster mahogany carved fantasy swirling with mermaids, dolphins, starfish and octopi, topped supremely at the crown of its headboard by a beautifully turned figurehead of the god Neptune, brandishing a 14 carat gold trident. Fingy had never seen anything like it, the mattress piled high with goose down pillows and snowy linens and topped with an alpaca blanket dyed the precise color of the Lake Huron depths that had swallowed his severed thumb.

He dreamed of that bed nightly as he struggled to fall asleep on his hard shelf bunk fitted deep within the ship's fetid hold, fantasizing of someday being able to rock gently off to dreamland snuggled in precisely the sort of luxury that his Captain enjoyed. And now here he was. He'd located the Captain's bed and purchased it for a song, and every night before he closed his eyes he looked up at the watchful presence of the great King Neptune gazing down upon him and whispered, "Keep us safe, yer Majesty."

On its maiden voyage to the Metropolis Of The West, the *Enquirer* had carried Fingy Conners and all his friends, including William Randolph Hearst, to the Democratic National Convention of 1896, for which Conners served as delegate from the Great State of New York. Captain Sam Golden guided the ship to Chicago through lake waters he knew at least as well as the back of his own hand.

But presently, this particular voyage had its own specific purpose.

Waiting to disembark, Fingy looked out and chuckled to himself as the *Enquirer* tied up amid the maneuvering of a gaggle of news reporters awaiting him on the Chicago docks.

He disembarked to hold court.

"Sir, Mr. Conners, can you tell us about the contract you've signed with the Montréal people?" queried one newsman.

Fingy replied, "Certainly. I have the support of all the large grain interests of Chicago and Duluth. The Montréal route will afford an all-water way to the sea, which can compete with the railroads because of its cheapness. Montréal is 300 miles nearer Liverpool than is New York, a decided advantage. Besides the three elevators at Montréal, we expect to build an elevator of 1,500,000 bushels at Port Colburn, Ontario, sixteen miles from Buffalo. Through-grain going to Montréal in large cargoes will be broken there."

"Are you starting a war with the railroads, the city of Buffalo, or both, Mr. Conners?" another reporter asked.

William J. Conners smiled broadly at the delicious thought.

"During the season just ended, boys, only a little more than 11,000,000 bushels of the vast amount of grain which came to Buffalo from the West by lake and rail was shipped east through the Erie Canal. The great bulk of it rather went by rail. The water route to Montréal will be much cheaper than any rail route, and the end result is that bread for your family will cost you less. Yes, you heard that right. *Less.* No, son, we're not trying to kill the railroads. We're just engaging in a little friendly competition, that's all. It's the American way, is it not? May the best man win."

The *Chicago Tribune* editorialized the following day:

> It may be that the labor troubles which Mr. Conners was involved in last season may prove a roorback, sort of a boomerang to the people, especially the grain scoopers and their leaders who tried to down W.J. by all means in their power. Looking at it from this end of the line it is easily seen that every extra bushel that goes through the Canadian Welland Canal will be so much less for the Buffalo scoopers to handle. Mr. Conners seems to be a fighter and one that will hit back harder than his best opponent every time. Besides, he has the influence and wherewithal to do it.

Chicago's *Tribune* apparently failed to realize that Conners' power and influence was not entirely without limits. Fingy Conners was as yet unaware that Willie Van Horne and Prime Minister Laurier had pounded the final nail into the coffin of his grand Canadian endeavor. And with the appearance of a bicycle messenger from Western Union at the front door of No. 12 Hamburg Street, bearing an urgent telegram from Ottawa, Alderman John P. Sullivan was granted his wish as expressed to Willie Van Horne.

JP would have the honor of being the tidings-bearer.

THE BANQUET

The great banquet was set for the Iroquois Hotel.

JP was starving, newly energized by the excitement of what was to come. He picked up the handsome eight-page banquet program, the cover beautifully printed by Fingy Conners' own Courier Litho Press, a full color reproduction of the stunning poster by Evelyn Rumsey Cary chosen as the official image of the Pan American Exposition.

JP opened it, and immediately his stomach began to growl.

MENU

Massachusetts Bays
Celery
Old Amorosa

Green Turtle Americaine

Kennebec Salmon, Hollandaise
Cucumbers   Potatoes, Parisienne
Varies   Varies
Liebfraumilch
P.A. Mumm & Co.

Filet of Beef Pique, Fresh Mushrooms
Green Peppers Farcie   String Beans
Pontet Canet

Vol-au-Vent of Chicken, a la Reine

Gem Peas
Moët & Chandon
White Seal

Sorbet Iroquois

Quail Sur Canape aux Cresson
Lettuce and Tomatoes Mayonnaise

Vanilla Ice Cream
Jelly Macedoine
Assorted Cakes   Bonbons
Fruit
Fromage de Brie and Roquefort

Amid the hubbub and distraction of men who had gathered to celebrate themselves, the Alderman withdrew the telegram from his breast pocket. He opened it just for as long as it took to quickly reread the soothing words that would change everything. Then he tucked it back into his coat and took another sip of his Moët & Chandon. The brilliant news had come from Willie Van Horne that very morning. The Canadians would build the Montréal grain elevators themselves with no interference whatsoever from Fingy Conners. The only person with whom JP had shared the splendid news was the Mayor.

Conners' grand plan was now just so much rubble, but he hadn't a clue.

A pall was cast as Fingy stalked into the Iroquois' banquet room, his disposition overconfident and overbearing.

As the director of numerous commercial enterprises, all of which performed better under his leadership than they ever had before he came crashing into the picture, his untarnished record of achievement spoke for itself. The malevolent sneer and primitive wharf rat aspect of the man were invariably present. Threat was always implied behind his suspicious smile. Slippery as butter when it came to having to atone for two decades of criminal malfeasance, imminent violence was a foreshadowed implication in his every steely glower and reticent handshake. Each man who encountered Conners had the deeply disturbing feeling at the initial locking of eyes that they were being probed and analyzed for future benefit or misuse.

JP observed that there were two kinds of individuals in the room; those who gravitated to Conners out of owing him or needing him for something, and those who were repelled by his mere presence whether for moral or social reasons. The latter did their utmost to avoid him. It was always an uncomfortable situation, encountering Fingy, which was exactly what Conners intended. But having to work with the man, confer and plan and allow his opinions and influence to pollute a splendid enterprise like the Pan American Exposition was too much for many of those present. They had worked tirelessly for two years, and now there hovered Fingy like some underwater mine, lurking, threatening, relishing an opportunity for destruction, anticipating sending the entire fleet to the bottom.

Fingy made it clear that Mayor Diehl was dead to him. And in recent times he barely paid any notice to the Alderman's existence either. When JP caught Conners' eye, Fingy quickly looked away. Eventually, the signal was sounded for the attendees to take their seats. The feast was served and gobbled and champagne and wine heartily enjoyed, and before the alcohol could finish its fine work on the crowd entirely, JP rose to speak.

As chief toastmaster, the Alderman would be making the welcoming remarks. Mayor Diehl, recalling now the fantasized scenario of publicly humiliating Fingy Conners that he himself had conjured during their meeting with Willie Van Horne at Niagara, suddenly gulped, realizing that it might well be just like the jokester of the City Hall to pick up the ball and run with it. Suddenly uncomfortable, the Mayor began to sweat a little.

JP had indeed been energized by the Mayor's humorous scenario that day at Niagara. The look on his face as he rose to speak was that of impending triumph.

"Mayor Diehl. Exposition President Milburn. Director Scatcherd. Gentlemen," he began. "I am honored and humbled to be able to speak here tonight in your esteemed presence, the most influential, forward-looking and hard-working of Buffalo men, responsible for bringing to fruition the grand idea of the great Pan American Exposition of nineteen hundred and one.

"When as President of the Common Council of this great city I offered the resolution directing the Corporation Counsel to draft a special act giving Mayor Diehl power to appoint a Provisional Committee to attend at the birth of this spectacular new enterprise, I had great hopes for the success of the venture. But not in my wildest dreams did I entertain the idea that we might have an opportunity to match, or might I even be so bold as to project, *exceed* the astonishing success of the Chicago Fair of 1893.

"Tonight we have as our honored guest, I am pleased to say, the venerable Mr. Daniel Burnham, the chief architect and visionary of the 1893 World's Columbian Exposition, the Chicago Fair's exquisite White City."

Applause and excited chatter greeted the architect's introduction. Burnham looked pleased with the ovation, and the Alderman continued.

"It was Mr. Burnham who conceived and built the most celebrated architectural jewel in our own beloved metropolis, Buffalo's Ellicott Square Building, which grandly occupies an entire city block just two streets away from where we are now seated. It is celebrated as the largest office building in the entire world. Fully occupied from the very day of its grand opening, within Mr. Burnham's breathtaking masterpiece, Mr. Thomas Edison set up his Edisonia Vitascope Theater, the first theater in the world exclusively dedicated to exhibiting the new moving pictures.

"Indeed, once Mr. Burnham agreed to honor us tonight with his presence, we conceived the idea of moving the site of this great feast to the heart of his masterpiece, to the Ellicott Building's grand interior courtyard, beneath that great sky-lighted glass roof. But alas, the banquet plans were already too far along, and the idea proved impossible to carry out within the limited time left us. Nonetheless, we are complimented just to be in the company of this imaginative and accomplished artist. Gentlemen, please join me in welcoming here tonight the esteemed genius, Mr. Daniel H. Burnham of Chicago."

Great acclaim thundered up and Daniel Burnham stood briefly to receive the deserved adulation of those who might dare follow in his successful exposition venture footsteps.

Alderman Sullivan continued.

"We could not have come as far as we have today if not for the enthusiasm, the civic pride and untiring efforts of all those assembled here. We are especially thankful to Exposition President Milburn, the Commander who has valiantly led this great army of businessmen, architects, artists, participating nations, laborers and supporting citizens to the threshold of victory."

Thunderous applause rang out. The Alderman paused for effect when the ovation began to subside, making sure that all eyes were his. He cleared his throat so that his words would not go unclearly heard.

"But we are especially honored this evening to welcome back—to once again enjoy the full undistracted attentions and boundless energies of Mr. William James Conners, now that the Canadian government has, regrettably, denied his bid to build for that country what would have been the greatest, most extensive grain processing facility in the entire world."

The relaxed atmosphere of the cigar smoke-filled room suddenly erupted in a wave of charged murmurs at hearing the momentous news. Everyone present had feared Fingy's plan and the devastation it would surely have wrought upon the city. Yet the untouchable narcissist Conners had the unmitigated sand to stride into that banquet room and sit there among them as an ally, gloating, pretending to support the endeavors of the united tens of thousands of Buffalo citizens to bring to life an undertaking which the megalomaniac's own planned single-minded Canadian endeavor might well have annihilated.

The Alderman continued.

"And thus, Canada's loss is Buffalo's gain, as it were. So welcome back, Fingy my friend, to the Pan American Exposition Company family. Let us all now raise a glass and drink a toast to all the senior members of this directors' board, these many fine and loyal citizens, the shining lights of our great city to whom we are indebted and tonight whom we are gathered here to honor. Here, here!" he shouted.

The Alderman brought his champagne to his lips to the booming of voices following his call, toasting themselves and each other. JP smiled as all joined with him, then turned and raised his glass one more time to Fingy Conners as their eyes met and locked, and the Alderman sipped again.

Fingy's champagne glass trembled in his infuriated hand, his face crimson with anger. The moment the toast was finished, he shot out of the banquet hall like a lightning bolt, practically dragging Kennedy with him, cursing and spitting his humiliation. He headed down Main Street to the telegraph station at his offices at the *Courier* to try and determine exactly what the hell was going on.

As Fingy stormed out, Alderman Sullivan and Mayor Diehl exchanged broad grins across a calmed sea of crisp white linen and sparkling silver.

DOMINION DAY

July 1st marks the date that marks Canada's Dominion Day.

In the week preceding, Ontario newspapers in Toronto, Hamilton, London and Niagara Falls were filled with advertisements placed by Buffalo shopping emporiums and hotels welcoming the hordes of Canadian celebrants who annually flowed over the border bridges to spend the national holiday. They arrived by train, carriage and lake steamer to celebrate their heritage by means of a shopping spree. The annual ritual proved a bonanza for the Buffalo businessmen whose advertised combined Dominion Day-4th Of July Sale produced the year's greatest windfall other than that of Christmas.

Herbert Alexander Meldrum was on site at his department store the morning of July 1 to personally welcome the Canadian shoppers. The façade of the ultra-modern establishment across the street from the Tifft House Hotel was alive with the fluttering flags of the Dominion and of the Province of Ontario. Canadian guests filled the elegant hostelry.

Mr. Meldrum's family was descended from an illustrious Scottish line and despite his being barely thirty years old he had made a great success for himself in the dry goods business.

Concurrently, old Joshua Lovejoy was suffering another bout of severe melancholy.

It was thought that the later in life that a woman gave birth the more prone to serious and regrettable mood problems her offspring might be. Joshua's mother was 46 when he was born. She died a few days thereafter. Throughout his long and painful sixty eight years his demons had trailed after him doggedly. Most vivid in his mind's recollection were the terrifying accounts of the murder and horrifying barbaric scalping of his grandmother Sarah Lovejoy on December 30, 1813 at the behest of the invading British and their Indian collaborators. Lovejoy's earliest memories from childhood were of the terrifying stories his aunt had recounted with relish, vivid with bloody detail, that had haunted his tormented sleep ever since.

The previous week he had visited the library of the Buffalo Historical Society and there discovered letters written by two sisters in 1876 whose family name, St. John, was familiar to him as relating to the stories of the incident his aunt had recounted. Curious, he sat down and began to read. For the next few hours he was unable to remove himself from the chair he'd occupied.

Far more elaborate and complex than the bare-bones version spun by his aunt, the recollected elements within the letters penned by the two St. John sisters who had escaped from the Indians on that fateful night, then returned to view the horrific aftermath, sent him spiraling downward like the whirling seeds shed by the great elm.

Lovejoy, smelling of spirits, teetered unsteadily out front of the Tifft House hotel, scowling at the well-dressed Canadian visitors. Sarah Lovejoy's house had been built right on the very spot the hotel now occupied. She had died in agony and terror on the very spot he now stood. With him he carried a sturdy box and a megaphone. He was dressed in the style of thirty years previous, the garments ragged, yet clean. His hair was dyed jet black and was so dull that even with oil applied to give it a sheen, it was obvious the hue was not naturally his own.

Lovejoy crossed Main Street and set up his Lautz Soap box outside the main entrance of the Meldrum Store and commenced with his tirade, shouting through a megaphone constructed of green shellacked cardboard.

"They call themselves Canadians in a transparent charade of distraction to disguise themselves from the onerous truth that they are in fact British, and enthusiastic Royalists to boot!" he bellowed.

The scurrying forms of lovely Canadian women and their well-dressed gentlemen escorts were at first taken aback. They hastened by, trying to avoid the vehement exhortations amplified by the horn. As Lovejoy's anger increased, the women became frightened. Those who were approaching the Meldrum Store from across the street or down the block turned and walked the other way.

"Shakespeare himself said it best," Lovejoy went on, "'What's in a name?' Those British scoundrels across the river over there thought that by takin' on a new name that this would change things? That somehow, their character would be transformed along with it? Canada, as they have more recently come to call their prison, is nothing more than a toady British colony, its inmates shiverin' with cowardice, a British possession terrified to stand up on its own, rollin' over on its pitiful stomach whenever its boss' depraved appetites demand satisfyin'!"

A sales girl at the front counter in the Meldrum store realized people were no longer coming through the doorway. She poked her curious head out to see the increasingly frantic Mr. Lovejoy preaching wildly, pedestrians detouring well out of their way to avoid his rancor. She ran back inside to fetch the manager, but as she flew down the aisle past Ladies' Silks, the manager could be seen approaching from the opposite direction on the arm of Mr. Meldrum himself.

"Sir," she panted as she ran up to the owner, "there's an insane man in front of the store scaring customers away!"

Meldrum would have none of that, and with his walking stick ready as a weapon, the doors of the emporium flung open to disgorge him almost into the lap of the dedicated Mr. Lovejoy.

"That my friends," shouted Joshua Lovejoy, "over there on the other side of the river so close that a child's toy arrow could reach it, lies Great Britain, and don't you dare forget it! Their festerin' colony on our very doorstep is rotten through and through!"

"Say you!" shouted Mr. Meldrum, "You come down off that box at once! You are frightening people away!"

"The worst oppressors of men in the history of this earth, that is the contemptible title that the English imperialists enjoy!" Lovejoy continued, undaunted.

Meldrum grabbed at Mr. Lovejoy's waistcoat and pulled. The manager lingered there not knowing what to do.

"Don't just stand there, Whitcomb! Help me get rid of this trash!" admonished the store owner.

Together the men tried to dismount Mr. Lovejoy, but a solid whack delivered from the lecturer's cane across Mr. Meldrum's head ended that. Whitcomb helped his employer up off the pavement and back into the store.

"Telephone the police!" Whitcomb shouted toward the direction of the telephone.

"The scourge of the entire globe!" Lovejoy ranted on, "That's what them people are! If them cowardly Royalists to the north had an ounce of gumption or a speck of backbone, don't you think they'd have declared their independensh long ago, the same as we...we have?"

Lovejoy stopped a moment to take a swig from his bottle, then resumed the tirade.

"It wasn't until thirteen long years after the start of our American Revolution in 1776 that we finally had a true government with George Washington as our President. Thirteen endless, arduous, bloody years during which we had to continue fightin' off them British scum any way we might, and still they refused to back away! They stopped our American ships at sea and on our Great Lakes and boarded them and kidnapped over six thousand of our citizens and enslaved them into their French war with Napoleon! White American slaves, forshed to die for the diabolical British! They took American boys as young as ten years old for cannon fodder! What sort of animals are them Britishers? What levelsh of cruelty have they not sh...schtriven mightily to attain?"

Increasingly besotted, he looked down at a refined gentleman clearly from a monied background.

"How about you? Are you a white slaver, *monsieur?*" he asked. "Hey my canuck fr...friend! I'm talkin' to you! You got any Americans locked up in your Ontario coal shellar, perhaps?"

Lovejoy's speech was beginning to heavily slur.

Detectives Jim Sullivan and John Geary had heard the commotion from up Main Street. They had been on high alert for pickpockets attracted to the city from all outlying regions by the promise of the bounty contained in the Canadian shoppers' purses and vest pockets and had just come from policing the Flint & Kent Store. They ran up to Lovejoy and ordered him to stop.

"You cease that tomfoolery right this instant, you!" shouted Jim, as Lovejoy's cane connected with his skull. It glanced off, landing hard on his shoulder, recalling an old injury.

"It's not as if the damn British navy is going to come a-sailin' up the St. Lawrence and begin bombardin' you spineless people!" Lovejoy continued. "You can end your evil ash...assosh...association anytime you choose, and yet you do not choose! What in God's name is wrong with you? What are you people waitin' for?"

His whiskey bottle at that very moment dropped to the walkway with a crash resulting in an explosion of glass shards. The heavy smell of drunkenness surrounded the orator.

Geary tackled the lecturer and toppled him like a rotted stump. Jim rose up from the sidewalk with the great urge to break a few of Lovejoy's teeth but the pathetic nature of the man's condition stopped him.

"You're comin' with us. I'll put you in wrist shackles if you so much as try and resist detention!" Jim warned angrily.

Lovejoy was suddenly crestfallen. He offered no resistance, but considering his inebriated state walked quite handily to the lockup. He toddled without coaxing straight into the opened cell.

"Them Redcoats and their red savages chopped the bloody scalp right off me dear sweet grandmother!" he sobbed as the door clanged shut.

Sullivan and Geary walked off to write him up.

Lovejoy looked around his cell, not surprised at where he had ended up, but disappointed he had not been allowed his entire say outside the H.A. Meldrum Store on Main Street.

With nothing else to occupy his mind, his tormented psyche replayed the old story, yet again, from the beginning.

THE EXPOSITION TAKES SHAPE

As of the first of August, 1437 applications had been received for permission to operate various kinds of concessions within the boundaries of the Pan American Exposition. Many of the applications were for shows of a kind that could not be permitted at a great moral exhibition such as the Pan-American was intended to be. Some were so utterly absurd as to tax one's ability to understand the mental processes of the applicant.

If the Exposition officials had carried out the proposition presented by A.H. Kilian of Indianapolis, visitors to the Exposition would have had the opportunity of gazing upon something extraordinary, but Mr. Kilian's idea was not acted upon for reasons which must be patent upon any respectful American.

Mr. Kilian proposed to erect a statue of George Washington 80 stories tall, having elevators running up both legs and through the body to the head, where various forms of amusement would be provided; to have restaurants, beer halls and shows of various kinds spread along from the hips to the chin, and to have a great stairway encircling the statue from top to bottom. Secretary Fleming turned down the idea, which at first he thought must be a hoax, explaining that it "did not recommend itself" to the officials.

Other ideas that were turned away included a gigantic baked bean pot fifty feet in diameter inside which people would be served beans put up especially for Boston people.

A man from Paris wanted a space three meters by ten to build a restaurant smack dab in the middle of the esplanade, disregarding the effect it would visit upon the overall artistic concept.

Another wanted a space three feet by twenty-five feet alongside one of the permanent structures, the Grecian-columned Albright Art Gallery, on which to knock together a lean-to from which to sell milk and pie.

George C. Tilyon of Coney Island, who was awarded the steeple-chase concession, planned to also show there a Negro he had picked up in St. Louis who could drink a bucket of water, then shoot it out his nose and mouth in imitation of a whale, a fire engine or an electric fountain.

A Texas man wrote that he was the proprietor of the only genuine four-legged girl in the U.S. and wished to exhibit her at the Exposition. Another asked for permission to erect a derrick at the brink of Niagara Falls that would swing people out over the cataract. Another applied to exhibit a family of claw-footed hook-handed humans.

New York publisher Roy Crandall, falsely promoting himself as an agent of the Exposition, announced a competition to choose a Miss Pan-American Beauty to represent North America on the official Pan-American seal. Anna McLean of Paterson N.J. was piqued at not having been chosen and thus killed herself by drinking carbolic acid. She had entered her photograph in a contest supported by the New York Sunday World. When she discovered that she was not among the finalists chosen, Miss McLean wrote letters to all of her friends and to the directors of the Pan American expressing her utter disappointment, and then dressed in her best gown, her hair beautifully arranged and wearing her grandmother's diamond brooch, drank the poison and lay down on her lace bed pillow to die in agony.

Underscoring the futility of her tragedy, the newspaper's scheme petered out without any winner having been selected after the Exposition's publicity department denied any connection whatsoever with publisher Crandall's beauty contest.

The city of Buffalo, having wrested the honor to mount the exposition from the determined clutches of Detroit, had to face the fact that the Queen City had no previous qualification in the field of hosting such an international fête. Buffalo's planners could only look to the Chicago Fair of 1893 as a guide for possible predicaments and complications. The challenge taken on by the city and its optimistic citizens was admittedly monumental.

When subscriptions were first offered in 1899 a huge swell of support welled up immediately. Buffalonians rich and poor, from captains of industry to immigrant schoolchildren, backed the grand exposition with enthusiastic pledges of hard-earned money. On the first day, nearly a half million dollars was pledged.

In July, when the fair was taking recognizable shape, Mayor Conrad Diehl, as top man in the hierarchy of esteemed citizens backing the exposition, experienced dreadful nightmares concerning fire consuming the entire scheme. He and Director General Buchanan were greatly agitated over the failure of the city's Aldermanic Committee on Fire to act upon their request for additional fire protection for the Pan American grounds.

The Mayor warned the committee that if action was not taken immediately, he intended to order fire apparatus transferred from city firehouses to be established on the grounds to protect the huge buildings rising there.

"I never saw a body of men so slow in acting on a proposition in my life as these aldermen in charge of fire," fumed the Mayor. "Petty jealousy and an enlarged imagination of their own importance seem to have completely carried them away. If they don't do something at their meeting this very night I will order the largest steamer in the Fire Department to the grounds tomorrow, even if it has to be put under a tent!

"Every night I fear that fire may occur on the grounds. Locomotive engines are passing frequently on the tracks nearby and a spark from one of those might start a conflagration which would wipe out all the work done thus far. After all the progress we have made, a fire there is a dreadful thing to contemplate. It will mean an end to the exposition, a shame put upon the entire city for the next few decades, and a great loss to the thousands of people in Buffalo who are stockholders in the company.

"Officials will be guilty of criminal neglect if anything occurs. They haven't a leg to stand on in the way of excuse. This matter was laid before them six months ago and they have done nothing as of yet."

Not being a member of the fire committee, Alderman Sullivan was free to rant and rail at the shameful lack of responsibility displayed by his colleagues. He assailed the aldermen for their holding out the hope that some of the exhibitors of fire apparatus themselves would provide the steamers free of charge, as had been done at Chicago, or that some unused apparatus might be rigged up for the purpose.

Fingy Conners' cohort, Alderman Kennedy, defended the committee's actions.

"They are a private enterprise and have a large amount of money," Kennedy said. "Why should the city go into debt to provide them with fire protection? It strikes me this question should not be considered too hastily."

At the same moment that Kennedy was justifying his months of stonewalling, forty-five railroad cars loaded with material for the mammoth Electric Tower, the iconic main feature of the exposition, were chugging slowly on their way into the grounds proper, adding to the consternation and urgency of protecting this major undertaking.

Meanwhile, a scheme was being authorized by the Exposition's Department of Publicity to throw pictures upward upon heaven's canopy over Atlantic City, where the legend "Pan-American Exposition, Buffalo 1901" would be seen beckoning from the clouds above throughout the entire summer and autumn of 1900. A contract with the Searchlight Publicity Company was signed to perform this feat as well as to project artists' renderings of the exposition via lantern slides by means of a huge searchlight onto clouds in the summer resort was readied. Nothing was said of the interruptions sure to be caused by an uncooperative sky.

Throughout Buffalo, scammers were out in full force working their schemes on the unsuspecting public. Two well-dressed young men claiming to be officials of the Pan-American Exposition Company representing the Bureau Of Public Comfort were making the rounds in the appropriate neighborhoods offering, for the trifling sum of $2, to put boarding houses on an official list which will be put in the hands of Pan-American visitors looking for boarding-houses.

Their suspicions aroused, Mrs. Elizabeth Brainerd and Miss Mary McCabe, proprietors of a boarding house at the corner of Hudson Street and Orton Place, summoned the police. Officers stood with the lady proprietors on the rounded front porch beneath a quaint turreted tower as they told the tale.

"These young men were very suave and very smooth in their manner," Brainerd said. "They informed us that we could not afford to lose the chance of having our house included on the official Pan-American Exposition boarding house list. They promised they would crowd our house for us during the Pan year if we would give up $2 now. They gave references from the Exposition Company as to their integrity. But I do not prove so easy, no. I told them I would look into the matter, and did not give them any money."

Mrs. Dora Crandall, who keeps a large boarding house at 310 Franklin Street, paid $2 and happened to tell of her investment to one of her boarders, Frank A. Converse, chief of the Pan-American Exposition's Department of Livestock and Agriculture. Converse informed his landlady that she had probably been fleeced, as the exposition company employed no official canvassers. Mrs. Crandall told the police that one of the men wore duck trousers, a blue serge coat and a straw hat, while the other was fashionably dressed as well in a brown suit and a fedora hat.

Throngs of sightseers descended daily upon the vast Exposition site to monitor the construction progress for themselves. Chief among them were citizen-shareholders keeping an eye on their investment. On the second Sunday in July hundreds of carriages were driven through the grounds on Amherst Street and no fewer than one hundred persons journeyed through the grounds in automobiles. People came on foot by the thousands, on bicycles, and even pushing baby carriages. Chaos was created when the crowds interfered with the movements of rail cars, drays and laborers rushing to make headway on the construction. The logistics thus far involved in digging lakes, lagoons and a canal system for accommodating gondolas on the property were daunting, and coordinating that muddy construction with the transporting of the vast amount of building materials was an arduous and complicated feat.

If as many people were to flock to the Pan-American in one day as visitors to the grounds did during this time of construction, then its success would certainly be assured.

For many weeks there had been a growing call to close the grounds to visitors and curiosity-seekers. What had been for months a vast field of mud had by mid-July dried and hardened in the midsummer sun and heat. Great clouds of dust stirred up from the incessant traffic. Smoking was strictly prohibited but both visitors and workers balked at the idea of not partaking in this particular addiction.

"No Smoking" appeared in gigantic letters at the entrance and throughout the entire grounds at every turn, but one did not have to venture far to see it disregarded by those in carriages as well as those on foot. Visitors squatted along the edges of the massive wooden framework of the largest buildings, some being so bold as to picnic in the interiors, smoking all the while.

The wisdom of the campaign to close the grounds to the uncooperative public having been confirmed with their own eyes, the Board of Public Works rushed in to furnish seventy eight hydrants with direct pressure, and to install a Snow pump in place at the adjoining power house, much to the relief of Captain Riley of the Exposition firehouse. Another firehouse on the opposite end of the grounds was being rushed to completion.

"These problems with careless behavior on the part of hundreds of people on any given day have caused the officials to decide to close the grounds to the public within the next few weeks," stated Riley in the *Commercial*.

"The reason is obvious," added Director of Works Mr. Carllton. "The people are getting in our way and it greatly increases the fire hazard. We are delighted to have the public with us, of course, but must look out for the safety of the buildings as well as our workmen. One shudders to think of what might happen from one lighted stub carelessly tossed aside."

Concessionaires were brought to fury by this proposal since great sums were being earned by the sale of food and drink as well as souvenirs to the army of looky-loos.

"As to the fire risks," they attempted to reason, "the exposition might better hire fifty extra policemen than to deprive itself of the cheap but effective advertising it is getting by admitting visitors. Everyone visiting the city makes a point of coming to view the progress on the grounds, and then departs to spread the news far and wide of its coming magnificence wherever they go. Such a policy will prove costly in the long run."

Fingy Conners' Buffalo *Enquirer* wrote, "The general opinion among the Exposition officials is that the Exposition is running too much of a risk in allowing multitudes to wander at will among the half-completed structures with their attendant debris, wherein the omnipresent idiot with his never-failing cigarette stub could start a blaze at the drop of an ash. An admission charge of ten or fifteen cents would exclude most of the young and rough element. People best positioned to do the Exposition good would not be kept out by the charge of a few cents."

Conners' other newspaper, the Buffalo *Courier*, argued that no amount of hired police could harness the 20,000 visitors who had overwhelmed the grounds just the previous Sunday, and too supported the plan to charge admission.

"For the time being, the Exposition grounds must be closed to the public to protect the unprotected structures. Then, after sufficient progress is made on constructing the exposition, admission tickets to tour the exposition grounds will then be sold, as has been the case with all the great expositions."

The Buffalo exposition's grand plan varied most significantly from the 1893 "White City" at Chicago by its color scheme of parti-colored effects in harmony with the Spanish-Renaissance style, but presently, 10 months before opening, little of that scheme could be recognized by even the most imaginative of observers. On the other hand much progress indeed had been made as to the ornamentation of the grounds with flowers, shrubs and trees, the landscaping being much further along than the progress on the construction of the buildings.

Steel girders for the Electric Tower littered the ground around its stone base, readied for the Passaic Rolling Mill Company's assembly.

The tower would rise to an imposing 36 stories, and it was estimated that workers would require 45 days to complete the iron framework. The girders required for the Electric Tower and the various bridges crossing the canals were delivered via the web of temporary railroad tracks laid throughout the grounds.

The frames of the huge Machinery and Transportation Building were already covered in sheathing and stucco. The pumps and boilers were being placed in the power building which had been completed two weeks previous and coating was being applied.

The tons of crushed stone covering the bottoms of the canals and the Court of Fountains was already laid. Visitors poured through the gates virtually unchecked, getting in the way of the workmen, obstructing progress, filing complaints, throwing their trash around, losing their children, stealing souvenirs and building materials, falling into the canals, defecating anywhere they found convenient, vandalizing and pulling pranks, smoking then tossing their lighted stubs in any direction without thought as to the consequence, and endangering themselves and all others daily.

Ground was broken on the Midway for the building serving as the landing dock of the airship *Lunette*, scheduled to make its initial trip to the moon on the opening day of the exposition. It was destined to be the largest and highest attraction on the Midway at 40,000 square feet. There was no lack of features planned for the Midway. The current 1900 Paris Exposition was proving so poor an investment for concessionaires that many were looking to America and Buffalo to get their money back in 1901. Over 30 Midway features at Paris had already closed shop because of the disappointing numbers of visitors. It proved a great expense to keep them open, especially with no prospect of any returns.

The work of building the Exposition Stadium was already well underway before any serious thought was ever given to exactly what use it might be put, increasingly giving the impression that the Exposition Company had a very costly white elephant on its hands. Time was when it was announced with a blare of trumpets that the Stadium would outdo the Coliseum of Rome in every feature, notably with regard to architecture and seating capacity. It was said that great competitive games in which all of the world's greatest athletes would participate would be an unrivaled feature of the Pan. A committee on sports was appointed quite some time back, but the most rigid of research on the part of the newspapers had yet failed to unearth anything in the shape of progress accomplished by them. The expense of building the stadium was so large that a daily profit of $2,000 was required in order to pay for it. Even the most optimistic of exposition officials declared there was no hope of getting anything like this sum out of the venue, and kicks were being made to halt its construction. It was then that the plans were amended to reduce its size and glory. All this would have been very well if only someone with the imagination of a Chinese Director of Telegraphs could point out any use for the building once it was completed. It seemed destined to be idly passed by as a monument to some misguided contractor in air castles. The grand plans proposed for an unprecedented international athletic carnival that Stadium boosters called "The Second Coming of the Greek Olympiad" fizzled finally, thanks to the Exposition Athletic Committee's being hobbled by inertia.

The best idea put forward to salvage the debacle was to bring in Buffalo Bill Cody's Wild West Show for the entire run of the exposition. This plan had the Midway concessionaires in a full fury of protestations at the temerity of officials in proposing to allow Col. Cody to encroach upon their territory, which they were paying for at the rate of $25 a foot.

At the end of July a deputation from Buffalo interviewed the Ontario government at Toronto and strongly urged the Canadians to at least send over to the exposition an agricultural, mining and timber exhibit, but the committee received little encouragement. The Canadians had no interest in participating, they said, but gave no reason. With virtually every country in the Western Hemisphere exhibiting at the Exposition—many erecting their own stand-alone buildings—it was a mystery how the largest country on this half of the planet had declined to even mount an exhibit in one of the theme buildings.

In an interview with a newsman from the *Enquirer*, Alderman Sullivan said, "If a country as poor as Chile can construct its own building to boast of its grand history, its unique wares, the exotic produce of its agriculture and all other accomplishments, how is it then that Canada fails to see the great potential of this Exposition?"

MEA CULPA

Mary Jordan Conners sat on the pearlescent pale blue and cream fleur-de-lys silk damask that covered her 18th Century French settee paging through the latest issue of *Vogue*. She was in her bedroom, the private boudoir that she did not share with her husband. It overlooked the large carriage house that their two remaining horses shared with the new automobiles. The corner bedroom overlooking West Ferry Street was larger and brighter, and had a beautiful semi-circular balcony, but the noise from the trolleys and the legions of Exposition people who were forever coming and going for meetings with Milburn in his mansion across the street had driven her to distraction. Peace and quiet in which to forge her schemes were more precious to her than square footage.

When Fingy needed to occasionally satisfy himself with her they did so in his room, on the sturdy oak four poster bed that he insisted be covered with his woolen blankets collected from western Indian tribes and the Pendleton Mills in Oregon.

The Indian blankets smelled of goat.

It was bad enough to have the man on top of her drilling away, but to have her naked hindquarters rubbed raw by Indian blankets during the height of Fingy's impressive passions was the very height of barbarism, taking place as it did by means of such a primitive act, she told herself. She didn't ever want him to know that at times, once in a while, during the height of her passion, she adored it.

It was a fine French dress fabric that she insisted be used to upholster the settee. The interior decorator told her point-blank that for a piece of furniture there were more durable options, other choices just as beautiful that would better stand up to the challenge imposed by her big well-fed rear end.

She laughed.

No one she'd ever known since her own father, especially these days, ever spoke so crudely and familiarly without regard for who she was or what she or anyone else thought about them. The fancy Monsieur Jean-Marie Lorrain was handsome, crude and wicked, and she loved that about him almost as much as she did his unerring eye for beauty and style.

Lorrain had apprenticed with Monsieur St. Ody, who in the 1860s up until his death had decorated all the best mansions of Buffalo's wealthy families. M. St. Ody was best remembered and widely praised for so well and quickly conjuring a beautifully serene resting place for the body of the beloved President Lincoln when his corpse arrived in Buffalo for his funeral. Now it was Monsieur Lorrain who was intimately familiar with the interiors of all the finest society households, as well as other delicious secrets hidden from view behind ponderous velvet drapes and massive oak armoires.

The sun was shining even though it was freezing out, so sitting in its rays as they poured though the double-paned glass in her boudoir allowed Mary Conners to close her eyes and imagine that it was summer. That precious season was still so very far off yet. This was a city where the sun's rays might not emerge from behind the clouds for an entire month or longer in winter, and when it did venture out, fully half of its beneficial countenance would be stolen away before it ever reached the ground by the thick cloud of coal soot that hung perpetually over the city.

The maid balanced the tray unsteadily as she knocked.

"*Entrez-vous,*" allowed Mary Conners, as lunch was brought in and carefully set up for her expected visitor.

Hannah Sullivan was extremely suspicious upon receipt of a solicitation from Mary Jordan Conners, inviting her to the Delaware Ave. mansion for luncheon. Hannah had initially demurred, immediately leery of the woman's motives. Despite their speaking together over a telephone, Mary had picked up on Hannah's hesitation.

"I need to apologize to you, Mrs. Sullivan, face to face, and I feel that the only fitting and respectful way for me to go about this properly is if you'll agree to grace me with your presence for tea at our beautiful home."

"Thank you, Mrs. Conners. But that won't be at all necessary. My Jim told me that he stood right there in your doorway as Fingy ordered you to apologize to me— *or else.* So we can just do away with the window-dressing and consider this telephone conversation to be such as it is."

Hannah Sullivan's intellect was not always an effective counter to such predatory, persistent and manipulative machinations as those so sharply practiced by the likes of Mary Jordan Conners.

There was silence on her part over the telephone for a moment. The surprised Mary Conners had assumed that the First Ward trash she routinely referred to as "that shanty-Irish old washerwoman" behind her back would jump at such a rare social opportunity.

She viewed Hannah Sullivan as being a woman defeated by life. Mary Conners was not introspective enough to understand that this opinion was simply her own invention. *How could someone endure so much, yet keep going on?* she had thought. *How else could a plain woman, the wife of an oft-absent policeman and the failed mother to four poor dead children possibly feel anything other than perpetually defeated and inferior?*

❧❧

Detective Jim Sullivan picked up the telephone at Headquarters.

"Police Headquarters, Detective Sullivan here."

"It's you," barked the familiar voice on the other end.

"Yeah, I'm busy. There's a fresh body waitin' for me over on William Street that's gettin' cold," replied Jim.

"Listen Jimmy, yous gotta get that girl of yours to accept Mary's invitation to come over here and have lunch wit' her."

"Fingy, let's you and me just look the opposite way while we let them two be. Let the girls have their fight. I swear it's the only real fun Hannah's had all year. They enjoy being enemies a hell of a lot more than they'd ever enjoy being friends. And really? I don't see friends in the cards. No way, never. And you don't neither, so don't you be shittin' me."

"Mary's got her mind made up and I won't have a fuckin' minute's peace until she gets her way. I'll give yous fifty bucks."

"Okay. I'll make sure Hannah shows. When...?"

Fingy hung up without saying goodbye.

❧❧

"Well, I don't care. I'm not goin' over there Jim. She's a horrible woman. I won't give her the satisfaction of me accepting her apology."

"Well you already did, according to her. Over the telephone she says you accepted her apology."

"I did no such thing! What a horrible woman! See what I mean? There's a perfect example of her connivin' and lyin'. I told her I wouldn't see her and that her telephone call could stand as an apology as far as I was concerned. I tell you, she and that Fingy are two peas in a pod. They deserve each other. My brother told me things, Jim. Dave's there all the time. He sees. He hears."

"Oh, God Hannah. Let's not start. Let's at least leave your brother out of it for once, okay? Aren't things already crazy enough? Just go over there. Think of it as an opportunity to get some new dirt on her. I'll give you ten dollars if you do."

"I wouldn't do it for twenty!"

"Okay, I'll give you twenty."

"Where ever did you get twenty extra dollars? Jesus, Mary and Joseph! Are you on the take? Jim!"

"Oh, Christ. Hannah. No. Just go. Slip five bucks to the maid and you'll get some good dirt outa her, I guarantee it. That'll keep you in ammunition for a while."

"Just what do you take me for, Jim?" asked the insulted wife.

"Somebody who likes to eat fancy food almost as much as she likes to dig up dirt," replied the knowing husband.

Hannah was speechless as she tried to counter with an effective retort, but she came up empty.

"Well, all right. I do like meself a nice luncheon. I'll telephone her."

✾❧❧✾

Mary Conners heard the bell at the West Ferry St. entrance. She got up from her perch on the settee and removed the throw pillow from the armchair intended for Hannah. She didn't want her guest getting too comfortable.

The maid led Hannah up the staircase and knocked on the open boudoir door. Hannah purposely did not wear her best dress. She tried not to look around the richly decorated room. She didn't want to give Mary Conners the satisfaction of seeing her awe and wonder at such a display of wealth and luxury.

She couldn't help but glance around a bit here and there, though. There was a beautiful English tea service that had been purchased from an antiques dealer in London during Mary's most recent shopping trip. A silver tray was set sky-high with a mountain of triangular crumble cakes and a large bowl brimming with clotted cream. And strawberries. *Fresh* strawberries. It was January. Where in the name of

God does a body ever find strawberries in January?

"Can I offer you a scone?"

Mary nodded toward the plate of treats, the signal for the maid to pick it up and offer the selection to Hannah. As she sat Hannah took one smelling of ginger and lemon and butter while eying another studded with chunks of chocolate. A huge vase of yellow hot house roses, all perfect buds, at least two dozen, filled a vase on the side table. The sun reflected their golden color onto Mary Conners' face, softening her harsh features a bit.

"And how are the children, Mrs. Sullivan?"

Hannah knew she was being steered into asking Mary to call her Hannah, so she didn't take the bait.

"They are wonderful, Mrs. Conners. All excited about the Exposition. Jim Junior is convinced the place will be brimming with beautiful girls, so he's got his eye on a position there." Hannah knew she was spouting and tried to pull herself back. *Don't volunteer so much*, she admonished herself.

"I should think a position in the New York State Building would be an ideal place for an industrious young man like your eldest, Mrs. Sullivan. I'm sure the Alderman could help him with that."

"Yes, they've already spoken, and the Alderman suggested that very thing," said Hannah, knowing Junior full well had his heart set on the fun of working at the beer garden as a sort of last youthful fling before buckling down to serious adult business.

"How about little Billy? He must be excited too."

Fingy and Mary's boy, William J. Conners Jr., had a heavy load to bear, even at age six. Fingy had already lost his eighteen year old progeny Peter upon whose shoulders he had intended resting everything. A football injury at the military academy he attended in Michigan turned into pneumonia, and he died before his parents could reach him—or so the confusing story went. Now, after that boy's death, it was all on little Billy's shoulders. And somehow, even at his tender age, Billy knew.

"Oh my, yes. He is fascinated by electricity, electric lights, electric motors. So the promise of the industrial buildings already has him excited," Mary said. My husband took him to the architect's office and the man had there a small scale model he had built of the Electricity Building, with all its little engines and whatnot and that's all that little Billy can talk about these days. My husband is having the man build another one exactly like it for Billy to play with."

Hannah thought to herself, *that must have cost him an arm and a leg. And with all the time constraints, how could the Exposition architect possibly humor Fingy like that?*

"That's nice," Hannah replied.

"Mrs. Sullivan, I hope you will accept my apology. I have been feeling poorly as of late and it has unfortunately affected my good humor. I know you'll understand."

Hannah nodded sympathetically. "Do you mean about your going through the change of life? Oh surely, of course."

Mary Jordan Conners spit her scone just about halfway across the room.

"What I mean, Mrs. Conners, is we all have to face it at some point. As for me personally, I can't wait until My Old Friend stops visiting."

Once she'd stopped choking, Mary Conners blurted "Mrs. Sullivan! I never! That is the rudest, most presumptuous thing anyone has ever said to me!"

Inwardly Hannah was giggling like a five year old clutching a giant sack of stolen Halloween candy, but she maintained a poker face.

"Mrs. Conners, I meant no insult. We are both women, after all. If we can't talk about it with each other, then who can we? We aged females need to stick together."

"Mrs. Sullivan, I'll have you know that I am still quite in my prime!" She darted her eyes toward the door, then stood abruptly. "I just remembered that I have another engagement I must attend to."

She rang her little bell and the maid instantly appeared.

"Will you please show Mrs. Sullivan out?"

The maid nodded.

Hannah quickly took one more big bite of her ginger scone and a fast gulp of her tea as Mary moved toward her to herd her out.

"Oh, that's too bad. Well, goodbye Mrs. Conners. It was lovely of you to invite me. I'll have to have you over to our place on Hamburg Street sometime soon—maybe after they finish dredgin' the river. Right now it stinks somethin' awful, them stirrin' up things from the bottom the way they are. Can't hardly keep my lunch down, some days."

"Goodbye Mrs. Sullivan," dismissed Mary Conners, as the maid escorted Hannah out and down the stairs to the Delaware Street entrance. The maid held the door open.

"You keep me posted about what's going on around here, Jennie," whispered

Hannah to the maid, "especially when it involves my brother." She slipped Jennie a five dollar note with her telephone number folded inside.

With the other fifteen she had left from Jim's bribe, she made her way downtown on Main Street to have a nice lunch by herself at the Hengerer's department store Tea Room on the seventh floor. She was starving—she hadn't even been welcomed at the Conners' long enough to finish a single crumble cake.

9-11

By mid-afternoon on September 11 the horizon had blackened ominously. Huge masses of heavy coal-black clouds were rolling in over the lake from the southwest. The light dimmed eerily over the Erie, the sky colored deep ebony, the water an unexpected lovely translucent aquamarine glowing between erupting frantic white wind caps.

The initial zephyr, preceding as it did the same hurricane that had just wiped Galveston clean off the face of the map and reportedly claimed ten thousand souls there, slowly began picking up. Early in the evening the Alderman was attending a meeting of the directors of the Pan-American Exposition downtown at the Ellicott Square while Detective Jim Sullivan was at Police Headquarters a few blocks away working the graveyard shift. From the top floor of Headquarters there was usually a clear view to be had out over Lake Erie. However, things did not look so good even when there had still been enough light in the sky to see. But now it was pitch dark. Doors were slamming with powerful force throughout the police building, sounding not unlike gun blasts, unnerving the men.

Windows on upper floors had been left open in the heat of the late summer day, and a sort of vortex inside the structure had been created. A great commotion was heard suddenly overhead as a scuttle on the roof was torn from its fastenings and was hurled about the rooftop like a toy, creating a great clamor. The patrolmen on reserve feared that the building was collapsing. Immediately after the scuttle was unleashed there came a series of crashes of breaking glass in various parts of the building. The panes in a few of the interior office doors shattered upon their slamming, so powerful was the gale's force. The men were sent running around through all the upper floors, and the basement too, making sure all the windows were tightly secured.

Jim had placed a phone call to Hannah a little after 9 o'clock, but the operator could not secure a connection. He then asked her instead if she might try his brother's number.

"Hello? JP?" answered Annie's panicked voice.

"No Annie, it's me, Jim. I couldn't get though to Hannah so I had the operator try you."

"Is JP there with you Jim?"

"No, Annie. Isn't he home yet?"

"No, and I'm here all alone with the kids, and they're frightened because of the terrible noise of the wind and all the shaking."

"The shaking? You mean, the house is shaking?"

"Yes! The wind gusts are furious here! I'm scared, Jim. That building across the street that the Pennsylvania Railroad was building is gone! It's been torn to pieces. The wood and scantling are flying though the air like straw!"

"Oh my God," gasped Jim.

Hamburg Street runs east and west, lining up perfectly with a very broad west-east corridor created by the Buffalo river. The river for a quarter mile runs straight out from the end of Hamburg street, funneling cool lake breezes toward the Sullivan homes during balmier times, but delivering devilish blasts of destruction during a tempest. Beyond its most western point where the river turns south, wide-open Lake Erie lay about a thousand yards beyond that, with nothing at all to obstruct its winds. The south bank of the river accommodates the siting of many dangerous industries, including the massive Buffalo Union Furnace Ironworks, with all its behemoth derricks towering precariously many stories overhead, the structures allowing for the direct delivery of material to or from waiting ships in the river. The plant's myriad assortment of towering smokestacks, offices, out-buildings, stockpiles of raw materials, mounds of refuse, and various vehicles were all being assaulted by the winds. Across Hamburg Street from the Sullivan houses, a brand new building had almost been completed for the Pennsylvania Railroad Company. Building materials had been piled generously about the grounds; metal sheeting and lumber, empty nail barrels, crates, wheelbarrows and scaffolding. These paraphernalia were now being widely redistributed over half the ward by the gale.

The Alderman's house was nearest to the corner of Hamburg and South Streets and the river. The two-story structure was receiving direct blasts of wind off the lake. Next to the Alderman's house stood Jim and Hannah's house, taller than the Alderman's again by half, so that their upper story could expect to be rattling even more strongly than what Annie was describing, Jim thought to himself.

"Where could he be, Jim? That Pan-Am meeting was supposed to be over by now," worried the alderman's wife.

"Annie, I'll go track him down. I'll go over there to the Ellicott Square right now and see what might be keeping him."

"Please, Jim. Send him right home. The noise is terrifying. The children are crying and I'm frightened. And I don't want him out on the streets with tree branches breaking off all about as they are."

"All right, Annie. Are Hannah and the kids okay? I can't get through to her."

"I'm standing at the parlor window as we speak and she's waving at me now." Annie parted the drapes and exchanged hand signals with Hannah across the way. "I'll run over there through the side yard and tell her you called."

"Be careful Annie. Tell Sophie you're leaving the house so she can watch you to make sure you get over there safely."

"Okay Jim. You be careful too."

"All right Annie, I will. Me and JP will be home as soon as possible."

Annie told Sophie she was going next door. "Keep the kids here in the downstairs parlor and out of the dining room, away from the windows, and don't let them go upstairs no matter what. Do you hear me?

"Sure, tak," said the Polish girl.

Annie signaled Hannah through the parlor window that she was on her way over. The blast that slammed Annie as she stepped from the shelter of her house nearly lifted her off the ground. She crouched low and scuttled between the houses almost like a crab. Hannah flung open the door and Annie shot in. It was a challenge to shut the door behind her, the wind was so fierce.

"Jim just called. The girl couldn't get through to your telephone. He's going to leave headquarters now and go look for JP at the Ellicott Square."

"Did he say he was coming home? He has to come home!"

"I'm sure he'll be coming back with JP, Hannah."

"I certainly hope so. Isn't it terrible Annie? Isn't this the same storm that just destroyed Galveston?"

"Yes, but we're two thousand miles from there, Hannah, so it must have weakened considerably by now, wouldn't you think? I would think so...although it certainly doesn't seem like it. I'm hopeful we won't get much more than a good fright from this."

"Oh, poor Bridget Mulroney!" remembered Hannah.

Bridget was one of the Island women Hannah had befriended recently. They met at church during one of Hannah's afternoon visitations. Shanty-Irish Bridget indeed lived in a shanty, right on The Beaches at the end of Michigan St. where she squatted with her common-law husband and her children. Her poorly built tiny hovel would be taking the full blast of the gusts, as well as the wicked tides. "The Beaches" was the name given to the strip of sandy real estate sandwiched between the lake and the canal. It was connected to the rest of the city but by a single bridge, at Michigan Street. Some 1.5 miles long and a couple hundred yards wide at its widest, it was an island in more ways than one. None of the shacks had electricity. The Celtic Rowing Club's house was just about the most well-built structure on that shore, and that was little more substantial than a typical summer vacation cottage. Kerosene lamps would be the only light on the Island during the storm, as dangerous as those lamps might prove to be with the winds so fierce. The Island was an idyll on a warm summer's day, but a veritable death trap during a storm.

Michael Regan had left work to go to his home on Louisiana Street earlier in the afternoon but with the worsening conditions had made his way back to Headquarters after supper. The director of the Yacht Club at the foot of Porter Avenue had called him about 8 p.m. telling him a number of boats had slammed into the pier, which itself was now underwater, and were sinking, and what could Regan do about it?

"What can I do about it?" he blustered. "We're police officers, sir, not the United States Navy! The entire city is suffering in this storm, and you want officers who have families waiting for them at home to come over there to put themselves in jeopardy so as to rescue rich people's yachts? Tell your people they should have taken them out beyond the break wall when they heard the storm was coming! Now let us go about our duties of trying to keep the citizens of this city safe, sir!"

"Sully, have you called home to Hannah yet?" Regan asked as soon as he ran into Jim.

"I did Mike, but couldn't get through. So I called Annie and she was in a tizzy because JP is still at that Pan-Am meeting at the Ellicott Square. I'd like to go over there now and send all those men home if they haven't left already."

"Yeah, sure, go on, get outa here."

It was just 2 blocks east and one north to the Ellicott Square building, but with the horses terrified and debris flying, it felt like a mile. At Seneca and Main streets a man was standing over a fallen horse, furiously beating the poor beast. The horse had been shocked by a downed electric wire and lay stunned in the street, still attached to the wagon he'd been pulling.

"Hey you, Stop that nonsense!" Jim shouted. "That poor horse is suffering enough as it is without you havin' to..."

Without warning a flash erupted and the man danced wildly as electricity coursed through his body. Then he collapsed on top of his motionless steed.

Stunned by the sight of his first electrocution, Jim surmised there was nothing he could do for either man or beast, lest he himself be shocked. He continued along on his way avoiding the dancing sparks as the guilty wire writhed on the pavement.

The Ellicott Square was warmly lit, the men made unawares of the intensifying storm as they sat cozily under the glass roof of the mosaic-paved courtyard. Nine or ten stories of solid building towering above surrounded and cocooned the men who sat in what could be best pictured as the bottom of a well, where the wind and flying debris would not reach, giving them little clue as to what was happening outside.

Jim entered from Main Street and ran across the spectacular tiled floor to the foot of the grand staircase where the Alderman stood enjoying his glass, his company and his cigar, and leaned in to tell him the news. The Alderman immediately climbed up the stairs for a bit of height and called for the attention of the loose and jovial crowd.

Jim then announced, "Gentlemen, it is imperative that you leave immediately and return to your homes. The storm is intensifying and it looks like it's going to be a real doozy. Please go to your homes now, quickly. There is no time to lose."

The revelers were a bit stunned as alcohol and good friends do tend to slow a man's reactions, but Jim wasn't about to hang around to encourage stragglers any further.

"I promised Annie I'd bring you directly home. So grab your briefcase, brother, and let's get the hell outa here."

The brothers ran out onto Main Street and climbed into the police wagon. Jim made a U-turn to head south just as the giant McKinley-Roosevelt election banner that had been strung across Main Street between the White Building and the Ellicott Square was blown down and blew right into the terrified faces of the horses. This elicited intense alarm adding to that which the animals already suffered. Jim stopped and jumped out to pull the huge wrapper from around the shrieking steeds as the image of Teddy Roosevelt grinned at him solicitously from the banner.

One advantage to living in the down-at-the-mouth First Ward was that it was located to the south, so none of the landed gentry would be trying to catch a lift from them. All the bigwigs lived north and west.

As they galloped down Elk Street they were just in time to see the derrick that confectioner Albert Behrends had for years been trying to get disassembled crash down onto his shop roof, where he and his family lived at the back.

"Jesus Christ! shouted Jim. We gotta stop!"

The horses were panicked and hard to control, but Jim was able to halt and secure them to a rail in front of the shop. He ran down the side alley to the back, just as Behrends came out, scratching his head.

"That goddamn thing!" he shouted above the howl of the wind. "I knew it was goin' t' come down on our heads at some point. I'll kill them bastards!"

"Is anyone hurt, Behrends?" asked Jim.

"No, we're alright, but there's a big piece o' sky where my roof used to be. What'll I do? It just keeps gettin' worse."

"Is the shop all right? If it is, then take you family into there for shelter, and keep away from the plate glass window and the display cases as best you might until this is over."

Several years previous, exploring for natural gas, test wells had been drilled at the rear of the saloon next door to the confectioner's shop. But when the project found nothing, the site was abandoned and the derrick just left there to rust. Now it was half inside the Behrends' kitchen.

Jim ran back to see the Alderman trying to calm the horses while at the same time keep from being knocked down himself, as much by the beasts as the wind.

"Let's go," Jim screamed above the whirling and crashing, and the two galloped down Elk to Hamburg Street, then straight home.

"Holy shit," cried the Alderman as they crossed the Erie Railroad tracks. Debris was flying everywhere. A roof, barrels, twisted metal, wooden planks, paper, shingles, scantling—all swirling around midair, the heavier things being pushed, skidding along the asphalt by the wind, adding to the deafening cacophony.

Jim had planned to return to headquarters after he checked in to make sure Hannah and the kids were safe, but the increasing velocity and frightening scene as the Buffalo Union Furnace Ironworks glowed and crackled too close for comfort and sparks flew in all directions, its ramshackle out-buildings being torn apart causing him to abandon his duty to the city in favor of guarding his family.

The Alderman ran inside No. 12 as Jim pulled the horses into the little barn at the back of his house next door, leaving the police wagon unattended on the street. This was against the rules, but he had no other choice. The world was ending.

Bolting inside, Jim found a terrorized Hannah and Nellie in each other's arms, but Junior and David sat calmly playing cards to pass the time. The electric lights were still on, surprisingly, at least for the time being. Conditions were much too unsettling for anyone to sleep.

Jim had made the right choice. Even if he had gotten back to Headquarters in one piece there would be nothing for him and the other men to do but wait out the storm anyway. The forests of trees that lined virtually every street in Buffalo had brought down the wires with their amputated limbs. For some few hours it was 1850 all over again.

By midnight the full storm was upon the city with sustained winds of 60 miles per hour creating a terrifying din. Whole blocks of street lamps were out. The police patrol system suffered severely, the storm cutting off communications between stations. At fire headquarters it was found that telegraph and fire alarm service was fully knocked out. By 3 o'clock the last of the electric lights went out and the city was plunged into complete darkness.

The huge Great Lakes passenger ships en route to or from Buffalo were tossed about and wildly pitched and canted by the mountainous swells churned up by the hurricane. Aboard the ship *Wyoming*, there was much excitement when her cargo shifted and the ship listed dangerously. For a time she was beyond control and lay roiling in the trough of the sea with every wave breaking completely overdecks. Passengers aboard the lake luxury liners were vomiting and terror-stricken.

Communication by telephone or telegraph was no longer possible. At 3:30, as families huddled terrified in coal cellars and interior closets, the wind reached its highest velocity, maintaining a blast of 78 miles per hour for a full thirty minutes, completing the job of imparting doomsday panic and wreaking havoc. It was widely agreed that no one had ever experienced anything like this storm.

At Crystal Beach, the amusement resort's pier was submerged and all craft in the area were broken and dashed onto the sand or beached inland.

"The water rose fully ten feet," said Manager John E. Rebstock later to a *Commercial* news reporter, "and at five o'clock this morning our dock was entirely underwater. All the small boats in the bay, forty or fifty, were completely wrecked. However, no one was hurt."

More than a few late summer vacationers were startled as boats ended up on the front porch of their beach cottages and campers begged those having more solid shelters to take them in.

As the sun rose, the wind diminished to 40 miles per hour. Citizens emerged from ravaged homes, sleepless and dazed, their adrenalin keeping them going. Rumors of the total destruction of the Pan American Exposition sent thousands of citizens swarming to the area to have a look-see for themselves.

The unsheltered and open site chosen for the Pan happened to be the windiest of places in Buffalo at any given time. No matter from which direction the wind blew, it had a full sweep across the grounds. From 3:30 until after 4 o'clock the fullest force of the relentless gale savaged the site, uprooting trees, destroying some buildings entirely and severely damaging others, filling the esplanade, the canals and the grounds' streets and walkways with tons of construction debris and broken tree limbs.

The United States Government Building was totally demolished, a large part of it having been blown into the canal upon the bank of which it had been erected. The Electricity Building suffered greatly as well; one tower of this structure was broken off completely, while the other was damaged so badly that it would need to be torn down and completely rebuilt. On the Midway, the entrance gateway tower was destroyed. The Manufacturers and Liberal Arts Building and the Horticultural Building sustained great damage. Only one building in the entire exposition had been insured against such a storm.

President Milburn of the Pan American Exposition Co. made light of the damage so as not to concern the thousands of entities who had invested heavily in the enterprise. His main objective, above all, was to preserve the Pan.

Initially it was reported that only two people died, but as the week wore on, floating bodies were recovered from various waterways or pulled lifeless from collapsed Island shanties. Thousands of itinerants had recently flooded the city in hopes of finding work constructing the Pan, with no one to miss them if they disappeared, since many were squatters. When all was said and done, no official tally of the dead was published so as not to horrify.

Lehigh Valley Yard detective Ed Moylan was surprised to receive a telephone call at the Tifft Farm two days following the storm after the wires had been strung back up. It was John Rebstock over at Crystal Beach. He was luckily alone in the office when the telephone rang.

"Hey, Moylan, they tell me you recovered from your fall an' are doin' just fine."

"That's right Mr. Rebstock. I'm back in the rail yards still keepin' the hoodlums in order 'round here."

"So how's about you come over this weekend and have a look at the scenic railway. It was beat up pretty bad in the storm."

"Well, to tell you the truth Mr. Rebstock, I'm not so sure I wanna be climbin' around on that thing right about now," replied Moylan.

"Ye ain't gotta be a-climbin' Moylan, atop nothin'. Yous just gotta be lookin' and tellin' others where to climb. You know, supervise. You built the goddamned thing. Who better'n you to have a look-see? I can't trust nobody else. Kin I be expectin' yous this Satraday mornin'?"

"No sir, I work at the Tifft yard Saturdays. I can get over there early Sunday though, bright 'n' early."

"But we need you sooner, Ed. I don't want to go ahead with any of the work without you inspectin' it first."

Ed could have had his Saturday off if he wanted. Since he lost his arm, even though he'd proven to everyone at the Lehigh that he was as capable as before the accident, they were always urging him to go a little easier around the rail yard. He would have liked to, truth be told, but now he feared he had more to prove than ever, and didn't want to risk missing even a day, or accept any special treatment. He was sure at the first sign of weakness they'd can him.

"Sorry Mr. Rebstock. Can't do it."

"Oh. All right. We'll have to wait then. We still got a good month of decent weather ahead to put things back in order. Best to make hay while the sun shines, right?"

"Ain't that the truth," laughed Ed Moylan. "I'll be there first thing Sunday morning, Mr. Rebstock."

PICKPOCKETS

From the Buffalo *Express*:

A stylishly dressed woman of middle age and a pretty miss were elbowing their way through a crowd of shoppers in a downtown dry goods store yesterday afternoon, when the experienced eyes of Detective-Sergeant James Sullivan fell upon them.

"Aha," exclaimed the sleuth, mentally.

"So these are the birds who have been flying away with the pocketbooks."

As The Express told exclusively a few days ago, many purses have been stolen from the pockets of the shoppers in the large dry-goods houses downtown, and it was suspected that a contingent of expert pickpockets had arrived in the city to be here for the Pan American Exposition. Day after day the best detectives of the force, who had been detailed to watch for the sleight-of-hand crooks, have been patrolling the stores where the crimes had been committed without getting a clew.

Detective Sullivan's heart bounded with surprise and delight when he recognized in the woman and the girl a pair of professional pickpockets and shoplifters who have been arrested dozens of times or more. They were Mrs. Anna Kurtzmann and her daughter by her second husband, Miss Clara Bork.

Sullivan followed them as they forced themselves through the crowded aisles. He watched their every movement. He paid particular attention to the actions of their hands. They carried shopping bags of robust proportions, and the detective was willing to gamble those receptacles contained stolen goods.

When he had seen them fumbling at the goods on several counters and crowding close behind well-dressed women, so close that their hands were invisible, he thought it time to arrest them. They started when he stepped up close to them and spoke to them, but then laughed when they recognized him.

"What do you want us for? We ain't done nothin'," said Mrs. Kurtzmann.

"Yous fly-cops are altogether too suspicious," said Miss Bork, saucily.

When they were searched in Asst. Supt. Cusak's office their shopping bags were found to contain a pair of shoes, three dozen handkerchiefs and a number of pieces of silk and dress goods. Later it was learned that the shoes were stolen from Forsyth's store on Seneca street and the handkerchiefs from William Hengerer & Co.'s. The other goods have not yet been identified.

The prisoners were silent as clams when questioned as to their doings during the last few weeks. It was thought to be a good plan to go to their house and search it. They live at 469 Sherman street. Detective-Sergt. Sullivan went there, accompanied by Detective-Sergt. Wright. It was a profitable business. About $500 worth of property of all kinds was found stored away in one of the rooms. It consisted of silverware, velvets, ivory knives and forks, corsets, pieces of dress goods, silks, cut-glass, imported dishes and a score of other articles.

The detectives also found about 26 tickets on different pawnshops representing articles which had been pawned; diamond rings, overcoats, clocks, lamps, suits of clothes, a sealskin cape and other property.

All the goods were taken to Police Headquarters. The women will be tried as soon as the property can be identified. They are old-time shoplifters and pickpockets and their pictures are in the rogues' galleries. It is believed they are responsible for some of the thefts of purses in dry goods stores lately.

THE PABST BEER PAVILION

"Just you behave yourself, Junior. That's all I'm going to say on the subject. I don't want you ever comin' home to this house drunk. You hear me?"

The Alderman rolled his eyes at Hannah's warning. Her overprotective nature was understandable but not appropriate regarding such a good boy. She was giving last minute instructions to Jim Jr., who was readying himself to be off to the Exposition grounds for his first day of orientation training at the Pabst Beer Garden.

"Leave the boy be, won't you Hannah? He's sixteen and anxious to get on with living his life," interfered the Alderman.

"Just how much training does one need to be at the beck and call of ignoramuses the likes of those from Saskatchewan and Tennessee?" sniffed Nellie, needling her brother. "You bring food and beer from the kitchen to their table and set it down in front of them, then jump back before all hell breaks loose. That's it. I've been doing the exact same thing right here in this very house since I was about five and nobody ever had to 'orient' me," she declared.

"Nellie!" exclaimed her mother. "Fourteen-year-old young ladies do not use that kind of language!"

"Well," responded Junior to his sister, "if they happened to be hiring finely brought-up lady swells much like yourself to do this kind of important work at the Pan, then I'm sure the likes of me would be plumb out of a job."

The large Pabst On The Midway Pavilion occupied a prominent corner on the North Midway, just inside the decorative Midway entry gate, a true crossroads of humanity if there ever was one. Its splendid watchtower shone two powerful spotlights after sunset, panning and beckoning the Pan's nighttime crowds with the Pabst's reasonable prices and ample accommodation. Located right next door was Barnes' Diving Elks attraction with its massive antlered mascot perched atop the building three stories up. Visible for a mile, you couldn't miss it. Around the corner, the other face of the Pavilion sat directly across from the building housing the Wonderful

Mutoscope.

It was April 26, and a very cold wind was blowing off the Lake. The unofficial opening of the Pan was set for May 1, just five days away. The exposition would then be opened to the public. This interim was designated a "dry run," a period in which all the wrinkles and problems could be worked out for the official Grand Opening on May 20th. Already the Pabst restaurant doors were open to crowds of curiosity-seekers who had been visiting daily since ground was broken. On Sundays, these paying previewers numbered in the tens of thousands, and not having foreseen this bonanza, the Pabst had to scurry to be up and running earlier than expected.

At the Pabst's busy lunch and supper hours an orchestra was scheduled to serenade its guests who were expected to number at their peak, 1200. At first glance inside the arched entry, Junior nearly turned and ran in terror, unsure how he could possibly enter this maelstrom and function capably as he had promised. The place was a veritable sea of tables and chairs. How could he keep track of his customers? The pavilion was largely empty of patrons now, but its vastness struck fear into his imagination as to how he could uphold his false claim at having accumulated broad experience waiting tables.

He saw a gaggle of boys and men congregated at the far side of the open dining area. He walked over to join them. They numbered half a hundred or so. A Prussian, Gustav Schutkeker, called for order. The Hessian had only a light German accent; his manner painted him as fair and capable.

"You vill each be assigned a station of twelf to feefteen tables. You vill be completely responsible for taking care of efery detail of your station. You vill haff a boy who vill report to you whose job it is to remove empty glasses and dishes and sveep up. Your job is to please the customer, of course, but to also encourage them not to linger once they haff finished eating. The more people ve can seat at each table the more money ve vill make, and the more money you vill make as vell. You cannot be rude to people, of course, but you are expected to know about efery attraction of this Exposition so that you can talk about each with great enthusiasm so as to encourage your customers to get up and go on their vay once they haff finished eating. Your job is to feed them and see to their thirst, then politely get rid of them."

And so, on and on went his spiel, doling out details on personal cleanliness, proper behavior, the system for submitting orders, and much more.

Junior was feeling quite overwhelmed even before Schutkeker had finished, but apparently other faces too revealed the same emotion to the speaker.

"Don't vorry. I know all these details seem to be very complicated and confusing, but you vill see that once the action begins, common sense vill lead you to do many of these tings natürlich. So now, you vill all follow me to the kitchen so I can introduce you with the cooks and the methods for submitting and picking up your orders."

As the crowd followed him, Schutkeker continued talking.

"Unless told to do so, such as in times of great crowding, you vill not encroach upon another vaiter's tables. Anyone caught taking tips from a table that is not his own vill be fired, once the Exposition Police haff finished vit you. There vill be no tolerance for bad behavior of any kind. Just remember, there are a hundred men vaiting to take over your place here, just vaiting for you to fail. You must not eat any of the food that people leave on their plates. You vill be fed a light lunch in the middle of your shift, but it must be eaten next to the kitchen vhere the customers vill not see you."

Junior liked Schutkeker, and although out of earshot others referred to him caustically by his permutation, Junior was invited to call him Gus, which he did. Schutkeker, a man free of false airs or superior attitude whom everyone else took to calling Shit-Kicker, in turn answered to the Big Boss, Herr Fritz Mueller, who was a much more stern taskmaster than he. Mueller too had lectured the group about honesty, citing the newly-installed invention, the cash register, as a necessary antidote to what had been so prevalent and widespread in days past.

"This machine vill keep you honest. I vill not be loosink my shirt on this enterprise!" Mueller bellowed to his employees. "Ve are all hier to make money!"

After that first long day, Junior's head spinning with dos and don'ts and rules and regulations, he politely declined the invitation of some of his fellow waiters to explore the Midway with them in favor of visiting the Electricity Building. The Exposition, with its unprecedented lighting scheme and a host of new inventions powered by electricity, had newly energized Junior's interest in the stuff. Making his way he passed the Photographer's studio, his other passion, taking mental note of exploring that building thoroughly as soon as possible as well.

This is going to be the greatest year of my entire life, he thought to himself.

Many buildings had not as yet installed their exhibits at this late date and some buildings were still being constructed.

Haughty Canada, submitting a last-minute design for a national building smaller than any other at the Pan, no bigger than a cottage actually, was given an appropriate spot on which to erect it: adjacent to the livestock barns in the farthest corner of the grounds. Canada had made herself the laughing stock of the Exposition if not the entire country, ours as well as her own.

"Serves 'em right," chuckled Jim Sullivan when reading the Canuks' complaints about the stench and the dark-side-of-the-moon building location in the newspaper.

As he entered the Electricity Building's cavernous space, five hundred feet in length, a strange and beautiful apparition assaulted Junior's eye, much like love at first sight. Lighted bulbs spelled out in giant letters GENERAL ELECTRIC COMPANY on the upper wall, the building's under-roof decorated with festive striped swag extending prettily from the center of the roof toward the outer walls. Here in the northwest corner of the Electricity Building was installed the Niagara Falls transformer plant, with a capacity of five thousand horse-power, the purpose of which was to transform the power delivered from Niagara Falls to a lower voltage so that it could be used for distribution about the grounds to operate the million lights, the Electric Fountain and the other electrical appliances.

A handrail guided Junior past a diminutive single-story classic Greek Headquarters building erected on the exhibition floor. Hypnotized by the equipment beyond it, he zoomed right past the odd structure with nary a glance.

A double row of nineteen ultra-modern transformers, all painted a glossy forest green, stood sentinel on the left like some regiment of steel soldiers from another world, while behind them along the wall loomed the massive switchboard by which the distribution of the current for the splendid illumination of the grounds was accomplished. The scene captured Junior's imagination instantly, both for its magnitude and the intensity of the currents handled. A narrow striped carpet acted as a pathway leading visitors on a walk though a massive round section of steel pipe, a field ring for the Niagara Falls Power Co., weighing 33,200 lbs. and manufactured by the Bethlehem Steel Co., then on through the rest of the building past all the electricity exhibits.

The development of electrical power was fully illustrated in a very comprehensive manner. Working models of many of the great power plants were on exhibition. Most noteworthy in the historic exhibit were the elementary dynamos and lamps and motors of just two decades previous, looking now as if something from the Stone Age in their crudeness and jerry-rigged appearance.

Comparing the historic exhibits, which appeared glaringly primitive to the extreme, with the finished and effective machinery of the modern section, Junior was enlightened with the startling velocity with which the world had moved in matters electrical during the previous two decades. The advances that had been made in less than twenty years laid out right there in front of his eyes boggled his mind, and at that moment he realized that Electricity was the Future, and that he was determined suddenly to be a part of this new age.

Toward the end of the hall he was excited to see an exhibition where visitors were able to watch the telephone girls at work. The switchboard was a part of the Buffalo Bell Telephone Company's system and the entire procedure of calling "Central" and getting the desired connection was shown in full view and carefully explained, clearing up any mysteries that might have remained in his mind about how it all worked.

His head bursting with ideas and new information, Junior was surprised finding himself turning the lock on the front door at No. 16 Hamburg Street.

So distracted was he that he didn't recall a single detail about making his way back home.

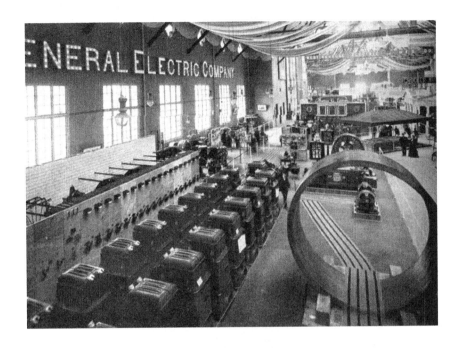

Inside the Electric Building: the transformers at the General Electric Exhibit.

MAY 20, 1901
OPENING DAY AT THE PAN AMERICAN
EXPOSITION

Excited children were up and running around the Sullivan homes on Hamburg Street while outside it was still pitch-black. The oldest kid, the Alderman himself, was more excited than any of the others, as he had been an instigator of the exposition scheme and had enthusiastically boomed the enterprise far and wide whenever provided any opportunity.

He climbed out of bed as Annie moaned, "Already?"

He stepped into his trousers. He parted the curtains and allowed the glow of the Buffalo Furnace Co. across the street to invade the room. Annie opened her eyes to the reddish light and wondered for the thousandth time if she would ever live to see the day they could move away from this hell-hole forever.

The wind was rushing down from the north, pushing all the smoke and stench to the south, allowing a rare morning when it was possible to actually stick one's head out the window and breathe in the fresh morning air if a person had a mind to. The only odor present was a fine one; it came from the grain elevators to the north, where the delicious scent of toasting oats filled the air.

As the sun rose it did not show its brilliant face, for it was a gloomy leaden day. This did nothing to daunt the population of the Sullivan homes nor of the city itself from the intoxicating prospect of the stupendous spectacle that lay ahead.

The Alderman had arranged for his own and his brother's families to have a prime viewing spot of the opening promenade inside the grounds just over the Triumphal Bridge. It was over that bridge inside the exposition proper, its span anchored by four absolutely massive colonnades topped with giant heroic sculptures of rearing horses and majestic figures, that the parade of exposition dignitaries would enter the grounds.

All the family members were present except for Junior, who was required to be at his station at the Pabst Pavilion.

"Junior's the lucky one," moaned Nellie as she stood in the chill breeze waiting for the procession to begin. She huddled against her mother for warmth and looked around to see what handsome boys she might view as Hannah and Annie gabbed excitedly and the kids made no effort to contain themselves; they wanted in, now. But they would have to endure the pompous procession of dignitaries first.

"Finally!" sniffed Nellie as the distant sounds of the 74th Regiment Band could be heard at the far end of the bridge. A sea of black top hats appeared, those belonging to Vice President Roosevelt, Exposition President Milburn, Mr. Scatcherd, Mayor Diehl, Fingy Conners and all the rest of the cream of society who led the way. These were followed by other important people, men and women, who had worked long and hard to bring this day to reality; the architects, decorators, landscape designers, colorists and planners. Following them were the aldermen in derbys and bowlers, a jovial gaggle of fellas joking and laughing together, in contrast to the more dignified and serious top hats who had preceded them.

Alderman Sullivan was easy to pick out of the otherwise indistinguishable crowd of dark suited, bow tied, cane-leaning aldermen and others by his massive orthopedic shoe and characteristic limp. As he passed his families, they cheered for him.

"Yay, Papa!" shouted his brood, led by the deepening voices of his eldest, Thomas and Daniel.

JP saw them from afar and waved excitedly only to have his attention stolen by something of greater interest at that particular moment: the camera man from the Thomas Edison Moving Pictures Company filming the parade, with him in it. He poked Alderman John Kennedy.

"Hey Jack! Look! It's the moving picture people! How grand!" laughed the animated politician, looking directly into the camera lens. "We'll have to go to the Edisonia Theater together to view ourselves when it's exhibited!"

Kennedy smiled disingenuously and said, "Yep, it's a corker all right, JP."

The dignitaries were followed by the 74th Regiment Marching Band, then by battalions of feather-capped admirals and other military men on horseback with sabres displayed, followed by columns of marching troops with rifles held to their right shoulders, pointed toward the heavens. There was much more to come, but the kids could no longer be contained, and they dragged their mothers away, into the hornet's nest of opening day bedlam where far more interesting attractions awaited.

The crowd numbered 101,687, making it the second largest opening attendance in the history of expositions. The restaurants were immediately packed end to end, creating a demand regrettably unanticipated. Despite meticulous preparations at the Pabst Pavilion, the Alt Nuremberg, and all the other dozens of beer halls, eateries and cafés, nothing approaching this volume of demand had been predicted. Cooks and waiters fell over one another in the pandemonium and many restaurants ran out of food entirely as early as 6 p.m. and had to close, their managers cursing the heavens for their being so short-sighted. They cried salty tears as the dollars flying out of visitors pockets landed into better-prepared competitors' laps rather than their own. Others made a practice of admitting a certain number of customers and then locking the doors, as hungry patrons made to wait their turn were becoming aggressive and abusive, shouting and cursing at diners sitting and enjoying their meal, screaming at them to hurry it up.

To the Sullivans, as they wandered wide-eyed across the Grand Esplanade munching popcorn balls, the exposition looked exactly like the painted pictures of it had promised, and then some. The gorgeousness of coloring on the fanciful Mediterranean-Renaissance style buildings, which provided the Pan its appellation The Rainbow City, as well as the lighting and fountain effects which had been so vividly portrayed previously only on paper, had now come to glorious life. The surging laughing crowds that artists had depicted in their illustrations and now jamming the buildings and pavilions were, it turned out, accurately represented.

At about 2 p.m. the sun finally came out, darting between the swiftly passing cumulus clouds, counteracting the chill breeze. The flowers and trees and formal gardens of tulips and daffodils were in full bloom along the curving walkways of the Grand Court, which was bordered by all the important buildings and cut down the middle by the gigantic lagoon and its spewing fountains. There were other ways of entry, but the approach to the exposition from across the Triumphal Bridge revealed a triumph of vision and design, planning and commitment to hard work by the many thousands who brought the fantasy land into being. The thirty-seven story Electric Tower straight ahead stood sentinel at the farthest end of the esplanade.

It was from the rise of the bridge that Hannah and Annie, now joined by the Alderman, gathered all the children at dusk, along with thousands of other spectators having the same idea, to view the birth of the illumination.

"When will it begin?" squealed the Alderman's ten year old Mazie, pulling at her mother's dress, ever anxious.

Pan American Exposition Illumination.

"Mazie, you calm yourself down or I'll take you directly home!" scolded Annie.

"Oh mother, don't be silly! You won't neither! You'd never miss seein' the show!" snorted the little brat, as Annie exchanged knowing looks with Hannah.

"Now Mazie, you do not speak in that tone to your mother, do you hear me?" scolded the Alderman.

Mazie hung her head in pretended shame and softly said, "Yes, Papa."

Suddenly as a murmur arose, a dull glow appeared on the crowns of the many small pillars all around the grounds, followed by a stream of light climbing swiftly up the dome of the Temple of Music and then trickling down the other side, leaving a fiery path.

A moment later, lines of fire, indistinct, rose-colored, flecked across all the great buildings, followed by a soft, faint glow bursting suddenly on the magnificent Electric Tower, giving the vast pillar the illusion of a gigantic oven through which a fire gleamed. The intensity of the illumination increased slowly, the lights changing color from pink to a warm bright yellow almost imperceptibly. And then, a giant searchlight blasted into illumination from atop the tower and began scanning the entire exposition grounds.

The crowd throughout the site, but especially those gathered on the Triumphal Bridge, could not contain their wonder at this unprecedented display of electric magnificence and burst into cheers involuntarily, their excitement echoed by other throngs gathered in other parts, all eyes fixed on the Grand Esplanade.

The Alderman was tired. He would have preferred to begin heading home at that point, but the children were in such a state of excitement that he knew he would find no peace once at home. Besides, his leg was throbbing and he needed to sit down.

"Let's go eat!" he announced to the hungry throng.

"Yay!" they cheered in response.

"Let's go see Junior at the Pabst, why don't we?" snarkily suggested his sister. "We can have fun makin' him wait on us."

"We'll do no such thing," announced the Alderman. "Reservations await us much closer at the restaurant in the Electric Tower! It is seven stories up in the sky, and the view is magnificent. I've already seen it."

"Oh boy!" shouted one and all, as the limping politician, his leg pulsing dully, hopped along to try and keep up.

"Is the same menu available in the Garden restaurant as in the main Tower restaurant, asked the Alderman as they were greeted by the maître d'hôtel.

The man, dressed in a tuxedo, responded, "No Alderman. The Garden restaurant has a more abbreviated version, because the space is so much smaller up there."

"Well, children, if we are going to eat as well as I feel the need to in my famished state, we'll be dining right here. Look how elegant it is!" he said, holding up the black menu with silver scrolling. "And look at that magnificent view out over the fountains!"

Indeed, situated only about eight feet above ground level, the Electric Tower restaurant was huge, with a menu to match.

A hue and cry went up from the children. Hannah and Annie did nothing to stop it.

"We want to go up in the elevator!" little Anne demanded. The others chorused in.

"So do we, JP," said Annie as Hannah nodded.

"All right," he groaned. "The Garden restaurant it shall be."

That'll be twenty-five cents," announced the elevator attendant.

"Whew!" said the Alderman. "It costs the same to ride the elevator as it did to see the entire exposition? Well, lucky for me I have my aldermen's pass. Here it is, sir." The pass allowed free admission to everything.

"Fine, Alderman Sullivan, but the pass is good only for you personally, not for the entire group."

He looked at all the anxious, expectant faces, quickly calculated the cost weighed against the animosity he would suffer if he denied his kin this once-in-a-lifetime family adventure, gulped hard, pried open his creaking change purse and counted out two dollars and seventy-five cents. It almost made him faint. The elevator ride up to the seventh level made him even queasier, but once they'd been seated and he'd had a few sips of wine, he calmed.

The children were ecstatic and awestruck, the women lost in wonderment. The great expanse of water contained within the basin of the Court of Fountains spread out expansively below in one vast flow of luminous golden-glowing liquid broken through by powerful jets from many fountains gushing. A fairyland of electric lights, millions of them it seemed, shone as never before anywhere in history. This was the greatest water illumination ever attempted. A gigantic spray six stories in height rose powerfully like a geyser in front of the Tower, the geyser's apex seemingly almost close enough to touch. Such a combined hydraulic and electrical display was only possible in the vicinity of Niagara Falls with the protean power that the great cascade was capable of producing.

The view did not distract the Alderman from noticing that people recognized him and tipped their heads in greeting, or also that the restaurant still had plenty of Connecticut Blue Point Oysters left.

All was right with the world.

A FREE LUNCH

Hannah and Annie had been planning for months to attend the Pan together, just the two of them. The scheme included leaving the children at home with Sophie as soon after opening day as could be arranged. Both women were excited by the promise of the naughty, the extreme, the dangerous, the exotic and the unbelievable.

There were many attractions they knew would be unsuitable for children, as well as those others best enjoyed minus the company of husbands or other members of the male species. They wanted to see for themselves the public drinking fountains, the first of their kind anywhere, and the Butterick pavilion, showcasing all the latest dress patterns.

Together they followed the daily accounts in the *News*, the *Star*, the *Commercial*, the *Courier* and the *Express*, the newspapers all competing for who could provide the most colorful coverage of the planning, building and presenting of the astounding attractions of the Pan American Exposition to the point of, the women were quite certain, exaggeration. Especially suspect were the attractions of the Midway which were described in the most outlandish and far-fetched manner.

"A 'realistic' Trip To The Moon? scoffed Annie. "Now, really! How realistic could it be if nobody's ever been there?".

Hannah countered by doubting that an enormous full-grown live elk could possibly be coaxed to voluntarily plunge off a high cliff into a deep pool, or that actual bullfights with matadors and raging bulls would take place daily at the Streets of Mexico amid the streets of Buffalo, New York.

"And how are the Arctic Esquimaux going to compete in dog sled races in the heat of summer?

One exhibit that intrigued both, and hopefully would not be unmasked as some faked sideshow attraction, was the Infant Incubator Building.

Said to be outfitted with the latest scientific equipment to keep babies alive who would normally die due the deficiencies of their premature birth, the infants were placed safely behind plate glass in individual capsules elaborately fitted with ventilating devices. Most curious of all, it was said the machinery was all automatic and that nurses need attend very little to the babes.

Hannah and Annie discussed this, initially fearing the possibility of seeing helpless babies on display suffering or ignored, knowing that witnessing such an exploitation would affect them terribly. But upon reading glowing opinions from reporters who had gone before them, and after learning that Dr. Roswell Park himself was overseeing the enterprise, they grew increasingly fascinated and eager to view this miracle of modern science with their own eyes.

At the last minute, Annie announced to Hannah that Mazie, Annie's oldest, wanted to come along.

"No," stated Hannah, flatly.

"Oh," responded the surprised Annie. "All right. I just thought..."

"Annie, we agreed, no children. I didn't even tell David we were going, because I knew he'd throw a fit. And besides...Mazie sassed me yesterday, so I'm not feeling very generous toward her right now."

Annie went silent. Never in their entire years together had Hannah said even one critical word about any of Annie's children, despite some rough behavior on the part of the older boys. She sensed something was not being said.

"No, that's fine, Hannah. We've been looking forward to this day as being just yours and mine, anyway."

🍂🍂🍂🍂

Mazie shot daggers from her eyes toward her mother and aunt as they walked out the door.

Even though the West Amherst Gate was a much more convenient entry, Annie wanted to use the spectacular Lincoln Parkway entrance over the Triumphal Bridge again, as the neighborhood along its approach was gracious and elegant, and she especially enjoyed seeing how the city's wealthier citizens lived.

"I promise you Hannah, someday I'll convince JP to buy us a house in this part of the city," she said wistfully, recalling the temporary rental they'd moved into on Depew Avenue during the dangerous time of the Scoopers' Strike. She felt that it was here in North Buffalo that she belonged, rather than festering alongside the filthy stinking Buffalo River to the south.

"Annie, if you want to use the Lincoln Parkway gate, you're going to have to pay for a wheel chair for us. You know I can't walk all that distance to the Midway.

Annie hesitated.

"Okay. Well, maybe we should use the West Amherst Gate after all, since the naughty things are all grouped conveniently together right there!"

The two giggled at the prospect.

"I'm guessing it's no accident they located the Exposition Hospital right on the Midway," Hannah laughed, as they passed the building.

"Kodak?" asked the young man, trying his best to look authoritative despite his baby face.

"What?" Hannah asked.

"Do you have a Kodak or other camera hidden away? You have to buy a permit to use it at the Pan."

The whole city was aware that this policy was being strictly enforced at the Exposition and a highly unpopular tax it was indeed. The entry fee was twenty five cents as it was, and yet they wanted double that amount in addition, just for the privilege of snapping personal souvenir shots for people's own memory albums. The Eastman Kodak Company tried to stop it, unsuccessfully. But being bafflingly shortsighted and having unwisely decided not to participate, to not erect a building or even mount an exhibit of their own at the Pan, Kodak exercised no leverage.

"No, we have no camera, young man," barked Hannah.

"Well, it will be confiscated if you do have one and don't purchase a permit. It's not worth fifty cents to lose your Kodak," sneered the officious youngster.

"What is wrong with you, boy?" snapped Annie, looking ready to pounce on the little pest. "Are you accusing us of something? Because my husband Alderman Sullivan will be very interested in removing you from your position here at the Pan if you are!"

Almost as if he'd been slapped, the boy jumped back and said, "No, no Ma'am. I meant no harm. I..."

"Shut up, you little vermin!" shouted Hannah, staring holes into him as the two stalked past him, insulted.

"The nerve of that little brat!" huffed Annie as she cradled the purse containing her Kodak a bit closer to her bosom.

They apprehensively approached the compact red brick building at the intersection of the Midway and the Mall, directly across from the merry Alt Nuremberg beer garden restaurant. They managed to ignore all the other barkers' excitable ballyhoo out front of every other midway attraction, but could not resist seduction by the persuasive solicitator and Dean of the outside talkers himself, the famous Mr. Alexander Donaldson. For fifty years Donaldson, who pronounced his Christian name *Alexandah*, had been perfecting the art of alluring enticement at every exposition since the London Crystal Palace of 1859.

The extravagantly mustachioed Donaldson strode back and forth, claiming to all within earshot "...while it is conspicuous for the absence of any unpleasant features, at the same time it is of an eminently instructive and interesting nature and well calculated to provide many hints to mothers and to females generally in the successful rearing of weakly infants."

The Sullivan wives were at first put off by the fanciful nature of the building, which was bedecked with dozens of fluttering flags, banderole and colorful pennants more appropriately suited to a Mutuals Rowing regatta than a hospital. Nor did they find endearing the enormous solicitous letters over the colonnaded entry that spelled out INFANT INCUBATOR. They hesitated before parting with their precious quarter.

Accurately assessing their procrastination, the illustrious talker encouraged as best he could, claiming that many a woman attendee arrived at this very place on the Mall clutching the one and only quarter she would ever spend for entry to any Exposition exhibit.

"Sir?"

"Yes, Madame," responded barker Donaldson.

"Is it really worth our while, then?" asked Annie.

"Why Madame, there is nothing else in this entire glorious, monumental, epic Exposition that will affect you more, or quite so deeply, and continue to do so for multitudinous years to come," Donaldson proclaimed, calling upon the air of absolute certitude emblematic of his profession.

He noticed Hannah shading her eyes as she looked up at the Alt Nuremberg's cylindrical tower across the way, a distinctive beacon for the well-heeled tourist at the Pan crazy enough to pay forty-five cents for an imported frankfurter when a ham sandwich could be had at the Pabst for merely ten cents.

"Is that creature up there real?" she asked.

"One day this April," Mr. Donaldson explained, readjusting his tall hat, "before

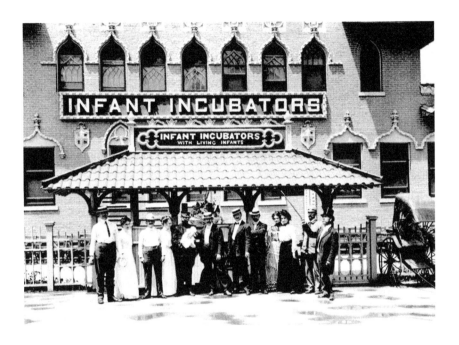

Donaldson outside Infant Incubators Exhibit.

the Exposition was finished, a woman whose age is a trifling subject, for time has touched her lightly, whose features yet mirror the buoyance of youth, a vision dressed to the tips of her ears in furs, was driven by this very spot in an open *barouche*. She glanced with the tragic eyes of Phedre lightened with merriment at the artistically age-mellowed walls of the Alt Nuremberg we view there across the way. She gazed up at that tower just as you do so now, and saw there, in a nest of pliant reeds, its long legs doubled under and its head poked to the west at half-elevation, a stork, the indispensable adjunct to all German villages. Then she looked over here at our red building bearing the conspicuous announcement: INFANT INCUBATORS. The woman in the carriage, the famous Mme. Sarah Bernhardt of Paris, France, regarded the two edifices and then said, 'Eez not ze stork on ze wrong beelding?'

The women roared with laughter.

"Although the actress continued on her way the stork has thus remained, having sat there ever since in the exact position faithfully watching over the babes it has delivered here to us."

The ladies giggled approvingly at Donaldson's colorful tale and handed over their quarter to the attendant.

As they shyly entered the doorway of the exhibit they were guided along the designated pathway by an iron railing designed to contain the wanderings of the overly-curious. The large main incubator room was bright and airy, painted snowy white, with a very high ceiling. The blue railings kept visitors corralled at the perimeter of the room along which the twelve incubators were arranged, leaving the spacious center of the gallery unoccupied. Circumscribing the large room below the level of the incubators ran a polished steel pipe about eight inches in diameter. At each incubator another pipe connected to this main pipe, a gauge at the side of each unit measuring delivered sanitized air to the babes. Another pipe followed a similar route above, near the ceiling. A pipe emerging from the top of each incubator withdrew stale air from each unit and sent it away.

Each little glass and polished steel cubicle housed a single infant. Every beribboned newborn was dressed in warm flannel from head to toe, save for their bright pink hands and their bald heads snugly cushioned on dainty pillows. They had been taken from mothers of low vitality when the conditions of food and air made their survival outside of this rarefied enclosure impossible.

Each pod was supported by metal legs that elevated the housing to a comfortable working height. Each unit had a double glass door in front and glass windows at the sides.

Two nurses in spotless white floor length dresses, their hair neatly gathered at the tops of their heads, wandered from incubator to incubator assessing the monitors, feeding the infants every two hours with a nasal spoon, and changing their diapers.

Two male attendants were stationed here as well, their contribution less than hand-lending, other than offering a spoken History of Modern Infant Incubation.

"The employment of incubators for the purpose of saving the lives of prematurely born or weakly infants, although much on the increase in all other civilized countries of the world, has not as yet become a general factor either in the United States or in Great Britain," the guide intoned. "France and Germany use such methods to a large extent and it is proven with satisfactory results. One of the most essential measures to preserve the lives of prematurely born or weakly infants is to protect them from change of temperature and cold. In bygone days these children were wrapped in wadding or sheepskin with the wool left on. In Silesia and Westphalia infants were sometimes placed in a jar filled with feathers. In the United States the cot or cradle was placed near the hearth, a custom which entailed the necessity of watching the fire by day and by night so that the temperature should be kept as constant as possible. Hot water bottles inserted in the bedding was a custom also largely resorted to. Devices of this nature, however, could not be relied upon; their success was too dependent upon chance."

"In 1878 the first attempt was made to construct an infant incubator on scientific principles. The celebrated Dr. Tarnier when visiting the Jardin d'Acclimatation at Paris was struck by the artificial *couveuses* for the rearing of poultry, and the thought entered his mind that a similar apparatus might be utilized for the rearing of children. He therefore ordered to be fabricated a *couveuse*, sufficiently ventilated and large, to contain one or two infants. Although defective in many respects, notably in the mode of heating, Mr. Tarnier's innovation was attended with a fair measure of success and many lives were saved by its agency."

A nurse who had been feeding an infant with a nasal spoon suddenly became quite agitated as the little one began to distress. She quickly grabbed the babe's feet and held him upside down, like a bat from a rafter. She then slapped him on the back as the child choked and coughed. The women present grew very distressed themselves seeing the infant struggle to breathe. The nurse then took the infant and draped him over her shoulder, patting him continually between the shoulder blades as his choking subsided, the child screaming with fright. Seeing the alarm on the faces of all the women who had stopped listening to the male guide she said, "The nasal spoon method sometimes causes an infant to inhale the mother's milk, and we must expectorate all the liquid from their lungs lest they contract pneumonia. Do not be alarmed. The child will calm in a few moments after I get him to clear his little lungs."

Annie and Hannah were unsettled. The guide continued his lecture. They looked to leave, but dozens of people lingering in front and behind caused them to remain.

"The heat of the incubator," the guide continued, "is regulated by a thermostat, the construction of which is so delicate that the slightest variation of temperature suffices to set it in motion. Consequently the heat within the incubator, never varies more than 2° F.

"To ventilate the incubator, there is a pipe which is conducted through the wall of the building so that no air but outside air is supplied to the infant within. This pipe delivers the air into a box at the side of the incubator, but before the child is permitted to breathe the air, it is first moistened and washed by being passed through a layer of absorbent material suspended over a utensil containing an antiseptic solution. In the same box is dry wool which takes up any physical impurities. A second pipe conducts the air from this box into the bottom and center of the incubator. Thus the air is washed, filtered, and warmed before it reaches the infant. So long as the lamp or gas burns, the temperature and ventilation within the incubator will be automatically maintained. Every two hours, by day and night, the infants are taken out and supplied with breast-food and their coverings cleaned."

Annie and Hannah had each birthed premature infants and both had suffered miscarriages. Visions of their past torment entered each woman's mind, but neither spoke her thoughts aloud to the other.

As they prepared to depart the room they were solemn, but not unhappy, knowing that their child-bearing days were not yet over, and thus the future looked brighter because of this new technology.

"Adjoining the incubator room you will next visit the model nursery, constructed principally of glass, in which there is a small pharmacy, contrivances for sterilizing milk, scales for weighing, miniature tubs for bathing, etcetera. It need hardly be said that scrupulous cleanliness is observed in every minute detail of this establishment. We can confidently claim that by means of this improved incubating system, eighty-five percent of prematurely and weakly born infants are saved."

Hannah observed that in the short time they spent there that the nurses washed their hands twice.

"I'm starting to get hungry," said Annie.

The brilliant sun blinded the two upon emerging from the incubator building. They shaded their eyes.

"Well," said Hannah, "I can't afford the menu at the Alt Nuremburg, and you won't let me go anywhere near the Pabst restaurant until Junior announces that he's comfortable about having us see him working there, and I'm already tired from walking, so what do you propose?"

"I propose," said Annie with a twinkle," that we next visit Fair Japan, right over there," she said pointing directly across the Midway's avenue to the beautiful red foreign construction. "And afterward I will treat you to a rickshaw ride on our way to a big surprise."

Hannah brightened right up. The Japanese jinrikisha cost double what the wheel-chairs did, a dollar an hour, and thus for the more affluent visitor it was considered *de rigueur* to utilize this convenience to get around the Pan.

Unlike everywhere else on the Midway, outside the Japan attraction there stood no emboldened ballyhoo, no strident barker promising more than could possibly be delivered. Its serene contrast to the garish Venice In America attraction built right next to it was startling.

"Chaos vs. serenity, vulgarity as opposed to refinement; it's like night and day between the two," opined Annie.

Next door to Fair Japan stood the Photographer's Building, the studio of the man who had won the official designation as Official Photographer for the Pan American Exposition.

"I wouldn't step foot in there, just to make my point. Why would I want to buy his photographs when I can take snaps of you standing in front of the same landmarks?" she said, patting her purse. "He wants a small fortune to come out with us and to make our portrait on the Esplanade? Ha! People want snaps of themselves and their children that they make themselves. Whose idea was it to have only him and his three employees to service the millions expected to visit?"

Hannah was uncharacteristically subdued. Annie waited for a strong opinion on the matter but it never came.

There was no fakery in the presentation or construction of the Japan exhibit as was the case on all surrounding sides, such as in the painted canvas icebergs of the Esquimaux Village, or the bizarrely fashioned papier-mache lunar inhabitants' homes of the Trip To The Moon. The Japanese construction was genuine; a true replication made of legitimate Japanese materials imported especially for this exposition and fashioned in certified Japanese style, put up by Japanese workmen and built as an actual sketch of foreign life. Thick bamboo walls shut out the frenzy of the Midway crowds busy running around in frantic search of increasingly exciting diversions, the barrier keeping at bay the Midway's idle bluster and fulsome nonsense. Inside, there was no artificial display of village life but rather a sublime serenity and beauty exhibited in its gardens, streams, arched bridge, tea house and beautiful Japanese maidens outfitted in stunning kimono.

In Fair Japan's bazaar, in place of the cheap trinkets found in the showmen-owned shops set up everywhere else on the Midway, beautiful objects were displayed and reasonably priced. There was no disposition to force a sale, nor abominable quotes as elsewhere were charged for sadly ordinary goods. Rather curiously the Japanese sales girls were somewhat reticent and diffident, a bit reluctant to let their merchandise go, as if unsure whether the customer deserved such a treasure, concerned perhaps she might not properly care for it.

Annie paid for a small jade vase to add to her collection of similarly-colored objects displayed in her glass-doored hutch in her dining room. Then a gong sounded and a quartet of young boys appeared in shorts and leggings and what appeared to Annie to be an abbreviated kimono worn as a shirt, made of the most beautiful jewel-toned silk. They removed the colorful kimono shirts to reveal white blouses underneath, then immediately set about bouncing all over the place as if their limbs were made of rubber. The oldest looked to be no more than fourteen, the youngest six. The older boy lay on the ground on his back with legs raised perpendicular, whereupon the six-year-old hopped atop his upturned feet as if they were a chair. The older boy set to spinning, flipping and somersaulting the little boy into the air from this position so speedily and with such abandon that it was hard to believe the little one could remain aloft. But remain aloft he did, never faltering, never slipping from his brother's feet until the older boy, completing the act, flipped the little one high into the ether in a complete somersault before the child landed squarely upright with his feet flat on the ground, without so much as a hitch or a wobble.

Hannah and Annie joined all the others standing and watching in enthusiastic applause, and Annie slipped each boy a dime.

"Let's go eat!" Annie then cried, as the women hurried out the bamboo gate and plopped themselves into a rickshaw. The little man pulling it darted off, maneuvering through the crowds with an expertise borne of negotiating frenetic midday traffic in Tokio.

The ride was bumpy. The asphalt that had been laid along the Pan's promenades was sunken and broken in many places due to the poor quality of the material itself and its incompetent installation. The paving contract having been awarded to the lowest bidder, the old adage 'You get what you pay for' was again proven. Plank roads had been laid in stretches where the delivery of heavy materials, such as the massive cannon for the Government Building, had torn up the paving altogether. The oriental conveyance halted none too soon at the north end of the Manufacturers and Liberal Arts Building, where a swarm of excited women thickly congregated.

"What's this?" complained Hannah. I thought we were going to eat? I'm almost ready to faint."

"We are going to eat, Hannah—right here...for free!" Annie happily replied as they entered the massive space over which hung a sign proclaiming FOOD SECTION.

"I thought we were going to rest our tired feet and sit and enjoy a leisurely meal, Annie," whined Hannah.

"Oh Hannah...this is so much better!"

Hannah noted to herself that the Alderman's skinflint ways seemed to be rubbing off on his wife.

Both women stood flabbergasted seeing the massive display greeting them upon entering the portal, an out-sized two-story confection of architectural ornament that overwhelmed all others around it, Henry D. Perky's famed Natural Food Company of Niagara Falls exhibit.

A full-size building within a building, its entrance was crowned by a huge SHREDDED WHEAT emblem within an oval bearing a beautiful life-size painting of an Indian grinding grain on the banks of the Niagara River. Living Indian Maidens stood at the ready, extending saucers of shredded wheat products to all takers.

In height, frontage, architectural design, skillful workmanship and artistic arrangement, the Perky exhibit momentarily arrested their attention. Admiring it for a few seconds, Annie abruptly said, "Shredded Wheat? Hmm. I don't think so. But I believe I smell gingerbread baking down this way a bit. Come on."

With those words Annie grabbed Hannah's hand and the two set out on their gastronomical adventure.

Up and down the aisles of all the many exhibitors women jostled each other anxiously to taste the wares.

"We can eat our fill here, Hannah, and at no cost!" Annie exclaimed. "Then after, we can walk over to the Electric Tower and take the elevator up to the roof garden and treat ourselves to a comfortable seat and a beer, or maybe some wine! We haven't had a chance to see that view yet during daylight."

Hannah felt a little uncomfortable in light of all the starving, albeit well-dressed creatures attacking the food counters, looking like so many baby birds craning their naked pink necks up from the nest in desperation to be fed.

"I don't know, Annie...this looks rather desperate..."

Having felt diminished by having to accept charity as a child, Hannah's old scars yet remained.

"Hannah! Let's have fun! These companies want us—no, they fully expect us— to eat their food, because they believe once we taste their delicious wares, we'll buy their goods in the stores next time we go shopping. We're doing them a favor, that's how they see it. They paid a lot of money for the privilege of feeding us a free lunch! The floorspace here cost them dollars per inch! So let's not disappoint them. You're a charitable sort, Hannah, so look at it this way. You can accomplish the two things you love most in life at the same time: eating, and helping those in need!"

Hannah couldn't help but laugh out loud at Annie's joke, as she had indeed become a bit more ample lately. But because Jim had made a similar joke not long ago, it gave her pause.

Nevertheless, free food at an international fair—and fine quality free food at that— was nothing to sneeze at.

They were at first surrounded by other reticent souls much like themselves, well-brought-up women and girls of refinement holding back whilst the food-grabbers, those having no pride at all it seemed, gobbled away.

"Ladies," Annie encouraged Hannah and those dawdling around them, "let's not tarry back here when there are so many wonderful treats awaiting us at the food counters!" And with that she led the Charge Of The Timid to compete with the more aggressive hordes for their share of the bounty.

The ornate gazebo created for the Heinz Pickles pavilion—57 Varieties—displayed towering pyramids constructed entirely of jarred pickles, India relish, and bottles of catsup. One of the counter girls was being engaged by an insistent woman.

"Yes, these pickles are grown for us especially, ma'am. That's why they are all of such an even size. No, really, I don't believe I could give you our pickling recipe. It's something like a patent, you know."

Across the aisle, Heinz' many other products attracted throngs of tasters, as did neighboring exhibits distributing gingerbread, crackers, prepared grain dishes, cough drops, coffee and candies of all kinds.

Much like the ballyhooers along the Midway, except that these were decidedly more demure, the lady attendants hawked their wares.

"This is one of a score of ways in which our rolled oats is prepared. It's the simplest way. So just think of what the others must be. Here, Ladies, try some."

Hannah and Annie took the small saucers offered them, with cream and brown sugar, and judged the rolled oats excellent.

"It's the way that our oats are rolled, recited the young miss attired as a Quakeress representing the Quaker Oats Company, "that gives that dish such a nice flavor. I thought you would like it. Just pour a little hot water on the oats, stir them up, and your breakfast is ready!"

Annie and Hannah moved on.

"This pineapple preserve is only one of eleven delicious fruits which are put up in the same way. This is merely to give you an idea of what our preserves are. We also have loganberry, cherry, peach, raspberry, strawberry, huckleberry..."

Annie reached out to take the tiny saltine, the size of a quarter and covered in pineapple preserves, between her thumb and index finger, as offered.

"No!" sternly admonished the counter-girl. "Palms up, ladies!" I'll drop it into your hand lest the preserves end up all over the counter!"

The army of women obeyed the General of Pineapple Preserves.

"That one's corset's been laced up a bit too snug if you ask me," Annie confided to Hannah, as they each dutifully extended a single gloved hand, palm up.

Plop! The little saltine landed as intended, with nary a drop wasted.

"This gingerbread is made of our famous flour," extolled the lady at the expansive Gold Medal Flour exhibit. "Yes, of course we put real ginger in it, but it is our flour that makes the bread so nice and flaky. You can cook it in a few minutes in any sort of an oven."

"'This is hot rags,' as Junior would say," said Hannah, imitating her son's slang. Can we please have another?"

"I'm sorry ma'am, we're only allowing one slice per visitor," the girl said loudly, looking around furtively before slipping two additional pieces to the ladies.

Hannah and Annie smiled their thanks and uttered pleasure sounds as they consumed their second helping of the delicacy.

"Is the recipe on the package?" Annie asked the girl.

"No—isn't that odd?" she replied. "They make this delicious bread to show the world how wonderful Gold Medal Flour is, yet the recipe isn't even printed on the package. I suggested on the day we opened that they have cards printed with the recipe, but as far as I know they haven't done that yet. Everybody asks for it."

"Well, thank you again, that was very sweet of you," Hannah smiled. The Gold Medal girl gave them a wink before turning to face a fresh throng barreling down the aisle toward the heavenly smell.

And so it went as Hannah and Annie made their way up and down four long aisles of scrumptious samples, amused by the hawkers' spiels.

"This apple butter is made from apples from our own farm, so you know just what you are eating. No, we aren't giving away jars of fruit today. We are afraid our samples won't hold out if we do that."

"Our tea is especially imported by us in limited quantities once a year. Yes, I thought you were a person who would appreciate the flavoring. No, I can't sell you a five-pound package today, but I can take an order for one."

Hannah and Annie retraced their steps to try again those counters that were too mobbed to approach the first time around, as well as revisit their favorites. They heard the pineapple preserves wench complaining to a news reporter who wore a tucked a *Buffalo Commercial* newspaper card in his hat band. On his coat he wore his Pan American Exposition pass with his photograph on it.

"You wanted to know the worst trouble I have with the crowds?" she moaned to the reporter. "Why, the only real trouble I have is to make the people hold their hands right. 'Hold your hands out straight, palms up,' I tell them over and over. People will try to take these tiny crackers by the edge, just as they would a big one, and the women are wearing gloves much of the time to boot, making the task even more difficult. It's too small to take that way. When they insist on doing it their way they usually get smeared with the preserve."

At the Baker's Chocolate booth, the girl was interrupted in her speech by a well-dressed middle-aged woman who said, "Are you Mrs. Baker?"

"No, I am not," the Baker's girl replied.

"Well, has she been here today?"

"No."

"Do you expect her this afternoon?"

"No, I don't. To tell the truth, I don't even know if there indeed is a Mrs. Baker. For all I know, Mr. Baker is a bachelor, or a widower. I've never met him."

"Well," the matron sniffed, "Why do you need an entire Baker's Chocolate Building out there," she waved vaguely toward the Esplanade where the fantastically ornate Baker's Cocoa Pavilion was located, "and take up valuable space in here as well? I should think he would have a wife to organize such affairs as this. That Mr. Baker needs a woman to straighten it all out," and immediately she turned on her heel to head off for some free gingerbread.

Then the same Baker girl was interrupted by another woman who asked, "Is that Oscar Astor who went to the Philippines to fight for his country?"

"Oscar Astor?" repeated the girl cluelessly. "Why of whom are you talking?"

"*Oscar Astor*, I said. There is a picture of a man in the next exhibit and his name is given as Oscar, and Astor is also mentioned.

"Oh, that's a picture of Oscar, the chef at the Waldorf Astoria Hotel in New York," explained the Baker's girl.

"And he isn't the rich man who went to fight in the Philippines?" she insisted disappointedly.

"No, he isn't any relation," said the Baker's girl, trying her best to dismiss the pest.

As the bothersome woman walked away, the Baker's girl cursed under her breath, "Jesus, Mary and Joseph! Some people!"

There was a war of words being waged between the American Coffee Company purveyors and the Postum true-believers, each trying to convince Exposition attendees that theirs is the healthier hot drink.

The coffee purveyor recited the pertinent facts as he knew them:

"There is a strange idea abroad in the land that it is much more wholesome to drink a hot liquid made of barley and wheat and molasses than to imbibe in an extract of pure coffee. If cereal coffee is drunk for any length of time, however, it breaks down the tissues in the stomach and induces a flatulent condition."

"It is a curious fact that real coffee has no injurious effect whatsoever on the man who smokes tobacco. The effect of either one seems counteracted by the effects of the other."

"The Portuguese who said he wanted his coffee as black as ink, sweet as honey and hot as hell had the right idea."

Hannah and Annie stopped what they were doing every now and then to take it all in. Every type of women seemed present here, huddled together, rich and poor, outlandish and plain, accomplished and commonplace. Women wearing diamonds elbowed women who might well have been their kitchen maids just to grab a free biscuit baked from the "finest baking powder on earth," free pancakes served by Aunt Jemima herself made from the only pancake flour guaranteed not to produce "sinkers," free soup from the only cans containing real tomatoes, free cheese, free mincemeat sandwiches, mustard and jam, free chow-chow, plum pudding, clam broth, baked beans, free sponge cake, Welch's grape juice, Kato, the "World's First Instant Coffee," free dinner rolls and biscuits, pudding and pickled lobster.

"So, what is it that my Mazie said to you," asked Annie suddenly. Hannah's comment had been bothering her. "I won't stand for any disrespect from that girl," said Annie.

"Oh, it was nothing. I corrected her, and that was that."

"Hannah, I know my Mazie, and if you corrected her, I cannot picture her being humbled. Quite the opposite. I don't believe 'that was that' at all. You have to tell me. She's only ten years old and getting more spoiled and snippy with each passing day —and I don't know what to do with her anymore."

Hannah let out a deep sigh.

"Annie, Mazie's been treatin' your girl Sophie like Sophie's her own personal slave. And by that I mean she's nasty and mean and orders her around. It's vindictive behavior. It's meanness solely for the joy she's gettin' from bein' mean. I promise you, if someone comes along who offers her a better position, Sophie will take it. You know how lucky you are to have her. She's loyal and sweet. She loves you and the children. But your Mazie is causin' her a lot of unhappiness. You need to have a talk with Mazie. You *cannot* afford to lose Sophie."

Annie felt like she'd been punched in the stomach. She had never witnessed

Mazie's mistreatment of Sophie, yet nothing Hannah said sounded far-fetched or out of character. With seven children, she couldn't imagine how complicated her life would suddenly become if Sophie quit.

"Thank you for telling me, Hannah. I wasn't at all aware of this. I will have some strong words with Mazie, believe you me. If I ever lost Sophie, that would be a real nightmare," shuddered Annie.

Hannah didn't reveal to Annie that Mazie had also called her a "damned busybody" and a "wrinkled old wind bag." Maybe some other time.

At Horlick's Malted Milk booth the women drank a tasty cup of the stuff, promising to purchase the product from that day forward for their families. At the Artistic Kitchen of the Washburn-Crosby Flour Company the entire process of bread making was presented. The finished loaves were removed hot from the Dutch Ovens in which they were baked, then sliced and slathered generously with fresh-churned butter and handed out happily to the eager crowd.

At the Erie County Preserving Company's booth Annie and Hannah feasted on a generous slice of mincemeat pie along with liberal allowances of the company's fine local Western New York preserves.

Eventually they were feeling full.

"Ooh...I shouldn't have eaten that mincemeat pie. It's just sitting down there like I swallowed a rock," Annie winced as they waddled their way toward the exit.

As they passed by Perkey's Shredded Wheat Pavilion on their way out they were invited to explore the upstairs level where lovely settees and divans were artfully arranged and strewn with large welcoming feather-filled cushions and pillows for the comfort of weary lady Exposition-goers such as themselves. They decided to rest a bit. As each settled into her chosen seat she expelled a great sigh of relief.

"Oh my, this feels soooo lovely," sighed Annie with pleasure.

Soon both were fast asleep.

PABST'S PREFERRED CUSTOMER

It took Junior almost a full month before he ceased waiting tables all night long in his dreams, running back and forth to the restaurant kitchen arms loaded with steaming plates up to the elbow. Throughout his entire night's snooze he would reenact the tasks required of him, fearful he would spill food on some fancy lady or drop a loaded champagne tray or be fired at any moment, his pockets suddenly empty of the daily gratuities. What he most loved about the job was its unique reward of his arriving home every day with fresh money in his pockets.

Memorizing the Pabst Pavilion's bill of fare, all its categories of Steaks and Chops, Cold Meats, Relishes, Cheeses and such was difficult enough. A Porterhouse single was 75 cents. A Sirloin was 50 cents—with mushrooms, 75 cents. Mutton or Pork Chops and Veal Cutlets were all priced at 40 cents, cheaper than a frankfurter cost over at the Alt Nuremburg restaurant.

Junior was familiar with the food names of course, so committing the fare to memory was not that difficult. But the Wine List served up a maelstrom of confusion to him, never personally having seen such a choice offered before. The wine menu listed more than twice the number of items as did the food menu; Liqueurs and Mixed Drinks, Champagnes, Clarets, Moselles, Brandies, six kinds of Pabst beer including Doppelbrau and Red, White & Blue, in addition to Guinness Stout and Dog's Head Bass Ale, and much more.

The staff was encouraged to push the imported G.H. Mumm & Co. Extra Dry Champagne, at $2.50 a pint and $5.00 a quart.

Junior scoffed at first that anyone would pay such sky-high prices for the French bubbles, but did as instructed anyway. "The better-dressed the customer, the more you recommend the higher-priced dishes and libations," stated manager Schutkeker.

Junior was stunned at how much Mumm's he sold. And how often these big spenders, running up a bill as high as $40, left him a quarter tip, while an Esquimaux man from the Midway attraction who had only ordered a 10 cent ham sandwich and a 5 cent coffee one day left him a nickel.

"The rich man leaves me a tip of less than 1%, while the poor man leaves 33%!" he exclaimed to his mother after returning home from a long hard day.

"That's exactly why the rich stay rich," explained Hannah, "and the poor remain poor."

Working at Pabst's was proving to be even more of an education than Junior had anticipated, especially concerning the ways and means of different people. He began to provide special service to his fellow Midway denizens, much to the rebuke of Herr Mueller, simply because they were much kinder customers compared to the tourists.

Only when Gus Schutkeker and Herr Mueller both informed him that he was doing a fine job, other than a few small criticisms such as his favoring Midway riffraff, could Junior begin to relax.

It was around that time that the fun began.

The nearby Alt Nuremberg restaurant was bigger, more popular and more expensive than the Pabst. The Alt had 85 waiters to the Pabst's 50. Nonetheless, the Pabst's great location and cheaper prices drew in the more common man, including many adjacent sideshow participants. At first, Herr Mueller wanted to seat these odd Midway people at the back of the restaurant out of sight. He didn't want his preferred customer to be offended by the entertainers' odd eating customs or strange national dress, their extra limbs or tiny stature, feeling such visuals might disturb their appetites. These Midway performers were certainly not to be seated adjacent to the Mall promenade itself, where they would be in full view of the crowds walking by and thus discourage them from entering Pabst's at all. Only the best-dressed and most refined citizens were meant to be displayed in full sight there.

As the participants at the various Midway attractions became more accustomed in their jobs, they began to seek distractions, some pleasant diversion from the usual, a welcoming place to gather among their own. Many found this camaraderie at the Pabst Pavilion.

Herr Mueller would have discouraged this ilk entirely had business been better than it was.

One of the Pabst's beer taps had been designated exclusively for guests of the management so that the inventory might be best kept track of. The waiters were encouraged to take good care of certain VIP guests, and a select trusted few, including Junior, were allowed to serve from this tap at their discretion.

Herr Mueller became concerned one day when upon checking the level of inventory from this tap that far less of it was depleted than he had budgeted for. The Pabst Pavilion was his baby, and he had invited all his friends and those he felt might be influential to come by and spend time enjoying themselves, but many did not take him up on his offer. At first he admonished the staff for their not recognizing the VIPs when they presented themselves. Soon enough though he found that these important people were simply not coming by in the first place, preferring instead the atmosphere at the Alt Nuremberg.

A babble of confusion filled the Pabst at times as scattered about the central courtyard Turks, Mexicans, Indians, Filipinos, Japanese, Arabs and Esquimaux mingled and relaxed and made themselves at home.

One day Junior's heart nearly stopped as little Chiquita The Doll Lady, in the company of her visiting mother, a full-sized human who curiously appeared younger than her dwarf daughter, waited to be seated.

For some reason this tiny miniaturization of an adult human made Junior queasy in the stomach. Junior was initially disturbed by this Midway curiosity, as he had never seen such a lilliputian, perfectly formed, proportionally correct, extremely wrinkled human before. And that voice! High and thin, emanating from such an elegantly-bejeweled little woman, with her cackling laugh sounding much more barnyard than country club. Chiquita was dressed in beautiful silk gowns and threw money around like it was water.

Junior quickly noticed that people on the Mall who had seen her enter Pabst's followed behind her and requested to be seated near her, and spent good money thereafter. Chiquita sat in Junior's section every time. At first she gave Junior fitful dreams as he slept, but her generous tipping, along with the tips of her admirers, soon helped dispel these.

Chiquita began to drop in regularly. She always ate heartily, typically ordering the single porterhouse, Lyonnaise Potatoes, a plate of brie with sliced tomatoes and a glass of sherry. She surprised Junior by finishing all of it, every time. Nothing was left on her plate.

He tried not to stare, but was intrigued by her eating habits, at once both fascinating and repulsive. She moved twice as fast as a full-size human; every gesture, her speech, even her walk. But most especially her chew. Her mouth moved at an extraordinary speed as she masticated. She cut her porterhouse as if with a sabre and pitchfork, so outlandishly huge did the eating utensils appear in her tiny baby hands. Junior had never encountered anyone like her before.

She usually left him a generous tip.

On her third or fourth visit she came in with a handsome boy over six feet tall, who mentioned to Junior that he was up from Erie Pennsylvania. Chiquita barely came up much higher than the boy's knee.

Things took an odd turn that very first day when they sat so close together that Chiquita might as well have been lounging in the boy's lap. As Junior set down her order of broiled chicken with German fried potatoes, he noticed that her tiny hand was deeply exploring the crotch of the teenager's pants. The boy was smiling.

As their meal leisurely disappeared, Junior returned to their table with a pint of Mumm's.

"Courtesy of the management, Miss Chiquita," he said as he place the champagne glasses and fresh linen napkins with a flourish. Those customers who had followed her in to the restaurant and had asked to be seated around her smiled their approval.

"Vat are you doing, Sully? Trying to get yourself fired?" exclaimed Gus Schutkeker back in the kitchen. "If Mueller finds out he'll get rid of both uff us."

Chiquita left Junior a dollar tip.

The following evening, balmy and beautiful, a delicious breeze softly stirring, Chiquita returned for dinner dressed in an extraordinary tiny elegant rose-hued silk ball gown of Parisian design. She wore a sparkling necklace that may have contained real diamonds. Again she was accompanied by the same towering teenage boy. People gaped. There was a fine table available right at the railing in full view of all who walked past.

"I have a lovely table ready for you, Miss Chiquita, the view from which I believe you might find highly entertaining, right over there," Junior pointed to the very public location, "but if you'd prefer your privacy I can instead seat you and the gentleman in the courtyard as usual."

"Oh no, we'd love to take the place by the promenade so that everyone can see me," she effused in a tiny high-pitched voice. She had tiny teeth, an extraordinarily pink tongue and was uncommonly wrinkled for someone said to be only barely in her thirties.

"Then, please, follow me," invited Junior as Herr Mueller appeared. Junior escorted Chiquita and her young lover to the table by the railing and handed them their menus, then made a small bow.

"I'll be back in two shakes of a lamb's tail," Junior said, "to take your order."

After he departed he was intercepted by Herr Mueller.

"Just vat do you think you're do-ink, seating that little Midvay curiosity out front? Are you tryink to drife people avay?"

Before Junior could defend his position, a group of six very excited, very well-heeled people, three couples visiting from New York City, ran up to them excitedly and asked, "Might we be seated beside Chiquita?"

Their eyes were glued on the little lady.

"Of course you can!" said Junior. "Ladies, gentlemen, please follow me."

Junior left the angry and now-confused Herr Mueller standing there scratching his head.

"Excuse me sir, are you the maître d'hôtel?" asked the elegant parasoled European woman on the arm of the refined aristocratic gentleman in the silk top hat.

A woman sitting at a table close at hand exclaimed to the others at her table, "Oh my Lord, look! Isn't that the Duchess of Kent?"

"Yes Madame, I am the maître d'. How might I be uff service?" responded Mueller.

"We would like to be seated over there, close to that extraordinary little person in the pink ball gown. Can you arrange that?"

"Why yes, madam, of course. Please come this way," said Mueller, relieved that a table with a fresh linen cloth was available just one table way from Chiquita's.

After seating the Europeans, Mueller ran back to where Junior was preparing a tray.

"Sullivan. Giff that little woman und her friend a pint uff the domestic champagne on the haus."

"Herr Mueller, might I suggest instead, considering her value as an attraction at this moment, that we provide her with Mumm's?"

"No!" he dismissed. "She von't neffer know the difference!"

Junior took a bottle of Mumm's from the ice box, placed it in a silver ice bucket and returned to Chiquita's table, shielding it from view as he passed Mueller.

With great ceremony he presented the champagne to Chiquita and her escort with a giant smile, popped the cork loudly to the satisfaction of all those around, and poured with great ceremony and a discreet wink.

The tiny woman clapped her little hands together excitedly before grabbing the stem of the glass firmly in both tiny fists. Junior had been careful not to fill her glass too full.

"Oh, waiter!" called a man at the table seating the six New Yorkers, "Will you bring us a quart of Mumm's as well?"

"Certainly, sir," answered Junior, staring at the hovering Mueller as he responded. Mueller had followed Junior with the purpose of scolding him but found himself instead converted.

"For us too, please. A pint," politely asked the gentleman escorting the European woman thought to be a Duchess.

"Coming right up," cheerily replied Junior Sullivan, who then ran and gathered two more waiters from the back section of the Pavilion sitting idle there, neither having any customers at their tables. Junior quickly told them of his plan as they followed him back up to the front.

"I'll split my tips with you lads if you'll fall all over yourselves providing Chiquita and all those sitting around her with the best service of their lives. I want to shower them with attention and service."

The reassigned waiters scurried.

Soon the elegant nature of those diners who surrounded Chiquita's table, and the sparkling vision of Chiquita herself in full view of the passing hordes, attracted a line of people at the entrance wishing to be seated near the celebrity and the glamorous personalities who had followed her in.

"But ve haff no tables at the moment," Herr Mueller explained, now aware of the brilliance of what Junior had arranged, "but you can be seated immediately inside if you vould like."

"No thank you, we'll wait," was the standard reply. And wait they did.

Others who had also initially been attracted by Chiquita and too hungry to wait, reluctantly acquiesced to be seated elsewhere, just so they might eat. They were escorted into the courtyard.

Almost immediately, Llavito the Mexican matador presented himself accompanied by a beautiful senorita, Columba Quintano, the dancing sobriquette, who was dressed in a wildly colorful costume beautifully embroidered with flowers and birds and butterflies in flight. All eyes landed on them upon their entering.

"*Señor, señorita, bienvenidos,*" welcomed Junior in his awkward high school Spanish. "Dinner? Of course. Come this way, *por favor.*"

Junior led them into the inner courtyard as all watched the beautiful couple glide past, then seated the exotic pair centrally for all to see, much to everyone's satisfaction. They were provided a table amidst the patrons who had opted to sit in the interior because they were too hungry to wait for a table near their initial attraction, Chiquita.

Junior provided these diners with something exciting to ogle and talk about. Their eyes lit up and they nudged each other as the beautiful Mexican celebrities were made comfortable.

As Junior passed him, Mueller grabbed him and said, "Keep Miss Chiquita here as long as you can. Brink her und her friend caviar to go vith their champagne. Offer them cake. Brink them sherry after dinner. Offer the young man a cigar. Just keep them out there as lonk as you can."

Junior delivered the caviar to Chiquita as Mueller watched.

"Your caviar, Miss Chiquita," Junior said loudly. "I hope it is to your satisfaction."

The surprised celebrity nodded graciously.

"Oh waiter," called a woman from the table of six. "Can we order caviar as well?"

"Certainly, Miss, I'll bring it right away."

Mueller stood there, beaming. He hadn't sold any caviar in days. He was forced to feed what had been left over in an opened can to his cat lest it spoil.

Junior delivered eleven orders of caviar that night.

The sudden rush of eager excited customers quickly converted Mueller to Junior's crafty scheme. He relocated one of his best waiters to where the Mexican beauties and their admirers had been seated and instructed the server and his helper to attend to the Mexicans like the VIPs they now were. Their tablecloth was discreetly changed out for a spotless one and an iced pitcher of brew was delivered from the VIP beer tap without being ordered.

"*Cerveza.* Compliments of the management," whispered the waiter, as the grateful matador and sobriquette looked at each other quizzically.

Upon suffering Herr Mueller's tirades instigated by the boss' frustration over the Alt Nuremburg stealing away his society-set customers, it was Junior who understood that the very best promoters that Pabst's could possibly wish for already surrounded them. The performers from the various attractions would become Mueller's new VIPs. These individuals had become celebrities in their own right due to all the daily newspapers' lengthy reports detailing the wonders of the Pan. The entire city was now familiar with the matador Llavito; with Isola Hamilton, the famed artists' model generously blessed with extraordinarily large breasts; Fatima, the little tempest; Esau the chimpanzee; and the substantially-muscled Cora Beckwith, champion woman swimmer of the world. No one, much to Herr Mueller's surprise, objected to the chimpanzee being seated at a table with his human friends.

Then there were the ballyhooers.

"Who better than a gee-gaw man who shouts out to thousands of revelers every day—visitors unfamiliar with the environs and eager for a good time, to send customers over to us?" reasoned Junior to Herr Mueller. The light went on in Mueller's eyes, and at the nightly meeting after closing he encouraged the staff from that day forward to troll the Midway for those personalities who could best send them the business he wanted by giving them their first beer for free, as well as every-second beer after that also. Treats were delivered to their tables periodically too, depending on fluctuating supplies and stores.

Junior had been right when he said, "You know, Mr. Mueller, the best show don't have to be goin' on out there along the Midway; it could be happenin' right here at the Pabst, if we just encourage it."

So, contrary to the original plan of convincing flush customers to leave as soon as possible after their meal in order to make way for other well-heeled diners who failed to materialize, the opposite tact was now taken.

"The more full the pavilion is, the more popular ve look," Herr Mueller concluded. "Don't hurry them out anymore."

It was one thing for Exposition-goers to see Chiquita on her Midway throne in her own venue, Chiquita's Palace, beautifully jeweled and costumed. There she ruled, surrounded by treasures presented her by European royalty, along with a landau and two miniature horses gifted to her the year before by President McKinley. Lately there was a brand new present of a miniature electric automobile which she used to zoom all over the Exposition grounds, waving to well-wishers wildly as she weaved between the pedestrians a little too close and a bit too fast. On her throne she was ballyhooed endlessly, gawkers staring in either disbelieving wonder or repulsion.

It was quite another though to see the tiny thing lounging at the Pabst at a table half-soused, with her towering seventeen-year-old lover's hand disappearing under the table and vice-versa, surrounded as they quickly became by intrigued, free-spending customers loving every minute of the dinner show.

It was as well wondrous to see the famous Geronimo sitting atop his horse at the Indian Congress, majestic, dignified, posing for photographs with dignitaries like William Jennings Bryant or Vice President Teddy Roosevelt, but perhaps more interesting to see him at the Pabst, relaxing with his friends, laughing, smoking, telling stories, trading insults with the waiters and acting nothing like the savage Indian of his purported reputation.

At the corner of the restaurant where the Mall and the Midway intersected, where passers-by could look in on the patio and clearly view the clientele, where Junior had seated Chiquita on the evening that turned the Pabst's fortunes, was the place newly designated for entertaining the house's preferred customer lately reconsidered. When this change was made and vividly-costumed, elegantly-dressed performers and celebrities poured in, trailed by Midway entrepreneurs the likes of Frank Bostock the Animal King, or the press agent Doc Waddell, business increased dramatically. Fair-goers couldn't wait to go home and tell their friends who they had seen or dined alongside, and what those people were doing—at the Pabst.

As word spread and interest in dining in the vicinity of exotic personalities like Selica the beautiful lady lion tamer, Mlle. Dodo from gayest Paree, the astonishing Gypsy Princess Stellita crowned in her priceless jeweled tiara, The Man in the Moon, Polatie the Strongman, geisha girls from Fair Japan, and even the Prussian Giant Guard from the Alt Nuremberg who had made new friends here and dropped by regularly, business boomed.

Now it was the Pabst Pavilion where people flocked to see and be seen. It had taken a few months, but the Pabst had become a cosmopolitan gathering place the likes of which few fair-goers had ever frequented previously or ever would again have the opportunity to in the future.

Since Pabst's business had increased less dramatically for lunch than for dinner, Junior suggested they invite others on the midway during the sparser midday hours who could not usually afford to eat at the Pabst, but whose costumed exoticism would help attract the paying customer. These included the hula-hula girls and boys from the Olupa halau in the Hawaiian Village, the Singalese stick dancers, the Japanese acrobats, and the Italian Adonis. Rickshaw drivers were encouraged to come in and have a free beer and to park their jinrikisha out front of the Pabst giving the impression that the place was being patronized by the hioty-toity customer who could not only afford a dollar an hour to be wheeled around the Fair, but could also afford to park his idle rickshaw as he dined.

Junior made four times as much money in tips during August as he had made in the entire previous period from late April to the end of July.

Herr Mueller would not be "loosink" his shirt after all.

As the Pan American Exposition wound down and colder weather set in, Chiquita disappeared from her lavish apartment on the Midway at about 11 p.m. on November 7.

Rumors spread that she had been kidnapped, which made the happy couple giggle.

Justice Thomas Rochford married the 26-inch tall, 18.5 lb. Chiquita, legally known as Alice Zenda, and seventeen year old boyfriend Tony Woeckener in the judge's home, at midnight.

Frank Bostock, King of the Midway and Chiquita's infamously possessive and physically abusive employer, was not at all pleased.

Neither were Tony Woeckener's parents.

EMMA GOLDMAN

"Sully, we need you at the Exposition to help out during the President's visit."

Those were words Detective Jim Sullivan didn't want to hear.

"Chief, I could sure use a day off. I been workin' eleven days straight. Hannah's not feelin' right and these huge crowds have made all our jobs ten times harder than before. I tell ya, I'll be happy once the Pan is over and done with."

Cusak looked at him wondering what was going on. It wasn't like Jim Sullivan to complain.

"Sully, everybody's workin' double shifts and havin' to pull extra duty, includin' me. It's either you go along with the President's detail to Niagara Falls tomorrow, or stay here and work the Exposition detail. Either way, we need your eyes.

"Six of one, half a dozen of the other," moaned Jim.

"Choose," said the Chief of Detectives.

"Okay Pat. The Exposition. It's closer."

"Good boy."

Hannah wasn't the only one feeling not so good, but Jim had to do his duty, whatever that happened to be.

"Oh, Jim." said Hannah. "You look so tired. You need a rest."

"I know. I feel it in my bones, Hannah. But I got no choice. What good can I be if I'm sleepin' standin' up? We're all exhausted. The whole department. Good thing McKinley's got his own men. Courtelyou, and the Secret Service. They're on the ball."

Publisher William Randolph Hearst's years of abusive slandering of President McKinley had stirred up a hornet's nest, most prominently among them a stinger going by the name of Emma Goldman. The East European jewess had strong ideas about socialism and anarchy and she wasn't afraid to speak her mind. The yellow newspapers, hungry for salacious material to sell their rags, attributed to her far more importance than her campaign against American capitalism deserved, allowing her to gain a prominence well out of proportion to her actual standing.

Goldman had emigrated from Kovno, in the Russian empire, to Rochester New York to join family members who'd preceded her. There she became polarized by the Haymarket Affair. A dynamite bomb had been thrown into a crowd in Chicago killing seven policemen. Although there was no evidence that any of those who were ultimately arrested threw the bomb, four of the men were hanged for the deed and one more committed suicide. After a gubernatorial election brought a new Illinois governor to office, John P. Altgeld vigorously condemned the trial that caused the arrest of the defendants as a travesty and pardoned those accused who yet remained in prison.

Goldman became a writer and a famed lecturer on rights for women, anarchist philosophy, birth control, free love, tolerance of homosexuality, and other social issues unspoken of in polite society. Her lectures attracted thousands of frustrated and angry people. Goldman's brand of rhetoric appealed mainly to immigrants like herself who had arrived expecting streets paved in gold but more often than not found them covered in shit, literally. Their American Dream shattered, they were looking for something or someone to blame.

William Randolph Hearst was an expert at pointing fingers in the wrong direction and fabricating stories out of thin air to promote sales of his tawdry penny sheet newspapers. So expert had he been in fact, that his bellicose ramblings had gotten the United States into a war with Spain.

Penny sheets, obviously given their price, were the most likely newspaper that a poor person might read. Hearst knew his audience, and gave the penny sheet reader precisely what he wanted.

Leon Czolgosz found Emma Goldman inspirational. He approached her after one of her lectures in Cleveland and attempted to become her friend, but seeing clearly that something was seriously off with him, suspecting perhaps he was an infiltrator like many police agents sent to spy on radical groups, she rejected his overtures.

Czolgosz felt he needed to somehow prove to Emma Goldman that he was worthy. And so he headed to Buffalo to attend the Pan American Exposition, pistol in hand.

SEPTEMBER 5, 1901
JAMES "BIG BEN" PARKER

It had been a long hot day for the President, but Niagara Falls had refreshed him a bit. Still, The First Lady was feeling poorly and instead of accompanying the President back to the Exposition, she decided to remain at the Milburn mansion on Delaware Avenue to rest. McKinley was eager to leave Buffalo and get his sickly wife back to Washington.

George Cortelyou, the President's private secretary, was anxious in a different way. A spate of assassinations in Europe had prompted him to cancel a number of McKinley's recent public receptions. But the President was thrilled and energized by the Exposition and the enormous crowds. He viewed the Pan as a unique opportunity to positively influence a vast audience in one fell swoop.

He insisted on going through with the public reception in the Temple of Music.

James Parker, a towering powerfully built Negro known to his coworkers at Bailey Catering as Big Ben, was delighted to find a place in the public reception queue only about 200 people back from the head of the line. He was certain with so few ahead of him that he would surely get to shake the hand of the President of the United States.

The man standing directly in front of him, a rather nice looking slight young white man, much shorter than he, gave him no suspicions.

Along the queue were stationed a number of Buffalo Police, the men sent in especially as an adjunct to the Pan-American Exposition Police Force in maintaining control of the mammoth crowds attracted to the fair that day by the President's visit. Included in this auxiliary force were Detective Sergeants Jim Sullivan and John Geary.

The sun was broiling, and since he was feeling poorly to begin with, Jim chafed standing in its cruel direct rays. His luckier partner John Geary was assigned inside the building. Jim regretted not having chosen to perform his Presidential duty at Niagara Falls instead, where at least there might have been a refreshing mist. Further up near the entrance to the Temple of Music lazed Detective Wright, cool as a cucumber, standing in the shade. Jim tried for some minutes to attract Wright's attention. Once he did, Jim signaled for Wright to switch places with him. Wright wasn't about to willingly stand in the hot sun so he pretended not to understand, quickly devoting his full attentions to keeping people in an orderly line.

Jim Sullivan did not take any special notice of the slight man with the handkerchief-bandaged hand as he passed him by; Jim's eye was drawn instead more strongly to the huge Negro standing directly behind him. Although the Negro looked benign, his powerful stature made Sullivan nervous. Attracting Wright's attention again, Sullivan pointed out the Negro so that Wright could size him up as he passed. But Wright found his attention directed rather to the smaller man in front of the black, the man with the bandaged hand. The small man was talking animatedly to the man in front of him, and Wright thought it hilarious to hear a polack and a wop, each with accents so thick that Wright couldn't understand either one of them, chattering away and perfectly able to understand each other.

Wright waited to catch the polack's eye to ask about his hand, but the little man never looked at him. At any rate with such an obvious injury he didn't look like he could be much of a threat to anyone. On the other hand, the big Negro standing behind him in line...*that* giant might prove a different story.

Wright signaled to Detective Geary standing ahead just inside the entrance to size up the six-foot-six-plus Negro as he passed. Geary gave Parker the once-over as he filed by but found no special reason to be concerned.

As he edged close to the President, James Parker noticed that Exposition President Milburn stood on McKinley's left, and thought he might like to shake that man's hand as well, considering his splendid achievement.

Parker had just been laid off from his job at the exposition's Plaza Restaurant with much regret being expressed by his manager, for Parker was a damn good worker. The Exposition was winding down and it was clear that the Bailey Catering Co. was not going to make the kind of profit projected so optimistically the previous spring, so the management was cutting back.

The 250-pound Parker was a modest man and a gentleman. He'd enjoyed a career as a Constable in Savannah Georgia previously, and before that he was a newspaper man for the *Southern Recorder*. He was known as an imposing gentleman of few words by the citizens of the east side of Savannah. In his role as Constable, his command to submit to arrest was always meekly complied with.

Dejected by his firing from the Bailey Catering Co., Parker decided to hang around and enjoy the Exposition as a visitor, since he likely wouldn't be able to afford to come back again as a paying attendee. Looking on the bright side, if he hadn't been laid off he'd never have gotten the chance to meet the President, so he positioned himself to be near the door of the Temple of Music when it opened at 4 p.m.

As the sun beat down mercilessly the line moved forward surprisingly quickly. Big Ben found himself third man from President McKinley. It was very hot inside the building, about ninety degrees. Most people had handkerchiefs out, fanning themselves, wiping their brows and necks.

Suddenly the line halted.

The Italian man who had been ahead of and talking to the Polish man with the bandaged hand in front of Parker would not let go of the President's hand and move on. He spoke effusively to McKinley, but Big Ben could see that the President's associates and his secret service men, most notably Mr. Ireland, were looking perturbed. Finally, as the Italian continued chattering away to McKinley loudly, even as he was being physically moved along, everyone, distracted by the Italian, and all eyes on him, heard two shots fire from the handkerchief-bandaged hand of the young man standing directly in front of Big Ben.

Stunned, it took people more than a moment to react.

McKinley leered at his assassin with an expression of absolute repugnance; the assassin's handkerchief was aflame.

Before anyone including the secret service men could pounce, Big Ben slammed the assassin from behind on the neck with one mighty hand and reached for the pistol still aimed at the President ready to fire again with the other. Instantly then a dozen men piled on the assassin driving him to the floor, but despite his slight build and the scramble of men atop him, Czolgosz attempted yet again to fire the pistol.

Once more, it was Big Ben who reacted in time. Parker knocked the revolver from the hand of Leon Czolgosz before the assassin could get off a third shot, sending the weapon sliding across the floor.

The President, with two bullets lodged in him, remained upright, and Exposition President Milburn and secretary Cotelyou led him to a chair to have a seat.

Chaos ensued.

Women shrieked and men bellowed. The electric ambulance was called from the

James Benjamin Parker brought down President McKinley's assassin.

Exposition hospital. Jim had heard the shots from his position outside and immediately reacted by charging the entry door and forcing his way in.

"Stay out!" he shouted to the crowd as they began to jam the entry. Losing no time, Detectives Geary and Solomon along with Mr. Ireland dragged the assassin out and away from the scene just as the ambulance raced up to take the President the short distance to the Exposition facility.

Jim was incredulous.

"Take him instead to the General Hospital!" he shouted, knowing that the small facility on the exposition grounds was in no way prepared or equipped to attend to such an urgent matter. No one seemed to hear him, or perhaps others thought they knew better. Perhaps if McKinley were splayed on the floor unconscious they might have reacted more urgently, but the President was seated and calmly speaking.

Pandemonium reigned as Detectives Geary and Solomon escorted Czolgosz away from the Music Hall. Knowing the crowd would be out for his blood, they sped their way through the unsuspecting hordes of fairgoers converging on the scene. They rushed the shooter downtown to police headquarters and into a jail cell not a moment too soon.

McKinley was hurried into the small hospital. The first surgeon to examine him there was Herman Mynter, who had been first introduced to the President only the day before. As Mynter examined the President's wounds, McKinley raised his head, smiled and said, "Doctor, when I met you yesterday, I did not imagine that today I should have asked a favor of you."

Other physicians quickly arrived, and just as quickly a decision had to be reached as to who would be appointed head surgeon. As a testament to the dearth of qualified physicians attending him, Dr. Matthew Munn was selected as chief despite the fact he was a gynecologist with no expertise in surgery of the upper abdomen where McKinley's wounds were located. Additionally, Munn had never before operated on a gunshot wound.

Surgery began at 5:20 p.m. with the President's personal physician, Presley Marion Rixey, holding a mirror to reflect the waning sunlight onto the President's wound because there were no electric lights in the operating room. There were also few surgery implements on hand.

Due to the great amount of fat in the President's midsection, Surgeon Munn was unable to follow the path of the bullet in McKinley's stomach, and gave up finally, deciding to instead close the wound without removing the bullet. He also failed to drain the wound from the second bullet, allowing a rich environment to flourish for which sepsis to set in.

Dr. Roswell Park, Medical Director of the Exposition and one of the country's most renowned physicians, had been performing a surgery in Niagara Falls when the emergency call came in, but by the time he was able to reach the Exposition site the surgery on President McKinley had been completed.

As doctors are wont to do, even a physician as esteemed and experienced as Roswell Park did not second-guess nor closely examine the work performed by Dr. Munn on the President, nor question thoroughly enough the details of his procedure.

Moreover, the President should have been taken thereafter to the General Hospital, but was instead inexplicably removed to the private home of Exposition President Milburn.

Secret service man Gallagher who was an eyewitness gave this firsthand account to the Buffalo *Commercial*:

"Parker struck the assassin in the neck with one hand and with the other reached for the revolver which had been discharged through the handkerchief and the shots had set fire to the linen. While on the floor Czolgosz again tried to discharge the revolver but before he got to the president the Negro knocked it from his hand."

At Police Headquarters on The Terrace the crowd had grown huge. Throngs had followed hot on the detectives' heels and were threatening to invade the structure. Police Superintendent Bull recognized the mounting crisis and realized a certain kind of respected personality was needed to handle the roiling mob.

"Send for Regan," advised city officials.

Michael Regan was called in to take possession of the situation. Charging into the crowd on horseback with a dozen mounted police behind, he cleared the streets surrounding the building inside of an hour and had the President's shooter taken quietly out a rear entrance and secreted in the old penitentiary on Trenton Avenue.

Regan then returned to headquarters and stood on the steps and shouted to the lingering horde, "Get out o' this and go home. Yous should be ashamed of yerselves. And most o' yous, bein' my very own neighbors!"

They did go home.

The once-defiled and demoted Michael Regan, who had been stripped of his Captain's rank and put back out on the street as a common patrolman for his enabling of the Sheehan election debacle of 1893, suddenly found himself on top once again, positioned to lead.

❧❧❧❧

Vice President Teddy Roosevelt was summoned and quickly arrived in town from his upstate holiday.

Jim Sullivan along with three other detectives was reassigned to shadow Roosevelt, whom as Governor of New York State they had protected on numerous previous visits to the city. Roosevelt had become familiar with the faces of the Buffalo detectives who'd protected him over the years and placed his full trust in these men.

T.R. was the house guest at the Delaware Avenue mansion of Ansley Wilcox, the home located several blocks down the street from the Milburn mansion where the wounded President lay.

Fatigue notwithstanding, Detective Jim Sullivan was electrified by the assassination attempt. Whether shadowing Roosevelt on his visits to the ailing President, or standing guard outside the Wilcox home, he watched like a hawk for any suspicious person or unusual activity anywhere near the Vice President.

A short while after his arrival, assured by McKinley's physicians of his impending recovery, Roosevelt left Buffalo to return to his family vacation in the Adirondack Mountains.

On September 10, Big Ben Parker appeared in the Pan American Exposition Mall, near the west gate. He had been presented with a season pass by the grateful Exposition Company. A group of people surrounded him, asking if he might sell pieces of his waistcoat and other garments. He politely retold his story to the crowd that had gathered and sold one button from his coat for $1. He provided a quote to the reporter from the *Buffalo Times* newspaper:

"I heard the shots. I did what every citizen of this country should have done. I am told that I broke his nose—I wish it had been his neck. I am sorry I did not see him four seconds before. I don't say that I would have thrown myself before the bullets. But I do say that the life of the head of this country is worth more than that of an ordinary citizen and I should have caught the bullets in my body rather than the President should get them. I can't tell you what I would have done and I don't like to have it understood that I want to talk of the matter. I tried to do my duty. That's all any man can do.

"I went to the Temple of Music to hear what speeches might be made. I got in line and saw the President. I turned to go away as soon as I learned that there was to be only a handshaking. The crowd was so thick that I could not leave. I was startled by the shots. My fist shot out and I hit the man on the nose and fell upon him, grasping him about the throat. I believe that if he had not been suffering pain he would have shot again. I know that his revolver was close to my head. I did not think about that then though. Then came Mr. Foster, Mr. Ireland and Mr. Gallagher. There was that marine, too. I struck the man, threw up his arm and then went for his throat. It all happened so quickly I can hardly say what happened, except that the secret service man came right up. Czolgosz is very strong. I am glad that I am a strong man also or perhaps the result might not have been what it was.

"I am a Negro, and am glad that the Ethiopian race has whatever credit comes with what I did. If I did anything, the colored people should get the credit."

THE PRESIDENT IS DEAD.
LONG LIVE THE PRESIDENT.

Death came painlessly or so it was claimed. Since early evening the night before the President had been unconscious with occasional lucid intervals. In his wanderings he spoke of home and his longing to be there. In conscious moments he asked for his wife, who came close and was comforted by him.

"It is God's way; His will be done," the President said to her. To his loved ones gathered round his deathbed he weakly bid "Good-bye all, good-bye." Then he lapsed into unconsciousness.

In the sick room the team of doctors toiled unremittingly to bring the President back to awareness and into a lucid state. They gave oxygen and stimulated him. When he again opened his eyes, without a moment to be lost they brought Mrs. McKinley to him for the final time.

She saw that he was dying but she did not falter.

Dr. Rixey was with her; she put her arms around her husband's neck and she kissed him, then crooned over him, patting his ruby face, smoothing his brow already losing the warmth of life. The President, eyes open, looked and looked at her, gazing as if when he finally left her behind, her picture would be forever with him.

He lapsed into unconsciousness even as he gazed at her, and Mrs. McKinley was led out of the room.

President McKinley died at 2:15 in the morning.

As Theodore Roosevelt hurried back to Buffalo to assume his duties as President of the United States, he informed his aides, "The men who were guarding me last week when I was in Buffalo, I want the same men in their same places again."

He was uncharacteristically nervous.

Among the reliable men T.R. had requested was Detective Jim Sullivan.

The whole city was bereft. First the terrible crime, followed by the optimism at the President's recovery, then suddenly, with only hours' warning, the shock of his death.

Buffalo, in the eyes of the many of the nation's citizens, was to blame for this tragedy.

Alderman Sullivan was ill himself at this time, and in the Common Council meeting presided over by Mayor Diehl, when the resolution of condolence was passed expressing the body's public statement of official grief, the Alderman's signature was missing, as he was bedridden.

To help out at home, Hannah took charge of the younger children during much of the day to keep the Alderman's house quiet and allow him his needed bed rest. Accustomed in recent years to her own small brood's lack of needing her attention, she felt overwhelmed, reminded what it used to be like when her own house was just as full.

Emma Goldman had been arrested in Chicago and was charged with conspiracy in the murder of the President of the United States.

When shown the Associated Press dispatch announcing the death of the President, Goldman, the anarchist being held at the Harrison Street precinct station, carefully adjusted her glasses, read the bulletin, and after a moment's pause, without any change in her expression, said, "Very sorry."

Not a single shade of regret or pity colored her countenance, witnesses said.

"I do not see how that can affect my case," she added, "if it is carried on lawfully and legally. They have no evidence against me. Chief Bull and Chief O'Neill have admitted they have none. They are holding me without evidence. The death of McKinley would only lengthen my term of imprisonment if they convicted me. I feel very bad for the sake of Mrs. McKinley. Outside of that I have no sympathy."

Buffalo Detective Matt O'Laughlin secured two affidavits from persons who attended the meetings held by Emma Goldman in Cleveland where she had been approached by the assassin Czolgosz. They were to the effect that her utterances were of an anarchistic and inflammatory nature. The affidavits were hoped to secure extradition papers for Goldman's removal to Buffalo for trial. Popular indignation caused the landlord who owned the house in which the Czolgosz family lived to order them out into the street.

Outside Police Headquarters where the assassin was being held, a crowd surged back and forth at the corner of Franklin and Erie. Daniel Girard, 20 years old of Cortland N.Y. fell unconscious from heart disease. Patrolman Dechart of the Fourth, and Connolly of the Tenth, carried him into Headquarters, where he was attended to by Dr. T.J. Martin, then allowed to depart.

Justice Murphy committed John Heintz age fourteen to the Rochester State Industrial School on the charge of petit larceny. The specific charge was that he stole 25 cents worth of nuts from a slot machine at the Pan-American Exposition. The *Buffalo Express* report did not mention for how long the boy would be imprisoned.

Rushing back to Buffalo upon receiving word of the President's fast-approaching end, Theodore Roosevelt's train arrived at the Exchange Street Station a little past one o'clock in the afternoon on September 14, the same station that had received the body of Abraham Lincoln 36 years before. There was no time to lose.

Roosevelt was met at the station by his friend Ansley Wilcox, whose guest he had been a few days previous when Roosevelt first arrived in Buffalo to visit the wounded President. It was decided that Roosevelt should continue on by train the short way from the Exchange Street Station to the Terrace Station to obviate a possible demonstration on busy Exchange Street.

From the Terrace Station the new President was escorted to his carriage along with his retinue. The carriages in Roosevelt's convoy were heavily escorted by a platoon of police, including Jim Sullivan, as it headed up Delaware Avenue toward Ansley Wilcox's home.

As the carriage passed Virginia Street, a block and a half from Wilcox's mansion, Wilcox leaned over and pointed to the house at No. 472.

"That's where Mark Twain used to live, T.R., when he resided here," Wilcox said.

Teddy, a Twain admirer, looked at the lovely home, at that moment thinking to himself that the structure was from a time much less complicated and much less sad than the present.

Little did he know.

Jim Sullivan too, turned and looked at the home as he passed, a flood of memories returning him to age seventeen when he was in the employ of Samuel Clemens at this very house.

A minute later the new President's carriage drew up in front of the black-shrouded columned portico of No. 641 Delaware, and Roosevelt went inside for a quick lunch with the Wilcox family. It was agreed that immediately following he must drive further up the street to the Milburn home to pay his final respects to the late President and to Mrs. McKinley, in preparation for the funeral.

To their dismay, Roosevelt ordered that the secret service and the battalions of police be discharged from further escort duty, but agreed to keep two mounted Buffalo police and four detectives, including Jim Sullivan.

The detectives and mounted police escorted Roosevelt and Wilcox the nine blocks north to the Milburn mansion, where Jim waited outside.

Roosevelt removed his top hat before entering the home. On the lawn some of President McKinley's male relatives lingered, having a smoke.

"My condolences, gentlemen," Jim said to them quietly, "My family is heartbroken."

The relatives nodded somberly in acceptance as Detective Matt O'Laughlin walked around the back to the Milburns' carriage house and inspected all sides to see if anything appeared to be amiss. Great crowds had gathered near the death house, but were being held back a respectful distance from the perimeter.

Inside, Theodore Roosevelt inquired for Mrs. McKinley, but did not see her. Nor did he carry out his original intention to view the remains of the dead President, lying at peace in the bed in which he had succumbed, upstairs. He spoke with acquaintances for about fifteen minutes, informing them of the change of plans, then left and entered his carriage, Jim and the other three detectives and the two mounted police following closely.

Judge Hazel soon thereafter arrived at the death house as also did Senator Chauncey Depew. They were told it was at the Milburn house that the swearing-in of the new President would take place. But Roosevelt had changed his mind, feeling the ceremony should occur away from the mournful death house.

Down the street, less than an hour later, Teddy Roosevelt stood in the library of the Wilcox mansion surrounded by Cabinet Members Attorney-General Knox, Secretary Hitchcock, Secretary Wilson and others. No one having had the forethought to summon a photographer, U.S. Secretary of War Elihu Root began, "Mr. Vice-president, I..."

His voice broke and then he stopped, remaining silent for a full minute, saying nothing, trying to maintain his composure. His fellow Cabinet members, gathered about, their eyes filled with tears, their heads bowed, mourned along with him the memory of the beloved man who had lost his life. Tears streamed down the cheeks of Secretary Root. Roosevelt, agitated and trembling, pulled nervously at the lapels of his frock coat.

Root then recomposed himself.

"I have been requested by all members of the Cabinet of the late President who are present in the City of Buffalo to request that for reasons of weight affecting the administration of the Government you should proceed to take the constitutional office of President of the United States."

Roosevelt stepped toward Root and said, "I shall take the oath of office in accord with the request of you members of the Cabinet, and in this hour of our deep and terrible national bereavement I wish to state that it shall be my aim to continue absolutely unbroken the policy of President McKinley for the peace, prosperity and the honor of our beloved Country."

Judge Hazel then took in hand a sheet of parchment on which was written the constitutional oath of office, and said, "Theodore Roosevelt, hold up your right hand."

Judge Hazel read the oath and Col. Roosevelt repeated it after him: "I do solemnly swear that I will faithfully execute the office of President of the United States, and will, to the best of my ability, preserve, protect, and defend the Constitution of the United States. And thus I swear."

Then there was a long silence as Roosevelt dropped his chin to his chest as if in prayer.

Judge Hazel next said, "Mr. President, please attach your signature," handing him the pen with which the new President used to sign his name.

After shaking hands solemnly, and conferring with members of the Cabinet, Roosevelt turned to War Secretary Root and asked him to take a little walk.

"It will do us both good," T.R. said.

Ansley Wilcox, said, "Mr. President, shan't I go along with you?"

T.R. responded, "No, I am going to take a short walk up the street with Secretary Root and will return again."

The men walked out onto the portico together as the house's great black volume of mourning bunting strung between the columns fluttered overhead in the breeze. An enormous American flag hung over the short stairway. When they reached the foot of the walk, a couple of uniformed policemen, along with Detectives Sullivan and Lynch who were dressed in civilian garb, began to follow them. T.R. turned and told his secretary, Mr. Loeb, to tell the men that he did not desire protection. "I do not want to establish the precedent of going about guarded," he said.

Jim tipped his hat respectfully at the request, but thought better of it. "This can't happen twice, Jerry. We need to tail 'im, regardless."

They allowed the new President to walk up the street half a hundred yards or so, then began to follow at a distance, looking fore and aft all the while, Jim and Jerry Lynch trailing behind the President, and Detectives O'Laughlin and Zimmerman across Delaware Avenue on the opposite side. The President did not object. Roosevelt and Root walked as far as the police lines, where bystanders recognized Teddy as he said goodbye to Root and began to create a fuss.

As Root continued on his way, President Roosevelt turned on his heels and quickly headed back down Delaware Avenue toward the Wilcox Mansion, completely alone. Jim and Jerry panicked a bit and caught up to him respectfully with the intention of following behind, but Roosevelt now invited them to walk alongside him.

"I was told by Mr. Wilcox that one of your men here used to be in the employ of Mr. Mark Twain as a boy?" the President asked.

"Uh, it...uh, yes, I was, Mr. President," Jim stuttered.

"Yes, Mr. Wilcox pointed out the Twain home as we arrived, and said you worked for him there for some years in fact?"

"Yes, sir, that is correct. More than two years."

"Well there, detective, Bully. Bully for you. Very humorous man, that Mr. Twain. One of my very favorites."

"Yes sir," responded Jim.

At that point Mr. Wilcox and two others, seeing Roosevelt walking back to the house, quickly approached them, and escorted the President away into the mansion.

That evening, Jim didn't arrive home until almost 10 p.m. He walked in, kissed Hannah hard, and asked for the kids.

"Junior and Nellie are in the parlor and David's asleep," she said.

"Nellie! Junior! Come in here," their father called out.

The two teenagers cautiously approached the kitchen, wondering what they'd done wrong.

"Wait for me here."

"What's going on, Jim?" asked Hannah.

Jim opened the door to David's bedroom and tip-toed in.

"Davey. Davey!" he loudly whispered. David stirred.

"Come, get up, just for a little while," Jim said, sliding his arms under his groggy boy to lift him up. "Your father has something wonderful he wants to tell you about."

ANOTHER PRESIDENT'S BUFFALO FUNERAL
SEPTEMBER 15, 1901

Jim was up again and out the door before dawn. He reported to Headquarters to join the army of Detectives and patrolmen assigned to McKinley's funeral detail. The Pan American Exposition was closed for the day out of respect for the dead President.

Hannah and the children dressed themselves in mourning black and piled into the Alderman's automobile, Junior at the wheel, to head for the City Hall where President McKinley's body would lie in state.

Rain was heavily pouring down.

President Roosevelt rose early and welcomed the Rev. Dr. Mitchell of the First Presbyterian Church for breakfast. T.R. was exhausted from the trials of the previous day but he dressed quickly for the funeral. His naïveté the previous day when he'd insisted upon his unguarded walk with Secretary Root down the Avenue was chastised. The President would from now on be heavily guarded. Jim Sullivan and the other detectives were newly relegated to peripheral duties as a small army of federal secret service men moved in.

Roosevelt, when the hour came, left the Wilcox home and traveled back up the street to the Milburn house to where the dead president still lay on a bier, undergoing preparation for transfer to his coffin. Teddy waited patiently as this ceremony was accomplished.

Thousands of people lined Delaware Avenue to view the cortege as it departed the Milburn mansion. The throng was silent as the coffin was carried out of the home and slid into the waiting hearse. Mrs. McKinley remained behind at the Milburn mansion along with her sister, Mrs. Barber, Dr. Rixey, and other close associates. The former First Lady, that morning after the death mask had been taken of the President, spent over an hour with his body. The removal of Mrs. McKinley from the room afterward was attended with some difficulty.

The procession was at first a bit discombobulated. The military units, Bluejackets and Marines from the USS Michigan, marched with less than practiced precision.

A battalion of white-helmeted Buffalo police on spirited horses led the way, followed by the 65th Regiment Band playing a funeral dirge. Then came the carriages of President Roosevelt and New York Governor Odell. Heads bowed and people sobbed as the glass hearse drawn by four horses made its way downtown. Two helmeted Buffalo mounted police held the bits of the hearse's two lead horses as they walked alongside them.

A downpour deluged the throng as the hearse approached the steps of the City Hall on the Franklin Street side, its two morning-coated top-hatted drivers soaked to the skin. Thousands of drenched mourners all around watched in silence. Street cars on W. Eagle Street slowed to a halt so that drivers and passengers could witness the historic sight. The rain poured down relentlessly, soaking everyone entirely, yet no one moved away. At the foot of the steps an Edison moving picture cameraman stood in the downpour cranking his camera as the hearse pulled up, recording the event for posterity.

The sailors who had trailed the hearse along the route opened its glass hearse doors, slid the heavy coffin out and hoisted the ponderous casket atop their shoulders, then ascended the granite stairs. The President, members of the Cabinet, and other important persons followed. The coffin would lie in state under the domed ceiling for public viewing. Once the casket was set in its place low and flat, the lid was opened and the deceased President's body checked over by the undertaker as to its suitability for presentation. President Roosevelt and the accompanying dignitaries then paid their respects, quickly departing out the Delaware Ave. side of the building for security reasons. Afterward the public was invited in. Roosevelt returned to the Wilcox mansion for a luncheon with Cabinet members, Governor Odell and others. After the meal the men spent an hour in the library in general discussion.

Jim and his fellow detectives stood guard out on the sidewalk on Delaware Avenue as an endless stream of callers tried to approach the front door to see the President. Notables were welcomed in by the dozen: Generals, Senators, Justices, men lobbying for a Cabinet post, a contingent of Civil War veterans and more. Many more callers were turned away before ever reaching the home.

Concurrently, thousands entered the City Hall via the Franklin Street entrance and were very expediently ushered past the bier, exiting on the opposite Delaware Avenue side. Those hoping to linger outside on Delaware Avenue were pushed along by the police so that a bottleneck would not be created. The driving rain helped scatter the lingerers until about two o'clock when the sun finally broke through. One hundred thousand citizens had passed the coffin by 11 p.m.

The following day Big Ben Parker returned to the reopened Pan-American Exposition as an honored guest. Reporters met him outside the gates but the modest giant solicited no acclaim. He said, "I happened to be in a position where I could aid in the capture of the man. I do not think that the American people would like me to make capital out of the unfortunate circumstances. I am no freak anyway. I do not want to be exhibited in all kinds of shows. I am glad that I was able to be of service to the country."

He did however hold dear a newspaper clipping quoting Mr. Ireland, President McKinley's secret service man's account of the incident that he kept in his wallet:

"[I was watching] this man who appeared to be an Italian, who had a short cropped heavy black moustache, he was persistent and it was necessary for me to push him along so that the others could reach the President. Just as he released the President's hand, and as the President was reaching for the hand of the assassin, there were two quick shots. Startled for a moment, I looked and saw the President draw his right hand under his coat, straighten up, and pressing his lips together giving Leon Czolgosz the most scornful and contemptuous look possible to imagine. At the same time I reached for the young man and caught his left arm. The big Negro standing in back of him and would have been next to take the presidents hand struck the assassin in the neck with one hand and with the other reached for the revolver which had been discharged through the handkerchief and the shots had set fire to the linen."

"Immediately a dozen men fell upon the assassin and was borne on the floor. While on the floor Czolgosz again tried to discharge the revolver but before he got to the president the Negro knocked it from his hand. As it went across the floor, one of the artillerymen picked it up and put it in his pocket."

But shamefully, forces were conspiring against the modest Parker, for many in the country could not abide a Negro being hailed and celebrated as a national hero.

The assassin Czolgosz had been saved from lynching by rabid crowds of Buffalonians only to be thrown to the wolves in a kangaroo court. His court-appointed attorneys were two elderly former judges who hadn't seen the inside of a courtroom in years. They petitioned the judge to limit the time spent in session to four hours per day because any more than that would create a physical hardship for them to endure.

This proved not to be a concern however since the entire trial from jury selection to the guilty verdict was neatly wrapped up in twenty-four hours. By the end of the day on September 24 it was all over.

Jim Sullivan found himself quite disturbed by the lack of examination in the case. "It's as if they just want to get it all over with as soon as possible, Hannah, never mind the pursuit of justice," he complained to her as she ironed.

"He killed the President Jim. So why should it even matter? There's no question he done it. He's lucky he's even gettin' a trial if you ask me."

Having been stationed outside the Temple of Music, Jim had not witnessed the shooting, but Detective Geary did. Together they talked about it in detail.

"What disturbs me, Geary," Jim said, "is that nobody seems to suspect the Italian who stood ahead of the shooter in the receiving line. I mean, all those involved have told how the Italian wouldn't let go of McKinley's hand and that it caused quite a stir, so much so that they had to physically move him along. This provided the perfect deflection for the shooter to carry out his heinous act. All eyes were laid upon the Italian and the disturbance he was creating, which opened a wide avenue from which the shooter could do the deed. Who was that Italian? Why is no one interested in finding him, just to make sure he wasn't in on it, to examine whether this was in fact the work of just one man?"

Geary nodded. He hadn't even considered that as a possibility, a fault which seemed to embarrass him right then. "Well, too late now," he dismissed. "Anyways, shouldn't them secret service guys 've nabbed him? In the chaos after the shooting that Italian fella just disappeared into the crowd."

Czolgosz's attorneys never offered the obvious defense of insanity as acceded in anarchist Emma Goldman's recollection of her own encounter with the disturbed admirer. Undoubtedly he did it, for there were so many eye witnesses. And yet despite all these eye witnesses to the assassination which left no doubt as to what Czolgosz did, suddenly the same eyewitnesses became unclear or downright forgetful about Big

Ben Parker's heroic role in the atrocity. Parker was never called to testify at the trial.

The first notable round in James Parker's deconstruction had been fired on September 13 in the *Buffalo Express*, when prominent Buffalo attorney James Quackenbush stated that he stood less than six feet from the President, and that secret service men Gallagher and Ireland, along with men from the 73rd Seacoast Artillery, took Czolgosz down. He denied seeing James Parker being any part of the take down.

Bizarrely, even secret serviceman Ireland, whose published statement taken the day of the shooting Parker kept in his wallet attesting to Parker's quick action, later testified he saw no Negro involved.

Local newspapers, most notably Fingy Conners' *Courier* and the *Buffalo Commercial* stated that the testimony presented in trial proved that Parker had nothing to do with the capture of Czolgosz, and accused Parker of profiteering under false pretenses.

The Afro-American community was outraged that Parker was not called to testify at Czolgosz's trial, charging that the secret service and the military were mortified that it was a Negro who took the assassin down rather than they.

A committee was formed at a meeting called by Reverend E.A. Johnson, pastor of Buffalo's African Methodist Church, on September 21, 1901. The audience was full of incensed black citizens, according to an article published in the *Buffalo News*, angry over Parker's being stripped of credit and recognition. They composed a statement that was published the following day:

"Whereas, there is a conflict of statements between the Associated Press and the Supreme Court of New York with respect or disrespect to the heroic act of James Parker in having thwarted the purpose of Leon Czolgosz in inflicting immediate death of our William McKinley. Whereas, we, the colored citizens of the City of Buffalo, N.Y. in this mass meeting assembled, that they very much regret the clash of statement in respect to the reported act of heroism on the part of James Parker, in that the Associated Press as a molder of public sentiment and as a herald of accepted facts. Reported said heroic act both in America and Europe, and that the Supreme Court, the arbiter of justice, entirely eliminated said James B. Parker from the part he is reported by the press to have played in this tragedy."

BILLY BUSTER & THE ENCHANTED HILL
1902

Fingy Conners was impressed as hell to say the least. But he just couldn't fathom removing himself all the way across the country so entirely, so isolated and so far away from all his businesses, especially considering the time and effort required to reach such a God-forsaken place.

The Buffalo newspaper publisher preferred his vacation resorts a bit closer to home and teeming with rich people and society celebrities. Conners didn't believe he could effectively supervise his varied empire from so far afield the way that William Randolph Hearst so confidently could. Fingy in order to rule needed to be there right in people's faces. His methods of persuasion were of a more primitive variety than Hearst's. And Mary and the girls, they would certainly hear none of it, spending any length of time way out here in the dust and heat, that's for sure, with all their fancy dresses, important parties and social obligations.

On the other hand, it did seem a perfect place for a boy. Little Billy would love it. Fingy imagined his son here with him as he slowly rocked on the veranda, the hawks circling overhead on the ascending thermals, the blue Pacific spreading its infinite azure volume far below, the silence of the place overwhelmingly peaceful. The Ranch was beginning to appeal to Fingy, all forty-eight thousand acres of it.

Its setting was undeniably spectacular. He could understand why Hearst had such a special place in his heart for it, this being his boyhood refuge and all.

The eighteen-room mansion on whose veranda Conners sat was a stunning edifice, a Victorian masterpiece, plunked down in the parched golden California hills right in the middle of nowhere. Its elegant period parlor was dominated by a huge formal oil portrait of Hearst's mother Phoebe.

The journey to get all the way up here from the harbor was taxing to say the least, even though the stunning sea of orange California poppies numbering in the millions through which the odyssey was made eased the eye, splotched here and there as it was with interruptions of deep blue-purple lupine. But as sore as he might have been feeling just about then, if he was serious about winning over W.R. with his master plan, Fingy had to endure the arduous trek no matter how long or how uncomfortable, and act like he enjoyed doing it.

Those last few miles though, climbing up along a hot, bumpy, spine-jarring narrow dusty trail in an imported horseless carriage had just about taken it all out of him. A time or two the car had inched too terrifyingly close to the edge for comfort. But now, though covered in dust, he was fine. Settled.

The automobile was a Marlborough steam engine chain drive, valued by Hearst at Rancho Piedra Blanca for its ability to climb a 25 percent grade. They did have to get out a few times to clear errant boulders from their path. The auto's canvas covering over his head kept that part of Fingy shaded, but his dark suit soaked up the broiling California sun, causing him to sweat considerably. His ruby face was now intensely crimson.

Reaching their destination it came as no great surprise when the laboring automobile slowed to a halt and Hearst's so-called "camp" turned out to be a spectacular eighteen-room California Colonial mansion. With six servants inside and God-knows how many scattered about the vast property, the house was surrounded by thousands of undulating acres of free-range cattle and exotic beasts from far-away continents.

Now as he rocked on the cool porch, sipping a lemonade, fog was beginning to roll in, blessedly. Its wispy fingers reached into the arroyos and canyons, tempering the mid-day's harsh rays, producing a soft light that muted the brazen yellows and silvery greens into translucent pastels.

The host stepped out of the front door and sized up his guest.

"Don't get too comfortable there, Conners," William Randolph Hearst commanded as authoritatively as his thin voice was able, gesturing as one of the Mexicans approached with three donkeys, fully saddled. Fingy rose unhappily from his shady refuge and just stood there a moment trying to fix his bearings.

Hell, no, he thought to himself.

"Ain't never rode no horse, W.R.," he balked.

"Well, these are donkeys Conners, better suited to the task. It's either this or walk. Believe me, you don't want to walk. Pancho will help you up. It's easy once you get the hang of it."

The ranch hand Pancho indicated that Fingy should put his foot in the stirrup, but Conners couldn't raise his leg up that high.

"Get him a stool, Pancho," said Hearst. "No. Wait. Rosamaria!" he called. "Bring the stool from the cocina!"

Out ran the cook with a small stool she used to reach the top shelves of the kitchen cupboards.

Once again, Fingy raised his leg and this time managed to hook his foot into the stirrup.

"Now, grab the saddle horn and pull yourself up," instructed Hearst.

Being minus a thumb, Fingy couldn't clutch like other people, so Pancho guided him, or rather, pushed him upwards. No one was more surprised than Conners when his ample butt landed in its intended place. He wanted to smile at his accomplishment, but the donkey was dancing sideways and he was terrified he was going to topple off.

"We'll take it slow, Conners. The donkeys know the way. Ven, Pancho."

Pancho hopped on his donkey and trailed a discreet distance behind.

Allowing Fingy's donkey to ride ahead as a setup for one of his favorite jokes, Hearst said, "My, my, Fingy, you certainly do have quite an attractive ass there! Would you let me ride it sometime?"

Conners couldn't help but laugh despite his physical agony.

They rode off on a slow amble while W.R. told stories about his father, his boyhood here at Rancho Piedra Blanca, his pet alligator George he had kept in his room at Harvard, and the many exotic animals he had collected and transported to the ranch as a diversion for himself, and hopefully, his future family with his new bride Millicent.

"Someday I want to bring in a few lions," he said matter-of-factly.

Fingy was too preoccupied by the struggle to remain sitting upright on his donkey to listen raptly.

"It helps to push down on the stirrups with your feet, as if you're ready to stand up. And don't fight the motion. Rock that big ass of yours back and forth in the same direction your other ass moves," he chuckled.

Fingy tried it and suddenly found himself more or less in rhythm with the animal. Just over the ridge appeared a series of fenced areas, each containing specimens Conners had only seen previously at the zoo or in pictures. There were zebras and ostriches, giraffes and ant eaters. The donkeys halted.

"Would you like to feed them?" Hearst asked.

"Nah. I mean, they're interestin' creatures 'n' all, but...don't they bite?"

"Sometimes," Hearst said. "You have to open your hand real wide and let them take the food, keeping your fingers well out of the way of those big teeth."

"Maybe some other time," Fingy demurred. What he was really thinking was that if he ever got down off this donkey he'd never get back up again, stool or no stool.

"My father purchased this spread back in '57, before I was born," said Hearst. "He was State senator from California, did you know that? Yep. He used to call me Billy Buster."

"Nope, didn't know that," answered the impressed dock walloper.

"Indeed. And this was our vacation home. He built the house some thirty-odd years ago, and we came up here every chance we got. God, I loved this place! All my best memories were here. Still are. I had a great childhood. The best. We'd all pack a big picnic and ride up to the highest vista point on the ranch, where the views are spectacular in all directions, and it's about 1600 feet clear down to the deep blue sea. The cool breezes manage to get caught right there at that exact spot and it is the most pleasant, the most idyllic location. Look," he said, pointing. "There it is, right up there. See? That's where we're headed next. Just wait, you'll love it."

Conners was feeling something akin to storm-tossed from the jolting and rocking of the donkey. He didn't relish riding all the way up to the top of the ridge currently being indicated at the tip of Hearst's finger.

They rode onward nonetheless. Soon the overpowering stench of chicken manure floated on the air currents and the murmur of thousands of hens created a combined sound something like an audience in a theater right before a performance.

"I have six thousand hens, Fingy," stated the tour guide. "We supply eggs and stewing chickens to markets all up and down the coast from Los Angeles to San Francisco. And we're expanding. You see, cattle eat a hell of a lot, and you need all this room that you see out there to raise 'em," he said, with a wide sweep of his long arms as if blessing all the distant hills and arroyos. The merciful fog had evaporated and the sun was now beating down full heat.

"But chickens, they don't take up much space at all, and pound for pound they can be just about as profitable as the beef. I know you couldn't raise cattle to this extent in New York, but chickens you could. Chickens make money, Conners. Chickens are good eating and they also produce eggs. The chicken earns a good profit. While you're

FINGY CONNERS AND THE NEW CENTURY

fattening them up they're laying eggs to help pay their rent. Everybody likes chicken and everybody eats eggs. Think about it. People have to eat."

Hearst's business tip struck a nerve. Fingy had always fancied the idea of someday becoming a gentleman farmer. That was the reason he'd bought that 350 acre lake front property back in Angola in New York. He just hadn't known exactly what to do with it until now.

They halted under the dappled shade of a Coast Live Oak with its rough bark and prickly leaves, the fallen litter crunching sweetly under the donkeys' hooves. It smelled lovely in the dry air and its shade was more than welcome. Fingy surveyed the chicken compound, a hamlet of neat coop houses furnished with nesting boxes arranged in tiers, the birds all nested in cozily. *Hmm. Tenement houses for chickens,* he thought to himself. He may have been looking at hens, but Fingy was suddenly seeing dollar bills.

"Hungry? Me too," said Hearst without waiting for an answer. "Let's head back to the house. Ever eaten tamales?"

Fingy held his breath. He might not have to endure the cruel journey all that way up to the Enchanted Hill after all.

"I'm pretty sure I had them things at the Pan American Exposition, at the Streets of Mexico village. Them was the mushy things wrapped in corn...corn paper?"

"Husks. You're thinking of corn husks. Yep. That's them. Maria makes marvelous tamales, all kinds. Wait 'til you taste 'em. And pasilla peppers, stuffed with queso. *Delicioso!*"

Fingy had no idea what the heck the man was talking about and didn't much care at this point. Arriving back at the house he was having as much a difficult time dismounting the donkey as he'd had climbing onto it. When his feet finally hit solid ground he winced at the stiffness in his inner thighs.

"That's a sure sign you're not spreadin' your legs apart often enough," Hearst guffawed.

Fingy was getting a little tired of the homo jokes.

"Don't be surprised if your shins are sore in the morning too," Hearst added, "and maybe your knees as well. Riding takes some getting used to. Let's have us an iced tea. Lunch is almost ready."

"Got nothin' stronger than tea or lemonade round here, Randy?" groused Fingy with a pained look.

"Certainly, Fingy. How's a Mexican beer sound?"

"Mexican? Can't you get no American brew out this way?"

Fingy Conners worshiped William Randolph Hearst—idolized him in fact. It was Hearst's template Fingy had adopted to chart the course of his own life. He'd hitched his wagon to Hearst and fully intended on riding the man's coattails into the White House.

When he'd first met W.R. in Chicago at the Fair of '93, Conners was immediately impressed with the thirty-year-old's boasting of his San Francisco newspaper. Hearst had revealed to him that he planned to soon purchase another in New York just as soon as he could find a suitable seller. Hearst planted a seed in Fingy that day, relating how through the ownership of newspapers he could mold public opinion and provide himself enormous political influence. Since then, Hearst also impressed upon Conners how he purchased the finest printing equipment to achieve the best reproduction, hired the best illustrators and photographers, and more importantly, the most popular writers of the day: Twain, London, Kipling and Creelman.

Fingy, anxious to make an impression, had chimed in, "Oh, one o' me best lads from me younger days worked for Mark Twain for a few years when Twain was the owner of the Buffalo Express."

"The Express. Yes. That *is* an interesting paper," Hearst said. Fingy took note.

Jim Sullivan would have had a damn good laugh knowing Fingy had elevated his status from "that crooked flat-foot" to "one o' me best lads."

What Fingy Conners had in common with William Randolph Hearst was a complete lack of interest in anyone's opinion of him or what he did, except for one example. Hearst had always openly conducted reckless dalliances with actresses and show girls beginning back in his teens. Unlike other men occupying his station in society who discreetly hid their mistresses, Hearst paraded his ladies around in public much to the horror of his family. For Willie-boy Hearst there was no need for the pretense of private dining rooms secreted away from prying eyes, nor covert bachelor apartments in lesser neighborhoods in which to engage in sexual dalliances. He lived openly with his girls and dined with them publicly at Delmonico's in New York or the American Dining Room at the Palace Hotel in San Francisco, which could accommodate 600 witnesses.

The thirty-five year old Hearst had up until recently been the gossip of New York for his very public five-year relationship with two underage chorus girls, sisters Millie and Anita Wilson, known on the naughty stage as the Sassafras Sisters.

It was said that the sisters' mother, Hannah Wilson, operated a New York brothel that was both Tammany-frequented and Tammany-protected. Worse, in 1903 Hearst married the then twenty-one-year-old Millie. Hearst's mother Phoebe, after waiting her son's entire life for him to grow up and come to his senses and take a suitable society bride, couldn't make it to the wedding; she forevermore shunned "Mrs. W." Millie's madame-mother. Fingy Conners was fascinated and envious, because this was the one example of Hearst's brazenness he dared not imitate.

William Randolph Hearst was credited with inflaming public opinion to explosiveness with his newspapers' false claim that the USS Maine had been blown up in Havana harbor by Spanish insurgents, giving birth to the battle cry, "Remember The Maine!"

Hearst in his newspapers called for war, but since he was not President, and the man who happened to be president at the time, William McKinley, was of a less impulsive sort than Hearst, McKinley did not act in response to Hearst's urgings. Hearst was infuriated and continued to mock, insult and rail against McKinley daily in his *New York Journal*.

The Maine falsehood greatly influenced the country into ultimately entering into War With Spain in 1898, a war from which both Hearst and Fingy Conners had profited handsomely. The terrible explosion on the *Maine* that claimed 250 lives was in truth accidental, but for Hearst's political and financial goals, his version of the story made for much more profitable copy.

The adventurer Teddy Roosevelt had sought and accepted a commission as lieutenant colonel in the U.S. First Volunteer Cavalry. His request accepted, he resigned his powerful position as Assistant Secretary of the Navy. As Assistant Secretary he had in fact conducted the office, and made startling strategic decisions on his own, just as the Secretary himself may have—had the Secretary not so much of the time been feeling ill or distracted or just plain disinterested. Why Teddy would leave such a powerful position to seek a military commission was not quite understood. Perhaps he had spent too much time commanding from behind a desk and longed to get his hands dirty.

Not to be outdone, Hearst wrote to President McKinley, the very same man Hearst had viciously denigrated in his newspapers, and offered at his own expense to equip a cavalry regiment of his own with which to enter into battle. When McKinley turned him down, Hearst then approached the Department of the Navy and offered his yacht *Buccaneer* fully armed and equipped at his own—or rather his mother's—expense, with himself as Commander.

Growing impatient as the Navy Department mulled over his offer, Hearst, without consulting the Department of the Navy or Congress or the President, took it upon himself to arrange to purchase a tramp steamer to sail through the Suez Canal where he would blow up the ship and sink it in place, effectively blocking further passage of the advancing Spanish fleet. Despite this being a violation of International law, the rogue warlord called off the plan when the Spanish armada was recalled and the plan for its intended passage through the canal canceled.

Willie Hearst was as obsessed with Teddy Roosevelt as Fingy Conners was with Willie Hearst. The difference was that Hearst hated Roosevelt for besting him at every turn and for continually being in his way politically. Teddy Roosevelt had graduated from Harvard with honors, whereas Hearst was kicked out for his failing grades due to his non-stop party-making and pranks. Roosevelt was just four years older than Hearst, yet by 1902 Teddy had already made himself a battle hero, the Governor of New York State, and now was President of the United States of America. Roosevelt had at present accomplished all that Willie ever wanted to, yet had none of it, and that made Hearst livid.

After Roosevelt had heroically charged up San Juan Hill with his colored Buffalo Soldiers, becoming a national icon in the process, Hearst sailed his yachts to Cuba, taking with him an Edison film crew, some close friends, and a gaggle of newsmen to engage in war irrespective of the fact the United States military did not sanction any such action.

An advance party sent earlier by Hearst and headed by famed journalist James Creelman had improbably rescued an eighteen year old beauty named Evangelina Cosio y Cisneros from a Cuban prison. She was the blameless daughter of an imprisoned insurgent, thrown into the dungeon, it was claimed, for rejecting the sexual advances of a licentious Spanish colonel. Hearst in his newspapers had made her a *cause célèbre*, bringing her to New York following her rescue to parade the freed captive through Manhattan's streets as she made her way to a huge Hearst-arranged rally at Madison Square Garden and a ball in the Waldorf Hotel's Red Room, followed by a reception with President McKinley at the White House. Hearst wanted people to know that W.R. Hearst didn't just publish the news; W.R. Hearst created the news.

Perhaps had Fingy Conners known the complete story of James Creelman, he might have not invested so heavily his own trust and aspirations in Hearst.

Hearst was quoted as saying of his world-famous journalist, "The beauty about Creelman is the fact that whatever you give him to do instantly becomes in his mind the most important assignment ever given any writer. He thinks that the very fact of the job being given him means that it's a task of surpassing importance or else it would not have been given to so great a man as he."

Creelman was said to have, upon meeting with him, lectured Pope Leo XIII on relations between Protestants and Catholics.

Hearst, preparing to personally head into war in Cuba as a soldier/journalist, wired Creelman in England to head for the embattled island to meet him there. He had sent his right-hand man Mr. Follinsbee ahead from New York, along with a dozen or so other *Journal* newsmen. Upon arrival in Cuba in his private yacht, Hearst connected with Creelman and Follinsbee and together they sought out a contingent of American soldiers advancing toward El Caney where the Spanish invaders held command over a stone fort, and joined them.

As they approached the fort, U.S. troops lay splayed on the ground so as to avoid the enemy's smokeless bullets. However, the less cautious Creelman, followed at a cautious distance by Hearst, decided on his own to forge ahead. It was told that Creelman was obsessed with capturing the Spanish flag.

"It was the thing I had come to get," Creelman stated afterwards. "I wanted it for the Journal. The Journal had provoked the war, and it was only fair that the Journal should have the first flag captured in the greatest land battle of the war. I looked up at the flag staff and found that the flag was not there. I rushed up to the Spanish officer and demanded the flag. He shrugged his shoulders and told me that a bomb had just carried it away. I was in terror lest someone else should get the precious emblem of victory first, so I hurried out the door to the verge of the hill, and there lay the red and yellow banner. Picking up the flag, I waved it viciously at the village and a volley from the main breast-works was the only reply."

Feeling an entitlement that Hearst's *Journal*, having been responsible for helping to incite the war to begin with, should be the first to capture the battle flag, Creelman waved it around in premature victory attracting considerable attention from the Spanish troops who promptly shot him. The bullet entered his shoulder and exited his back.

Hearst was thrilled.

Creelman wrote of the incident, saying that as he lay on the ground seriously wounded, bleeding, and in great pain, Hearst, wearing a "straw hat with a bright ribbon on his head, a revolver at his belt and a pencil and a notebook in his hand," leaned over him, face beaming, and said, "I'm sorry you're hurt but wasn't it a splendid fight? We must beat every paper in the world!"

Hearst then opened his notebook and took an interview with the grievously wounded Creelman. He scribbled his story into his notebook as Creelman moaned in torment waiting unavailingly for medical ministration. Then Hearst promptly abandoned him where he fell and boarded his yacht and set sail for Jamaica to telegraph his story to New York, deserting both Creelman and Fossinbee in the deadly chaos to fend for themselves.

On July 5, 1898 Creelman, not knowing where Hearst was or even if his letter might reach him, wrote,

"Dear Mr. Hearst,

After being abandoned without shelter or medicine and practically without food for nearly two days — most of the time being under constant fire — you can judge my condition. My shoulder was as you know. That I am here and alive is due simply to my own efforts. I had to rise from my litter and stagger seven miles through the hills and the mud without an attendant... Mr. Follinsbee stayed one night with me and got a fever. We are both here without clothes. I must get to the United States in order to get well. I expect no gratitude but I do expect a chance for my life.

Faithfully yours,
James Creelman

Later that year, in a very lengthy and lavishly illustrated feature in the *Review of Reviews Volume XVII* in which Creelman was hailed as a world-conquering adventurer, subtitled *The Hero As Journalist*, Creelman neglected completely to mention any bit of Hearst's abandonment of him and Mr. Fossinbee in Cuba. Feeling perhaps that continuing in the employ of the famously generous and well-paying Hearst was the more expedient goal, he thought better of revealing to the world what a capricious and fickle manchild Willie Hearst really was.

In the sixteen-page article, Creelman's description of the battle of El Caney and its personal outcome for him read vividly. Although most of his account of the harrowing aftermath rings true, Creelman's claim of the journalist himself valorously commanding the U.S. forces at the forefront of the battle, his tale accompanied by an elaborate illustration rendered in the epic heroic style depicting his aggressively leading the charge of the American army up the hill toward El Caney, reeked of pure hogwash.

Fingy Conners might have been provided a clue as to what he might personally expect from Hearst—if indeed he wanted one—by considering Hearst's vicious and virulent treatment of President McKinley, a man Conners admired. But Conners rather obviously chose to ignore the fact that Hearst had evaded a lynching at the hands of any number of mobs who held Hearst accountable for complicity in the President's assassination, not the least prominent of whom was President Theodore Roosevelt himself.

Fingy in fact had quite liked McKinley personally and had eagerly supported him to the point of requiring his entire force of dockworkers, numbering thousands of men, to march in a political parade on Presidential candidate McKinley's behalf, despite Conners and most of the workers being Democrats.

After their initial meeting in Chicago in 1893 Fingy wasn't able get Hearst's newspaper idea out of his mind. Conners was convinced that in order to get where he intended to go, he, like William Randolph Hearst, had to buy himself a newspaper.

So, in short order, he bought three.

Now here he was, ten years later, a guest of Hearst at his ranch in California. Hearst had recently decided to run himself for Congress from New York's 11th District. He didn't need a caucus or a convention or powerful friends to put his name in nomination because he owned the right newspapers. He simply declared himself a candidate in print. The people's candidate; independent of any political machine, free from any party Boss the likes of Democrat McCarren or Republican Hannah, beholden to nobody, able to finance his own campaign with his own money, or rather, his mother's, owing nothing to anybody else other than her.

His own New York newspaper glorified him, positioning him as a pro-labor, anti-corporation man, and began paving his way to attaining genuine Washington power.

This same path too was a longtime dream of Fingy's—winning, or stealing, a powerful political office for himself, and William Randolph Hearst was his ticket, at least for now. The two powerful New York newspaper publishers from opposite ends of the state agreed to a mutually beneficial alliance.

"After you win your Congressional seat, Randy, I wanna boom yous fer Governor," enthused Conners. "I got big plans of me own, and if you include me, I can promise you the governorship of New York. And after that, nothin' can stop yous from ownin' the key to 1600 Pennsylvania Avenue."

Hearst chuckled at Conners' hubris and at Fingy's underestimating his wild ambition; the entitled Hearst's plan was to run himself for President two years hence, in 1904.

"I'm way ahead of you, Conners," Hearst said, ambiguously.

W.R. sized him up as they sat eye to eye, concluding that this odd little thug may yet indeed prove himself to be of good use somewhere along the way.

He raised his iced tea glass and Fingy clinked his beer schuper against it.

"Great minds think alike," toasted the soon-to-be member of the United States House of Representatives.

"Better don't yous ferget it," replied the former saloon boss.

THE BURDICK MURDER
1903

Detective Sergeant Jim Sullivan looked around, memorizing the scene, taking in every detail.

Edwin L. Burdick, President of E.L. Burdick & Co. and the Buffalo Envelope Company and prominent member of the Elmwood Avenue social set lay dead on the sofa amid bits of skull.

The man was naked except for the solitary item of clothing that he wore, a blood-spattered undershirt, pulled up under his armpits. Multiple pillows had been placed under his crushed cranium. Others, blood-stained, were scattered about.

The wounds in his head, twelve in number, had been delivered with great force. A contusion at the front at the hairline seemed to be from the initial blow, with those at the side of the skull appearing to have been inflicted more seriously. The back of the head and the base of the skull contained a network of compound and multiple fractures, indicating that blow after blow must have been rained down upon the head in quick succession as he turned to flee from his attacker or to shield himself. The deadly flailing must have been applied with great strength and fury to have produced such onerous damage.

The pillows had absorbed a copious amount of the victim's life's blood; his dead body had been covered with pillows when the deed was complete. Over these was draped a beautiful Turkish rug.

The family physician, Dr. Marcy, the first to be summoned and the first to arrive on the scene, found Mr. Burdick's head wrapped in a quilt. He removed it to attend to him and placed the quilt at Mr. Burdick's feet, draping it over the arm of the couch. At the foot of the sofa on the floor in a heap lay Mr. Burdick's stockings, garters and underdrawers. Nothing of value seemed to be missing. Two of Mr. Burdick's fingers on his right hand were broken and bleeding, most likely the result of trying to shield himself from his attacker's murderous blows.

The theories already being spouted by Chief of Detectives Cusak and Detective Wright ignored evidence clearly visible that anyone with two eyes could see for himself, but Jim held his tongue.

The den was fancifully decorated with a profusion of Turkish rugs laid down on the highly-polished floor. Figured burlap covered the walls. The ceiling was hung with gold-flecked cloth swagged from the chandelier and fanning out toward the four walls which were decorated with oriental swords and other relics collected on world cruises. There were also some pictures of ballet dancers in color and photographs of several women acquaintances. The den served as the victim's smoking room.

Jim studied the remnants of a light repast that was arranged on the small table placed between two leather armchairs. A matching footrest lay overturned on its side. The top drawer in a table at the head of the couch where the body lay was left open. In the drawer were some letters, a few papers, and some odds and ends. More letters and papers were strewn about indicating they had been pulled from the drawer in haste and left where they landed. The detectives believed that certain papers or letters had been taken from the drawer.

Curtains had been ripped from the window. A small brown six ounce druggist bottle from a Washington Street liquor store was less than half filled with Manhattan cocktails. An emptied glass sat there as well, along with a platter of several partially-consumed pieces of Camembert cheese, a pile of tarts, and the new small square woven salty biscuits from the Niagara Falls shredded wheat company.

Hannah loves those, Jim noted to himself silently.

In the corner was propped a golf bag. Cusak examined it, asking Katie, the victim's maid, about it. She scrutinized the bag and noted that one of the golf sticks was missing.

"I cleaned in here yesterday afternoon, detective, and the putter was right here in the golf bag at that time. Now it isn't here."

The door of the den was of the pocket style that disappears neatly away into the wall. It had been found closed that morning by Maggie, the other servant, after she discovered Mr. Burdick's bed had not been slept in. The door of the den faced the front entry door of the fourteen-room house. The entry was discovered earlier by Maggie to be open to the winter cold. Blood was splattered on the inside portion of the den door. Maggie had also found a kitchen window opened as well.

Upstairs in Mr. Burdick's bedroom the bed remained neatly made, but clothing,

EDWIN L. BURDICK: VICTIM OF THE MYSTERIOUS ASHLAND AVENUE MURDER.

Mr. Burdick was found dead in his Turkish den, on the ground floor of his house at No. 101 Ashland avenue, about 8 o'clock on Friday morning, February 27th. He was lying on a divan, almost completely undressed, with a quilt and some rugs wrapped about him. The skull had been fractured and was almost pulverized in places by repeated blows, as if his assailant had continued the attack even after the victim was dead. Life had been extinct several hours.

including trousers and a shirt, lay discarded on the floor, as if he had quickly disrobed there.

Stepping outside the house, Jim scanned the neighborhood of beautiful residences along Ashland Avenue, one of the city's finer addresses, but the bucolic surroundings betrayed nothing hinting of the harrowing scene that was present inside No. 101, nor of the violence that preceded it.

In the house at the time of the murder were Mr. Burdick's mother-in-law, his three young daughters and two servant girls. Despite the horrible violence that took place in the den, no one had heard anything unusual the previous evening after retiring, nor any time during the night. The mother-in-law's name was Mrs. Marie Hull. Mrs. Hull insisted that Mr. Burdick hated Camembert cheese, and that it made no sense that it should be there at all. She also said that Mr. Burdick never drank liquor with food, that he always consumed his drink without accompaniment. He preferred martinis, and did not drink Manhattans, the cocktail contained in the bottle.

The den was a bit crowded. Detectives Cusak, Sullivan, Devine and Wright, Dr. Marcy, and Medical examiner Howland all had access to the body. Each examined the victim independently; the pillows, the clothing items, the papers, photographs. Things had been picked up and moved around from their original positions by each new examiner. Each detective independently went through Burdick's desk. The victim's coat was found draped over the back of a chair. Detective Wright went through the pockets, removing an envelope, papers, and a revolver—a 32 caliber, loaded.

Chief Patrick Cusak had retraced the scene independently of Jim Sullivan. When both had finished they compared notes. Cusak asked his detective, "So what're we thinkin' here, Sully?"

Jim Sullivan was a stickler for fine detail, which is why Cusak had grabbed him when the call came in. Dogged and determined, Jim was willing to invest whatever shoe leather it might require to track down clues.

"Pat, I'm inclined to consider that Mr. Burdick was upstairs undressin' himself for bed when he was called downstairs by a knock soft enough so's not to wake nobody else, if we're to believe the story that nobody in the house heard nothin'. Considerin' the deadly violence that went on here, I'm findin' it difficult to believe that none of the six women in this house woke up. That in itself is pretty suspicious. He didn't shout or cry out? How's that possible, unless he was surprised from behind and disabled by the very first blow? I believe he must've been expectin' this person's visit, and it must've been initially friendly, judgin' by the food and drink here, and the fact his pistol was tucked away. Otherwise I don't imagine he'd feel comfortable comin' downstairs in his underclothing to admit an unexpected caller."

"Sully, with his mother-in-law and three daughters in the house doesn't it seem odd that he wouldn't just at least put his trousers on? Or a robe? I mean, if he was in the middle of undressin' anyways? Evidently he admitted the caller, who he most assuredly knew well enough to allow that individual to see him in his underwear. I know these folks are different from you and me, but..."

Jim picked up the Chief's thought.

"...but who runs around the family home in their underwear, fixin' food and drinks for a midnight visitor when all their female family members are just steps away? My kids ain't never seen me in *my* underwear, Pat."

"Me neither, Sully."

The medical examiner, Dr. Howland, was still appraising the scene. He examined the quilt that Dr. Marcy had found wrapped thrice around the victim's head.

"Why would the killer stop and take the time to wrap up Burdick's head? Was he tryin' to save him after the fact, tryin' to bandage it?" wondered Cusak, appraising the bloody quilt.

"Only someone who cared about the man might do such a thing," said Sully. "Burdick for sure knew his killer, intimately so it seems to me, judgin' by this gesture. A robber woulda run right outa here lickety-split. This killer took the time to wrap Burdick's damaged bloodied head and place pillows underneath. Maybe the killer had second thoughts and tried to stop the bleedin'."

"You mean he was still alive after this wallopin'?"

"I'd say so," replied Sully. "Why bandage a dead man?"

"Then, maybe it's not a bandage after all, but just a way to muffle any sounds Burdick was makin' as he died, to provide the killer more time to get away," theorized Cusak.

Sullivan nodded his approval at that possibility.

"Oh. Looky here," Dr. Howland said.

The medical examiner had lifted the bloody quilt. Underneath lay a pair of Mr. Burdick's neatly folded trousers.

"Hmm. So maybe he wasn't runnin' around in his underwear after all. He might've undressed right here, Sully."

THE FIRST WARD II

"Unless someone undressed him after the fact," countered the detective. Sully didn't think that made sense, but kept it to himself.

They looked over the trousers carefully. There was blood spattered on the walls, the couch and the man's undershirt, but none was apparent on the trousers. Not even after having been covered by the bloodied quilt.

"So," said Jim, "Burdick may have not been in his underwear when he admitted the killer."

"Can we be certain?" asked the Chief. "We can suppose that because his clothes have been removed that he was the one who removed them. That leads to a conclusion that a woman might be the killer. Or, what if the killer was a clever man who arranged things to appear as if a woman had been here? Burdick's underwear could've been removed after he was dead rather than before."

Cusak and Sullivan looked over the body once again to reassess.

"Look there," said Sullivan, pointing. "Blood."

"Sully, there's blood everywhere, man."

No, I mean there on his leg. On both legs. Looks like thumb prints to me."

"Holy shit," whispered Cusak, his mind churning. "It looks like the killer grabbed him there with bloody hands, then...pulled him away from the head of the sofa. See how much blood is pooled in this spot up here?" he said, indicating the arm of the sofa, "and how little is evident under where his head's now restin'? Burdick was moved once he was disabled."

Sullivan picked up the white underdrawers and inspected them inside and out. No blood. Not a speck.

"Since the bloody thumb markings are in a place that would have had to come in contact with his underwear as they were slipped off him," Sullivan said, "and there's no blood anywheres on the underdrawers, then that could only mean he was already naked when the thumb markings were left there."

Cusak was becoming quite exasperated, sighing heavily with frustration as he reconsidered all the evidence gathered thus far, some of it in opposition and none of it adding up to anything conclusive. It was all very confounding, in fact.

"Beats me, Sully. All the evidence indicates to me that a woman was here. If this meal is some contrivance, as the old lady's opinions about it might indicate, a diversion created after the killing took place, that tells us that the killer was not only intimately familiar with the floor plan of this house and where things were kept, but that they did not take their escape immediately after the crime, or felt they needed to, as would any usual killer. So maybe the killer is still right here in the house. Maybe Burdick attacked the maid and she let him have it."

"Sorry Pat, I just don't see any actual evidence at all here that supports a conclusion that a woman killed Burdick, or that a woman was even present. There's evidence, and then there's circumstance. The meal, the naked state of the man—these aren't evidence, these are just circumstances, perhaps intentionally set up here to confuse things, to mislead us."

"Hmm. Not so sure I agree, Sully," countered Cusak a bit sullenly.

The Chief assessed the food arrangement again and recalled the doubts that Mrs. Hull had voiced about the items. "She stated her son-in-law hated this kind of cheese, and also that he never drank while eatin' food, nor did he drink this kind of cocktail."

Something didn't look right to him about it, the way it was all arranged, but he couldn't say exactly what.

Cusak summed up his thoughts thus far.

"Okay. This is what I got. The killer first caved in Burdick's head, splatterin' blood everywhere includin' all over hisself, then afterwards he felt confident enough that no one had woke up to then go into the kitchen, wash off the blood and fix this meal, and bring it back here to the scene? That makes no sense. None o' this makes no sense. What kind o' killer would not wanna immediately take his escape after the deed—especially with so many people present in this house? How could the killer be so certain no one in the house heard nothin' and that nobody'd be comin' down them stairs to investigate?

"Maybe after the deed was done," continued the Chief, "he was ready to run right outa here, but paused first to listen at the doorway and make sure no one was about to come downstairs and investigate who might recognize him leavin'. But, findin' no sign anybody'd heard nothin', he calmed hisself and then set about coverin' his tracks."

"Or, as you already suggested, it was someone who was already livin' in this here house," chimed in Jim. "What about the old lady? She's actin' mighty secretive and she's not sayin' much. And where's the wife by the way?"

"And why is this man naked?" Cusak wondered again, obviously thinking that this detail held the key. "Did he take his own clothes off, or did somebody else? They say Burdick loved the ladies, so I don't think he would disrobe for a male visitor, Sully.

There are trousers and a coat here with no blood on them, as well as clean trousers and a shirt on his bedroom floor upstairs. So, which outfit was he last dressed in? And do we think a woman really could've done this much damage to him, especially an old lady? His skull is destroyed. That tells me there was an enormous amount of anger rained down upon this man. So we got to find out who in his life was so angry with him. Angry enough to inflict this degree of rage to his head."

"With blood, brains and bone fragments splattered about the room here," surmised Sullivan, "the killer would have had to be similarly covered. Yet no blood can be found elsewhere in the kitchen or anywheres else in the house. How did someone covered in blood and brains go into the kitchen and fix this meal without leaving a trace?"

They proceeded toward the kitchen again and examined the kitchen sink to see if there was evidence of blood that may have been washed off there. There was none.

Cusak just shook his head. It was all so very perplexing.

"Looks only one way to me, Sully. Sex. It has to be sex. What else could it be? Who takes off their stockings, garters, and trousers during a midnight luncheon with a casual visitor—and then folds them neatly? If Burdick had been in the heat of passion, then the clothes would be strewn about willy-nilly."

"And if the killer took them off him after the fact, why would they fold them neatly, managing to get no blood on them?" countered Sullivan. "And what woman could overpower him, Pat? He looks to be an able-bodied man."

Jim glanced over at the drinks again.

"Maybe the drinks were spiked, and when he fell under the influence, maybe that's when the killer took his chance grabbin' the golf stick and whalin' on the poor bastard from behind. He was stunned, too stunned to cry out, and his bein' sedated, the killer let loose with a furious barrage that quickly disabled him before he could even make a sound. We need to have this glass checked for somethin' that might have been added. A sedative of some sort."

"There's no sign of the missing golf stick anywhere," added Cusak. "Maybe the killer took it away. We need to search the grounds outside."

"Well, these wounds might have been inflicted with a golf iron, Pat, a nine iron maybe, but not a hefty putter. The indentations in his skull are too narrow and too deep into the bone. A putter would make a much wider impact wound, befitting its large girth."

"Okay," exhaled the stymied Chief. "How about we go ask the old lady a few questions?"

Cusak led his detectives out of the room, leaving medical examiner Howland to continue with his work.

The grandmother was in the parlor, huddled on the couch with her three granddaughters.

"Mrs. Hull, we have some questions," said Cusak, catching her eye, then nodding toward the children. Mrs. Hull took the hint and asked the girls to go up to their room. She rang for the cook. "Keep an eye on the girls, Maggie."

Detective Cusak asked Mrs. Hull where Mrs. Burdick was.

"My daughter is in Atlantic City," curtly responded the dead man's mother-in-law.

"Atlantic City? How long has she been there?"

"Oh, since a few weeks before Christmas."

"We're at the end of February presently, Mrs. Hull. These girls have not seen their mother in all that time?"

"No," she answered without emotion or concern.

"She didn't spend Christmas with her own children?"

"No."

"Were Mr. and Mrs. Burdick having marital problems, Mrs. Hull?"

"Yes. Edwin ordered my daughter to leave the house."

"And yet *you* still live here?"

"Yes, of course. Someone has to raise these girls."

"So you have a good relationship with your son-in-law despite the fact he ordered your own daughter out of the house?"

"Yes. In fact, Mr. Burdick called me mother," she noted.

"How do you account for that?"

She formed an inscrutable smile. "I don't know if I *have* to account for that, now do I, officer?"

The servants had discovered the double-hung kitchen window open that morning. Police would later note that the snowdrift that lay piled on the outside sill had not been at all disturbed or imprinted. The window thus appeared to have been opened from the inside, perhaps a ruse employed by the killer to mislead police into thinking that the house had been broken into.

Sullivan took a closer look.

"How do we know that this snow didn't fall here after someone had already come through this window?" postulated the Detective. "This is a big house. Someone could have climbed through the window much earlier in the evening and hidden themselves, down in the basement, or in a closet, waiting for their opportunity."

The cook, Maggie Murray, was questioned at length next. She was told to start her story from the beginning. She stated that once she'd discovered that his bed had not been slept in, she searched the house looking for Mr. Burdick, but could not find him anywhere. When she slid open the door to the den she discovered it to be in such disarray that she was immediately frightened. Mrs. Murray said she saw what appeared to possibly be a human form under the rug and pillows, lying prostate on the couch. She did not endeavor to approach it.

Instead, Mrs. Hull was summoned.

Hull stated she went to the den and called out loudly, "Ed! Ed!" but after receiving no response she said, "Maggie, I fear something's happened. I do not dare go in there. We've got to call Dr. Marcy! Go!

Dr. Marcy was the family physician.

Despite the presence of Mr. Burdick's clothing in the den where his body was found, Detective Cusak nevertheless gave a contrary statement later that afternoon to the newsmen that had gathered:

"From what investigations I have made I would conclude that Mr. Burdick was called down stairs by a ring or a knock at the door after he was ready for bed, for he was clad only in his underclothing. He had evidently admitted someone he knew well and took the visitor into the den for a talk and to partake of the luncheon found there."

***

Arthur Reed Pennell was up and about quite early on the morning following the murder.

"Lizzie," the esteemed attorney said to his servant, "I do not want you speaking to anyone about me or Mrs. Pennell."

To anyone else this might seem an abrupt directive, but Lizzie Romance was quite used to it. The Pennells had an odd relationship and conflicting statements and requests made by her employers over the years had inured Lizzie to their unique ways. She simply did as she was told. Even if there was no good reason for it, it no longer interested her to wonder why. It was easier to just to do.

A knock came at the door. Lizzie looked to Mr. Pennell. "I'll answer that, Lizzie. You attend to your work."

Mr. Pennell opened the door and found the furnace man, Mr. Porter, making his usual Friday morning call to perform his duties.

"Oh, Mr. Porter. I do apologize. I already attended to the furnace earlier. Your services won't be needed this week."

That was the first time in the two years since the furnace man had been attending to the Pennell's convenience that Mr. Pennell had gone and cleaned out the ashes himself. Ashes which might have contained remains of the burning of bloody clothing.

Pennell got himself dressed and ate breakfast. Afterward he changed into a suit and went out to the garage, climbed into his runabout, and exited down the narrow driveway silently in his green Baker Electric. He nearly clipped a woman walking down the sidewalk, her arms laden with packages. He didn't bother to sound his horn, nor did he touch the brake. Mr. Pennell was decidedly of the type who expected the world to make way for him.

He drove downtown to the Iroquois Hotel barber shop for a trim and a shave. Afterward he walked down Main Street a short way to Walbridge's to buy a gun. It was noon.

E. W. Fox was in charge of the firearms department in Walbridge's store. Two other clerks, named Edmunds and Boehler, were also present as Pennell entered their department. Pennell walked hurriedly past them up to the east end of the store where the revolver case was located and said to Mr. Fox, who was behind the counter, "Give me a cheap revolver."

His manner was nervous, abrupt and strange. He did not exchange the usual greetings with those present, whom he knew quite well. Pennell merely glanced at a weapon that caught his eye and not even asking to examine it said "That one will answer. How much is it?"

Mr. Fox told him that the price was $5. Pennell pulled some bills out of his pocket and paid for it. While waiting for the revolver to be wrapped up, Pennell paced up and down in a highly nervous fashion wringing his hands. When the revolver was delivered to him he took it and hurried out the store without saying another word. After he left, Mr. Fox said to Boehler and Edmunds, "Did you notice how queer Mr. Pennell was acting? He seemed to be in a remarkable hurry, didn't he? And he didn't purchase any bullets. Odd, that."

Pennell walked back to his automobile. From there he drove down Kensington Ave. toward the city line, considering his situation as he went. The huge pit that was the Hannah Gehres Stone Quarry caught his eye for a moment. Before too long he arrived at the automobile factory. He explained a problem he was having with the Baker to the agent, who directed a mechanic to take the car. Mr. Burdick was led into the waiting area after asking to use the telephone.

"Might you have today's newspapers for me to read?" he asked.

"Sorry sir, no. All we have are those issues of Colliers that you see there on the table."

Carrie Pennell had mentioned to her husband that she was anxious to see the ice scenery at Niagara Falls before the approaching spring caused it to disappear, and asked him the previous week if they might go together. The repairs on the Baker would take the entire day, so Pennell conceived the idea of taking the urban railway car to Niagara Falls and have Carrie meet him there.

When she came to the phone he said, "Darling, why don't you take the express car to Niagara Falls and I will meet you there, and we can see the ice scenery together?"

Carrie was elated. Any time Arthur might spend with her rather than at his office, or with Alice Burdick, gave her renewed hope for holding on to her troubled marriage.

She stopped and bought all the newspapers detailing the murder of their friend Edwin Burdick the previous night, then boarded the car.

Pennell met his wife at their Niagara destination at about 3 o'clock, whereupon they set out for Prospect Point. He was preoccupied but pleasant. She knew his moods and patiently waited for this one to pass. They always did, eventually. They walked past the Prospect House, the handsome couple enjoying the admiring glances of the sightseers whose attention was momentarily stolen away from the frozen spectacle by their fine appearance. The Pennells decided before eating that they would first appraise the falls.

Carrie and Arthur made their way along Prospect Point in tiny steps, for the walkway was smooth as glass with a solid paving laid down by the freezing of the ceaseless mists that descended upon everything. The danger of slipping and falling was imminent. The rails at the edge of the precipice were encased in a thick armor of transparent ice many inches thick. Months of below-freezing temperatures had transformed the relentless spray of Niagara, thickly enveloping the trees, buildings, railings and walkways, turning the area into a fairyland of wonder. Bizarre sculptures created by Mother Nature dotted the landscape where telegraph poles, fences, hydrants and other man-made objects normally stood, their likenesses transfigured by a formidable encasement of ice.

Carrie wanted to take the footbridge out to Goat Island mid-river, but the pathway was too hazardous, her husband thought, and the distance too far to cover before dark, so Arthur convinced her instead to return to the warmth of the Prospect House and a pleasant window table by the flaming hearth. The waiter brought the menu. Arthur studied the cover, an illustration of a naked woman suspended in midair supporting herself within the arc of a rainbow created by the Falls' mists.

They enjoyed a lovely dinner together in the octagonal dining room beneath the dome. Carrie had the Restigouche Salmon Hollandaise with a wax bean salad and banana pudding for dessert. Arthur ordered the fried and breaded Lamb in Tomato Sauce, green peas, and fried eggplant, and no dessert. They decided on a quart of Claret but didn't finish it. Afterwards Arthur carefully studied each newspaper's account of the previous night's murderous activity on Ashland Avenue for any clues as to what the police might have discovered, if any.

His initial assessment from his perspective as an attorney was that already at this early stage the Buffalo police were proving themselves, as always, reliably incompetent.

That was a relief.

The papers stated that the police suspected the murderer was a lone woman. A police officer had spotted a lone woman out walking at one o'clock in the morning, just a block from the Burdick home. At the time, even though the officer recognized how unusual and risky it was for a female by herself to be walking the icy streets at that hour, he did not approach to stop or speak to her, but was nonetheless absolutely certain now, despite the sight distance and the darkness and the fact she was heavily bundled against the freezing cold, that he could absolutely identify her if he ever saw her again.

Pennell scoffed as he read that the police had already targeted this poor woman as their killer and were now hell bent on finding her.

"Typical of those amateurs!" he sniffed.

HOME INVASION
MARCH 1, 1903

As thousands of spectators milled past the murder house all day long on Ashland Avenue, a modest funeral service took place inside on the last day of February. It was presided over by Rev. L.H. Powers, pastor of the First Universalist Church where the late Mr. Burdick had a pew.

Late that evening, once the Ashland crowds had thinned, Burdick's body was removed to Koch & Drullard's undertaking rooms. Unnerved by the throngs of people milling outside her home, Mrs. Alice Burdick arranged for her late husband's body to be obscurely transported from the undertaker to the New York Central Station the following morning and placed on a car headed for Syracuse, shielded from the eyes of the curious.

The following morning, Sunday March 1st, after a sleepless night, Alice Burdick, her mother Mrs. Hull, the three Burdick daughters Marion, Carol and Alice, and the two servants, Katy and Maggie, arose before daylight on that saddest of days. They left their grieving home for the depot to take the 7 o'clock train.

They boarded a car to accompany Mr. Burdick's remains to Canastota N. Y. for burial in the family plot. They were met at their destination at the Canastota depot by Edwin Burdick's mother, Harriet Lewis Burdick. It had always been the custom of Ed Burdick to give much to the wants of his mother. Harriet Burdick was certainly going to miss that. Ed Burdick's father Henry, a wealthy farmer, had predeceased him some years earlier. Also present at the depot were his sister Mrs. A.J. Willet and various neighbors.

As the family stood together at Mount Pleasant Cemetery it seemed a natural inclination that each member, compelled by circumstance, might be wont to contemplate her own demise. Alice Burdick imagined her three daughters sometime in the future, much older and with their own families, standing at her gravesite saying their last good-byes to their elderly mother. Little did she realize then that it would be she who would be standing at her daughter Marion's grave at Forest Lawn Cemetery just eight years hence.

After the graveside service, the family turned right around again and returned to Buffalo the same afternoon.

That same day, Sunday, Chief Cusak led officers on a search of the homes of Attorney Arthur Reed Pennell, insistently named by Burdick's business partner Mr. Parke as the illicit lover of the murdered man's wife and probable murderer of Mr. Burdick.

As well, they conducted a search of Mrs. Seth Paine's home, the outrage of her domicile based on nothing better than the police having seen a signed photo of Mrs. Paine in the murdered man's den. The police spent far more time at Mrs. Paine's home than they did the Pennells', having convinced themselves of the simple logic that a female acquaintance who mingled with the Burdicks socially was more likely the murderer than the adulterous attorney who was fucking Burdick's wife.

The lawmen virtually ransacked Mrs. Paine's home from garret to basement, finding nothing of value to the case.

Late that night, after an arduously lengthy day of great strain without rest, prostrated in mind and body with saddened hearts, the Burdick family returned from the train depot to their lonely and shadowed fatherless home. The household quickly retired, the weak and suffering women and children seeking some respite from the shock and sorrow of the previous few days in the sleep of the exhausted.

A certain faction, led by Detective John Wright, he having eagerly adopted an early theory originally proposed by Detective Jim Sullivan, was of another mind. Wright was convinced that the killer of Edwin L. Burdick was one of those women residing in the Burdick home on Ashland Avenue. Rogue officer Wright devised a breathtaking plan to force the culprit's hand.

That night at midnight as the bone-weary and depleted occupants deeply slept, and while Ashland neighbors still unnerved by recent events tossed and turned, a sizable army of Buffalo's Finest, led by Detective Wright, quietly crept up to the Ashland Ave. house and completely surrounded it.

Upon Wright's command, each man took his club and began pounding the side of the house full force in a deafening, terrifying staccato attack. Simultaneously the front doorbell was rung loudly without cessation and the front door was shaken and rammed violently as if trying to force an entrance to the house. Loud blows resounded through the grieving home from the beating of clubs at the side door and all along the home's perimeter upon the clapboards.

Inside, the children awakened in absolute terror to the thunderous clatter of dozens of nightsticks slamming and violently shaking the house. They screamed and cried. Their elderly grandmother was horrified by the vibrations and the pandemonium, thinking it at first to be an earthquake. The servants scurried in sheer panic up the stairs to cower with the female family as Mrs. Alice Burdick cradled her girls in her arms against the bizarre onslaught. Only when Maggie the cook was ordered to look out the window was it discovered the attack was being conducted by uniformed officers normally charged with protecting a grieving and vulnerable family rather than terrorizing it.

Led by a detective better known for his troubled personal life and excessive drinking than his crime-fighting expertise, Wright had become convinced that the women in the house were hiding the truth of what had really happened, intentionally making fools out of his police department.

Alice Burdick ordered the traumatized maid Katie to go down to the front door and demand to know what this assault was all about. At the same time Alice ran to the telephone to call the police to demand emancipation from the renegade band.

The women waited together expecting to be rescued from the blue mob, expecting the good cops to race up Ashland Avenue at any moment to rout the bad cops and berate the thugs for doing such a horrible thing to an already shocked and stunned family, a family no longer having any man living in the house to protect them.

But no good Samaritans showed up.

When Katie opened the door a crack to commence her exchange with the terrorists, she was knocked to the floor by the human wave of the invading army, who forced the door and stepped on her as if she were no more than an obstruent dog.

The officers began shouting loudly for Mrs. Burdick and the elderly Mrs. Hull to show their faces. When they appeared at the top of the stairs the police rushed up to grab them and drag them off to the No. 14 police station. Upon remonstrating, they were forced out the door in their nightclothes into the freezing cold.

Frantic, Mrs. Burdick screamed and cursed at the police. Ashland Avenue neighbors cowered behind window curtains, shocked and filled with fear and horror, disbelieving what they were seeing and hearing from their hiding places.

"We've just buried the father of these poor children," Alice Burdick protested, "and we and they are exhausted and spent. Leave us alone! What on God's earth is wrong with you?"

"You just come with us, now. Stop fighting, woman!" demanded Wright.

The grandmother too pleaded, asking that the police defer their arrest until morning, promising that the women would come in to the station of their own accord once they had arranged for the children to be cared for.

Wright was in a fit of adrenalin-fueled fervor at this point and unstoppable, the scene he was instigating clearly some panacea for the unresolved troubling circumstances clouding his own life.

At the police station, there in the early hours of the morning, Mrs. Hull and Mrs. Burdick were subjected to all the ingenuities of the "third degree." Finally, after several hours of inquiries, and forbidden by the police under threat of incarceration from contacting their attorneys Hartzell & Hartzell, they were permitted to return to their violated home.

Without any apology whatsoever, their bizarre invasion, the police later justified, was intended to shock the inhabitants into revealing the truth of the matter, somehow it never dawning on the assaulting Neanderthals that quite the opposite effect, on both the women as well as the entire city, might well be the result.

The women were now all thoroughly mortified and hysterical, understandably so, and would be furthermore and lastingly untrusting and fearful of any and all authority for the duration of the entire investigation.

Somehow the press would not find out about this stunning attack for many weeks to come. The distant, oddly-paralyzed personalities displayed by the members of this family, outraged and irreversibly damaged at the hands of the Buffalo Police Dept., would from this point forward have the cruel light of public judgment and scrutiny unjustly shined upon them by a sensational press and an ignorant judgmental public, totally unaware of what absolute hell the police had visited upon this house that awful Sunday night.

Once the Burdicks had returned home from the police station, Alice tried to comfort Marion, her eldest daughter, age sixteen. Marion grunted as she violently pushed her mother away, causing her to stumble backwards and fall to one knee. Then she slapped her mother soundly across the face. As she stalked furiously out of the room she vomited just one single expletive without looking back.

"Whore!"

❦❧❦❧

The March 1st and 2nd issues of the *New York Times* ran two unflinchingly resolute headlines based on the Buffalo police's baseless conclusions: BURDICK MURDERED WITH A GOLF CLUB and BURDICK WAS KILLED BY A WOMAN, despite there being no proof whatsoever to support either determination.

Hannah Sullivan stood behind her drapes, watching and waiting. Once the Alderman had left for work and disappeared up the street, she walked next door to visit Annie. Devoting many pages to the murder, Hannah delighted in reading aloud from the newspapers to Annie as she readied herself and her children for their busy day. Hannah was enthused about helping out next door, lonely now that little David, her and Jim's youngest, was now in school.

She began reading: "The finding of the steel-tipped golf stick with which it is almost certain that Mr. Burdick was killed and the fact that the bone in Burdick's skull was found by the medical examiner to be remarkably thin, make it more reasonable to suppose that the crushing blows upon Burdick's head could have been delivered by a woman."

Hannah looked up from her newspaper with mouth comically agape. She was appalled.

"Are they joking, Annie? A *woman*? Jim told me that Burdick's wife was having an affair with her attorney, and yet that particular suspect is being completely overlooked here? And how do they conclude the golf club was definitely the murder weapon at all? Based on what? And just because there's cheese sitting there and the man's skull bone is thin, that's proof to them that a woman killed him? Makes me embarrassed for Jim to have to work with these tomfools, let me tell you. You and I could do a better job than these idiots."

She went back to her reading.

"Oh, my heavens! Listen to this."

Patrolman Meyers claims he saw a mysterious woman walking on the east side of Ashland Ave. at about one o'clock in the morning and concluded that her direction indicated she had come from or past the Burdick home. As she neared the corner where Meyers stood he said she turned out into the middle of the street staying in the middle of the road for some long distance past the policeman. He did not stop her, yet he claimed he got a good idea of her appearance.

"It's the middle of the night, in the middle of the week, and this Meyers fool sees a woman out alone at that hour and doesn't approach her to talk to her, to see if she might be alright? To ask if she could be lost or in trouble? To ask why she's out in the freezing cold and dark all alone? Isn't that the very reason we have patrolmen on the beat out on our streets at one o'clock in the morning in the first place, Annie? And because this woman looks...*looks?* ...as if she might be coming from the general direction of the murder house, that's conclusive proof to the police now that she's Burdick's murderer? There's not a word printed in any of these newspapers about the attorney that Burdick's wife was having her way with. My Lord! It's all so idiotic that it sends me into deep despair, Annie, thinking we're counting on these knuckleheads to be in charge of our city. To protect us. Instead, they're obscuring the most obvious culprit, and as a diversion have invented from out of nowhere a chain of assumptions, each based entirely on the silly theory that preceded it, and the end result is absolute chaos."

Annie did what she always did whenever Hannah got this worked up over something. She tilted her head and reprimanded her by contorting her mouth into a shape that conveyed, *are you listening to yourself?*

"Hannah, Jim's *your* husband—not mine. Why not tell him how stupid Buffalo's police detectives are? Go ahead. See where that lands you."

Their laughter was as much about the unlikelihood of such a provocation as it was regarding the foolishness of the male gender.

"Female detectives, that's what this city needs!" declared the budding suffragette.

"Men are idiots," summed up Annie, categorically.

FEMALE TROUBLE
MARCH 4, 1903

The *New York Times* printed "It is still believed by many laymen that the police as of yet are utterly at sea in the case, although Superintendent Bull is quoted as saying an arrest—the arrest of a woman—may occur at any moment."

Sixteen-year-old Marion Burdick had not spoken ten words to her mother for over a year now, not since that dreadful day she had secretly followed her to the house at No. 123 Seventh Street.

There, Arthur Pennell awaited to throw her mother down and lustily ravage her. It was right after the new year, when her mother, vainly attempting to make up for her many long absences from the household, had just hosted a dance in Marion's honor the day after Christmas, 1901. Alice made sure that her extraordinary gesture toward her daughter was noted prominently on the *Buffalo Express'* Society Page for all to see.

Marion suspected that her mother had been betraying her beloved father for quite some time, but never expected it to go on for as long as it did. She had hoped her mother would tire of the dangerous adventure and return home so that they might all become a real family once again. Marion was biting her nails to the quick and the younger girls wetting their beds. Only Marion was old enough to recall when there existed true happiness in this house, when she often saw her father and mother kiss each other longingly. She could not recall the last time her stomach was not tied in knots as she walked up the front sidewalk, home from school.

Nevertheless, Marion was not prepared under any circumstance for what her young eyes would witness when she peeked through the window that day at No. 123.

She had grown angry in light of her mother's increasing disrespect and heartlessness toward her father, whom Marion worshiped. At the same time, her mother was removing herself from the entire family, from her own mother, her own daughters, abdicating the entire care of her children and the household. Marion's mother was never home anymore when her daughters returned from school. On weekends she would disappear from the family house in the morning and not reappear until evening, or sometimes not until Monday. She disappeared on Thanksgiving, her empty chair at the dinner table a painful reminder. She would disappear often for a week or more at a time to travel to New York, New England and other destinations.

To the girls it seemed almost as if their mother had died.

Marion observed her father closely during her mother's demoralizing absences, waiting for him to do something about the situation. She was both mystified and enraged that he seemed not to even take notice. He never commented or wondered aloud where his wife might be. Both he and Grandmother acted as if it wasn't happening, despite the obvious bleak moods being suffered by Marion and her sisters. Perhaps in compensation during this unsettling time Father became even more loving and attentive toward his daughters as too did Grandmother toward her son-in-law.

Marion's father these days spent much time in solitude and contemplation when he was in the house, sending the girls off to do their homework after dinner, when all his daughters really wanted and longed for was the comfort of a caring parent's interest and company.

A few times Marion had sneaked up when she saw the pocket door to his den not fully slid closed and peeked through the gap. There she watched him for many long minutes, smoking, staring into space, sipping his drink, drumming his fingers, the veins in his forehead bulging, his pale white face contorted into a morose frown mirroring his unspoken loss and resignation.

She hated her mother for doing this to him. For doing this to all of them.

One day, when her father had gone to Indianapolis on business, Mother had the brazen audacity to invite Arthur Reed Pennell into the house for dinner with the family. Outrageously, she sat him at the head of the table in Father's customary place. Grandmother was furious, hardly taking a bite throughout dinner. After the meal was finished, Grandmother told the servants to take the girls up to their rooms to do their homework. Then Grandmother laid into her daughter with a fury over her having become so extravagantly reckless.

"What sort of example do you think you are setting for your girls, Allie, might I ask? You bring this strange man here into their father's own house and introduce him to the girls as if this were not the most immoral, improper, heinous thing imaginable for a mother to do? I am warning you, my daughter. You are destroying your family.

You have betrayed your children tonight even more terribly than you have double-crossed your own husband. You have brought your sin into the only safe haven these girls have ever known, ruining it. Rubbing their innocent young faces in it. And mine as well.

"I don't know you anymore, my Alice. What kind of daughter does such a thing to her own mother? Your kind, sweet Ed takes care of me. I am getting old. Ed has taken me generously into his home and treats me as if I were his own mother. He provides a home for me here with my grandchildren. He has been a profound blessing to me. I should be the happiest woman in the world, and I would be if not for your shameful obsession. Yet this is how you have chosen to go about living your life, with no regard at all for any of us. Your selfishness is appalling. I fear that Marion will actually come to hate you, if she does not do so already. You are the very embodiment of a narcissist, my child."

All throughout the grandmother's tirade Arthur Reed Pennell just sat there at the head of the table where Ed Burdick rightly should have been, sipping his wine, gloating, enjoying immensely the turmoil his wildly inappropriate presence had instigated.

Mrs. Hull had long recognized in her daughter Alice, even as a very young girl, disturbing traits of egoism.

The grandmother had been intrigued by the story of Narcissus ever since she herself was a little girl. Narcissus disdained those who loved him, instead devoting himself to his own reflected beauty in a still pool, dying there rather than abandon it. The story made no sense to her at the time. It seemed to her, back then, to be just another inscrutable fable.

But increasingly, as she watched her own little Alice grow from childhood, Marie Hull recalled and revisited that tale, it causing her to diagnose a terrible selfish isolation in her daughter wherein Alice excluded those who loved her the most.

In full adulthood, after marrying and birthing three beautiful daughters of her own, Alice Burdick found herself unhappily imprisoned at mid-life, feeling less appreciated than she thought a woman of her magnificent assets deserved. Her youth and beauty had begun to fade. She became increasingly panicked by this. Unable to fathom any better reason, certainly none within herself, she'd concluded that her husband was chiefly to blame for her deterioration.

Alice's roving eye was attracted to a brooding man at the Red Jacket Club, a handsome attorney ensconced in a marriage of convenience to a very plain yet well-to-do New England woman who stood to inherit her family's fortune. Being with Arthur Reed Pennell made Alice Burdick once more feel young and beautiful. Her spirits lifted, she yearned for his company more and more, and began to dress younger and adopt a more modern hairstyle to attract his eye.

Alice Burdick and Arthur Reed Pennell gravitated toward each other, both having grown disillusioned and unsatisfied with their respective marriage partners. Together they embarked down a terrible path that would at its end leave three people dead and two families devastated.

Marion wished her father would beat Arthur Pennell to a pulp, then take her childish mother over his knee and strap the life out of her, whipping her backside bloody. *Why does Father not do something?* she screamed to herself inside her head. *Why does he allow her to do this to all of us? Why won't he stop her?*

She became confused by her feelings, the great love she felt for her father being at odds with her anger with him for not being a man and fighting for his family.

Marion was of a tender age when as yet it had not been fully impressed upon her that she and her sisters had already lost their mother, and that Grandmother had lost her only daughter as well. Marion had not been made aware of the extremes to which her father had gone previously to win his wife back, or the terrible lies the scheming Alice Burdick had told while conniving to have it both ways, or the humiliation she had caused her husband and mother, flaunting herself so publicly as she did with her paramour.

These truths had repeated themselves many times previous in fact. Marion's mother was, as Grandmother feared, a true narcissist whose own happiness took precedence over the welfare and survival of her entire family. She had often boldly demonstrated this in recent years by deserting her children for weeks at a stretch with no remorse or care. She made it clear that she was more than willing to discard her own three daughters for the far more gratifying pleasures of passion and fulfillment of the flesh.

Edwin Burdick hugged his sobbing teenage daughter and tried to comfort her, remaining outwardly serene while boiling inside.

"And do you recall the address of that house, Marion?" he asked, swallowing hard.

"Yes, Father. It's 123 Seventh Street."

Ed Burdick had for some time confided in his business partner Mr. Parke his findings concerning the sordid activities of his wife and Arthur Reed Pennell. One day after Mr. Parke inquired about a large man who had come to their office on a number of occasions, Ed flat-out told him that the man's name was James Boland of the Mooney-Boland Detective Agency of New York City. He had hired Boland to tail his wife and her lover on their trysts to New England, Atlantic City and New York's Waldorf Astoria and other Manhattan hotels.

On one particular day the previous November, Burdick revealed to Mr. Parke the anguished details of his much-loved daughter having witnessed with her own innocent eyes the two adulterous beasts fornicating together. He related with much emotion how little Marion had agonized all by herself with no one to talk to concerning that devastating scene, holding inside her the terrible secret for almost a year. Parke was horrified and incensed.

"That was injuriously, cruelly indiscreet of your wife," Parke proclaimed. "No child should ever have to witness something so treasonous, so wounding. A young girl's mind cannot possibly recover from such a dastardly thing, much less her heart. Not ever!"

The accommodating Mr. Parke then proposed that he just so happened to have a few friends of his own who would themselves be very agitated by the story of Alice Burdick and Arthur Reed Pennell, friends who might wish to help Ed Burdick exact his retribution.

Soon thereafter one Wednesday Alice Burdick informed her husband through the servant girl that she would be gone for most of the afternoon. He knew now exactly where she was headed. Ed Burdick gathered Mr. Parke and friends together to drive his automobile to Seventh Street. They parked the auto down the street in the shadow of a towering elm and waited. Soon Arthur Reed Pennell's Baker Electric glided silently by, coming to a stop in front of No. 123. He alighted and went quickly inside, using a key to unlock the door. Ten minutes after, Alice Burdick arrived in a hired coach, and she too went inside. She also had a key.

After some fifteen minutes had passed, the men believing that the couple would most likely by this time be distracted within their coital exuberances, they sneaked quietly up to the house and broke in.

FINGY CONNERS AND THE NEW CENTURY

Hearing an angry commotion, Mr. Pennell, ever chivalrous even when naked, aided Alice in pulling back down her skirts, then opened the window for her to climb out. He himself made the mistake of pausing to put his shoes on, providing the invaders the extra second required to snatch him as he tried to follow her.

Many eager hands pulled him back inside.

The Seventh Street neighbors, attracted to their windows by all the ballyhoo, watched open-mouthed as the refined Mrs. Alice Burdick tumbled disheveled out the first floor bedroom window painfully into the upward-turned branches of the bare hedges, then righted herself before running down the street, stumbling as she attempted to rearrange her costume mid-leap. She ran and ran, until finally reaching Holy Annunciation Church, where she entered to take sanctuary and tend to her bloody scratches with holy water from the marble font.

Arthur Reed Pennell endured his resultant beating like a man, hopelessly outnumbered as he was. His goal was to emerge from it as undamaged as possible so that he might finally put an end to the one and only obstacle to his true happiness.

Pennell had wearied of waiting and sneaking around, of taking what barren comfort he might in the swoon of romantic poems celebrating star-crossed lovers' suffering and suicide. The ungodly act of self destruction was presented as a possibility that he and Alice had discussed. They considered carrying it out together, or so Pennell was led to believe by her. It would have interested him to discover that suicide was a folly that someone the likes of Alice Burdick would in no way whatsoever have ever allowed herself to be a participant, as befitted the high esteem in which she held herself.

Instigated by Pennell's unstable ramblings on the subject, Alice Burdick wrote her lover a letter soon after this discussion and demanded he put up a bond of $25,000 for her as a substantiation of the seriousness of his commitment to her, claiming she feared he would never leave his wife for her. In fact it was an insurance policy of sorts, something to ease her through her contretemps in case he followed through on his deadly romantic delusion.

More recently though, concerning that particular undertaking, he had substantially amended his attitude, reasoning, *if I'm prepared to kill myself, and to ask Alice to join me in the act, why not rather merely kill Ed Burdick and be done with it? Why should the good people be the ones to die?*

MARCH 5, 1903

"Well, I'm off to New York now, honey. What can I bring you back?" asked Jim Sullivan as he kissed Hannah goodbye.

Hannah nodded toward the baking pans and waiting ingredients, their resulting combination predestined for Jim's birthday cake, now put on hold for the time being.

"Bring *me?* It's *your* birthday, Jim! Don't them people you're workin' with have no heart at all?"

"Can't be helped, honey. It's work. I'll get you somethin'. Just tell me what you'd like."

"Oh. Well...maybe just pick me up a little something from Tiffany & Co.?" she winked. "Anything that's got a bit of sparkle to it."

"Yeah, if I was goin' to New York to rob a bank, I might just visit the Tiffany people on your behalf," he coughed, "but..."

"Don't forget this," Hannah said, handing him his dogeared copy of the Official Guide of the Railways and Steamship Lines of the United States. "When will you be back, Jim?"

"I'll be getting into Manhattan too late in the day today to meet with Boland, so I'll see him first thing in the morning and if all goes as planned I could well be home tomorrow night. But I expect it's probably more likely I may end up on the night train tomorrow, especially if that storm arrives as predicted. Don't worry."

"I always worry, Jim. You know me."

MARCH 6, 1903

After a big bacon and eggs breakfast around the corner at the Liberty Street Diner, Jim climbed the stairs at 130 Broadway and knocked on the door of the Mooney-Boland Detective Agency.

The Burdick murder and the circus surrounding it was the talk of Manhattan, with the *Sun* and the *World* both affording it screaming front page headlines, while the *Times* did its best to walk a gentler path somewhere acceptably midpoint between conservatism and exploitation.

Chief of Detectives Cusak had a few days earlier wired the agency to ask for particulars concerning the work the private detectives had done for Edwin Burdick.

Jim presented to Mr. Boland, as an introduction, Boland's own telegram to Cusak. It read:

EMPLOYED BY BURDICK TO ACQUIRE GROUNDS FOR DIVORCE ACTION STOP SUGGEST YOU SEND MAN TO NEW YORK FOR DETAILS STOP

"Well, here I am Boland. In the flesh. Now what can you tell me?"

James Boland shook Jim Sullivan's hand. He was a massive man—tall, rotund, imposing; a florid-faced fellow who appeared to be no stranger to the bottle.

The story that Boland related almost floored him.

"More than three months ago," Boland said, pausing, trying to relight a cigar stub with some difficulty, "Burdick appeared here in my office and handed me a bunch of letters he said he'd found in his home. They were written to his wife, from a Buffalo lawyer named Arthur Reed Pennell. From what was in them it was pretty clear the two had been having a love affair for some time. Burdick came to me very distressed by his young daughter's having followed her mother to what turned out to be a love nest, where the girl witnessed with her own eyes something unspeakable through a window.

"Burdick wanted me to come to Buffalo and secure solid proof of it, evidence which would enable him to get a divorce in this state."

So Boland had done precisely that. He traveled to Buffalo and without too much difficulty was able to dig up verifiable facts which would convince any judge that the careless and blatant Alice Hull Burdick was indeed having an adulterous sexual relationship with Arthur Reed Pennell.

"For one thing, I was able to trail them to two different love nests, one on Whitney Street at the corner of Carolina, and the other at 123 Seventh St., which they maintained under false names. With this information in hand, Burdick charged his wife with her conduct and she got out—went to Atlantic City.

"Burdick then informed me of her whereabouts and authorized me to continue my surveillance over Mrs. Burdick at the New Jersey resort and anywhere else she might go.

"That proved interesting as well," Boland continued. "I trailed her several times here in New York, where she used to meet Pennell at any of several hotels. One night Pennell was standing alone at the bar of the Hotel Roland, and I stood next to him and ordered a beer. He got in his cups and I heard him say to the bartender, 'There's this fellow up in Buffalo I intend to get—even if I go to the gallows for it.'

"I immediately notified Burdick about his threat, and he replied saying that henceforth he would go armed. When he sent me a check a few weeks ago he enclosed this note here," said Boland, handing Detective Sullivan the paper, "saying he was about ready to put the whole matter in the hands of a lawyer, and that both his wife and Pennell knew of his intentions."

Jim Sullivan listened with rapt attention. He was relieved. It seemed to him that Boland's information just about tied up the case. Jim had been troubled from the beginning by Cusak and Wright both insisting on the pointless idea that a woman had killed Burdick, when he himself had quickly given up on that theory. It was clear to Sullivan that the most obvious assassin was gloating right there in plain sight.

All they had needed to do was go after the most logical suspect from the very beginning and the police department would have avoided a whole lot of grief and mockery. They'd had enough information about him to suspect his intent within twenty four hours of the crime, yet they failed to bring him in, instead obstructing genuine justice by chasing down some so-called mystery women, thereby bringing nationwide ridicule to the department. Newspapers from the Atlantic to the Pacific had mercilessly ridiculed the Buffalo Police. And all for what? To protect the man responsible for doing this? Why? Why invest so much effort to destroy the life of an innocent woman to protect a killer? Who was the Department higher-up, or politician, protecting Pennell? Who was behind this crime to cover up another crime?

Jim began to wonder if Cusak and Wright were in on the conspiracy, so insistent were they as to their stupid working theories. And if so, why was he being kept in the dark?

Pennell, Jim decided, upon learning what private detective Boland had discovered, became desperate at the prospect of the impending public scandal over a divorce, and concocted some ruse to get Burdick to invite him into the privacy of his own home, the place he could most clandestinely carry out the deadly crime.

The detective wondered though, after all Burdick had found out, and after purchasing a revolver for self defense, why would he let this lunatic anywhere near him, much less near his family? Certainly Alice Burdick knew of Pennell's plan. That she'd allow it to take place within bullet range of her own mother and daughters was absolutely chilling to Sullivan, he being in indeterminate mourning for his own sadly missed children.

Jim played out the likely scene in his mind, imagining Pennell employing his wily attorney ways, catching Burdick off guard with some persuasive proposal or false promise or bribe, completely surprising Burdick with the first blow, then rapidly walloping the life out of his reeling victim. After, realizing that no one in the home had been roused from their slumber, he staged the famous diversions to lead the police astray: the small luncheon, the open window, the entry door left ajar. Jim couldn't imagine however any sound reason for rearranging the body the way it had been, or the removal of the clothing. But a man who had just killed another would most likely not be in his right mind regardless after such a thing. He in fact would be highly agitated if not panic-stricken, and his decisions at that moment might not make sense upon review later after the fact when a clearer head prevailed. Pennell had simply improvised as best he could on the fly.

Jim suddenly felt foolish, recalling that, when he and Cusak had shown up to speak with Pennell, how craftily Pennell deflected suspicion away from himself by making claims about the women whose names Jim and Pat Cusak themselves had offered him. The detectives had revealed their cards, offering ammunition for his lies, playing right into Pennell's hands. The detectives provided Pennell with the very information he required in order to divert suspicion away from himself and buy some time in which to scheme, like any cunning attorney possessing his courtroom-honed skills indeed could.

Jim wired his Chief as to his discoveries and added that he would arrive back in Buffalo about noon the next day.

BIRTHDAY BOY
MARCH 7, 1903

As the Burdick fiasco continued spinning wildly out of control, the reputation for corruption and ineptitude that was now an international mortification for the Buffalo Police Department continued to solicit derision and sardonic jabs in the press all across the country, and beyond.

Arriving in Buffalo a little past noon, Jim headed right over to Police Headquarters directly from the Terrace station, stiff and weary from the long journey and feeling every one of his fifty years.

"Hannah invited me to yer birthday party tonight," Cusak brogued. "She told me not to be bringin' anything, exceptin' fer you, lad" he smiled. When he was talking serious business, Pat Cusak's Irish accent was almost indistinguishable. But when the mood lightened up, the brogue flowed forth like beer on St. Paddy's Day.

"That Hannah. What better way to guarantee I'm home on time tonight than to invite my boss along?"

"Crafty lady ye got there, Sully. But I'll be bringin' us a bottle anyways."

"Wait 'til you taste her cake, Pat...it's moist as mornin' dew, with lemon curd filling between all the yellow layers, covered all over in an inch of meringue light as air, and heaped heavy with handfuls of shredded coconut. It's spectacular."

Jim savored the approaching feast for a moment, then got back to business.

"But let's first get movin' on this Pennell thing right away now before any more time's wasted. I'm absolutely convinced he's the killer."

"You have to be knowin' somethin' first, Sully. Because I'm about ready to chew me own moustache off. I took your dope to the Commissioner. Well, he was shocked at the thought of a man as prominent as Pennell being thrown into the jug. He warned me we better be careful. How's that for politics?"

Jim searched his boss' face for any sign that Cusak knew more than he was admitting to, hoping he was wrong about his friend.

"I've already asked Pennell for an alibi," Cusak continued, "and what he gives me is pretty weak. Says he was home all last Friday evening, but there's only his wife to back him up, and she's a bit hazy about the whole thing."

"Well, Pat," said Jim, "let's you and me pay another visit to the Commissioner. Now that I got first hand knowledge of all the dirt Boland was able to dig up, includin' what he witnessed with his own eyes, we can't just be allowin' Pennell to skate away because the Commissioner's fearin' a little scoldin' from his new poker pals down at the Buffalo Club."

The two marched over to the Commissioner's office together and Jim laid out everything that Boland had found out about the many various clandestine rendezvous conducted by the adulterous couple. Together the detectives urged the Commissioner to take Arthur Reed Pennell into custody immediately. The Commissioner reacted abruptly, even defensively, making the hairs on the back of Jim's neck stand up. The bureaucrat claimed he was unsure despite all the damning statements, wary of the "consequences" and said he needed the weekend to think about it all.

"But Commissioner, he's as guilty as sin and walkin' the streets. We can't keep embarrassin' ourselves chasin' ghosts. The Department's a laughing stock! In New York they think we're fools! We got our guilty man!" insisted Jim, as Cusak tried to shut him up with a look.

"I'll let you know my decision first thing Monday morning, detectives. Be patient. We can't afford to make any more mistakes," evaded the Commissioner.

As they spoke, the Commissioner's door was open a crack to the outer office where his secretary, the widow Peggy Shedler, pricked up her ears to hear what the detectives had to say. The moment the detectives left, she poked her head into her boss' office.

"Commissioner, how about if I shut your door over for twenty minutes to give you some peace and quiet? I'll keep everybody out of your hair for a while. Have yourself a little catnap."

The Commissioner smiled in grateful agreement, and once he heard the door click shut behind her, he laid down on his divan. He closed his eyes, trying to figure a comfortable way out of this predicament.

Peggy picked up the telephone and dialed the house on Cleveland Avenue.

"Arthur, it's me, Peggy. The Commissioner is being pressured into bringing you in for questioning, perhaps as early as Monday. I thought you should know, so you can prepare," she warned.

"Thank you, Sis. Everything will work out. Don't worry. Just you wait and see."

"I wish Papa were still alive, Artie. He'd tell us what to do," his sister said, sadly.

❧❧❧❧

That evening the electric lights burned brightly at No. 16 Hamburg Street. Jim had no trouble blowing out all fifty candles blazing away on the towering layer cake to the boisterous cheering of all the salivating children.

The Alderman's brood was wild with second helpings of cake washed down with Coca Cola, the younger ones running around playing cowboy and Indian with little David, the older ones slipping out into the backyard to sneak a quick shared smoke before the cold drove them back inside.

Gay music tintinnabulated from Jim and Hannah's Victor Monarch Deluxe, which played flat-disc gramophone records. Not to be outdone, from next door the Alderman carted over his own machine, the competing Edison device that played phonographic wax cylinders. The Edison apparatus allowed the unprecedented ability for the consumer to record his own voice.

The Alderman was enthralled with his Edison, having fallen in love with the sound of his own intonations, not too surprisingly. His excuse to Annie for the expensive purchase was that he needed the machine to practice and refine his speeches. After all, he was continually being tapped to preside over various functions and festivities as toastmaster, not to mention reciting his many self-serving arguments in the Council chambers at the City Hall. But for his own amusement he had also taken to secretly recording himself singing popular songs of the day in the privacy of his office, hiding the guilty cylinders away in their protective cardboard tubes in a locked desk drawer.

And indeed, surprised at hearing his voice resonating a bit thin and a little high and sounding nothing at all like the same voice he heard from inside his own head as he spoke, he was able to use the device successfully to practice lowering his register and improve his speech making.

When the family had traipsed from next door to Jim and Hannah's with the Edison tucked under the Alderman's arm, Annie rolled her eyes at Hannah and shook her head dismissively, silently mouthing *Sorry*.

"I thought everyone would enjoy hearing my speech castigating the railroads!" JP enthused.

Annie took Hannah aside, fuming at her husband.

"Even at his own brother's fiftieth birthday party he manages to find a way to make himself the main attraction," she whispered.

Hannah whispered back, "I'll take care of it."

"There'll be none of that here tonight JP," Hannah stated definitively. "No work, nor any work talk, nor any related wink or nod will be tolerated around here tonight. That goes for everybody. Detective Cusak? Agreed? This here's a *family* party."

"But..." argued the Alderman.

"But nothing, JP," responded Hannah, abruptly cutting him short.

Cusak elbowed Jim and chuckled. "Now I understand why yer so well-behaved."

❧❧❧

The day previous, Friday, Mrs. Seth Paine, whose home had been ransacked the previous Sunday by the police who'd found nothing, had nevertheless been placed under virtual house arrest. Her home was surrounded by patrolmen based on nonexistent evidence: a signed photograph of her that was present at the murdered man's home and a short tuft of hair that was found on the couch where his body lay. The police positively attributed the hair to Mrs. Paine, announcing as much to the newspapers who ballyhooed this damning clue, despite the fact it was the wrong color and length. The hair, consisting of 20 strands just 2.5 inches long, would soon enough be proven to have been detached from the murdered man's skull upon its being battered.

It wasn't just Hannah and Annie shaking their heads in dismay anymore. Jim too was deeply disturbed by the goings-on.

Dr. Seth T. Paine, the accused's husband, seething over the invasion of his home and the baseless accusations of the police, retained an attorney, W.N. Webster. Webster issued a statement to the newsmen regarding the actions of the Buffalo Police Department. This statement was reprinted nationwide:

> "They have broken more statutes than any officers I ever came across in conducting the investigation of a crime. They have intercepted telegrams and opened letters belonging to persons whom they dare not charge with any crime. They appear absolutely ignorant of constitutional law. How blunderingly they have gone to work to unravel this Burdick murder case!"

As Jim sat that previous Friday getting an earful courtesy of Detective Boland in New York, Marian Hutchison was arrested and locked up based on little more than the fact that she had worked for a few weeks at Burdick's Buffalo Envelope Company, a firm which employed 70 people. No other employee was arrested.

Hutchison was dragged out of her rooms and away from her family on Tupper Street and tossed into a cell personally by Police Superintendent William S. Bull at Police Headquarters downtown, despite Bull knowing full well that Arthur Reed Pennell was the likely murderer.

The aptly-named Bull swore to attorney Philip V. Fennelly—the same attorney not-so-coincidentally representing the outlandishly also-accused Mrs. Seth Paine—and to Marion Hutchison's sister Florence, who accompanied the attorney to police headquarters, that he had no idea where Miss Hutchison was, when in fact she was languishing a few steps away in a locked cell.

"She was kidnapped!" screamed Florence, lunging at the smirking Chief of the Buffalo Police Department. "You dare call this corrupted place America?" she shrieked. "Our family will have our retribution on you dirty coppers!"

Attorney Fennelly was rightly appalled by this second outrage coming directly on the heels of the first.

The Hutchisons, natives of London, Ontario, were horrified to discover that the promise of the slogan "Land of The Free" applied only to those who hadn't as yet been singled out for random illegal kidnapping and debasement by rogue civil authorities.

Marion Hutchison was a church choir singer; tall, refined, and attractive. She had been removed from her home by force, taken to police headquarters, stripped of her clothing and intimately searched and kept locked up in a prison cell against her will for five hours, then released only after much anguish and a writ of habeas corpus having been sued out by Attorney Fennelly.

After Fennelly first arrived at police headquarters demanding to see his client, the police denying any knowledge of the whereabouts of Miss Hutchison, Mr. Fennelly then called on District Attorney Coatsworth. Coatsworth also denied any knowledge of the whereabouts of Marion Hutchison, further outraging Attorney Fennelly.

It's for this very reason I don't trust myself to carry a pistol, he reminded himself as he stalked out.

From the District Attorney's office Fennelly proceeded to go before Supreme

Court Justice White who issued a writ of habeas corpus, directing the police to bring Miss Hutchison before that court. With writ in hand, Fennelly went back to District Attorney Coatsworth's office to serve it, but Coatsworth hid himself away from the attorney's sight.

"He's gone for the day," lied his assistant.

Fennelly then called again at Superintendent Bull's office.

"I want to see Miss Hutchison," Fennelly said.

"Mr. Fennelly, you can't see her," responded Bull.

"But I will see her," demanded Fennelly, after producing the writ.

"When is this returnable?" asked Bull.

"Forthwith," answered Fennelly.

Fennelly returned then to Justice White's chamber at City Hall with Marion's sister Florence. Concurrently, Marion Hutchison was taken there as well from her cell at police headquarters by Detective Coughlin. Marion was not handcuffed, for that would confirm to any onlookers that she was under arrest, but Coughlin sternly warned her about the terrible consequences of her trying to escape. He sneaked her into a back entrance at the City Hall to minimize there being any witnesses to the trouncing of the young woman's civil rights, and made his way to Justice White's chambers. There Attorney Fennelly and Florence Hutchison awaited, only to find that Justice White had since departed to the Ellicott Square to attend a luncheon.

Fennelly telephoned White at the Ellicott Square and asked if Marion could be brought before him there.

"Is the young woman under arrest?" asked White.

"I don't know that," replied Fennelly, "but I will go ask the officials that question."

Fennelly laid the ear piece down on the desk and went into Justice White's private office where Marion Hutchison was being guarded by Detective Coughlin and five other policemen.

"Justice White is at this very moment waiting on the other end of the telephone line to hear the answer to this question, so hear it well: Is Miss Marion Hutchison under arrest?"

Fennelly returned to the telephone saying the officers had stated the girl was not under arrest.

"Then tell them to release her at once," said Justice White.

When he did so, Fennelly was told by the fiendishly grinning officers that Marion

Hutchison was not under arrest at all; that as a matter of fact she had never been under arrest and that she had been at complete liberty to leave whenever she so pleased.

"You had me locked in a cage naked, like an animal! You took my clothes away! I was not allowed to leave, you damned liars!" she screamed, infuriated.

As the attorney quickly hurried from the room with a vengeful Hutchison sister at each elbow, Florence seethed, "If I only had my revolver with me these dirty scum would all be lyin' dead."

Fennelly didn't try to shush her, as he might anyone else promulgating something so provocative, for he knew at this point the cops would be foolish to drive this debacle any further off the cliff than they already had.

The *Syracuse Journal* wrote, "It was admitted that there was absolutely nothing against her. The police brazenly denied that she was under arrest, despite admitting they had her locked in a cell against her will."

The *Rochester Democrat Chronicle* ridiculed the Buffalo Police, beginning its front page headlined account of the latest fiasco with the mocking "Exploding theories and vanishing clews do not at all discourage the Buffalo police authorities working on the Burdick murder case."

The *New York Times* published a bizarrely elaborate statement furnished to them by the Buffalo Police Department that went far beyond merely suspecting that some unrealized mystery woman murdered Ed Burdick. They now claimed a full profile of the "murderess.":

> The suspected woman was in severe straits for money. Her necessity was such that when she wished to do some house furnishing she bought her goods on the installment plan. She also borrowed money from a money lender. It was quite a large sum, and she gave security. One of the payments on the mortgage was due just before Burdick was murdered. A lawyer, who acts for the money lender, received money in payment. The police suspect that the payment left the woman penniless, and that she appealed to Burdick for more funds. When he refused, she killed him. In any event the police believe her straitened condition is established, and they are giving it great importance.

At his job at the Biograph Company in New York, after weeks of reading of the bumbling absurdities committed by the Buffalo Police Department in the *Sun,* the *World* and the *Times,* actor, singer, clown and set designer, Michael Sinnott got an idea that he soon enough would take with him out west. Rechristening himself Mack Sennett, and with the financial backing of the New York Motion Picture Company, he founded Keystone Movie Studios in hilly Edendale, California. Putting his idea to work he came to enjoy great success in the movies directing the hilarious antics of the fumbling, blundering Keystone Cops.

THE CULPRIT

Finally, having had both of their two favorite female suspects begrudgingly disallowed them, police attentions and those of the newspaper vultures at long last turned toward the only logical suspect from the very outset, Attorney Arthur Reed Pennell.

Mr. Parke, the late Ed Burdick's business partner, disgusted by the police department's white-glove treatment of Pennell and appalled at their relentless harassment of completely innocent women, including one of his own employees, gladly gave his story to the press. Perhaps also, certain police personnel, insulted, disheartened and fed up with their superiors' criminal shenanigans, also cooperated.

Parke revealed to the *New York World* the Mooney-Boland Detective Agency's findings as to the adulterous couple's many activities including the addresses of their many love nests around town, the bartender at the Roland Hotel's sworn statement attesting to Arthur Pennell vowing to "get" Ed Burdick even if he had to "go to the gallows" for it, and summed up by directly accusing Pennell as the obvious killer of Edwin Burdick. Every other newspaper picked up the story.

Pennell was incensed, feigning grave insult to his sterling reputation. The injured party composed his own statement about the murdered Ed Burdick, intended for the press:

"I did not like him and he did not like me, and we both knew it and I have told the police frankly that we were not on good terms. His death coming at this time was one of the worst things that could have happened to me. Some say that it comes with ill grace from me to abuse a dead man, but Burdick was no saint, and when the time comes that I must make a statement in the newspapers in defense of myself from what other newspapers are printing about me I intend to let people know just the kind of man he was, and then perhaps some of them will turn a little of their time to him that they now are devoting to prying into my affairs."

When asked by a reporter about a letter, recently produced, that he had written to Alice Burdick in his own hand in which he stated "I feel that I must kill Ed Burdick," he stormed off in a rage.

How did they even get their hands on that letter? he wondered. *Did Allie willingly give it to them?*

The grounds around the Burdick house were not searched by police until three days after the murder. By that time, hundreds of footprints left by the milling-around of the city's curious citizens had preceded their examination, obliterating whatever evidence or clue the snow might have preserved.

In a garbage can in the rear of the house the police found a label from a bottle of cocktails that Burdick had purchased the day of his murder, but they found no bottle itself. Somehow this compelled the police to now decide that Burdick's head wasn't caved in a dozen times with a golf club after all, but rather with the mysterious missing cocktail bottle. The search was now on for the police department's latest theoretical murder weapon.

Ed Burdick had obtained irrefutable evidence that his wife had been having intimate relations with his once-close friend Arthur Reed Pennell. He reached his limit of tolerance on December 2nd and demanded she get out of the house for good.

She did not protest, having already been tossed out twice before, each of those times forgiven by her husband, and each time taken back again by him upon his receiving false promises from her that she never intended to keep.

Nor on December 2nd did Alice Burdick seem at all concerned about what might become of her daughters, for she was thrilled for the opportunity to celebrate Christmas with her paramour openly, away from all that other business, without having to concern herself with her family's heartbreak or their agony over her betrayal of them.

Clause four of Mr. Burdick's will appointed his business partner Charles Parke and one Risely Tucker as guardians of the Burdick children, ignoring any claim of Mrs. Burdick, the surviving parent. Attorneys for Parke and Tucker raised the point that in view of Mrs. Burdick's illicit relations with Pennell that she was morally not a fitting guardian for three impressionable daughters.

MARCH 10, 1903

By Monday afternoon the Police Commissioner, crucified by the newspapers for his inaction regarding Arthur Reed Pennell, could delay the inevitable no longer and ordered Chief Cusak to arrest him. Pat Cusak and Jim Sullivan went immediately to the Austin Block where Pennell's office was located but found no one there. Next, they visited his home on Cleveland Avenue but the servant, Lizzie Romance, said that the Pennells had gone out and did not know their destination.

Arthur Reed Pennell seemed to his wife Carrie to be inappropriately jovial, considering. In light of the Burdick murder, with the condemning eyes of the whole nation increasingly focused intently upon him, his photograph featured prominently in the Sunday papers around the country, the attorney became agitated and depressed.

But come Monday morning his demeanor indicated that the veil of gloom and doom was lifting.

"Let's go to the Falls and have us a lovely dinner again at the Prospect House," he said brightly to his wife.

Carrie had not left the house in days because of the lingering crowds out front on the street. Curious pedestrians insisted on walking past the house at all hours on a street that normally saw little foot traffic and she was angry that the police had done nothing to prevent it.

"Let's just see if we can forget all this malarkey for a few hours and enjoy ourselves, darling. What do you say?" Arthur Pennell encouraged.

"Oh, yes, Arthur! Let me just have fifteen minutes to freshen myself and change my frock!" responded the grateful Mrs. Pennell.

The couple soon after entered the carriage house and climbed into their Baker Electric. Mrs. Pennell was bundled up in her fur coat and muffler and wore goggles against the chill breeze. Pennell was an expert at maneuvering the steering arm of his

Brass Era Baker Electric, effortlessly guiding the compact car around tight corners just as adroitly as he did obstacles lying in the street. Carrie Pennell found it thrilling.

"Why are we going this route?" she asked, as he turned onto Kensington Ave. heading northeast.

"Because I have a surprise for you, darling," he said with a big smile beneath his handlebar moustache. He squeezed her gloved hand with his own.

"What? Tell me, Arthur!"

He laughed and shook his head no. "You'll see soon enough, my love."

Kensington Avenue was paved straight as an arrow for as far ahead as the eye could see. There was no traffic to speak of. Arthur wanted to stop for a drink at Volk's Saloon but Carrie did not want to be seen going in there.

"You go, Have your whiskey. I'll wait here in the auto."

He did. In ten minutes or so he returned.

Rain began pouring down. As they passed Bailey Avenue, Carrie giggled and reached into her husband's crotch to gently squeeze his genitals, so exhilarated was she by the mystery and the speed. She felt his area swell. Despite the deluge, Pennell threw back the top suddenly, fully exposing the couple to the elements, and accelerated to the car's top speed, twenty five miles per hour. Carrie buried her hand even deeper into that warm nook as the rush of cold buffeted them.

As the runabout approached the Hannah Gehres Stone Quarry, Pennell unexpectedly flipped the tiller steering mechanism, jumping the curb and sending the car sailing off the 30 foot precipice roadside. Carrie had no time at all to react save for a truncated scream. The chasm speeded toward her face before she even had time to blink. She closed her eyes a split second before solid rock collided with her cranium.

She was dreaming, wasn't she?

Carrie Lamb Pennell was vaguely aware that someone was picking her up and placing her on a litter. She could not see, and was only barely cognizant. She winced with pain at being roughly handled, bumped and jarred as her rescuers struggled to carry her up from the bottom of the quarry to the waiting ambulance above. She was driven quickly to the Sisters' Hospital, but her awareness of any matters that might be of concern to her faded away just as they were carrying Carrie through the facility's doors. Mrs. Pennell suffered a fractured skull, concussion of the brain, a compound fracture of the left elbow, a disfiguring scalp wound with flesh excised, and multiple cuts and bruises.

Arthur Reed Pennell meanwhile remained crushed and broken exactly where he'd landed, pinned under the automobile, his brains spilling freely out of his gaping skullcap, the glistening grey mass cleansed of blood by the pelting of the incessant downpour. He had been left behind in position by the ambulance men for the time being, awaiting the arrival of the city Coroner Mr. Danser.

Mr. Pennell suffered the fractures of all the facial and cranial bones, compound and comminuted fractures of the right thigh, left elbow, left shoulder, fractures of the third through fifth ribs at the spine, a compound fracture of the left knee and left wrist, and a deep yawning gash down his back between the shoulder blades.

Carrie Lamb Pennell died the following day from shock.

Besides recovering Arthur Pennell's engraved gold pocket watch still ticking, in his snakeskin wallet were found eight visiting cards engraved with his name, an identification card issued by a life insurance company, $35 in greenbacks, sixty-nine cents in the change pocket-book, and in a separate compartment of the wallet was a mass of newspaper clippings with bits of poetry, the subjects of which were love and death.

The green Baker runabout was the same automobile in which Pennell had often taken his paramour, Mrs. Alice Burdick, joy riding. It too was dead.

With the news of this startling event spreading like a wildfire through the city came the deduction that Mr. Pennell, hounded by the association of his name with the murder of Ed Burdick, and worry over the disgrace that had been thrust upon him, had taken his own life and that of his devoted, perennially forgiving wife.

There was nothing remarkable found in Pennell's pockets to support the idea that he had intended self-destruction. No inkling had been given to any of his friends or associates, or so they claimed, that he'd formulated any such exit scheme. His automobile veered suddenly and accidentally, it was theorized—perhaps as he reached for his hat blown off by the wind—and leapt over the curb and into the quarry before its intended path could be regained. The Baker landed upside-down and the Pennells were delivered there horribly mangled.

Arthur Reed Pennell carried $215,000 insurance on his life, all of which was made over to his plain-faced spouse, the woman who clung to him though all his troubles, forgave him time and again for his indiscretions with Alice Burdick as well as with the other women who'd preceded her, and had promised, even after her good name had been dragged collaterally through the scandalous mire of the Burdick investigation, to stand by him.

The unwavering devotion of Mrs. Carrie Pennell elicited much comment.

She was a member of a well-known New Haven Connecticut family and recently had come into an inheritance of $150,000. Her husband's small legal practice, which he paid little attention to between his dalliances with Alice Burdick, could not support his wife in addition to his mistress. He was said to be an excellent chauffeur, often seen zooming along Delaware Avenue and through the parks. He had never had any accidents. He loved his Baker and was known for chasing children away who might approach to lay their dirty fingers on it.

"The only thing unusual about their going out last night," said their maid Lizzie, "was that usually Mrs. Pennell told me the hour at which they would return. But yesterday it was Mr. Pennell who gave the order."

The Pennell home had been thoroughly searched by the police after the Burdick murder, and the prominent attorney had been watched for several days afterward. He continued his schedule and business as normal and to live together with his wife to all appearances as usual. After his death the police searched the papers and belongings in his office in the Austin Building, located just a block over from Police Headquarters, directly across Franklin Street from St. Joseph's Cathedral. They also then once again keenly plundered the Pennell home on Cleveland Ave.

The four insurance companies that held Pennell's policies sought to have his death ruled a suicide so that they could deny a payout to his heirs.

The matter went to court.

MARCH 14, 1903

Hannah and Annie had together devoured the police statements given the press and the quoted testimonies of all the witnesses at the Burdick murder inquest featured daily on the front page of all the city's newspapers. When they got together to add it all up and talk about it, they were troubled by all the blatant contradictions and discrepancies, and discussed these in great detail.

Jim was very short tempered when it came to the case. He'd snapped at Hannah when she cornered him about the inconsistencies she'd noticed. He had not confided in Hannah his own many personal doubts and qualms.

The Sullivan wives really heated up after the police so viciously went after Mrs. Paine and Miss Hutchison. In fact, all of the city's females suddenly felt frightened and newly vulnerable, especially upon learning the police had no logical reason whatsoever to target either of the two women.

But when Jim slipped and told Hannah about Police Station 14's midnight raid on the Burdicks' Ashland Avenue home, all hell broke loose. He tried to take it back. He weakly attempted to paint the raid as justifiable, not that he thought it was, but anything to avoid getting Hannah riled up again. But it was too late. The cat was out the bag. Incensed by the police's targeting of women, she sallied forth.

"Jim Sullivan! You dare defend to your own wife that such actions of the police, as illegal and terrorizing as they were, should be condoned simply because men with badges committed the act? How do you feel so above it all that you believe something like this cannot or will not ever happen to me or to our children? Do you even hear yourself when you blather such nonsense? How do you not possibly feel for that poor family? Those children? Awakening to the crash of fifty nightsticks pounding on the outside walls and doors in the middle of the night. The terror they must have felt! I would have had heart failure if it happened to me! Did your police brothers suspect the old lady had a gatling gun waitin' for 'em mounted at the top of those stairs? That those little children were a mortal threat to the well being of the neighborhood and therefore the house needed to be attacked under the cover of blackness at the midnight hour and its women carted off as if having conspired treason?"

Jim was trying his damndest to keep the lid on his temper. Hannah wasn't quite done.

"When will this damnable police nonsense end, Jim? Why don't you get your brother to find you some honorable position with some firm or company that doesn't run roughshod every single day over the good people of this city?"

That did it.

"That's enough from you now, Hannah! What do you expect me to do anyway? Exactly what, Hannah? I am fifty years old! Should I apply for a position in one of Fingy Conners' enterprises, or with the murderous railroads, for Christ's sake? What *honorable* company do you have in mind exactly? How naïve can you be? Show me where the goodness and where honor lies in this dirty world, Hannah, and I will go seek it out. I will stop being a police officer and give up my security and my pension that provides for my wife and children should I die or become injured so I can more honorably sell brushes door-to-door or file papers at the Catholic Diocese office, or, or..?"

Hannah didn't respond.

Jim continued.

"Every day I catch criminals and put bad people in jail, Hannah. Every single day! People who otherwise would be following you or my own children on the streets waiting for their next opportunity to brick you. Hannah, you talk about your books of psychology and what they supposedly reveal about people, but you have no concept of the inherent illnesses of the mind! I am not trying to make fun of your knowledge, or of you reading German books by crackpots like that Freud fellow. Perhaps you understand something in these characters that I do not. But you do not have a complete picture, nor do you intend to. You are satisfied picking and choosing your specific points of contention, disregarding other facts that figure into the case."

"That, right there!" she retorted, "That's what I am angry about! I asked you a pointed question regarding that police assault on those poor Burdick women and you clouded it in a puff of smoke to divert me away from the issue. I'm talking specifically about the police invading a private home in the cold dead of night that contained only grieving women and children who had only that day returned from traveling across the state to bury their dead father. There is no justification for that, or their terrorizing tactics! An army of police pounding on the side of a house at midnight with their clubs, terrorizing the women and girls asleep inside who were already thoroughly terrorized over a murderer having entered their home while they slept, slaughtering, brutally bludgeoning their beloved father while they were mere yards away? That police invasion was lunacy! It isn't just the Burdicks who are injured now; the entire neighborhood hates the police for doing this. *Are we next*, they must all be wondering? There was no threat, no danger, from anyone, toward anyone! It's yet another case of the police having neither evidence nor clues, so as to make some show of their authority they just close their eyes and throw a net out there and drag in whatever poor soul happens to get caught up in it. It's shameful, and pathetic, and damned lazy! The police were the thugs and the hoodlums in this case, how can you stand here and defend that?"

She had him.

He paused to choose his words carefully as he seethed.

"Hannah, there are bad cops, I agree. And sometimes I have had to do questionable things myself for no better reason than because I have been ordered to in order to keep my job so I can keep my family together. A few times I have stepped over the line just to get a bad man off the streets, I admit, that being to attend to the greater good. We do not live in a perfect world where everything is clearly illuminated as to its absolute goodness or badness. But I will ask around tomorrow and see what was the reason behind that invasion. Because...because, yes. You are right. That does seem insane no matter which way you look at it. I don't blame you or any other woman for being terrified over that. I will try to find an answer, even if the answer does not put your mind at rest."

"My mind can never be at rest, Jim, just so long as nonsense such as this is allowed to go on and the police act as hired Hessians for whatever bosses happen to own them at the moment. I came to the conclusion back in the nineties with the Sheehans' and Fingy Conners' murdering of people and your brother's police exam scandal, that the only way to put a stop to this criminal behavior is for women to have the vote."

"Oh, God. Hannah! Not again!"

"Don't you 'Hannah' me, Jim Sullivan! If half the people in line at those voting booths had been women with babies in their arms, there would have been no Sheehans and no Fingy Conners! There would have been no police clubbing women over their heads just because they demanded to vote their own mind. The only solution to stop all this corruption of our police and the politicians and the terrible things that endure in this city and in this country is for women to have the vote. I promise you, this world will become immediately more peaceful the very day that happens."

"Well, good luck. Because it won't ever happen."

"Jim Sullivan, how dare you say that to me! Negro men have the vote, but white women do not? Is that right by any stretch of your imagination? All citizens have the same rights, supposedly, but in reality half are forbidden to vote! The half that I and your daughter happen to belong to!"

He remained silent. He knew he wasn't going to prevail.

"The world is changing before your eyes, Jim, and women will no longer sit back and watch dangerous decisions being made in their names and the names of their children by bad men. That invasion of the Burdick home is deplorable in every imaginable way. Police men invaded a private home. *Male* medical students invaded the home of that poor Negress a while back and tried to kidnap her to conduct medical experiments on her like she were some dog in the street! *Male* students dug up Mrs. Carey's grave at Holy Cross Cemetery and carted her body off to chop it to pieces in their dissection room. Then, *male* doctors insisted that the body was not hers despite her own husband and sister standing right there in front of them testifying otherwise! How preposterous! *Men* are defiling women and destroying this world! Your beloved martyred President McKinley allowed the lie of the Maine being blown up by the Spanish at Cuba! That was a fabrication now well known! How many thousands of our precious boys died in the resulting war because they heard the cry 'Remember The Maine!'? How many of our own sons, yours and mine, and our nephews will die in the next? I'm glad that lunatic shot McKinley! He deserved it for sending innocent boys off to die!

"Hannah! This is insanity. Take ahold of yourself, God damn it! Where the hell is all this coming from?"

"Oh, Jim, every women knows that! Everything that men do when it comes to war is just insane. I'm just disgusted with it all! I didn't give birth just so that my precious boys could go off and die for some politician's lies!"

And with that Hannah stormed out of the kitchen and into the bedroom and slammed the door behind her with a force that shook the whole house. Jim leaned against the sink, exhausted.

He audibly exhaled.

He thought for some minutes there, motionless, as the faucet dripped. She'd asked him twice now to fix it. He ruminated and worried. This conversation began with the Burdicks and ended with a government conspiracy. Jim feared that Hannah might be becoming unstable once again, that she may indeed have inherited the frightening traits of her mother. This certainly wasn't the first time her frustration was the cause of an explosion between them.

But right then, he needed to get to work for the four o'clock shift. The supper Hannah had been preparing was sitting there uncooked. He made a cheese sandwich. Young David came in from school.

"Pa! I got an A!" David produced a drawing of a house and a tree and a yellow sun in a clear blue sky that was an idealized representation of their own home, although theirs rarely knew a sky above that was not murky with smoke and soot.

"That's very artistic, Davey. An A! I'm proud of you, son."

David beamed at his father's praise.

"Where's Ma, Pa?"

"Your mother has a headache, Dave, so try and be quiet. She went in to lie down for a few minutes. You go change out of your school clothes and wait for her to get up.

"OK!" said David as he darted joyously out of the room.

Jim had to leave for work soon.

When he finished his sandwich he went to check on Hannah. He knocked gently at the door.

"Hannah, I gotta go to work now. The kids are comin' in."

She rose from the bed and melted into his arms.

"I'm sorry, Jim. I don't know what comes over me sometimes. I read too much. Way too much. Too many terrible stories in the newspapers."

"Don't fret. We're a family and we love each other. I won't let anyone or anything hurt us. I promise. I know that Burdick thing scared the hell out of you. I understand that. Completely. I really do."

"I didn't make you your dinner..." She was on the verge of tears.

"I had a nice sandwich, honey. It's okay. I put a flame under the chicken pot. Check on it, will you? Just don't worry so much about what all goes on out there in the big scary world," he said nodding out the window, "because everything's just fine in here. Just fine. Hear me? Little Davey got an A for his drawing. He's proud as hell and chompin' at the bit to show it to you."

Hannah smiled a weak smile, wondering what might be wrong with her, blowing up over things she could not change or control.

"I'll wait up for you," she said.

"Don't, honey. You and the kids need your sleep. Everything is fine. I promise. You and me. We are fine."

He smiled and kissed her on the forehead as if she were a misguided child, and descended the stairs to the front door. Zeke followed him but Jim sent him back up the stairs.

"You keep an eye on yer mother," he commanded. The dog understood.

Hannah walked over and lingered in the window watching Jim head up toward Elk Street, worrying how much damage she may have just caused.

After feeding him his supper she went next door with little David to visit his cousins. The Alderman was who-knows-where.

"He's downtown at the Iroquois, Hannah. Some Democratic nonsense-excuse to eat and drink and smoke cigars and shout their anger over matters Republican," clarified Annie.

As usual Annie and her girl Sophie had the household composed. It occurred to Hannah that she never spoke much to Sophie.

"Sophie, where are you from, dear?" ventured Hannah.

"Poland," Sophie responded.

"Yes. No, I mean, what city?"

"No city. *Country*. Village. In north. Pogódki. Fifty kilometers of Gdansk."

"Oh," Hannah smiled. "Is it nice there?"

"No. It's lonely."

Hannah had never heard of Gdansk.

She refocused her attentions on Annie.

"I fought with Jim again."

Annie said nothing. She only sighed.

"I was screamin' like a banshee at one point, about that police attack on the Burdick family and suddenly I realized just how badly turned around I've been by that story. I wish Jim had never told me about it. I have bad dreams over it now, cops rushing up the stairs in the middle of the night with clubs, hitting me, shouting.

"I realize now there are really only two kinds of cops, Annie—the bad cops, and the ones who look the other way."

Annie showed no reaction.

"And Jim is lookin' the other way. Which means, in my gut, I know somethin' like this is bound to happen again, because nobody's even talkin' about how insane this was, much less apologizin' to the family for it, or tryin' to make up for it in some way. If no one talks about it, if nobody admits it was wrong, then they must all believe that this kind of thing is acceptable. That's what's frightened me so deeply, Annie, and that's what set me off on him. I would have told him that, but he was already gone to work when it finally dawned on me."

"So? What do you expect Jim to do about it, Hannah? Realistically, I mean? He's just one man," said Annie, spooning apple sauce into baby Mildred.

"Realistically?" Hannah shrugged. "Nothing. What *can* he do? Fight the entire department? He'd lose his job—if one of the bad cops didn't decide to shoot him beforehand. I mean, if the newspapers haven't even reported this outrage, what does that tell us? You can't tell me with all them neighbors around there packed in so tight that somebody didn't tell someone they knew at one of the newspapers about it. People are whisperin' about it only now, as if it's only some crazy rumor. I should feel safe being the wife of a police detective, Annie, but I feel the opposite. I know too much to feel safe."

Hannah paused a moment, then said, "We women need to have the vote Annie."

"Hannah," grunted Annie, straining to hoist the toddler into her lap, "I'm surrounded by children who need me twenty-four hours a day. I don't even have time to think, much less parade up and down the state with Mrs. Cady-Stanton."

"She's dead. The poor dear died last year." reminded Hannah.

"Well you know what I mean. The suffragettes. Your kids are in school now, and I think...well, maybe you just need something of substance to fill up your time these days. That's what all this thinking and worrying is about. When you had babies crying for you to pick them up every five minutes I'll bet these things never crossed your mind."

Hannah did not take offense.

There was some truth in Annie's observation. Hannah was searching for what to do with herself, now that her children didn't need her so much. But she *had* thought about these things before, she really *had*. But like Annie nowadays, she was so preoccupied back then with babies sick and well, alive and dead—that there was no opportunity to think a whole lot, much less actually do anything about the way that things were.

But now there was.

❦❦❦❦

On March 14, the bodies of Arthur and Carrie Pennell arrived in Brunswick, Maine at 2 p.m. and were immediately removed from the train to the cemetery at Pine Grove. Mrs. Pennells' mother, Mrs. Carrie Lamb, her children Henry, Charles and Gloria, and a cousin were the chief mourners. Two score friends also stood at the grave, where the cover of Carrie Pennell's coffin was lifted for a viewing; Arthur Pennell's was not. Flowers and evergreens covered the double grave, including a large square from the class of '87, Yale College, Arthur Pennell's alma mater. William M. Pennell, sheriff of Cumberland county and Arthur's cousin was in charge of the burial arrangements.

THE BURDICK INQUEST

"Under law we are compelled to hold this inquest," Judge Murphy announced in his opening statement to the court. "We charge no one with this crime. The purpose of this investigation is to lay this crime, if possible, at the door of someone."

The Burdick family was well represented by Hartzell & Hartzell, and John C. Hubbell. District Attorney Coatsworth conducted the examination of witnesses. Chief of Detectives Pat Cusak sat beside Justice Murphy, prompting the judge to ask several questions during the day.

News reporters from the *San Francisco Call*, the *New York World* and all points between scribbled furiously into their notebooks.

The crowded courtroom was peopled by the stridently stylish; the ladies adorned in an enviably beautiful mode reminiscent of the Easter Parade, the men attired in dashing suits and brilliant white or boldly striped shirts with lay down or wing tip collars and shimmering silk ties. It was a fashion parade.

The first witness questioned was Mrs. Marie Hull, mother-in-law of the murdered man. The little woman with the neat gray hair, blue eyes and determined expression was gowned in black entirely from head to toe. She wore a long, voluminous mourning veil on her head which she lifted from her face upon commencing her testimony.

The authorities had expected that the petite and frail-appearing Mrs. Hull, when put on the witness stand, would collapse under the steady and merciless fire of questions and would betray some incident, some fact, which would lead to a solution of this profound and baffling case.

But she did not.

For two hours and eight minutes Mrs. Hull was subjected to a relentless, irritating storm of repetitive queries. She was asked to review in the minutest detail the tragic incidents of the discovery of the battered body of her only daughter's husband. She was compelled to rehearse the troubles and quarrels of the Burdick household, to recall the indiscretions of her daughter and the supposed sins of her son in law, which have been her life's sorrow. She was required to picture the horrors of the little den, the chamber of death, and to point out in photographs the very spot where Mr. Burdick lay slaughtered. She showed little irritation or fatigue and did not become confused. She did resort to using smelling salts on occasion, particularly upon being shown photographs of the bloody murder scene, but the aged family matriarch never once lost her composure. Sighs of sympathy and pity for her rippled repeatedly through the courtroom. Women spectators almost cried as District Attorney Coatsworth, implacable and resolute, plied the elderly woman with questions which almost accused her of complicity in the murder. Through it all Mrs. Hull maintained a composure that was remarkable. Her hand trembled occasionally, but not a tear dropped from her eye, not a sob escaped her. She answered every question with emphasis and composure and exited the witness stand with a little smile and a firm step. Not one incriminating word was uttered by her; not a single phrase interjected which might aid the authorities in placing responsibility for the crime.

More than a few of those present however interpreted her stoic placidity as coldheartedness; a testament, in their jaundiced opinion, as to her cooperation in the cover up of the terrible murder.

Next on the stand came Dr. Howland, the medical examiner.

"At what time did you arrive at the Burdick home, Doctor?"

"At about nine o'clock."

"And who did you see there?"

"I saw Chief Cusak, Detective Sullivan, Detective Wright and Dr. Marcy."

"Dr. Marcy, the Burdick family physician?"

"Yes sir."

Were any of the family members present?"

"No, they were upstairs, I believe. It was a shocking scene."

"And what did Dr. Marcy say to you when you arrived?"

"Dr. Marcy was sitting having his breakfast, and when he saw me arriving he jumped up quite animated and rushed to me before I could set foot over the threshold. He told me that something had been going on there and that Mr. Burdick was dead."

"Dr. Marcy was sitting down, having breakfast?"

"Yes, he was sitting at the table having his breakfast."

"After just seeing Mr. Burdick's head caved in...in the adjoining room?" asked the Justice.

"Yes, your honor."

"All right. Go on."

"Dr. Marcy requested that I make it appear that this case was one of suicide, rather than murder. He said there had been a good deal of gossip in the neighborhood respecting the relations existing between Mr. and Mrs. Burdick."

"Suicide? Were there any indications at all that it might be a suicide?"

"No sir, absolutely none. After examining the body I told Dr. Marcy that it was impossible to entertain the suicide theory even for a minute."

"And then what did he say?"

"He was very disappointed. I told him that a man does not commit suicide by beating his own skull in from behind."

"Why would Mr. Burdick's own physician want to betray him in this way?"

"I do not know. I found it very odd and quite disturbing, to be honest, considering the violence that was so apparent at the scene. Mr. Burdick's killer needed to be captured quickly and sent off to prison, not be encouraged to roam freely so he might have an opportunity to strike again. That would be a terrible, unforgivable injustice. There were children present in that house when Mr. Burdick was beaten to death! That Dr. Marcy's request was so preposterous and outrageous did not even seem to bother him in the least little bit. Dr. Marcy should have been his patient's most ardent protector, his advocate. It's shameful. Mr. Burdick suffered a terrible death. It was prolonged, in my opinion."

"What was prolonged?"

"His suffering. There is one other thing Dr. Marcy told me," he continued. "He said when he went into the den that morning, the curtains were drawn and it was dark in there. He tried to raise the curtain, but could not, and had to tear it down. He also told me a quilt had been wrapped three times about the head of the murdered man. He also said he found blood on the floor."

Mr. Coatsworth revealed to the court that evidence showed Mr. Burdick's body had been moved by the murderer after the deed. Dr. Howland said he noticed blood on the couch, on the floor, and on the doors of the den.

"How far was the head of the dead man from the blood pool on the couch?" asked Coatsworth.

"About fifteen inches below the blood pool on the couch. The only item of clothing he wore, an undershirt, had ridden up almost to his neck, evidence that he had been dragged away from the murder spot by the legs."

Dr. Howland then said he saw Detective Wright remove a letter from the dead man's pocket, and that he heard Dr. Marcy say that old Mrs. Hull was subject to heart failure.

"As Mrs. Hull was giving her statement to the police," Howland continued, "she hesitated quite a few times, and each time, Dr. Marcy had to prompt her."

"Prompt her? For what reason?"

"I have no idea. He repeatedly interposed himself whenever the detectives attempted to talk to Mrs. Hull or the children. And it was he who first asked, when told something had happened to Mr. Burdick, if Mrs. Burdick was at home. As if he might have suspected her initially."

Dr. Howland said he saw no weapon nor any blood anywhere outside the den. There were blood stains on the dead man's legs that appeared to have been made by bloody fingers.

"Do you think he was killed on the couch?" queried the District Attorney.

"Yes."

"When he was killed, was he lying on the couch in the position in which you found the body?"

"Judging from the location of the wounds," Dr. Howland testified, "he must have been in a very different position at the time he was struck."

"Do you believe a woman could have committed this murder?

"No sir. I do not. That theory is just ridiculous."

"At what hour did you affix a time of the murder?"

"About 2 o'clock."

"Policeman Meyer encountered a "lone woman" walking away from the direction of the Burdick house on the night of the murder at one o'clock. But your finding is that Mr. Burdick was murdered an hour after that."

"Yes sir. I believe the report of the lone woman as a suspect should be laid to rest based on my determination."

One of the last to see Burdick alive was his attorney George G. Miller who took the stand next. The attorney had been retained by Burdick to act on the divorce proceedings against his wife. Their case was scheduled to be heard on March 3rd, he said. The murdered man and Mr. Pennell had held a meeting together in Mr. Miller's offices a few weeks before the killing. Miller had an appointment with Mr. Burdick

Alice Burdick takes the stand, examined by D.A. Coatsworth as the judge Thomas Murphy looks on.

the evening he died at 6 p.m. on February 26 at the Burdick home.

"Mr. Burdick was ready at all times to sacrifice his own interests for those of his children. He carried a revolver, but I never heard him say that he feared harm from Pennell. At that conference held at my office, Pennell made one or two statements from which an intimation of suicide could be drawn, although I never heard Pennell say precisely that unless the divorce action was withdrawn he would kill himself and Mrs. Burdick."

In her testimony, Lizzie Romance, the Pennells' maid, said that the night of Edwin Burdick's murder, Mr. Pennell was with his wife in their room reading at 7:45 p.m. She said she saw them again at 10 p.m. when she passed their door, but did not see either of them again until the following morning. She testified that although her custom was to iron and care for Mr. Pennell's clothes, and that she had pressed Pennell's trousers, she could not now recall what he was wearing on either occasion. She had not noticed whether any of his trousers had gone missing. She could not say whether Pennell went to the furnace the morning after the murder, or whether or not the Pennells left the house after 10 p.m. the night of the murder, for the Baker Electric automobile was virtually silent in its operation. In the history of her employ she claimed she had never once heard cross words exchanged between Mr. and Mrs. Pennell. Furthermore, she did not notice anything unusual in the manner of either Arthur Pennell or his wife on the day they left for the auto ride that ended in tragedy for them. It was upon Miss Romance that Arthur Pennell had relied to corroborate his alibi for the night of the murder.

Mr. Burdick's business partner Charles S. Parke was called next. He produced an uproar when he stated without hesitation "The murder was committed by Arthur Pennell or a hired assassin."

After Mr. Parke was excused, Mrs. Burdick was called to the witness stand. Parke had stared holes right through her as he testified, and continued to do so as he returned to his chair, but Mrs. Burdick refused to look at him.

A loud murmur filled the room as she made her way to the stand. District Attorney Coatsworth was relentless and without pity as he exposed her lies and evasions, forcing her to tell her story of her relations with Pennell from the time he first had his way with her in 1898 until 1901 when these sexual relations were begun anew after Mr. Burdick had forgiven her and taken her back into the home for the sake of their children.

Mrs. Burdick stated that she had married Ed Burdick in 1886 and that they had three children. She met Arthur Reed Pennell at a card party in 1897 to which Mr. Burdick had accompanied her. She traveled alone to New York and New Haven with Mr. and Mrs. Pennell in 1898, Mr. Burdick being detained in Buffalo then due to business obligations.

Mrs. Burdick swore under oath that no unusual friendship ever sprang up between herself and Pennell.

In response to her lie, District Attorney Coatsworth produced a piece of correspondence. It was a love letter written by Pennell to Mrs. Burdick. She turned deathly pale.

Coatsworth asked, "Mrs. Burdick, do you recall receiving a letter from Arthur Pennell in 1900 written at New Haven, in which he said, 'Yesterday I was at the gateway on the campus grounds where more than two years ago I drew you in, in the darkness'?"

"No, sir. I do not," she emphatically replied.

Coatsworth then turned and withdrew from his leather portfolio the letter from which he had just quoted. She began to tremble at having been found out. Forward from there she took the District Attorney's examination of her quite hard. Many of her answers were made in a near-whisper.

"Do you recognize this as being in Arthur Pennell's handwriting?"

"Yes."

"Do you now recall the incident?"

"Yes. I recall that he took me into a darkened doorway and kissed me."

"Did you recoil? Did you push him away?"

"No, sir. I kissed him back."

The female spectators, who outnumbered the male variety two to one, quite audibly gasped.

Letter after letter was produced, all written by Pennell to Mrs. Burdick. She tried to deny having ever seen some of them. One referred in very affectionate language to Pennell having found her gloves in his coat pocket. In another written from Shelter Island he said he would telephone her just to hear her dear voice. She claimed she did not remember his calling.

"What did Pennell mean in this letter," Coatsworth asked, pulling it from a pile of many in Pennell's own hand, "where he says he hoped to see you Wednesday morning at 1-2-3?"

"I do not know."

"Doesn't it refer to a house number on a street in this city? Seventh St. to be exact?"

"I don't know."

"In 1900 there were several houses in this city where you used to meet him?"

"There may have been two or three."

Coatsworth drew another letter from the pile, this one dated September 17, 1900, postmarked New Haven and addressed to the witness. Mrs. Burdick admitted receiving the letter. In it Pennell wrote:

"I shall try to telephone you tomorrow morning, and on Thursday if all goes well I shall know the exquisite happiness of seeing you. I have had your dear picture in the locket to look at, and that has been awfully sweet and comforting."

Pennell referred to Mrs. Burdick in the letter as "My love, my life, my dearest one."

"Did you give him a locket with your photograph in it, Mrs. Burdick?"

"No sir."

Coatsworth then produced a letter written on Waldorf-Astoria stationary and postmarked New York City.

"Do you recall receiving a telephone from Mr. Pennell on this date?"

"No sir," she whispered.

"In this letter, Mrs. Burdick, Arthur Pennell writes, 'I just came from telephoning you and hearing your dear, sweet voice. Am I foolish to telephone you from way down here? It was worth all it cost me! I realize more and more that you are the only woman in the world for me. Thank you, dearest, from the bottom of my heart, for the beautiful locket containing the image of your pretty face. I know the trouble you went to in order to obtain this, and I will treasure it close to my heart forever."

Coatsworth paused for effect, then asked, "Mrs. Burdick, do you remember getting this letter?"

"No, sir."

"In this same letter," the District Attorney continued, "Pennell says, 'Only a day more and I shall once more see the lovelight in your eyes and experience the paradise within your arms.' What does he mean by that, Mrs. Burdick, by 'the paradise within your arms'?"

"I don't know," she answered quietly.

"Pretty strong language, wouldn't you say Mrs. Burdick?"

She did not respond. The courtroom went dead silent, waiting, adding drama to her refusal to answer.

Another letter was produced. Mrs. Burdick was by now as white as a sheet and looking as if she might faint at any minute. Coatsworth took no mind of it, and asked, "Do you recall receiving this particular letter from Pennell, also written at the Waldorf?"

He showed her the letter. She studied it for a moment.

"No, sir, I don't."

"Then I'll read it and we'll see if it doesn't refresh your recollection. 'As I looked into your beautiful eyes last night, I feared there was some trouble hidden there. I did not know, but I feared it was because of some other reason than because I was going away. If there was, dearest, I wish you would tell me. There is that in the manner of your husband toward you that makes me fear sometimes that I might kill him'."

"*Now* do you recall receiving this letter?"

"No sir. I have never read those words before."

"You claim you never heard Arthur Pennell ever once say anything about killing your husband, getting rid of him, anything to that effect?"

"No sir."

"Did your husband know you were receiving love letters from Arthur Pennell?"

"I don't know. I had the habit of keeping my personal papers locked in a box."

"When did your husband first come to know about your intimacy with Arthur Pennell?"

"It was on New Year's Day 1900 when I told him in reply to his question that I had been out walking with Mr. Pennell."

"Wasn't that quite imprudent of you to reveal that?"

"Yes. It was."

"At that time did you give Pennell's letters to your husband for him to read?"

"I don't know."

"Did you remove some letters from your locked box and place them in his hands in anger?"

"I unlocked it."

"How did you happen to unlock it?"

"He forced me to."

How did he 'force' you?"

"He took me by the throat."

Mrs. Burdick did not remember how long after this incident that she rented a box in a safe deposit company's vaults. It was not when her husband had her by the throat, but more recently, after she had received papers about her husband's activities from the private detectives she claimed Pennell had hired.

Edwin Burdick had not started divorce proceedings, and she claimed she did want to get a divorce from him. She no longer had any love for Burdick, but she did love Pennell and expected to marry him. She said she expected him to get a divorce from his wife.

"Did Mrs. Carrie Pennell consent to her husband's asking for a divorce?" asked the District Attorney.

"Sometimes she did and sometimes she didn't."

Mrs. Burdick went on to say that she had never talked with Mrs. Pennell about the matter. She said that it was Pennell who'd hired private detectives to shadow Mr. Burdick. She said it was after realizing he was being investigated that her husband sent her away from their family in May of 1901.

Coatsworth then produced a letter from Mrs. Burdick to Mr. Burdick written from Atlantic City on May 27, 1901 in which she promised never again to see Arthur Pennell and begged her husband to take her back. In it she promised that "hence forward I will be a true and loving wife." She wrote that she could not promise that Pennell would leave town but that Pennell would decline to do anything that would mean a loss of his self-respect.

Another letter written by Mrs. Burdick to her husband referred to her being taken back into the family home, and in it she promised never again voluntarily to see or communicate with Arthur Pennell. She made a plea on behalf of the children. "I promise to be a good girl to you," she wrote.

Coatsworth waited a few beats, then asked, "Were you a good girl to your husband then? Did you stop seeing Pennell? Stop communicating with him?"

"No, sir."

Mrs. Burdick claimed she wrote these promises in good faith but failed to keep them.

Another letter was read aloud to the court in which Mr. Burdick declined to take her back.

In yet another letter Edwin Burdick wrote saying that she could not be trusted, that he had loved her truly and honestly long after she had stopped loving him, but that if she truly tried that she might win back both his love and his respect.

It was read aloud to the court:

"You wear a ring given to you by Pennell over your lawful wedding ring, that which I myself placed on your finger on our wedding day. I put no faith in Pennell's promises to you, and I believe you only wish to return home to me and to the girls for as long as it takes Pennell to free himself from his wife. You have not solely betrayed your husband. You have betrayed your children, your girls, who look to their own mother as a guide as to their moral behavior in life. Is yours an example any mother would wish to employ as a guide for her daughters?"

The resulting murmur from audience in the courtroom sounded like angry bees exiting a hive to organize an attack.

In other letters, Burdick wrote that he forgave his wife for the wrongs she had dealt him, that he vowed to fight for what little honor she had left him, and stated his intentions to fight for custody of the children. He insisted that any counter suit would be heard in open court, so that all the details of her sexual affair with Pennell would be made public, believing that this might shame her into repenting.

It worked, as three weeks after the date of this letter Burdick took his wife back yet once again. She did return to her family but returned also to Pennell's lustful arms. She claimed it could not be helped, that Pennell was constantly soliciting her, and she began meeting him alone in the house on Seventh Street.

They were there together one day when Edwin Burdick showed up with a gang of his friends, as they had been tipped off to the lovers' tryst by his daughter. Mrs. Burdick escaped by jumping out the window before he could catch her. She ran directly to church to seek sanctuary there, believing her husband would not assault her in a church. She did not hear until afterward that Burdick's friends had collared Pennell as he was jumping from another window, having unwisely taken the time to put his pants and shoes on. Mrs. Burdick had simply pulled up her skirts to receive his lovemaking, and thus was able to flee more expediently. The group pummeled Pennell after dragging him back into the house.

Mrs. Burdick admitted meeting Pennell in yet another house on Seventh Street after that particular incident, but insisted "that was all."

She changed her story yet again after Coatsworth read a statement from Pennell admitting they had begun meeting at a house on Whitney Place 'two or three" times after being discovered on Seventh Street. Coatsworth then grilled her about additional meeting places he'd found clues of, but she claimed no memory of any of those in which the District Attorney insisted they had also rendezvoused, including the cozy office at Ellicott Square.

It was not until all these incidents had taken place that Burdick expelled his wife from the home for the final time just after Thanksgiving. She had refused Thanksgiving dinner with her family, instead sneaking away to see Pennell. Her most recent exile took her back to Atlantic City where she remained waiting for Pennell to make his move until she received the news of her husband's murder.

"These letters from Pennell, Mrs. Burdick...did your mother ever read them?"

"No. My mother was not aware that I was receiving letters from Mr. Pennell."

"Not aware? How could that possibly be? Weren't these letters brazenly delivered to your husband's home where your mother lived? Delivered at a time of day when your mother was there to receive the mail but your husband was safely away at work?"

"I don't know."

"Did your mother Mrs. Hull know anything of the relations between you and Pennell?

"No, sir. Nothing"

"Did she ever say anything to you about Pennell?

"The night I went away she told me she blamed Pennell more than she did me."

"Blamed for what? You just testified that your mother knew nothing."

"I don't know."

"Did your daughter Marion ever say anything to you about Pennell?"

"No, sir."

"Don't you recall that your own daughter told you she thought you were doing wrong?"

"No, sir."

"Isn't it true your own daughter slapped you across your face and called you a whore?"

The courtroom exploded at the speaking of the word, and it took a full minute for the room to calm.

"Have you received any information as to who killed your husband?"

"No, sir."

You're positive about that?"

"I am."

"Has anyone told you who killed your husband?"

"No, sir."

"You swear you have no knowledge of information as to who killed your husband?"

"I do."

"You never heard anyone say that he or she was going to do it?"

"No, sir."

"Then how do you explain Mr. Pennell's letter in which he wrote to you, "I fear I must kill Ed Burdick.""

"I do not know."

"No, Mrs. Burdick. You just testified you never heard anyone say he or she might kill your husband and yet Mr. Pennell wrote these very words to you in his letter. That is perjury, madam!"

"No it is not. You asked me if I heard anyone say that they were going to kill my husband. And I have never heard anyone say any such thing. Mr. Pennell wrote it, he didn't say it."

"That's all." Said a disgusted Mr. Coatsworth.

Next, Mrs. Burdick was questioned by her own attorney, Mr. Hartzell, who was determined to shift focus away from Mrs. Burdick and place it elsewhere.

Alice Burdick said that Pennell had learned from her husband at the charity ball they all attended together that he, Burdick, had possession of all the letters that Pennell had written to his wife. Pennell was greatly angered by this and demanded that Burdick give him the letters.

"Did he fear the revelations of a divorce action?"

"Yes, very much."

"Who went with you to the Charity Ball?"

"Mr. Burdick, the Pennells and quite a party."

"Who assigned the partners at that ball?"

"Mr. Burdick."

"He seemed to want to throw you together?"

"He did always."

"Now, this den of his was his special pride?"

Yes, sir."

Now, at the Red Jacket Golf Club, who did you normally associate with?"

"Pennell."

"With your husband's knowledge and consent?"

"Yes, sir."

"And with whom did Burdick associate?"

"With other women."

"Now, in all these associations with Pennell, did you seek him out or did he seek you?"

"He sought me."

"He was infatuated with you?"

"He was."

"Were you ever in a compromising position with him?"

"No, sir."

"Were your relations with him ever immoral or criminal?"

"No, sir."

"Did Pennell ever make any improper suggestions or solicitations to you?"

"Never."

"Your friendship was just that, a platonic friendship? Nothing more?"

"Yes, sir. Nothing more."

"Pennell was always the perfect gentleman?"

"He was."

"Then why was he afraid of the divorce proceedings?"

"He was afraid of being humiliated."

"After you returned to Buffalo from Atlantic City and promised your husband that you would be a good girl, did you resist Pennell?"

"Yes, of course."

"Did you refuse to make appointments with him?"

"Most certainly."

"And did he then relentlessly and constantly solicit you, and importune you, and waylay you until you were forced to yield to his harassments?"

Yes, sir."

"Was Mr. Burdick fond of the ladies?"

"Yes, he was very fond of them."

"If Pennell or any other person had made any threats against your husband, what would you have done?"

"Why, I would have warned Ed!"

"Pennell never made any such threats?"

"No, sir."

Mr. Burdick and Mrs. Pennell were friendly?"

"Yes, sir, very friendly."

"And would he have admitted Mrs. Pennell to his house at any time?"

"Yes, sir."

"Even at night?"

"Yes, sir."

"Without any fear?"

"Yes, sir."

"Mrs. Pennell has been to your house many times?"

"Yes, sir."

"She knew the layout and contents of the house very well?"

"Yes, sir."

"And she was familiar with the dining room and the den?"

"Yes, sir."

The door of the den faced the front entrance door to the house?"

"Yes, sir."

"And a person could tap on the window of the front door and attract the attention of anyone in the den without ringing the doorbell?"

"Yes, sir."

Next, Alice Burdick was questioned by the Court. Justice Murphy asked questions prompted by Chief of Detectives Cusak.

"Didn't you know that Mrs. Pennell loved her husband and wanted to remain married to him?" asked the Justice.

"No. She may have, once."

"Did you and Mrs. Pennell never have a conversation on the subject? Didn't she feel that you had wronged her?"

"No, I don't think that she did. She knew I was not to blame. She knew it was all Arthur's fault."

"Mrs. Pennell would not agree to a divorce when Mr. Pennell asked her because she loved her husband very much, isn't that correct?"

"No sir. I don't think she did. It was because she dreaded the scandal and the publicity that surround divorce proceedings."

"Isn't it true that Pennell told you that Mrs. Pennell was at Mr. Burdick's home the night of the murder?"

"No, sir."

Didn't anyone tell you that she was?"

"No, sir."

"Do you know that Pennell was there that night?"

"No, sir."

"When Mr. Burdick made you give him the box containing the letters you'd received from Mr. Pennell, what did he do with it?"

"He turned the box over to my mother without removing the letters."

Called to the stand next, one by one, were the three daughters of Edwin and Alice Burdick; Marion age sixteen, Carol age thirteen and Allie age ten. The girls were calm, composed and spoke clearly. The wisdom of putting them through this public vetting and what value if any their testimony might have was in question in the minds of many, especially as the two younger girls had no direct involvement in the interactions of the adult parties. Marion, the oldest, responded only with the least number of words necessary to answer the question, clearly unhappy and uncomfortable with being examined so publicly.

Her attitude too was interpreted as frigid and detached, arousing suspicion and animosity among some members of the citizens' gallery and the press.

Marion snapped back at the District Attorney when he harangued her needlessly, putting the exact same question to her in ten different ways, in contrast to her mother and grandmother unemotionally tolerating Coatsworth's endless badgering.

No one at this point knew, except her dead father, Mr. Parke, and detective Boland, that she had followed her mother to her love nest, and she was determined that no one would discover this. The entire matter was to remain between her and her parents. She revealed nothing of what she had witnessed, taking her account of the incident to her grave soon enough thereafter.

The inquest was adjourned until the following day.

HANNAH & ANNIE IN THE COURTROOM

Hannah and Annie were excited to have garnered tickets to the Burdick inquest with the help of their husbands' influence. The public demand for entry was overwhelming. Sophie the servant girl was home with the Alderman's small ones, and Hannah and Jim's young David was securely at school. The women excitedly perused the finery worn by the many women and men present. Some had crossed over into outlandish choices in a bid to be noticed apart from the others. The newspapers had begun to pay as much attention to the peacockery and strutting of the adorned inquest spectators of both genders and the various ways in which they were dressed and wore their hair as they did the scandalous inquest itself.

The two brothers' wives sat together at enthralled attention in the courtroom, their focus sometimes diverted to someone's hat or shoes during particularly banal intervals of testimony.

District Attorney Coatsworth's stinging question reverberated around the room, aided by the silent pause taken by Alice Hull Burdick, the dead man's philandering wife.

"No, sir," she finally said, emphatically.

"You swear you have no knowledge or information as to who killed him?"

"I do."

Mrs. Burdick was much improved over the previous day. She was stronger, calmer, more confident.

She denied Coatsworth's insistence that she had provided her lover a key to her family's house. A key that might have allowed him to enter the home and murder her husband as her mother and children slept mere feet away just up the stairs. Coatsworth insisted that Mrs. Burdick had several duplicates made of her house key for her paramour while they were in New York on a tryst to allow him to enter the house. He reworded his question in a number of ways, hoping to trip her up, but no matter what form it took, she denied any such activity, or even that her key had ever left her possession for a moment.

The District Attorney read again from letters that were exchanged between Mrs. Burdick and Pennell in which he said life was "not worth living without her," and that "death would not be unwelcome."

She claimed no knowledge of a document found in her safety deposit box contracting Arthur Pennell to pay her the amount of $25,000 in the event of his not being able to marry her. It was contained amongst her important papers, in a vault no one else had access to, yet she disavowed any knowledge of its existence.

She said that on the Tuesday evening before the murder, Pennell had left her in Atlantic City. He had taken the night train back to Buffalo, arriving Wednesday morning. She said she knew nothing of her husband's murder until she received a telegram from her mother, Mrs. Hull, on Friday morning. She rushed back to Buffalo hastily and arrived early Saturday. A brief message of sympathy was delivered to her at her mother's house that same day, signed by Pennell. Alice Burdick claimed that was the last she ever heard of Arthur Pennell.

With all of the principals in the case now dead, Alice Burdick was free to invent. She claimed it was her husband who was the wanton philanderer, and it was his behavior that drove her to her "special friendship" with Pennell. With the dead Mrs. Pennell unable to respond, she painted a picture of Carrie Pennell as a suspect in the murder, arriving at the family's home to multiple private meetings with her husband in his den "with doors closed."

"I believe that Edwin's door was open to Mrs. Pennell anytime day or night," she stated.

"There was an occasion about two years ago when you and Mr. Burdick had quite an altercation at your house?" Coatsworth asked.

"Yes, sir."

"And after that it was necessary for him to wear a piece with Cotolia court plaster on his head?"

"No, sir."

"Did you not at that time strike him over the head with a chair?"

"I did not."

"You received a letter from your husband from Indianapolis in January of last year?"

"Yes, sir."

"I will read it:

'Received a letter to-day from A.R.P. of the contents of which you are familiar. I shall decline to have an interview with him. I do not intend to return home again.'

You wrote a letter in reply, Mrs. Burdick, in which you pleaded with Mr. Burdick not to move forward with his plan to sue for divorce, stating that the divorce proceeding would crush the children, especially little Marion. I quote you here, 'My God, Ed, this must not be. You cannot be so cruel to us. You have been generous; continue to be so.'"

Mrs. Burdick admitted she had written it.

"That letter was sufficient to induce him home?"

"I had an interview with him afterward. I asked him to come home and he said he intended to."

"And after that, you continued to meet Pennell?"

"I do not remember."

"Well, allow me to refresh your memory, then. It was right after that you held your clandestine meetings with Pennell in the houses on Seventh Street."

"Not right after, no."

"On what date was it that you jumped out the window on Seventh Street?"

"December 2nd."

What church did you run to?"

"The Church of The Ascension."

"And what did your husband say to you when you returned home to your family that night?"

"He told me I would have to leave the house and advised me to communicate with Pennell. I went down to his office and Mr. Burdick went with me. I remained away for several days and then went home. I had another talk with Mr. Burdick and he told me that I could stay the night."

"He was very kind to you even after all that had happened?"

"He was."

Alice Burdick testified that she was served with divorce papers the following day. She packed her things for good and was taken by Pennell to The Prospect House at Niagara Falls. She claimed Pennell did not stay with her at the hotel nor that they had dined together despite the fact that he remained in Niagara Falls that night. She returned to Buffalo to meet with her mother at the tea room at Adam Meldrum

& Anderson department store. There her mother told her that Mr. Burdick had informed her that he had expelled his unfaithful wife from the home.

Afterward she left on a train for New York where she met Mr. Pennell. Interestingly, Mrs. Pennell accompanied him, but Mrs. Burdick claims that despite their all being there for a week, and meeting with Mr. Pennell daily, that she never met or spoke with Mrs. Pennell. Mrs. Pennell wrote at least two letters to Mr. Burdick in Buffalo from New York pleading with him to take back Mrs. Burdick for the sake of the children, citing their "need for a mother's love and care,"—something the children had experienced precious little of in the years that their mother had been wantonly carrying on with Pennell.

Alice Burdick then returned to Buffalo yet again, this time to claim the contents of the safety deposit vault. While there she telephoned her husband and asked him to meet her at the Genesee Hotel, which he did. She had not retained an attorney. She said she allowed Pennell to make any and all decisions concerning the divorce. She wrote a letter on December 12 in which she said that returning home would make no difference for the reason that Pennell said she had no defense and that the divorce would be granted by mutual agreement.

Ed Burdick had told his wife that if she made no defense that he would agree to her having custody of the children half the time. For that reason she decided not to make a defense.

"Afterward I changed my mind and decided I would make a defense and save my honor."

"Save your honor?" exclaimed Coatsworth with raised eyebrows and mock incredulity.

"Yes. My honor."

"Isn't it true that you decided to make a defense not to defend your so-called honor, but because Pennell told you in no uncertain terms that Carrie Pennell refused to grant him a divorce?

"No, Mr. Pennell decided I should make a defense. He decided that himself, without me."

"And you just agreed to everything he said?"

"Yes, sir."

She said Pennell told her he would leave his wife and go out West and get a divorce from Mrs. Pennell there and then marry her.

"Did Mr. Pennell have any means of his own?"

"I do not know. He was a silent man, and told his business to no one."

Even though Alice Burdick had known him for seven years and had traveled extensively with him alone as well as with him and his wife she claimed to know nothing at all of his personal finances.

"When did you first hear that Mrs. Pennell had inherited a small fortune?"

"I did not know that about her."

"Pennell never told you his wife was a wealthy woman?"

"No."

"He never spoke of a plan to separate his wife from her money?"

"No sir."

"You claim, Mrs. Burdick, that you did not engage Mr. Thayer, Mr. Pennell's law partner, as your attorney in this divorce matter."

"That is correct."

"Yet you went to his office to secure something?"

"Yes, but I did not see him or speak to him."

"What papers did you receive at his offices?"

"I don't know. I never looked at them. They were legal papers of some kind, which I placed in my safe deposit box."

"Without even looking to see what they were?"

"Yes sir."

"Is it not true that these papers were a bond?"

"No."

"Did not Mr. Pennell give you his bond?"

"No, sir."

"Do you mean to say that he did not give you his bond to secure the payment of $25,000?"

"Not that I know of."

Do you mean to say he did not agree to support you in the event that your husband secured a divorce?"

"No, sir."

"And didn't he agree to give you a bond for $25,000 to support you through life?"

"No, sir, not that I know of."

"Didn't Pennell give you a letter of introduction to Attorney Thayer?"

"No, sir."

Mr. Coatsworth then produced a copy of said letter of introduction, made in Pennell's handwriting, to Mr. Thayer.

"Your husband somehow got the key to your secure box in the safe deposit vault, didn't he?"

"Yes."

"And this is a copy of a letter he found in your box!"

"I do not know. I never saw it."

Coatsworth next produced a copy for the witness to identify of a bond for $50,000 given by Pennell to secure the payment to her of $25,000.

"That came from your safe deposit vault also, didn't it?

"I do not know."

Don't you know that such a bond was in that box?"

"I do not."

"Isn't it strange that your husband could find that bond in your locked safe deposit box but you could not?"

"I do not know anything about that."

She claimed she didn't know that a provision had been made by Arthur Pennell to make a payment of $25,000 to her and that he never paid her that sum. She claimed she didn't know if he had signed any of his insurance policies over to her.

Around and around they went, with Alice Burdick recalling so many meetings with Alfred Pennell in New York and Atlantic City as to confuse even the most rapt listener.

While they were together in New York City, she said, Pennell never gave her any money, but he did pay her expenses. She met him in the parlor at The Fifth Avenue Hotel one day to sign papers. She claimed she had no idea what these papers were, that she always signed whatever Pennell asked her to. He accompanied her to the train station on February 23 to send her off to Atlantic City. He then returned to Buffalo.

Mrs. Burdick swore she never heard from him after that. The night of the murder she claimed she was tired and went to bed early and slept until 8 o'clock the next morning.

❧❧❧

Hannah and Annie discussed the inquest proceedings all the way home on the streetcar. They agreed there was something amiss; the dazed and detached aura about all the females, especially the grandmother and the daughters. Others around them had been especially noticing of this as well and were vocal about what they believed it signified.

Outside the court, a sanctimonious woman was heard to say, "How is it that such a horrible thing could happen in that house and yet not a tear is shed for that man in court! Those snippy daughters are as cold as ice!"

Another man was loudly proclaiming that all of the females in the Burdick home were obviously involved in a conspiracy, judging by their unemotional testimony.

"Them girls know a lot more 'n what they're lettin' on, by golly! You mark my words! They're all in it together."

That kind of talk made Hannah very uncomfortable, knowing what she did about the Burdick home invasion. When Jim had first revealed to her about the midnight raid she was sent into a rage over it, but so far the incident was still virtually unknown by the general public. No newspaper had yet printed any account of the incident, which for certain must have left a chilling deficit in these women.

"Why should they trust anybody at all now, after that, Annie? Especially since the whole thing has been kept quiet. They must be wondering why no one has learned about it. I would imagine they'd all be on pins and needles permanently over there at that house, wondering *what next?*"

Annie said, "I know...like that Canadian Hutchison girl too who they dragged in and stripped naked. If all these busybodies at the courthouse knew what really had happened to these women, they might not be so convinced they're the ones qualified to judge. These poor Burdick daughters are still in shock, I think, it appears to me. Frozen with fear and grief.

Hannah and Annie were back again the next day, Hannah beginning to feel a wee bit dowdy compared to all the other finely turned-out murder enthusiasts.

A letter dated December 22, 1902 was read that Mrs. Carrie Pennell wrote in which she asked Mr. Burdick whether he was absolutely crazy in taking the burden of pressing the divorce proceedings, pointing out to him that her husband did not value life too highly.

She wrote that Pennell intimated to her that he might commit suicide and take Mrs. Burdick with him.

Mrs. Burdick herself hinted at suicide in a letter written six days later to her husband.

She now claimed she never discussed suicide, neither hers nor Pennell's, to Pennell or anyone.

In one of Pennell's letters to "Dearest Allie" that was written from Portland Maine he said, "This trip has not been a happy one for me. None are, or can be, without you. I shall go on despairingly, but calmly, for I am not afraid of a fate which only your coming to me can avert. I shall see you Saturday. If only I could meet you alone again as I used to, then I should be willing to die. For an hour with you is worth death or life."

The testimony by the disgusting Dr. Marcy, the physician who tried his utmost to cover up the crime, was an eventful day for Hannah.

"He's obstructing justice!" she fumed to Annie and others sitting around them on the streetcar on their way home. "Marcy tried to mislead a police investigation. Who does he think he is, deciding that the "good name" of a adulteress should be protected at the cost of capturing a good man's murderer? And what would have been the end result if poor Mr. Burdick was believed to have committed suicide? What would that have done to his children? That Marcy cretin should have his medical license taken away permanently."

Hannah had became polarized by the actions of Dr. Marcy for whom she was now oozing with contempt. She vowed at one point to make it her life's work to discredit and shame Dr. Marcy for the rest of his days.

No one else however seemed to wish to hold Marcy responsible for his outrage. The police did not arrest him or charge him with conspiracy, fraud, interference in a murder investigation, obstruction of justice, collusion, or anything else he so richly deserved.

Jim told her, "Let it rest, Hannah."

Hannah decided it was up to her to make this monster pay. She would make it her mission. What if it were her, or her own child who'd been murdered, then shamed in death by an accusation of suicide by some entitled imposter?

"How would you feel Annie, if someone like Fingy Conners murdered JP and a jackass like Marcy tried to cover it up by claiming your husband killed himself? What would that do your poor children? What would Burdick's daughters be thinking every day if they were led to believe along with the rest of the world that their poor loving, forgiving, generous father had committed suicide? 'My father killed himself,' they would all be saying to themselves every day. 'Did I do something wrong? Was I not a good daughter? Was he so disappointed in me that he'd rather to die?'

"Children always blame themselves, Annie. How is it that they will not punish that man for what he has done, conspiring to stand in the path of justice and scar Burdick's girls for the rest of their days, and a physician no less who in his oath pledged to do no harm? I am hoping to read his obituary soon."

"Hannah..." Annie attempted to calm her.

"I am so angry I could just spit, Annie."

"You know Hannah, they say that one way to get the anger out is just to write it down. You could write a letter to this Marcy idiot, and allow all your anger to flow out through the pen. You can call him every vile name that applies. Then, you burn the letter. I've done this very thing with JP a number of times when I was so mad at him I was afraid I'd haul off and slug him in front of the kids. It really does relieve a huge burden, Hannah. I can even help you write it if you'd like. It would be good for both of us, I think. It would be fun, in fact."

So together the following day they opened a couple bottles of Magnus Beck at the kitchen table, a peace offering that Hannah's brother David Nugent delivered free from Fingy Conners' brewery to their door every Saturday, and sat and composed a damning indictment of the Burdicks' medicine man while Sophie kept an eye on the little ones next door.

The essay was suitably vile and crude, addressing every aspect of the likely results of Marcy's unforgivable attempt to subvert the truth of what really happened to poor Ed Burdick.

"With friends like you, Dr. Marcy, neither the Burdicks, nor anyone else for that matter have any additional need of enemies," Hannah wrote while both giggled like tipsy schoolgirls. It was an indictment so cruel that if he ever read it, it would make his skin crawl. Most damning of all was Hannah's ending, the threat to bring him to justice "if it takes me the rest of my life!"

IT'S IN THE MAIL

A week later Hannah was sick again, having picked up a microbe of some sort, no less after haughtily lecturing everyone about how her superior health measures had virtually eliminated illness in their home. She was now humbled.

"One of them awful people on the streetcar gave this to me, I'm certain of it," she complained to her daughter. "It was that dirty man who had dog poo all over his shoe."

At hearing the word "dog" Zeke raised his head from his lying position at Hannah's feet. He'd hardly left her side since she'd gotten sick, somehow holding his bladder for many long hours past his usual walk time until someone remembered to take the poor fellow out.

Nellie was feeling guilty about spending so much time with her girlfriends, ogling boys, while her mother was left to do all the work around the house. She was sure it was her being so overworked that caused her mother to be ill. She hated walking Zeke because he was too strong and pulled on the leash, and Hannah wouldn't hear of her precious baby being allowed outside to roam unaccompanied or untethered.

Hannah used to be quite a strict parent in her earlier days. But after suffering so much loss, she cherished those children who remained, and admittedly let them just about get away with murder.

Having inherited a bit of her mother's paranoia, Nellie began to fear perhaps that God might be testing her with this threat, and like a whirlwind set out to make up for lost time. She fetched the carpet sweeper as Zeke ran to find a safe place to hide from the devil contraption. The noise multiplied Hannah's headache, but it was so rare that Nellie pitched in with housework voluntarily that she just covered her head with a pillow and bore it. Hannah was surprised to feel herself drifting off to sleep despite the racket. She felt awful.

Tackling the roll top desk next, with papers and bills and newspapers spilling out all over, Nellie set to organizing the mess into proper piles before deciding what to do with it all. There was an unpaid Frontier Telephone bill due the next day, and a bill from Dr. Buswell too. In between she put a chicken in a pot along with potatoes and carrots for dinner, hoping it would be done on time for when her father got in from work.

Hearing his slow heavy steps climbing the stairs finally, Nellie positioned herself in front of the pot, stirring it nonchalantly as if not aware of his being there.

"Well, I never thought I'd live to see the day!"

"Oh, hi Papa. You're home. I was just cooking dinner."

"Surprisingly, it does smell a little bit like a dinner," chuckled the Detective, "but knowing my daughter, I suspect it could just as well be a big pot of cold water."

"Very funny. I can cook some things, you know, Pa."

"Yeah, I heard that rumor somewhere out on the street, but—and I say this purely as a professional detective—I've yet to unearth any solid proof of it."

"All right, Detective Sullivan, you'll see. I'll show you. It'll be ready in fifteen minutes and then you can just eat your hat."

"I might just be forced to, if that pie you made for last Thanksgiving was any preview."

"Papa!"

"Just kidding honey. How's your Ma. Is she asleep still?"

"Yes. She's got nothing left in her to throw up, but I've been making her drink water and I got a little apple cider in her."

"Atta girl."

"Pa?"

"Yeah?"

"I organized the desk and some bills are due, can you write some checks and I'll mail them out tomorrow?"

"What bills are those, Nell?"

"Frontier Telephone and Dr. Buswell."

"Oh. Sure, honey, right after supper, so long as my hat doesn't start repeatin' on me right away."

"Oh, Pa. You're terrible!"

The next morning, Nellie managed to get her mother to eat some oatmeal. Hannah sat up in bed for a bit and tried to read the newspaper, but soon enough wanted to go back to sleep.

"Take Zeke out, Nellie, please."

"Ma, I was gonna walk up to Elk Street to mail some bills. Pa wrote out some checks last night. I'll take Zeke along with me."

"Don't let him pull on the leash. If you make him mind, he will heel. Trouble is, you spend so little time with him, he's not used to you being in charge. He's a good guard dog, Nell. Nobody will bother you with Zeke by your side."

Nellie prepared to set out for Elk Street. Hannah was already asleep again and snoring. There was an envelope sitting in the cubby, sealed shut, with the name Dr. Marcy on it. Nellie didn't know any Dr. Marcy. So she looked the name up in the City Directory. She found it, and added the address to the envelope, attached the heavy leather leash to Zeke's collar, then headed off to the post office.

SIGNED, SEALED, DELIVERED

The troubled man approached the desk at Police Headquarters where Detective Sullivan sat nose to the grindstone, head down.

"Are you a detective?" asked Dr. Marcy.

"Yes I am," said Jim looking up at the excited visitor.

"Oh, it's you, Detective Sullivan. I didn't recognize you at first."

"Yes. How are you, Doctor? Can I help you with something?"

It's that idiot Marcy. Just my luck, Jim said to himself.

"Well, I hope so. I've received a terribly threatening letter from a crazy woman, and I'd like to file a complaint against her and have her arrested."

Dr. Marcy was sweating in spite of the spring chill.

Jim took the letter and began reading, finding the penmanship somewhat familiar. The oft-heard phrase "if it takes the rest of my life" rang a bell, right before he saw the signature, Hannah Nugent.

Captain Michael Regan recognized Dr. Marcy from across the room and approached from behind Jim to pay his respects.

"What's the problem here, Sully?"

"Well, Captain. I'm afraid it's quite serious. The good doctor here has received this alarming letter threatening his life from one Hannah Nugent."

"Whoa. Your *wife*, Hannah Nugent?"

"Yep. 'Fraid so."

"Oh my Lord," whistled Regan. "Don't that beat all?"

"That's your *wife*, Detective?" shouted Dr. Marcy, as everyone turned to look.

Jim sighed deeply and nodded his head in resignation.

"Oh, there's no mistakin'! That's her all right," Jim said, still reading. "Jeez, wait! This part right here sounds pretty grisly if you ask me, Captain. Listen: 'Someone should pull off your penis by tying it to a dray and stampeding the horses.' Yeah, I've even gotten that from her once or twice before myself. Ouch!" Jim grimaced as he crossed his legs tightly.

"Well, she doesn't *exactly* threaten my life," he said, backtracking, "but she…"

Both men interrupted.

"Oh, no! Make no mistake, Doc. She's threatenin' your life all right. Her words might not say that exactly, but here, between the lines…*believe* me. I live with the woman. She's cuckoo. It's all indicated right here in black India ink—and as I said, right between the lines. Plain as day."

Again, Regan whistled and stood there, rubbing his chin, shaking his head back and forth mournfully.

"Didja know she hit Detective Sullivan here with a cast iron skillet once and damn near took off his arm, Doc?" offered the Captain.

Dr. Marcy just froze there, stupefied.

"Oh, yeah, boss. Oof! That was a close one. And that butcher over at the Broadway Market, when he tried to sell her that bad pork? The meat cleaver incident? I won't soon forget that."

"Thank God for them quick-thinking polacks and krauts over there! Them people—they recognized all the signs right away—you know, because it's part of their national disposition after all. They tackled her before she could do any serious damage."

"Well, she *did* break some of his fingers, didn't she?"

"Well, yeah, but she didn't chop none off, thank the Lord."

"Oh yeah, that's right. I remember now."

Feeling the policemen were getting a bit off track, the doctor brought them back to the matter at hand.

"Well, what should I do about this?" he pleaded. "Getting a terribly threatening letter like this? It's illegal!"

"Look. No return address, Sully. She's one smart girl, that one."

"What do you need a return address for, detective? You're married to her, you said," cried the alarmed doctor.

"Oh, Dr. Marcy! Have you never heard of double jeopardy! A man can't testify against his own wife!"

"Sully, that's spousal immunity yer thinkin' of," corrected the Captain.

"Oh yeah. I meant to say spousal immunity."

"Well, the Captain here said he knows her also, so he can be the one to testify.

Right, Captain Regan?" countered the doctor.

"Well, Doc, I can't say for certain that I recognize the writing here as being that of Detective Sullivan's wife," he said, turning the letter upside down and inspecting it every which-way.

"She signs her name as Nugent, Sergeant. You must recognize that name! It's not a common name!"

"It's *Captain*, not Sergeant."

"Oh, yes, forgive me. *Captain*. For some reason I always become flustered whenever anybody threatens to kill me."

"Yes, of course, Doctor Marcy. I do too," said Regan. "And I do know that name. Nugent. *Nugent*. Oh, *now* I remember. This here Hannah Nugent's brother is..."

Regan raised his eyes to the ceiling and tapped the letter against his temple as if in deep thought.

"Yes, that's right. Hannah Nugent's brother David Nugent is married to Fingy Conners' niece. Have you ever heard of Mr. Conners, Dr. Marcy? William J. Conners?" inquired the Captain.

A sudden gloom overcame the good doctor's expression.

"Uh...*Fingy* Conners? Uh, well, um. Yes. Yes I have."

"Yeah, them two, they're very close, closer than any brother and sister that I happen to know, I can tell ya that much. The Nugents. Quite the...*unusual*...family, I'd have to say. Uhh...and there certainly *are* strong rumors out there about Fingy Conners, you know, I have to admit that. But I'm not convinced they're entirely all that true. Right Sully?"

"No. I mean, yeah. I always assumed they were true. You know, if they print it in the newspaper, some of it's bound to be true, right?"

"Really?"

"Yeah, boss. That's how we know how to sort truths from lies. The newspapers. Hey, remember the guy they found in the Hamburg Canal, eyes poked out, arms chopped off, with mud snakes living inside his chest where they'd cut his heart out?"

"Oh, yeah. I remember that one. *Nasty* situation. That wasn't Fingy Conners, though, was it? I thought it was that mass murderer from up there in Toronto, that guy who killed all them people in that crazy house near the Chicago Exposition, back in...'95...wasn't it?"

"No, '93."

323

"Yeah, '93."

"Hmm. Say, I got an idea," piped up the Captain.

Dr. Marcy looked hopeful.

"What we can do for you Dr. Marcy, is we can take you over to see Fingy Conners right now and you can show him this here letter and demand that he do something to keep that family of his in line, or else you'll be pressin' charges against 'em."

"Isn't Conners that fella that beats everybody up?" gulped the doctor.

"What? Oh, no. Not *everybody*. No, you just have to be very stern with him. Hold your ground like a man. He respects that. You just tell him in no uncertain terms that you have had it with his crazy family and their shenanigans and you expect it all to stop, every bit of it. His ears'll prick up to that kind of reasoning, I promise you—he'll listen *but good*."

"Yeah, I hafta agree with the Captain here, Dr. Marcy. Fingy'll listen hard to whatever you got to say. And he *never* forgets a face," Detective Sullivan concurred.

Dr. Marcy seemed to need a few moments to consider.

"Well," he finally said, "maybe I shouldn't bother him right now. He's a very busy man I hear, running those newspapers and all. Maybe I'll just write him a strongly-worded letter later on."

"Well, if you insist," said the Captain, looking disappointed. "But how about if we just keep this here letter at Headquarters as evidence, you know, in case anything *does* happen to you? You certainly want to be able to prove she threatened you if something does...well...*occur*."

"Uh, certainly. You're the police. You know best. You keep it, and please, um... well, I have appointments at the hospital now, so I have to go. Good day, gentlemen. Thank you."

"You bet, Dr. Marcy. And thank you for coming in to inform us of this menace. We'll take care of it. You, sir, are a fine citizen."

And as Marcy exited, without saying another word Sullivan went back to his papers and Regan returned to logging calls into his telegraph blotter.

❦❧

Zeke met Jim at the entry door with his deep bark and his lethal tail whipping around wildly. Jim's knees ached too much to stoop down to receive kisses, so he cuffed Zeke's ears affectionately instead. He held the door open while the dog anointed a bush near the front gate, then together they mounted the stairs. After putting his things down, Jim went right into Hannah's room to check on her, Zeke nudging him along at the backs of his knees with his wet nose as he walked. A chewed stocking lay on the floor at the foot of Hannah's bed.

"Hello there, honey, I'm home. How you feelin' this afternoon? Any better?"

"Yes, dear. I am feeling a little better. How was your day?"

"Oh, not bad at all. Except...well...there was this one troubling incident down at Headquarters..."

"What's that?"

"Well, this poor doctor came in, all upset, sweating, white as a ghost, holding a letter he'd received in the mail from a raving lunatic. Some crazy woman. I mean a real nut case, threatenin' him and callin' him every disgusting name in the book."

"Well, what did you do?"

"Well, I told Dr. Marcy that I would do my best to track down the horrid sort of woman who would write such a vile letter, making all those accusations about his character...uh, well, wait a second...let me..."

The Detective fumbled in his pocket and pulled out the four-page letter, sorting though the leaves.

"Oh yeah, here it is, see? She's threatenin' in this part to have wild horses pull his penis off... and then there are these foul insults about his mother being a prostitute..."

Hannah went even whiter than the deathly pale she already was.

"Ever hear of somebody named 'Hannah Nugent', dear?" asked the detective.

"Oh my God. How...? Nellie!" she called. "You come in here right this minute!" Hannah laughed for the first time in more than a week.

THE PENNELL INQUEST

The inquest into the deaths of Arthur Pennell and his wife Carrie convened on April 10th, 1903 and was presided over by Justice Murphy. The intent was to shed some light on whether the incident was a murder-suicide or an accident.

Arthur Reed Pennell's stenographer Wallace G. Omphalius read a statement five typewritten pages in length from notes dictated by Pennell on his final day of life. The *Buffalo Express* stated that in view of the facts established at the previous Burdick inquest, much of the statement "is not to be taken seriously, for its falsity is apparent."

In it, Pennell had stated that Burdick was murdered by an unknown woman who was invited to his house at midnight. He denied any knowledge of or complicity in the crime. He assailed Burdick and charged him with intimate relations with other women. He defended himself by insisting his relations with Mrs. Burdick were purely platonic and that he merely acted as no more than her legal adviser. He touched on the subject of the Ellicott Square offices, quarters he claimed were leased for his business but were in fact yet another love nest for himself and Alice Burdick.

It was Mrs. Burdick herself who gave him the lie about this through the letters they exchanged that she had saved and hidden away and that were read aloud to the court at the Burdick inquest. Pennell claimed in his statement that there were no meetings between the two at the Ellicott Square, thereby shining the light of untruthfulness over the entirety of his five-page manifesto.

The version of the Pennell statement that was read in court was but a copy. The original of the statement, with evidentiary additions made by the dead man and revealing revisions penned in his own handwriting, did not appear in evidence despite its availability. For whatever reason the copy statement, which disclosed much less about the man's state of mind and intent than did the original, was admitted in its stead.

A portion of this statement was devoted to a diatribe assailing the discoveries about Pennell's and Alice Burdick's misadventures made by detective James Boland of the Mooney-Boland Detective Agency:

"In reference to the alleged statements of a New York Detective Agency, whose main business seems to have been to give their clients' secrets to the public, I desire to say that, without knowing what arrangements were made with them by any person, any statements on the part of such agency tending to reflect in any way upon myself or any other person involved are unqualifiably false and have no basis in fact. They are made up of those unfounded statements of this class of parasite which have become of such doubtful value that even in the courts it is now almost held that the presumption is against their credibility."

About the newspapers' coverage of the Burdick murder Pennell wrote:

"Finally, it may be said that the crime is as great a mystery to the writer as to any one. Terrible notoriety and publicity has been brought upon people, more especially women, who have entirely undeserved it, and great wrong has been done to all concerned, especially to the family which has and must suffer most. For that we must thank the spirit of yellow journalism, which does not hesitate to violate every principal of truth, honor, chivalry, justice and sanctity in those efforts to make news and sell papers which makes that style of journalism one of the sickening things of modern civilization."

❧❦❧

Thomas Penney, the former Buffalo district attorney and currently the attorney for Fingy Conners and all of Conners' enterprises, attended the inquest. Penney claimed to be acting as attorney for the Pennell family, regardless of the fact that no family members were called in for testimony nor were any present in court. Penney had in fact sent the late Arthur Reed Pennell's brother, J. Frederick Pennell, back to Maine before the inquest convened in order to keep him from having to be questioned.

During the inquest, Thomas Penney himself maintained an odd and aggressively obstructive stance, compelling those present to question why, at an inquest no less, he would be so protective of his late client and fellow attorney in death, and raising the curiosity of what questionable collusions the two advocates may have shared that might be revealed directly or indirectly by undesired testimony here.

Things took an adversarial turn as District Attorney Coatsworth questioned witnesses who had seen Pennell the day of his death.

Dr. E. G. Danser, the medical examiner, was the first witness. Dr. Danser testified that on the evening of March 10th he was called to the quarry on Kensington Avenue to take charge of the body of Arthur Reed Pennell. He said he found the body on the floor of the quarry under the automobile. The skull was crushed and the dead man's brains had been entirely expelled out onto the ground.

The body, especially the head and the face, was horribly mangled. Nearly all the bones in the body were broken. He said that when he arrived at the quarry that Mrs. Pennell had already been removed to the Sisters' Hospital.

Frank Jerger was the next witness. Jerger testified that on the afternoon of March 10th he saw Pennell's electric Baker "come down Kensington Avenue from the west, going east. I was at the barn in the yard. After I first saw it, it went straight up the avenue about 1,000 feet, then came back and went north on Bailey Avenue. Then it came back and went south on Bailey about 1,000 feet to the land of the Equitable Land Co., turned around and came back up again. He remained in the area I judge at least an hour, and he went as slow as the wheels would move along all the time that he was there. That was a little after 4 o'clock. It wasn't just raining at the time, it was pouring down. That's how I remember that it was the same wheel."

At this point in the inquest Attorney Thomas Penny insolently interrupted, "I object to a lot of the testimony that is not relevant to the issue here."

Justice Murphy, surprised by this peculiar and thoroughly unwarranted outburst, replied, "You have no right to object at all."

Mr. Penney countered, "But I think, your Honor, that we have at least a common law right to enter objections here to a lot of irrelevant testimony."

Judge Murphy shot back, "I think I am quite capable of conducting this inquiry, Mr. Penney and deciding what is relevant and what is not. We are going to find out all about this case. There is a question here as to whether his death was accidental or suicidal and I am going to take this man's story."

The witness Mr. Jerger then continued, saying that he was standing in front of his barn while watching the automobile as the rain poured down and saw the auto stop in front of Volk's Saloon, at about 4 o'clock in the afternoon.

Attorney Penney at this point attempted to question the witness, but the judge had Mr. Jerger step down. The Judge then turned his attentions to the antagonistic Mr. Penney.

"You have no right to examine the witnesses under the law," stated Judge Murphy.

Mr. Penney said, "But I insist."

Judge Murphy—"Well, I won't permit it."

Mr. Penney—This is a most irregular proceeding. It has been irregular all through from the beginning.

Judge Murphy—"Well, if you don't like it you can get out of my courtroom."

Mr. Penney—"Well, I won't get out."

Judge Murphy—"Well, I'll put you out."

Mr. Penney—"I'd like to see you do it."

The Judge scoffed at Penney but allowed him to remain, and continued the inquiries.

The saloonkeep Mr. George Volk, proprietor of the tavern where Arthur Pennell stopped for a drink, said that Pennell entered his saloon at about 4 pm on March 10 and had a whiskey and a cigar.

A boy named James Reilley testified that he saw Pennell's automobile stop in front of Volk's Saloon and that Mrs. Pennell was a passenger. Mr. Pennell entered the saloon, he said, leaving his wife sitting in the auto all alone. Some time later he saw Pennell emerge from the saloon and get back in the auto.

"Just before he got in he said something and he and Mrs. Pennell laughed," said the young witness.

A witness named George Campbell testified that he was sitting at the front window of his house when he saw the Pennell automobile pass slowly. It went up the street and back again, then as it went up Kensington Avenue, the driver, Mr. Pennell, threw the top back, despite the fact that the rain was pouring down. At that point the auto was about 300 feet from the quarry, Campbell said, and "After the occupants put the top down they increased the speed." Then, Mr. Pennell put his hand up to his head, as if he reaching for a hat that might have blown off. The automobile "swayed" at that point, then careened over the cliff.

A newsman with the *Albany Journal* newspaper claimed knowledge that an hour before taking his fateful drive, Pennell had conducted an anxious conversation over the telephone with a female; that the information given to him by that female made a strong impression on him, indeed, it weighed heavily on his mind, and that the subject of that conversation was the midnight murder of his former friend, Edwin L. Burdick.

Mr. Babcock of the automobile company from whom Pennell had bought his machine testified that the Baker runabout was "perfectly manageable and in perfect condition and repair. In fact, it had been in the factory being refinished and was turned over to Mr. Pennell again the Saturday before his death, good as new."

The official findings of the Pennell Inquest as to whether the automobile accidentally or was intentionally plunged into the quarry were termed "inconclusive."

HARTZELL & HARTZELL HAVE THEIR SAY

On April 20, almost two months after the murder of Ed Burdick, the *Buffalo Express* published a lengthy article which revealed finally and at long last details of the actions of the police assault on the Burdick home on the night of March 1st, and the unconscionable behavior of the gang of thugs involved.

Upon learning the details of this bizarre fiasco, Buffalo's citizens were universally appalled and their historic fear and mistrust of the police department renewed.

Whatever fragile faith had been recently and tenuously set to ticking again between the police department and Buffalo's citizens, after decades of corrupt allegiance to the likes of Fingy Conners, Jack White, the Sheehan brothers and other criminal ilk, this outrageous event effectively reset the clock back to zero.

The attorney-brothers Hartzell & Hartzell, who represented Mrs. Marie Hull and Mrs. Alice Burdick, summed it up in the *Express* article:

Who can picture the horrors of that night?

Who can imagine the terror that filled the hearts of these tender women and children as officers of the law pounded on the doors of that stricken home with their night sticks, the sounds reverberating through the silent house as though a legion of murderers clamored and strove for admittance?

And when these men forced their way in they ran through the hallway and up the stairs shouting roughly. 'Get up! Get up! We want Mrs. Hull and Mrs. Burdick! They must come with us to the police station!'

Of all the unreal situations and the shocking conditions that have appeared in this tragedy from first to last, there has been none more terrifying or revolting than their midnight raid upon the Burdick home by the supposed 'guardians of the peace'! What home is forthwith secure in its sanctity and privacy? What recompense or amends shall be had? What shall prevent its recurrence in your home or ours?

Buffalo has achieved much, but it has much to achieve. The principle that 'Every man's home is his castle,' wrought into the English law at such heroic cost and claimed by our young nation as its birthright suddenly becomes in Buffalo but a myth.

In a single night this community casts off the acquired civilization of centuries. In a single night we leapt backward through the years to the darkest period in history.

Might again makes right. Law is only the manifestation of the arbitrary will of those in power.

Liberty is a faint spark, feebly flickering in the night of intense blackness. The rights of man are but an empty dream.

The word of Christ is untaught.

The Golden Rule lies hidden in the monasteries, and the words 'Love thy neighbor as thyself', and 'Do unto others even as ye would have them do unto you' is unknown to men."

❧❧❧

From the Rochester Democrat and Chronicle:

A particularly striking example of a new kind of questionable entertainment, the crime-play, is a melodrama entitled "Over The Quarry Brink, Founded On The Great Buffalo Mystery," now being played at a Buffalo theater.

This play purports to tell the story of the murder of Edwin L. Burdick, and is built on the theory that Mrs. Burdick was the author of the crime. It represents Mrs. Burdick as an evil woman wrongdoing her husband and finally procuring him to be murdered by one of her associates. As Mrs. Burdick, against whom no such accusation has ever been authoritatively made, is living in Buffalo presently, the utter abominableness of producing this play, especially in a Buffalo theater, need not be particularly pointed out. The law of criminal libel probably covers such an extreme case as this and it is to be hoped that it will be invoked in behalf of Mrs. Burdick. Conspicuous examples ought to be made of the author and of the producer of 'Over The Quarry Brink.'"

MILWAUKEE

The civil insurrection that Hannah Sullivan had anticipated would surely ensue upon revelation to Buffalo citizens of yet another outrageously intolerable and illegal police action never materialized. Precious little reaction, short-lived, came of the Hartzell Brothers' passionate statement printed in the *Express*.

Hannah couldn't quite understand it. This inaction only again reiterated in her mind the emergent need for women to win the right to vote. She had come to realize that people were naturally inclined to shut out from their thoughts any disturbing reminder of things they believed they could do nothing about. This may have explained why the police raid on the Burdick family house went ultimately unpunished. Women having the vote would surely change things, Hannah believed. Fingy Conners owned the police, the municipal judges and the politicians and had ruled over all for almost a generation. The police had demonstrated time and again that they were not protectors of the citizens as they had so sworn in their oath, but rather served as a standing army to politicians requiring protection from the righteous wrath of the citizens, from the penalty of law, and from all common standards of human decency.

Likewise, politicians were not servants of the citizens as vowed in their campaign promises, but rather servants of those who had bought them with surprisingly paltry sums of cash and cheap trinkets, whose primary objective was keeping the citizens under their thumbs.

❧❧❧❧

Hannah missed her brother.

David J. Nugent had been banished to Milwaukee along with his wife, Fingy's niece Minnie and their children. There Dave was put in charge of Fingy's dock operations, in the beginning unhappily so.

Fingy's intent was to get the flashy blatherskite Nugent out of Buffalo while his attorneys wrangled to overturn his conviction and his two year sentence to Auburn

Prison. Among First Ward men Dave Nugent had evolved into a folk hero of sorts. He was a charismatic figure and never gave any outward indication of distress or care over his legal predicament, so confidant was he in his place in the scheme of things—and in Fingy Conners' able maneuvering. It was habitually commented by newsmen in their reports about him that he was very well dressed and remarkably youthful appearing. Overconfidence made him cocky and drew attention to him wherever he went. His attorney Mr. Hoyt was not happy about Dave's boasting and his colorful profile in the community. He'd heard that in the saloons that Dave and his cousin Dick frequented he had been entertaining the clientele with dramatic new enhanced renditions of his ill-fated attack on the *Mather*, putting his case in peril.

Together Fingy and Hoyt came up with the plan to get him out of town.

Milwaukee was a big change. He'd never been there before. He had no friends in Milwaukee, and the workers under him, loyal to their longtime previous boss, took it poorly when Nugent strutted in, moved his predecessor out of his office, and took over operations.

The Nugent children were bereft at being uprooted from friends and family, but Dave's wife Minnie was downright distraught. Her antagonism toward her husband and his narcissistic behavior coming as it did at great cost to her and the children had only expanded in recent years. Her temporary exile to Milwaukee was something to endure with teeth gritted. She told herself it would only be for a short while. But soon enough she was horrified to find her husband expressing his actual preference for the place.

For the first time since he was a boy Dave Nugent was out from under Fingy's judgment, direct management and eagle eye while at the same time enjoying The Boss' full protection and support. More so, he was able to exercise better control over his family, especially Minnie, as she no longer had Fingy to conveniently run to whenever disagreements rose up between her and her husband. Minnie was forced into stricter subservience now that over 600 miles separated her from her uncle.

Good news came for Dave Nugent in January upon Attorney Hoyt's victory at winning a new trial for him and his 16 shooters. The Apellate Division set aside Nugent's previous conviction and sentence. The decision was based on grounds that the court that had indicted Nugent was not regular in that a notice of its convening had not been published as required.

Dave returned to Buffalo, and with Hoyt at his elbow, surrendered himself to the

District Attorney for arraignment to plead to four indictments that had been found against him. He was described by newspapers as looking "as stout and young-faced as ever. He bore no sign of anxiety or worry when the D.A. formally informed him that the grand jury had found four indictments against him, three charging him with assault and one with rioting."

The judge set his bail at $3000. South Buffalo building contractor William H. Fitzpatrick became surety on the bond. Fitzpatrick and Fingy Conners were business partners in the building of hundreds of homes in the new South Buffalo section of the booming city.

As expected, Fingy once again had prevailed.

Hoyt's strategy was for Dave and five of his cohorts to change their plea from not guilty to guilty to the lesser charge of rioting; the remainder of the gang pleading guilty to unlawful assembly. The plea change was made in order to avoid a trial. The men were arraigned in groups before the judge. They consented to have sentences imposed at once. Justice Kruse imposed a fine on David Nugent and his fellow conspirators of $250. The amount was posted by Fingy Conners. Thus, the Criminal Term of the Supreme Court efficiently disposed of the criminal cases. Nugent and all the rest walked free.

Their victim John Molik on the other hand received a life sentence of pain and disability, thoroughly uncompensated.

"I don't know what to think anymore, Annie," Hannah said.

"It's complicated," Annie responded while tying up a pork roast.

"What do you think, Annie? I mean, David has crippled a man. Mr. Molik has a bullet too close to his heart for surgeons to remove. That's what President McKinley died of. A bullet they couldn't retrieve caused the onset of sepsis. That's what I read. And who gets the money from the fines the Justice imposed? Shouldn't that money go to the Molik family by all rights?"

"I don't know. Is David staying here in Buffalo now that he's free?"

"Of course. His family and all his friends are here. But what do I do now? Just because a court excuses him doesn't change what he done. Little David thinks we can all go back to the way things were, with his Uncle Dave welcome as before. I don't know what to tell him now."

"Tell him the truth."

"I already did."

"No, I mean the truth about how you feel about all this. Say those exact words to him. Otherwise his understanding of right and wrong will be confused. You have to tell him that the court failed in its duty because what he did was terrible. He has to learn some time that justice does not always prevail, and here's the perfect example in his own life. In his own family."

"He misses his uncle, Annie. I miss him too. But..."

"Your responsibility is to your own child, not to your full-grown brother who *acts* like a child."

"You don't understand...the things that happened to him when we were little and got split up when our parents died. I feel responsible."

"Hannah, must we, *again?* You were only three years older than him. A child yourself! It wasn't your duty to raise him! You are not his parent. The Manahars took him in—and that's that. You have to stop blaming yourself. Your brother made all his own decisions. Yes, Fingy Conners had his influence, but your brother was a hoodlum before he ever met Fingy Conners. Haven't you ever stopped to consider why, if your family circumstance turned your brother bad as you claim, then why didn't them same circumstances turn *you* bad?"

Hannah had no response at the ready for such logic.

After a minute of silence Annie reiterated, "Am I wrong about that?"

"No," Hannah admitted reluctantly.

"You can't blame the Manahars, Hannah. They saved David from the orphanage after your parents died just like the Sheas saved you. How lucky you both were not to end up there! We both know our husbands' awful stories about when they were put in the orphanage. You can't blame Fingy—I mean, entirely—because David was trouble long before he ever landed on Fingy's doorstep. And you can't blame yourself. So, who's left? How about blaming your brother for his own foolishness? How about blaming your brother for making so many bad choices? Isn't it about time you shrugged this heavy burden off your shoulders and put it on him where it rightfully belongs? I admit I feel sorry for those poor kids of his, Hannah, I really do. But as for Minnie," she added, "that girl knew exactly what she was gettin' into."

✾✿✾

"Hannah!" her brother called. He was standing out on the stoop, knocking hard on one side of the door as Zeke barked and raged on the other. Hannah startled. She was awakened from her nap. She went down the stairs and unlocked the door.

"Zeke! Quiet. It's okay! Shh!"

She opened the door with one hand and looped the other under the dog's collar to hold him back. It was quite clear the two disliked each other.

"Oh, Sis. Did I wake yous?"

"I'm glad you did, Dave. Little Davey'll be gettin' home from school in a few minutes anyway. Come on up."

"Okay, but I can't stay. I gotta catch the train to Chicago."

"How come you're goin' to Chicago?"

"That's where I change trains for Milwaukee."

"Are you goin' back there to pack up?"

"Pack up for what?"

"For movin' back home, silly."

"Hannah, I ain't movin' back. I got responsibilities now. I'm headin' that whole Milwaukee operation. I got that place runnin' like a well-oiled machine. That lummox Hastings I replaced nearly had it run into the ground."

"What about Minnie and the kids, Dave?"

"Oh, they're fine. The kids are settlin' in. They got new friends."

"Well then, what about us? We're your family too."

"Come on now, Hannah. I know what's goin' on here. Jim don't want me round here no more. I'm a bad influence, or so's I been hearin'!" he laughed ruefully.

"Dave..."

"Gotta go, Hannah. Kiss the kids for me. Come see us this summer. We got a beach cottage twenty miles north of the city, right on the lake. It's beautiful up there. You'd love it."

"Oh Davey!" she began to cry.

"Aw, Sis. Don't. I'll be comin' back here on business a few times a year. It'll be like I never left. Gimme a kiss now."

Hannah hugged him tight. He kissed her on the cheek.

"Yer my best friend, Hannah," he said. "Don't know what I'd've ever done without yous."

She cried as she watched him get into the automobile he'd borrowed from Fingy and drove away, waving, the car sliding sideways on the ice, he wrestling with the steering arm to get it under control so he could move forward.

❦❦

"What's the matter Ma? You been lookin' glum all week long."

Oh, Junior. Nothing, really. I'm all right. Just a little sad that your uncle's decided to stay in Milwaukee."

Jim Jr. was fully aware of the complications caused by Uncle Dave and blamed him rightly for causing so much pain to the family. He for one was glad his murderous relation decided to remain in Milwaukee.

"It's for the best, Ma. For everybody. Say, I'm plannin' on goin' to the Exposition grounds Sunday to make photographs before they've torn it all down. Why don't you come with me? It'll be fun to see it again, all deserted and taken apart."

"Why would you ever want to photograph it like that, Junior? In such a state! How sad it will look in pieces in the snow with nobody there. I want to remember it the way it was in its glory."

"Oh, come on, Ma. You won't forget how it was just by seein' what it's become. All good things must come to an end, right? Even the Pan! It'll be really interesting, you can't deny that. Just bundle up good though. Just in case. That exposition property is the windiest spot in the whole county."

She didn't want to go, but couldn't remember the last time she and Junior had done something together, just the two of them.

"All right. I will."

❦❦

Junior maneuvered the sleigh into a place aside the old Temple of Music where President McKinley had been shot. There the horse would be shielded from the biting wind. He tucked a quilted pad under the horse blanket for extra warmth and tightened the straps. Before setting off they fed him two apples, then Junior said, "We'll be right back, Milo."

Milo stomped his hooves in protest and watched as they ambled off through the snowy pathways without him.

"It's so eerie. I can't believe we're just about the only ones here." Hannah said.

It wasn't depressing as she feared it would be. As Junior set up his tripod she poked her head into now-empty spaces where, strangely enough, much yet remained. Chairs, light fixtures, display cases. She'd read that people had come in to strip the place but armed guards chased them off. Many exhibitors had made no provision for dismantling or ridding themselves of the items needed for their exhibits and just abandoned the lot, much to the covetousness of local people entertaining salvage plans, thus far unconsummated.

Hannah recalled her visits the summer before, especially being transfixed by the exotic peoples from all over the world the likes of which few in the city had ever encountered before, and never would have either if the Exposition hadn't taken place. Eskimos, tribal Africans, Hawaiian women with breasts bared, fancy New Yorkers in their finest regalia, famous stage actresses, top politicians, Arab and Japanese acrobats, Indian savages of many tribes, Mexican bullfighters, Incas, high-diving elk. What an experience!

They returned to the sleigh and continued their tour, dodging piles of lumber and the occasional fellow trespasser with an eye out for souvenirs not yet taken away by workmen.

The Chicago House Wrecking Company had begun their work the day the Pan closed, the enterprise having bought everything in its entirety lock, stock and barrel—literally—and engaged in placing the material in marketable shape for resale. Its advertising listed trusses, skylights, sash and doors, pipe, electrical apparatus, iron and felt roofing of every kind, fire hosing, fire engines, alarm boxes and related apparatus, flags, flagpoles and bunting of all nations, plumbing materials, urinals, cast iron cesspools, water hydrants, an Otis elevator, 3000 iron beds, 5,000 bed sheets, 20,000 kitchen chairs, typewriters, stamping machines, cuspidors, pumps, dynamos, smokestacks, relaying rail, 300,000 incandescent lamps, steam road rollers, surveyors' instruments, trolley wire and equipment, automatic sprinklers, search lights, push carts, greenhouses, street sweepers, ambulances, boats, gondolas, oars, and hundreds more items.

Their advertising promised rock bottom prices for seasoned lumber and all manner of construction materials, a bonanza for those companies or individuals in the building trade. Sears Roebuck was a major customer, refurbishing and recycling the materials for the custom home building kits sold through their catalogs.

As Junior photographed the distant towers of the Triumphal Bridge, an armed guard approached and rudely shooed them away.

"Go on, get outa here or I'll lock yous up, yous two! Yer trespassin" 'n' takin' what don't belong t' yous!"

"The only thing we're takin', you no-account, is photographs!" Hannah scolded. "Unlike them men I'm seein' over there! Just look at 'em! They're loadin' lumber onto a dray, bold as can be right in front of your eyes, yet you leave them to it. Might it be that you're afraid to approach four grown toughs, so instead you impose your wrath on an old woman and a child?' Well, shame on you! Your mother must be proud! Now go and do your job and leave us to our Sunday amusements!"

Junior blushed. He was far from a child and his mother rather far from an old woman, mostly. Her dressing down effectively mortified the guard. He spat in protest, turned around and began walking away.

"Just don't let me see yous 'round here when I get back or I'll take your Kodak!" he threatened.

"Weasel! Coward! Milksop!" Hannah taunted, unloading all her most recent disappointments on the guard. "Go, get on with yous! Pick on somebody else!" she shook her fist.

"Ma! What are you doin', fer cryin' out loud! You're gonna get us in trouble! Let's get outa here. I got what I came for."

Hannah tightened her chin strap and giggled. Her tirade had disarranged her somewhat.

"So did I, Junior. So did I."

"

Pan American Exposition in the snow previous to being dismantled.

The San Francisco Call

The New York Herald devoted almost an entire page to the story on this day.

The US Government Pavilion was destroyed in the storm of 9-11

INTERIOR OF THE INFANT INCUBATOR BUILDING
SHOWING EIGHT INCUBATORS, EACH CONTAINING A LIVE BABE

The Infant Incubators at the Pan American Exposition

The Triumphal Bridge on opening day at the Pan American Exposition

Below: Strolling along the Grand Court

Pan American Exposition, out front of the Alt Nurnberg restaurant. Note sandwich vendor in foreground, one-legged man on crutches, wheelchairs for hire. Inferior materials and workmanship caused the walkways to sink and crumble, here replaced by planks.

Above: President McKinley's coffin is carried up the steps of Buffalo City Hall. The Edison Moving Picture cameraman is seen at bottom of photo. Below: Mourning bunting decorates the Ansley Wilcox house on the day that Theodore Roosevelt was sworn in as President as Cabinet Members gather.

President McKinley (in top hat) tours Niagara Falls hours before being shot.

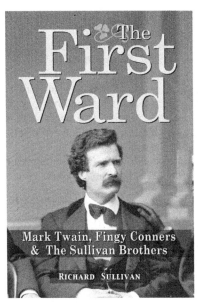

The First Ward

"...engrossing. The First Ward is vividly cinematic." — LA Weekly

"...engrossing saga..." — Publishers Weekly

"Sullivan has found a clever way of taking what we know and building a story around it. Samuel Clemens is brought to life with real believability... wonderfully involving." —Buffalo Spree magazine.

Based on real people and historical events, the immigrant Irish of Buffalo's First Ward and their offspring struggle to claim their share of the American Dream via less than honorable ways. Murder, disease, violence and terrible injustice were part and parcel of everyone's lives in the struggle to survive in hopes of achieving success— whether it be on the straight and narrow, or not.

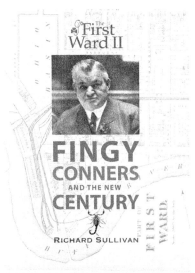

The First Ward II: Fingy Conners & The New Century

The saga of megalomaniac William J. Conners continues as he pursues further millions via backroom deals and illegal alliances. Based on actual historical events and the real people who drove them, **The First Ward II** documents the rivalry between dock-walloper turned millionaire Fingy Conners and two brothers who emerged from the Buffalo Orphan Asylum to claim political power, Alderman John P. Sullivan and Detective Sergeant James E. Sullivan. Their lives intersect with the giants of their day; heavyweight champion of the World, cousin John L. Sullivan, humorist Mark Twain, US Presidents William McKinley and Teddy Roosevelt, and publisher William Randolph Hearst. Additionally, the murder of Edwin Burdick grips the nation's attention and Detective Sullivan finds himself in the thick of it.

The First Ward III:
Murderers, Scoundrels
and Ragamuffins

The abduction and murder of a little girl changes the freedoms that parents formerly allowed their children. The city is in an uproar as a Chinese laundryman is falsely accused of the crime. Anti-Chinese sentiment explodes, affecting Asian immigrants as far away as Toronto.

Buffalo's Old Home Week celebration is wildly successful, effectively doubling the city's population during the long celebration during which it is claimed by the police that crime was non-existent.

The railroads commandeer the city's streets, laying over 150 miles of illegal track within Buffalo city limits, bringing chaos and death.

Alderman Sullivan's son is the victim of sexual abuse. When President Taft comes to town, Detective Jim Sullivan zealously guards his charge. Famous cousin John L. Sullivan, heavyweight champion of the world, arrives in town and joins the fun at the Mutual Rowing Club's Calico Ball.

The Murphy clan seeks revenge for Fingy Conners' hired thugs murdering one of their own. Fingy Conners' only son meets tragedy. Fingy establishes a charity fund for the families of firemen killed in a terrible blaze, then schemes to keep all the money for himself. Fingy becomes Chairman of the Democratic Party of New York State. *Collier's* Magazine outs Fingy Conners as a murderer.

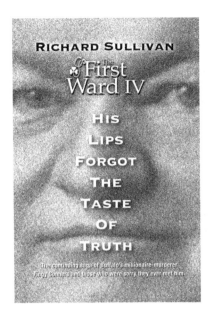

The First Ward IV:
His Lips Forgot The Taste Of Truth

A sweet Syrian child is horrifically murdered. Over the course of an entire agonizing year the sick killer sends more than a dozen postcards confessing the vile crime to the local police chief—who inexplicably ignores them.

Richard Sullivan's 4th installment in his turn of the 20th Century ancestor-populated The First Ward series finds every principal character standing at a personal crossroads.

Lying millionaire-politician Fingy Conners' obsession with dominating the lives of all those around him escalates into dangerous territory as he intensifies his grab for political power. Conners' ultimate goal? The White House.

Fingy Conners, Alderman JP Sullivan, Detective Jim Sullivan, Police Chief Michael Regan and State Treasurer John J. Kennedy all variously face dire circumstances having career-ending potential.

Hannah Sullivan's concepts of right and wrong are further challenged by her murdering brother's latest abominations.

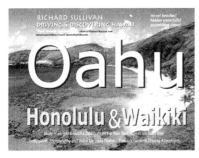

Driving & Discovering Hawaii: Oahu:

Winner, Travel Journalism Award For **"Best Hawaii Guidebook"** by **American Airlines** and the **Hawaii Visitors and Conventions Bureau.** Named **"Best Hawaii Guidebook"** by the Los Angeles Times, the Chicago Sun-Times, the San Diego Union-Tribune, the Orange County Register, the San Jose Mercury, and The Oregonian. Read the **RAVE REVIEWS** on AMAZON.com

Los Angeles Times:
"I'd be surprised if there is a hidden byway or corner of beach or town that Sullivan has not revealed here --even on the leeward side of the island, which remains relatively unknown to visitors."

Chicago Sun Times:
"A must read is Richard Sullivan's Driving & Discovering Oahu, the best guidebook on the market."

San Diego Union-Tribune:
"Visitors contemplating a driving trip around Oahu will greatly enhance the journey by packing along this guidebook by Richard Sullivan... The text is fresh and insightful and the photo tips are of tremendous value to anyone wondering where to stop for the best views in unfamiliar territory."

Orange County Register (CA):
"...the best guidebook on the market."

Driving & Discovering Maui and Molokai

Another beautiful guidebook from award-winning author and photographer Richard Sullivan. Each photo is numbered and its exact location pinpointed on an adjacent map, making this Maui and Molokai guidebook your best bet for unforgettable sightseeing and great restaurants, as well as vacation photography and video.

"A picture is worth a thousand words...which is why the 300+ beautiful photos in Driving & Discovering Maui and Molokai guidebook make this the best available, and a real bonanza for photographers searching for their best island shots. Nobody puts the "guide" in guidebook like Richard Sullivan" -photnet.com

Driving & Discovering Hawaii: Oahu Spectacular Beaches

Oahu Spectacular! Beaches is loaded with links to Google Maps for each beach:
— Google StreetView images for each beach as it will be viewed from the highway from both directions so you can easily recognize it from the road **(many Oahu beaches have no signage)**.
— Daily updated wind, wave, tide, and general conditions of each beach.
— 360 degree view of the beach where available.
— Satellite view of the area does double duty by also showing the exact spot the photographer stood to take the photo.
—Hawaii's Greatest Driving Adventures Map to the island's beaches with detailed notes on each.
— Each Beach Page provides a beautiful photo as well as icons depicting the **attractions and amenities** available there (swimming, surfing, restrooms, food trucks, etc.). GPS coordinates help you find your way. Everything you need to choose, find and determine current conditions at your desired beach destination is just a click away! Don't go to Hawaii without it!

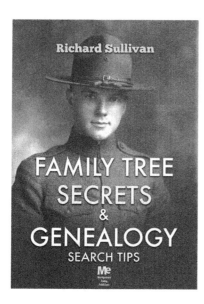

Family Tree Secrets
& Genealogy Search Tips

Richard Sullivan uncovered such an avalanche of information on his previously-unknown ancestors that he has turned their saga into the historical novel trilogy, **The First Ward**. Garnered from the author's own personal experience in researching over two hundred family members he shares his knowledge here with those who are tracing their family genealogy.

Sullivan suggests traditional as well as non-traditional modes and areas of research and provides tips to avoid repetition and frustration that will result in a broader research net being cast. The author provides links **(LIVE links in the eBook version!)** and includes a wealth of clever sources, as well as tips and tricks to apply when using online search engines to maximize both the researcher's time and discoveries. His narrative clearly explains how he connected the dots, demonstrating how he utilized one find to lead to another, and then another.

you really *can* turn back the clock.

Reclaim
Your Youth

no magic pill.
no secret formula.
no bull.

Growing Younger After 40

richard sullivan

Reclaim Your Youth:
Growing Younger After 40

People have bizarre opinions about muscle and their own bodies, especially their deterioration. Who in their right mind wants to get weaker, less attractive and more vulnerable as they age?

Don't conflate increased muscle mass with becoming a bodybuilder! *Everybody* needs to be stronger—and strength training can save us from a world of hurts down the line, as well as add years to our lifespan— healthy, pain-free, active years.

It's notable that the masses have no problem with getting fat or the diminished capacity that comes with adding overweight, but derisively claim repulsion at adding and strengthening muscle.

Science reminds us that the more robust our muscle mass, the faster we burn fat, the more vigorous is our immune system, and the stronger and more agile we are.

The elderly don't fall down because they're old—they fall because their leg muscles have **atrophied** to such a degree they can no longer hold themselves upright. Increased muscle mass is your guarantee that you'll still be walking—and running— when your contemporaries may be using walkers.

Looking great *below* the neck is just as important as from the neck up. **Reclaim Your Youth** isn't about magic pills or the Secrets of the Hollywood Stars, because these things don't exist.

Looking and feeling great are all about eating more nutritionally and less recreationally, challenging our muscles so as to reverse their decline, and questioning old habits and misconceptions that have accelerated that decline.

Made in the USA
Middletown, DE
01 December 2021

53891379R00199